VOYAGES

The Writing of a Life

The varying economic circumstances of Mrs. Moodie's life largely determined her writing. A more detailed consideration of significant events in her life will serve to show how consistently they are involved in her narratives, especially those in this collection. The Stricklands came from the yeomanry of the British north counties. Susanna's grandfather, bereft of hereditary lands by the return of a relative with prior claims, moved to London. Born in 1758, her father, Thomas Strickland, became a dock manager for a London shipowner, but was advised to retire to the eastern counties for his health. Susanna, the last of six daughters born to Strickland's second wife, Elizabeth (née Homer, 1772–1864), and their first Suffolk child, was followed by two brothers. She spent her first five years in a rented house, at which point her father bought Reydon Hall, outside Southwold on the Suffolk coast. The Hall is described in "Rachel Wilde" and "Trifles from the Burthen of a Life," and it, the town and the county appear throughout her writing with their initials and a dash. Her stories and sketches, apart from her historical sketches and a very few others, are set in this locale.

With his London capital Thomas Strickland established business connections in Norwich, Norfolk, with a near relation of his wife. Initially his investments thrived and Reydon Hall, a country estate with tenant farms, marked his ascent into the gentry. But Norwich was especially affected by the post-Napoleonic Wars depression and Strickland was forced to spend more time there than anticipated to oversee his investments. Early in 1818 the business with which he was involved failed and on 18 May he died, leaving his family the Hall, worthless stock and no liquid assets. Several sources attest to the difficult financial circumstances in which he left his wife and children. These events, determining Susanna's future, haunt her writing. She depicts a fall from economic grace in more than a dozen stories. Sometimes she combines loss of caste with a father's death; more importantly, this loss is the cause of emigration in "The Vanquished Lion," "The Broken Mirror," "The

Sailor's Return," "The Well in the Wilderness" and "Trifles from the Burthen of a Life."

Susanna Moodie's account of the lives of the Wilde children in "Rachel Wilde" accords with accounts of the early lives of the Stricklands. All the daughters except Jane are represented: Susanna as the eponymous heroine, Catharine as Dorothea, Sarah as Selina, Agnes as Ann and Elizabeth as Lilla; the sons Samuel and Thomas appear without being named. The Stricklands had a good library and before his death their father, assisted by Elizabeth, took an active role in educating his younger daughters. He so controlled their reading, however, that when Mrs. Moodie has Rachel familiar at seven with Shakespeare and Homer (in Pope's translation), she names two of the few poets he allowed his girls to read. They were encouraged to study history, particularly English history of the Civil War and Restoration. The account of the Wildes' reading reveals how the Strickland girls compensated for their father's ban on merely ornamental or entertaining literature. History became romance. Susanna was later enthralled with "the romance of history."[2]

Rachel Wilde's story spans the years 1808–1815, from her sixth to her twelfth year. Mr. Wilde's loss of "a large fortune" through "commercial speculations" (Chapter I) is described more fully in Chapter VIII, set in 1814. Here are details about the father's business venture with an in-law, his "failing constitution" and the reduction of "his comfortable establishment"; but he is still alive at the end of the story. A sketch of the girlhood of another Rachel in "Matrimonial Speculations" parallels the girlhoods of both Rachel Wilde and Susanna Strickland. In this version the father dies and the mother, seeking to improve her family's economic status by repairing the breach with her well-to-do blood relations, sends Rachel to an aunt in London. Susanna made her first trip to London at the age of sixteen. The visit in "Matrimonial Speculations" occurs in early 1820; this and Rachel Wilde's first trip away from home are probably based on Susanna Strickland's experiences. In the course of these journeys, both heroines come up against wealthy tradespeople, whom they have been taught to despise; these confrontations dramatize the extent to which they have been set

VOYAGES
Short Narratives of Susanna Moodie

CANADIAN SHORT STORY LIBRARY, No. 15

Edited by John Thurston

University of Ottawa Press
Ottawa • Paris

Canadian Short Story Library, Series 2
John Moss, General Editor

Printed and bound in Canada
ISBN 0-7766-0326-4

Canadian Cataloguing in Publication Data
Moodie, Susanna, 1803-1885.
Voyages

(The Canadian short story library; 15)
ISBN 0-7766-0326-4

I. Thurston, John Harry, 1955- . II. Title.
III. Series.

PS8426.O63V69 1991 C813'.3 C91-090234-8
PR9199.2.M65V69 1991

Series design concept: Miriam Bloom

Book design: Marie Tappin

CONTENTS

Acknowledgements

Thank you to Leslie Monkman for encouragement, insightful criticism and patience; to Jack Healey for giving much, with nothing but this in return; to John Moss for support and backing; to Leslea Keevil for being my worst, best, critic. Janet Shorten and Jenny Wilson at the University of Ottawa Press have earned my gratitude for their care and good judgment. My parents and my son have given me reasons to do what I do, even when they have had little to do with it. Finally, my thanks to Debra Weinber who, in more ways than I can admit, makes my work possible.

INTRODUCTION

Susanna Moodie (née Strickland) is well known for *Roughing It in the Bush* and, to a lesser extent, *Life in the Clearings*, accounts of her New World experience. However, little attention has been paid to the remainder of her extensive output. She began publishing in the 1820s alongside the popular women writers who broke the ground in which the more durable works of the Brontës and Elizabeth Gaskell grew. Similarly, the seeds of *Roughing It* may be found in Susanna Strickland's writing for the new fashionable magazines in England. As with the earlier popular writers, much of her work for both British and colonial magazines is conventional, romantic and predictable, while her best-known book is exploratory, realistic and open-ended. She earned her popularity through her skill in satisfying the expectations of her audience. But some of her short prose shares those features of *Roughing It* that are now more valued. Her more interesting sketches and stories vacillate between demonstrating comforting clichés and grappling with difficult lived particulars. Tentative acts of discovery, they produce the disjunction between literary and social conventions and the individual experience with which those conventions fail to deal. Gaps and contradictions are never more apparent than when she uses her life for material. And much of her short fiction is autobiographical, generically less like the fashionable romances it appeared alongside than like *Roughing It*. While her short narratives illuminate her canonical text, they also stand as examples of the craft of fiction in the first half of the nineteenth century.

Susanna Strickland was born on 6 December 1803 in the county of Suffolk, England.[1] Her father had attempted to elevate himself and his family to gentry status but he suffered a financial loss early in 1818 and died that spring. His wife and their eight children were left in reduced circumstances. In the late 1820s Susanna and four of her sisters began to supplement the family income with earnings from their publications. At the end of the decade she experienced an emotional and religious crisis which she eventually resolved in the spring of 1830 by leaving the Church of

England and converting to a Dissenting sect. That summer she met Lieutenant John Wedderburn Dunbar Moodie, a half-pay officer from the British army whose Scots family had lost its land. Having obtained Susanna's consent to emigrate — one of the few ways for fallen gentry to improve their circumstances — Moodie married her in April 1831. (I have chosen the convention of referring to her as Susanna Strickland until her marriage, and as Mrs. Moodie thereafter.) On 1 July 1832 they set sail from Edinburgh for Upper Canada.

That fall the Moodies and their eight-month-old daughter settled on the Lake Ontario front, near Port Hope. After eighteen months, dissatisfied with the neighbourhood, they took up land north of Peterborough among a more congenial society of middle-class immigrants, including Mrs. Moodie's brother, Samuel, and her sister, Catharine Parr Traill. Backwoods farming was not to their liking either, however, and within four years they were seeking a way out. Following the Upper Canadian Rebellion of 1837, Moodie served as a captain in the militia at Toronto. On the basis of this and subsequent service, and on her own contribution of loyal poems to the turmoil, Mrs. Moodie petitioned the Lieutenant-Governor for a permanent position for her husband. In the fall of 1839 J.W.D. Moodie was appointed Sheriff of Hastings County and was stationed in Belleville. In January 1840 Mrs. Moodie, now with five children, rejoined her husband, from whom she had been separated for most of the previous two years. This move did not, however, usher in the season of comfort and content for which she longed. Moodie's tenure as sheriff was plagued by the unceasing machinations of a local elite, until his resignation in January 1863. The Moodies never achieved financial stability or social rapprochement, and when J.W.D. Moodie died on 22 October 1869 his wife was left to the care of her children and sister. Mrs. Moodie relied mainly on two daughters who had married well, since her three surviving sons lacked economic security themselves. She died at a daughter's home in Toronto on 8 April 1885.

adrift in the British class structure. Rachel Wilde, "the daughter of a poor gentleman," asserts that "Papa never visits with tradespeople." The older, more circumspect Rachel of "Matrimonial Speculations," another daughter of "a poor, proud gentleman," does not verbally express her repugnance; she simply retreats from her new-found relations the day they meet. Mrs. Moodie not only emphasizes the vulgarity of these tradespeople compared to her heroines' gentility, but through their wealth she highlights the two Rachels' poverty. Throughout her writing these two contrasts are deployed together. Her uneasiness about class arises from loss of gentry status before she could ever become accustomed to it, and this also accounts for the obsession with wealth and caste in her work and the shrillness of some of her opinions.

Mrs. Moodie does not represent her life between 1820 and 1832 in her autobiographical fiction. The subtitle of "Rachel Wilde," "Trifles from the Burthen of a Life," becomes the main title for the continuation of Rachel's narrative after her marriage to Lieutenant John M —— and the birth of her first child. Writing was one of Susanna's main pastimes between her father's death and her marriage. In a memoir, Catharine provides an account of the early writing ventures of herself and Susanna that is similar to the concluding chapter of "Rachel Wilde." Both narratives tell of the discovery of the blue paper, the oral readings of the manuscripts and the reaction of the oldest sister. *Spartacus*, a children's book which Susanna said she wrote when she was thirteen, was her first publication, achieved with the aid of her father's friend in 1822. After an hiatus of a few years, she published a series of five children's books in the second half of the decade. By 1828 all of the sisters, except Sarah, had published one or more children's books, and Catharine, Jane and Susanna all connect writing with their economic dilemma.[3] Susanna went from children's stories to verse and prose publication in a series of magazines and annuals. Her first book for adults and only collection of poetry, *Enthusiasm, and Other Poems*, appeared in 1831. During her last years in England she never lacked a publisher and could justifiably say of herself, as she says of Rachel Wilde, that "the world . . . gave the meed of praise."

Mrs. Moodie's last words about Rachel Wilde, pointing ahead to her transformation in "Trifles from the Burthen of a Life," tell how she abandoned fame for love, marriage and emigration; but in Susanna Strickland's case, a religious crisis caused her to question her literary ambitions much earlier, before she met J.W.D. Moodie. This crisis, too, had social and economic implications. The Dissenting sects drew their parishioners from the middle class, but businessmen who could aspire to gentry status often belonged to the Church of England to avoid limits on the rights of Dissenters. Thomas Strickland was a member of the Established Church. While his older girls became High Church, from the mid-1820s Sarah, Susanna and Catharine had various involvements with Dissenters, involvements that disturbed their older sisters' sense of propriety. Only when Susanna joined a Congregationalist chapel in April 1830 did she solve a religious dilemma which had begun over a year before (letter 22). Late in 1828 she had broken off an engagement to be married; early in 1829 she had given up writing; in the summer she had written of becoming a missionary and was called "a mad woman and a fanatic" by a close friend; she had destroyed her plays under the pressure of "fanaticks," as she later termed them, who told her it was "unworthy of a christian to write for the stage"; she had rejected all aspirations to fame and devoted her "talents to the service of God"; by the fall of 1829 she was suffering from some obscure illness and frightening her sisters by "fainting away." The evidence of religious disturbance (and associated social and psychological trauma) combines with the concept of "enthusiasm" developed in her writing to situate a period of Low Church Evangelism in Susanna Strickland's life.[4] Her older sisters, their High Church affiliations reinforcing their social pretensions, were scandalized. Her Evangelical moment precipitated her fall from the Established Church altogether into Congregationalism, one of the original Dissenting sects. While the outcome of this storm would have been accepted by her friends among the Dissenters, it would have made overt her rejection of her sisters' pretensions. In Congregationalism she found a religious body more suited to her economic status, and recovered both her mental equilibrium and her literary aspirations. Her collection of poetry was now in the hands of a Dissenting printer.

Soon after her conversion, Susanna Strickland and J.W.D. Moodie met at the London home of an anti-slavery activist with whom she had become friends. Moodie knew this man from South Africa, where they had both been colonists. In London to seek a wife and a publisher for a book on the colony, Moodie planned to return to his thriving South African farm. He was successful in both quests, except that his fiancée dreaded Africa.[5] She vacillated between what were for her two mutually exclusive options: marriage and emigration or spinsterhood and England (letters 29, 31). When Moodie agreed to change their destination from the Cape to Canada and she chose the first option — marriage and emigration — Susanna Strickland believed, like Rachel Wilde, that she was also rejecting her literary career. The methods Lieutenant M —— uses in "Trifles" to force his wife to accept emigration with him seem to be the same methods that Lieutenant Moodie used on Susanna. In the expansion of "Trifles" into the novel, *Flora Lyndsay*, however, Mrs. Moodie's autobiographical heroine resumes writing during the trans-Atlantic voyage, and her author, of course, did not abandon writing when she emigrated. Perhaps it was her only means of resistance.

Mrs. Moodie's fictional self-representation ends at the colony's threshold. She resumes the story of her life in the openly autobiographical prose that culminates in *Roughing It* and *Life in the Clearings*.

A Life of Writing

Susanna Strickland Moodie had two main periods of literary productivity: the first, begun in 1827, ended with her emigration; the second, begun with the move to Belleville, ended with her consolidation of periodical work into a series of six books, starting with *Roughing It* in 1852. Her attempts to resuscitate her literary career in the 1860s failed. At each stage, her career was directly and indirectly connected with her social and economic position: it provided the possibility of improving that position through material return and social recognition; it constituted the site of her struggle to reconcile herself to that position. The tension between the desire for independence and the reality of constraint in *Spartacus* is resolved by romanticizing the slave-hero. The hero of *Hugh Latimer*, another children's book, shares with Susanna Strickland a grandfather who lost the family farm and yeoman rank, a father who died penniless and a mother struggling to support her family. The recognition of Hugh's worth by wealthy patrons leads to his social elevation, demonstrating not only that the true basis of gentility is morality but also that the good ultimately gain the material confirmation of their inner worth. The contrived plot is justified, here and elsewhere in Mrs. Moodie's fiction, as proof of God's control over the seemingly random operations of contingency: romance becomes realism when Providence is actively believed in. None of her separately published children's books is short enough for inclusion here, but most of them show their heroes curbing their revolt against circumstance by succumbing to the middle-class concept of duty, again demonstrating lessons that she herself was trying to learn.[6] But her compulsion to write was also an investment in the power of writing to lift her out of the social position humility dictated she should accept, and to that extent was itself a prolonged revolt against that position.

The professionalization of writing and the demand for women authors for the new fashionable magazines and annuals of the 1820s and 1830s added substance to this investment. Susanna Strickland's first signed publication for adults was a sketch published in *La Belle Assemblée*, whose alternate title, *Court and Fashionable Magazine*, and self-description as "Containing Interesting and Original Literature, and Records of the Beau Monde" succinctly locate it in the social and literary world of its time. In the spring of 1827 she mentions having sent a sketch to *La Belle Assemblée* and thinks of "becoming a regular contributor to the Mag" (letter 2). "Sketches from the Country. No. I. — The Witch of the East Cliff" is in the July issue. This piece and three of the four that follow it are melodramatic stories which old, county characters narrate. Only the fifth, "Old

Hannah; or, The Charm," comes close to the conventions of the sketch as they were being established, most popularly, by Mary Russell Mitford, whom Susanna Strickland admired and with whom she corresponded. "Old Hannah," included in the present selection, is the only one of these sketches not based on local legend. It also contains the greatest amount of autobiographical information. As the conventions of the sketch dictate, it lacks the developed plot which constrains the previous stories in the series.[7]

Susanna Strickland published some forty items in *La Belle Assemblée*, most of them verse. Of the prose pieces, two others are represented in this collection. "A Dream" demonstrates the importance she placed on experience beyond that of the rational waking mind, and also reveals her early preoccupation with fame. This sketch thus relates to her interest in the supernatural mentioned in "Old Hannah" and present in "The Witch of the East Cliff," and to her belief in omens as exhibited in "Rachel Wilde" and "Trifles." The other piece from *La Belle Assemblée*, "The Pope's Promise," is not as one-dimensionally didactic as most of her non-autobiographical fiction. Neither the Pope nor the shoemaker deserves his elevation in this story. When the shoemaker chastizes "a rich community of Franciscan monks," his words are charged with the author's displaced anger at the laxity of some Anglican priests. Counter-Reformation Catholics were legitimate targets for early nineteenth-century British Protestants, but the vehemence with which these monks are castigated suggests that her target was a professional clergy closer to home. An evil character in *Mark Hurdlestone* considers the "five rich livings" held by the local rector sufficient incentive for seeking a life of luxury in the Church of England, and the Reverend Dr. Beaumont in "The Doctor Distressed" is the object of a similar, although more muted, satiric intent. That Mrs. Moodie republished "The Pope's Promise" as "A Historical Sketch" shows how casual were her conceptions of both history and the sketch.

Shortly after her first contribution to *La Belle Assemblée* Susanna Strickland began writing for the annuals or gift-books, one of the first triumphs of capitalist commodity publishing. She continued to submit her work to the annuals until 1831, the year this phenomenon peaked with sixty-three different titles vying for the market; that December, she had at least seven pieces in four different annuals. Her five stories for the annuals in 1831 all deal with problems created by poverty. Her comic anecdote, "My Aunt Dorothy's Legacy," may relate to her own anticipation of an inheritance. There are also close parallels between the careers of Tom Singleton, a character in the story, and Thomas, the youngest Strickland. Legacies feature again in "Matrimonial Speculations" and *Mark Hurdlestone,* and in autobiographical guise in "Trifles" and *Roughing It.*

Ornate engravings were a main selling point of the annuals, and the fashionable writers who were sought in preference to more literary authors were sometimes commissioned to produce poems and stories illustrating already engraved illustrations. Mrs. Moodie wrote "The Vanquished Lion" and a poem to accompany illustrations in *Ackermann's Juvenile Forget Me Not* for 1832 (issued in 1831). The picture of a mother saving her infant from a lion, glossed only on the last page, provides a pretext for the rest of the story. In the opening paragraphs the mother's explanation to her son of the family's financial failure and necessary emigration produces what Mrs. Moodie knew of the economic and social causes of her own dilemma. She was married and pregnant when she submitted this story and in it she condenses her own experience and that of her mother by having the father of the story, instead of dying, decide to emigrate to the Cape colony. The attempts by this fictional mother to deal with the prospect of emigration anticipates Mrs. Moodie's own attempts, reiterated up to twenty years later in *Roughing It.* Reliance on God's inscrutable design ameliorates a fully determinist vision. Providence is the last resort for a woman who feels that control of her life is in the hands of others. The mother's grief is never resolved in the story. Her psychological distress at its opening is detoured into physical distress at its close. When next she occupies the foreground, she is before the lion, praying for the release of her child. The success of her prayers proves that God is listening. Mrs. Moodie must not have tested Him by praying against emigration.

Her religious crisis was probably the reason Susanna Strickland ceased to publish in the worldly *La Belle Assemblée* in 1829. The annuals were noted for their piety and many explicitly religious series offered her opportunities to publish; thus, writing for them would have fulfilled a moral, rather than a literary, ambition. During 1830 and early 1831 she gave expression to another commitment, writing poems and reviews for her friend in the Anti-Slavery Society who edited the *Athenaeum*. She transcribed for him *The History of Mary Prince*, and the exchange between Rachel and another character in "Trifles" concerning a book of the same title probably occurred in Mrs. Moodie's own life. Late in 1830, her new religious identity intact, she re-entered the fashionable periodicals through the *Lady's Magazine*, perhaps edited by her sister, Eliza. Her three stories in the *Lady's Magazine* may have been published as a result of Eliza's disposal of her papers after her emigration. The problem of the legacy in "The Doctor Distressed" is compounded for the Harfords by the son, Harry, being discharged from the army on half-pay. This was J.W.D. Moodie's situation when he became a prospective son-in-law to the Stricklands. This story was incorporated in "Matrimonial Speculations" and the ending changed to extend its autobiographical significance. The Reverend is widowed in the second version, but does not die. The Harford son and heir does not wait for the disposal of the doctor's fortune, but solves his financial problem by emigrating with a wife who accepts the move as a condition of marriage.

All but one of the pieces Mrs. Moodie published in North American periodicals and newspapers prior to her work for the *Literary Garland* were poems, many of them reprints. She contributed one story to the short-lived *Canadian Literary Magazine* in 1833.[8] Her first prose piece for the *Garland*, "The Royal Quixote," a long and rather tedious story about King Gustavus Adolphus of Sweden, a favourite historical figure of hers and her guide in "A Dream," was, she says in a note, written in 1824. She was always extremely frugal with her writing, seeking publishers for earlier work, published and unpublished, and forging periodical fragments into longer works, as she did for all her books. Once she began to publish in the *Garland* she had no difficulty becoming one of its main contributors, supplying both new work and old. The *Garland* was written by and for a small group of recent middle-class immigrants who wanted to satisfy conceptions of their gentility which had been frustrated in England. In the wake of the rebellions this group believed in its destiny as a new elite, tempering the extremes of the fallen oligarchy without succumbing to the temptations of agrarian radicalism. The British political principles of hierarchy, a balanced constitution and responsibility were part of a continuum which easily measured literature according to its piety and gentility. These values, and her conventional expression of them, deaden Mrs. Moodie's verse in the *Garland.* As her career with this periodical continued, however, she began to publish more prose than verse, and through her prose she eventually went beyond the limitations of the literary tradition the *Garland* attempted to transplant.

"The Sailor's Return," subtitled "Reminiscences of Our Parish" and labelled No. 1 as if to initiate a series, is the first of Mrs. Moodie's *Garland* stories in this collection. She plays with a pose of parish chronicler long enough to introduce Amy Morris, who tells her own story. Amy's is a conventional story of thwarted love, but in the thwarting her experience touches upon her author's. The economic failure of Amy's fiancé's family is solved by the providential provision of the opportunity to emigrate. Amy's expression of the fear that emigration permanently severs loved ones is only one of Mrs. Moodie's voicings of the same fear throughout her writing. She frees Amy from what could have been a prolonged engagement to an absent lover by ending his emigration in shipwreck. Mrs. Moodie covers this lapse in the divine design and attempts to transcend sentimental conventions by having Amy disprove her own assertion that "the heart is incapable of feeling a second passion." The mix of sketch and romance, of fiction and non-fiction, of various levels of first-person narration, while it makes the story somewhat disjointed, shows Mrs. Moodie experimenting with her form and exploring options that her own decisions had foreclosed.

In "The Broken Mirror," published two years later in the *Garland*, her own experiences are displaced into another exploration of the Cape colony option. This story demonstrates that "Providence is always true to those who remain true to themselves" and claims to be "A True Tale." The disposal of the mirror that makes the Harden family fortune in the colony and gives the story its title is asserted in a footnote by Mrs. Moodie to be based on fact. The temporal and spatial setting, and the nationality and religion of the Hardens, suggest that she got the anecdotal kernel of the story from her husband.

The Moodies began the *Victoria Magazine* in 1847, hoping to find a market among poorer settlers and thus avoid competition with the *Garland*. Overall, the material in their periodical, a large proportion supplied by them, does not distinguish it from its rival. An exception, "The Well in the Wilderness," Mrs. Moodie's first story in the *Victoria Magazine*, while another story of emigration under economic duress, is her only fiction set in North America. But as a result of bringing her fiction so close to home, the benevolent Providence, which has hitherto been behind the happy destinies of her emigrants, disappears. Wild animals never appear in her Old World fiction; her repeated expression of fear of them in her autobiographical work suggests that they are emblematic of her terror of the unsettled parts of the world.[9] In 1831 Providence was a presence powerful enough to save the mother in "The Vanquished Lion" from the beast in the jungle; in 1847, fifteen years from England, the beast and its jungle devour Providence. The one time Mrs. Moodie tried to bring her fiction to North America she produced a shocking image of loss of faith in God's ability to engineer happy plots for immigrating heroines.

Mrs. Moodie devoted much of her creative energy in the years 1847–1851 to producing the series of sketches included in *Roughing It* and *Life in the Clearings*. Those that focus on characters other than herself have the unity of short stories, but they are unified by plots that destroy their protagonists. When she transformed the sketches into a continuous narrative of her life, she could not discern the larger plot which would link them and redeem that life. She was too realistic to impose a romance plot and could not confront her life as a tragic plot.

Plot failure is also evident in the autobiographical fictions about her life prior to immigration, which Mrs. Moodie began publishing in 1848. "Rachel Wilde," serialized in the *Victoria Magazine* and diffuse and plotless throughout, is brought to an arbitrary close. It is a reconstruction of her girlhood as a young artist, and the artist, worshipping Napoleon and Milton's Satan, is an outcast and a visionary. The isolation Rachel generates for herself at the home of the tradesman and the isolation generated for her at the home of the gentleman are both due to the uncertainty of her class status. Mrs. Moodie juxtaposes the development of the artist with an exposition of economic determinism. While she does not connect the two, the first three paragraphs of the story delineate a theory of environmental determinism which asserts that character is conditioned by circumstances. Missing is any plot that would recover determinism by translating it as Providence. When free to invent a plot, as in "The Broken Mirror" and others of her more conventional stories, she could demonstrate the existence of a benevolent God. When she was living the plot out, no such easy solution was available. A "Domestic Sketch" in the last number of the *Victoria Magazine*, "The Quiet Horse," is based on her experience, whether or not the event it depicts actually occurred. The story provides an image of the expedients to which the Stricklands were driven, and it demands comparison with Susanna's epistolary anecdote of using a donkey to draw their chaise. The story's moral that "No one looks well or acts well out of his own sphere" applies to Mrs. Moodie's forced departure from the sphere within which she was raised.

Mrs. Moodie published excerpts from her life text, both documentary and fictive, in 1847 and 1848. She published no new prose for the next two years, probably because, as indicators in *Roughing It* suggest, she was engaged in producing that book. In the spring of 1851 she published the first instalment of "Trifles from the Burthen of a Life" in the *Garland.* This story, like "Rachel Wilde" loose and unplotted, lacks thematic wholeness and simply ends, as arbitrarily as the other story, with the emigrants boarding ship. The penultimate paragraphs strain to discern God's design in this story and in Mrs. Moodie's own life. The first two ships on which the M —— s almost embarked both meet disaster. As in "The Sailor's Return," Mrs. Moodie does not wonder why emigrants secondary to her plot are not guarded by Providence and, as in "The Vanquished Lion," the providential rescue of her main character from physical disaster does not dissipate her fear of the social and psychological disaster of emigration. While her fabricated stories constitute successfully integrated redemptions of determinism by attribution to God's benevolent order, her autobiographical texts, rather than taking over pre-established designs, seek to establish a design which is never quite there in the record — hence her inability to achieve satisfactory closure in these texts, including *Roughing It* and *Life in the Clearings*. Loosed from the contrivances of plot, she demonstrates the very unprovidential nature of her life.

Mrs. Moodie revised "Trifles" to become *Flora Lyndsay*, published in 1854 by the same firm that published her two Canadian books in the two preceding years. She expanded the first version in three ways: she added a number of character sketches, the best known being that of "Miss Wilhelmina Carr" which takes up three chapters in the novel; she extended the narrative to encompass the trans-Atlantic voyage, ending with the ship anchored in the St. Lawrence; she inserted the story of "Noah Cotton" — the last third of the novel — on the pretext that her heroine wrote it on the ship. She drops nothing from the first version and her revisions do not alter Rachel's dramatic struggle to cope with emigration. Mrs. Moodie described *Flora Lyndsay* to her publisher, in terms which also apply to "Trifles," as "a bundle of droll sketches of our adventures out to Canada and preparations for our emigration," and also acknowledged its incompleteness: "This should have been the commencement of *Roughing It*, for it was written for it, and I took a freak of cutting it out of the MS" (letter 47). At the end of the novel she refers to her continuation of it in the documentary work. In *Life in the Clearings* she also refers to its more famous predecessor and in a letter says that the two might have made up one book (letter 49).

As Mrs. Moodie was producing her life text in the late 1840s and early 1850s, her publishing relations were becoming unstable. After twelve issues the Moodies' trouble with the publisher of the *Victoria Magazine* made its future uncertain; plans for a second year were soon dropped. Their magazine would have been unprofitable because of many of the same factors that made the *Garland*'s demise imminent. An indigenous business and professional class was re-establishing political stability without aid from the middle-class immigrants of the 1830s, most of whom would have become assimilated to North American ways by 1850. Interest in nurturing a genteel British literary tradition, outdated even in its homeland, was fading. The *Garland* failed in 1851 and by this point Mrs. Moodie had a British book publisher. She lost this publisher after the five books following *Roughing It* failed to attain a comparable modest success; by 1855 she was without a publisher. She published again in the early 1860s, but as a nationalist sense of Canadian writing was awakening she returned to her British youth for material. Two late sketches of men she knew in the 1820s conclude the present volume. Her output was slight in these years, and she placed her last piece in 1872.

Rereading the Writing and the Life

Just as Mrs. Moodie developed *Roughing It* from a series of discrete sketches into a prolonged narrative, so too she began "Rachel Wilde" with self-sufficient "trifles" or sketches. She headed the first two chapters No. I and No. II, and they could stand on their own like the individual pieces in her many series of sketches. If she was beguiled into fully accounting for her early life only well after she began the accounting, this would explain the inconsistencies in narrative voice and the transparent device of the found manuscript. Perhaps she was unintentionally led into writing her life history, but once she began she produced a fairly complete account up to the late 1840s. Implicitly acknowledging the most important events in her life, she devotes the most pages to her father's financial failure and death, and to her marriage and emigration. She develops more or less consistent personae in her autobiographical texts — a misunderstood artist for "Rachel Wilde," a submissive wife for "Trifles," an heroic backwoodswoman for *Roughing It*, a detached observer for *Life in the Clearings* — and these personae are more or less convincing alibis for the separate existence of these texts. But none of her autobiographical texts is complete in itself, not even the three books of her Canadian trilogy. These texts are instalments in a serial writing project directed at aligning their author's perceptions of her life with the social and economic realities of that life. This life writing project includes sketches in which she is only an observer. The project is also deflected into some of the fictions in which she uses autobiographical details as a basis for exploring options she did not take. The project necessarily remains as unfinished and contingent as the life it shadows and the history it attempts to capture.

Fictional explorations of options not taken, the New World unravelling of romance plots and their replacement by tragedy, the discovery that Providence does not support and thus ratify all emigration schemes — writing was Mrs. Moodie's quiet way of resisting decisions about her life over which she felt she had no control. A striking number of her stories and sketches begin with questions asked by one character of another; the first half of *Roughing It* is structured on dialogue as interrogation. These seemingly formal features further manifest the power of words to probe the assumptions identity relies upon, and they also reveal that this probing is not always consolatory. Mrs. Moodie had reason to fear the exposure of self-doubt that writing risked. How could she acknowledge that the decisions she was forced to make in her late twenties may have been the wrong ones?

A closer consideration of the faith Mrs. Moodie placed in the supernatural and non-rational can disclose the subversion enacted in her writing. Catharine and Susanna in their youth were enthralled by astrology and by stories that Reydon Hall was haunted. Susanna opens "The Witch of the East Cliff" by noting her pleasure in ghost stories, and she later writes of Rachel Wilde's converse with ghosts, witches and fairies. The sketch on witchcraft is matched by another about a successful summons of the living by the dead. Rachel Wilde vaguely believes in "second sight," and Mrs. Moodie wonders if a family of backwoods neighbours "were gifted with secondsight" (*Roughing It* 440). She deals with magic in two of her *Garland* serial novels. She gives premonitory weight to "A Dream," and in *Geoffrey Moncton,* after a long digression on dreams as "revelations from the spirit land," a character has a dream the exact prescience of which is confirmed (68). In the pseudo-scientific discourse of the period oneiromancy was linked with phrenology and Mrs. Moodie confirmed her belief in the latter in letters, *Roughing It, Life in the Clearings* and "Washing the Black-a-moor White."[10] She based two early poems on a successful experiment in telepathy conducted with a friend, and expressed her happy belief in spiritual communion with the absent in a letter (letter 4). In *Roughing It* she confirms her ability to communicate spiritually with her husband in Belleville and devotes several pages to establishing the truth of "this mysterious intercourse between the spirits of those who are bound to each other" (493). She fulfils the conception of the artist as visionary, developed in "Rachel Wilde," most explicitly in her poetry, but she makes prophetic statements in her prose as well. She believed there were many "mysteries of the mind" (*Geoffrey Moncton* 322, 326), and these and "the mysterious nature of man" (*Roughing It* 494) could not be analysed rationally, but might one day be better understood. These uncontentious beliefs force us to take more seriously the statements she builds on their foundation.

Among the "mysteries" of Mrs. Moodie's mind the one that bears most closely on the question of her writing as resistance is her belief in premonitions and omens. Many characters in her conventional fiction have premonitions which, foreshadowing plot developments, turn out to be accurate. In this collection, the "something" that "whispers" to Mrs. Harden in "The Broken Mirror" predicts that the family "shall have luck" with the mirror. The disposal of the mirror in the Cape colony proves to the family that they are under "providential care." Mrs. Moodie's fiction contains no omens of disaster, but Amy Morris's "want of confidence in the wise dispensations of an over-ruling Providence" is affirmed by the loss of her fiancé in a shipwreck en route to Upper Canada. The storm that rages the day the M —— s try to depart in "Trifles" strikes Rachel as "a bad omen," but her husband reacts angrily to her "childish" belief in such "an exploded superstition." While Rachel grants that reason will not support "her favorite theory," she nonetheless insists that "we are all more or less influenced by these mysterious presentiments." When they miss their ship for Scotland a second time, Rachel has another premonition: "I should be quite disheartened if I did not believe that Providence directed these untoward events." This time her husband inclines to her opinion despite his "disbelief in signs and omens." In a brief exchange inserted at this point in *Flora Lyndsay*, Mrs. Moodie's autobiographical heroine suggests an interpretation of this second omen: "Is it not a solemn warning to us, not to leave England?" (105). Here, and at all but one other point in "Trifles," Lieutenant M —— overrides his wife's wishes, whether they arise from premonitions or from more capricious foundations.

In *Roughing It* Mrs. Moodie begins her narration of the events leading up to emigration by insisting that everyone has "secretly acknowledged" the power of the "mysterious warnings" which "the human heart" receives (206). She declares her faith in these warnings and hints that she would have been "saved much after-sorrow" if she had paid "stricter heed" to "the voice of the soul." Her digression prepares for the introduction of one such omen. On the last night in England her "inward monitor" warns her not to emigrate: "how gladly would I have obeyed the injunction had it still been in my power" (207). The only time in "Trifles" that Lieutenant M —— gives in to his wife is when "the dread of going in the *Rachel*, took a prophetic hold of the mind of her namesake." In this story Mrs. Moodie can only credit Providence for having saved the M —— s from death by cholera on the first ship they missed and from death by smallpox on the *Rachel*. She confirms the omen that saves them from these disasters. But what of the omens sent by Providence to Rachel and Mrs. Moodie telling them they should not emigrate at all? She never disputes them. In neither text does she ever claim that God watched over her own emigration. Was she, in 1851 when she was writing both of these passages on premonitions, secretly saying to herself and all who would read her that the omen she received on the eve of emigrating had been right? Was she afraid that by giving in to the demands of J.W.D. Moodie she had strayed from a romance plot authorized by Providence into a dangerously unplotted life?

Mrs. Moodie was no more than historically accurate in consistently connecting emigration with loss of caste. Nonetheless, her obsessive return to moments of fall and departure brings home what doubts and anxieties plagued that small, educated group of fallen gentry who settled among the mass of poorer immigrants in Upper Canada in the 1830s. Her sketches and stories show, among other things, that not all immigrants were willing to accept the inevitability of their exile from England, and they bring us to certain insights that bear directly on roughing it in Upper Canada.

Note on the Text

Besides her six books, Mrs. Moodie published five serialized novels and over seventy sketches and stories of various lengths. Another editor would make different choices for a collection of her short prose. I have chosen those pieces in which she is most engaged with her own experience, but other principles of selection have also come into play. No sketch that became a part of either *Roughing It* or *Life in the Clearings* has been included. Many stories have been excluded because they are either too long, too slight or too conventional to warrant attention. I have tried to provide examples from all of the various genres in which she wrote, and from all of the major periodicals in which she published prose. The selections are arranged in chronological order according to the first known publication date. This information and information on any subsequent appearances of the individual pieces are given in a note to each. The house styles of the periodicals that first published these texts have been retained. I have not attempted to improve, correct or modernize Mrs. Moodie's prose and have made alterations only in clear cases of error, usually attributable to careless printing.

Notes

1 Besides her own writing, there are many texts containing information about Mrs. Moodie. The following have been most useful to this introduction: Jane Margaret Strickland, *Life of Agnes Strickland* (Edinburgh and London: William Blackwood and Sons, 1887); Catharine Parr Traill, "Reminiscences of the Life of Mrs. C.P. Traill Written by Herself" and "A Slight Sketch of the Early Life of Mrs. Moodie," Public Archives of Canada, Traill Family Collection; Mary Agnes FitzGibbon, "Biographical Sketch," *Pearls and Pebbles; or, Notes of an Old Naturalist*, by Catharine Parr Traill (Toronto: William Briggs, 1894), iii–xxxiv; Una Pope-Hennessy, *Agnes Strickland. Biographer of the Queens of England 1796–1874* (London: Chatto and Windus, 1940); Carl Ballstadt, "The Literary History of the Strickland Family," diss., University of London, 1965; Audrey Morris, *The Gentle Pioneers. Five Nineteenth-Century Canadians* (Toronto and London: Hodder, Stoughton, 1968); Michael Peterman, "Susanna Moodie (1803–1885)," *Canadian Writers and Their Works: Fiction Series 1*, ed. R. Lecker, J. David and E. Quigley (Downsview: ECW, 1983), 63–104; Carl Ballstadt, Michael Peterman and Elizabeth Hopkins, eds., *Susanna Moodie: Letters of a Lifetime* (Toronto: University of Toronto Press, 1985); Carl Ballstadt, "Editor's Introduction," *Roughing It in the Bush* (Ottawa: Carleton University Press, 1988), xvii–lx. References to Mrs. Moodie's letters are incorporated in the text, using the numeric designations provided by the editors of *Letters of a Lifetime*; references to her book publications, also incorporated in the text, are to the following editions: *Flora Lyndsay* (New York: De Witt and Davenport, [1854]), *Geoffrey Moncton* (New York: De Witt and Davenport, 1855), *Life in the Clearings* (Toronto: McClelland and Stewart, 1989), *Mark Hurdlestone* (De Witt and Davenport, [1854]), *Roughing It in the Bush* (Ottawa: Carleton University Press, 1988).

2 *The Romance of History* is the title of a book Susanna Strickland reviewed in the *Athenaeum* in late 1830. Her defence of this book against "matter-of-fact people" who

object to the taking of "unwarrantable liberties with historical events" and to the mistaking of "fiction for fact" makes it clear that romance, not history, is the pertinent category in considering her own historical sketches and stories.

3 Catharine turned money earned on her first book over to her mother "to eke out the now reduced income of the home" (FitzGibbon xv). Jane believed that "poverty was the means of bringing forth" the sisters' talents (quoted in Pope-Hennessy 18) and Susanna makes the same point in *Roughing It* (209).

4 The information and quotations are from letters 8, 10, 12, 17, 18, 61, 19, 20. Susanna Strickland develops her concept of religious enthusiasm in the title poem of *Enthusiasm.* She expresses a prose version of this concept through the voice of a heroine with autobiographical features in *Mark Hurdlestone.* The Dissenting sects were rationally inclined and only the Methodists and Anglican Evangelists were enthusiasts in her sense.

5 J.W.D. Moodie describes his South African settlement, his return to England and his decision to emigrate to Canada in his *Scenes and Adventures, as a Soldier and Settler* (Montreal: Lovell, 1866) viii–ix and in one of his chapters in *Roughing It* (232–34).

6 The only published discussion of her children's books is by Peterman (68–69).

7 See Carl Ballstadt, "Susanna Moodie and the English Sketch," *Canadian Literature* 51 (1972): 32–38 and Peterman (68–69).

8 "Achbor: An Oriental Tale," originally in the *Canadian Literary Magazine*, is available in *The Evolution of Canadian Literature in English: Beginnings to 1867*, ed. Mary Jane Edwards (Toronto: Holt, Rinehart and Winston, 1973), pp. 167–72, and so has not been included in this collection.

9 In an exchange about the Cape colony added to "Trifles" before it became *Flora Lyndsay*, Mrs. Moodie has her autobiographical heroine speak about her "terror of the wild beasts" (7–8). J.W.D. Moodie in *Roughing It* says that his wife was against emigration to South Africa because "wild animals were her terror" (233). The mother in "The Broken Mirror" cites "the wild beasts" as a reason not to emigrate to South Africa. In *Roughing It* Mrs. Moodie mentions a "dread of encountering wild beasts in the woods" which she "never could wholly shake off" (295) and describes her "cowardice" during a walk with her husband at night in the woods when a bear followed them (426–27).

10 Letters 3, 4, 47, 63, 69; the phrase "the truth of phrenology" appears in both *Roughing It* (335) and *Life in the Clearings* (193).

A Dream

I had been confined to the house, during a fortnight, with an intermittent fever. It is one of the properties of this disorder to produce troubled and unquiet slumbers, and even waking fantasies, that present to the eye the grim heads of beasts and monsters; and the most grotesque and horrible caricatures of the human countenance, which seem perpetually to be making mouths and grinning at the patient. As the fever ran high in the day, I was constantly troubled with these phantasmagoria at night; and, waking or sleeping, incessantly under the dominion of the night-mare.

The dream that haunted my imagination last night was so extraordinary, that I could not resist an inclination to record it upon paper.

I found myself in the centre of a large and well cultivated plain, watered by a noble river, the dead flat of the landscape interspersed with woods and houses, while towns and villages appeared in the distance. While I stood musing alone, and marvelling where, and in what country I might be, I was joined by a plain dignified-looking man, whose majestic countenance bore the stamp of melancholy, and of secret care. On asking the stranger's name, he told me he was the unfortunate Gustavus, the exiled and dethroned King of Sweden; and that he was travelling to regain his kingdom. His was a name which I could not hear when waking without emotion, and my interest was not a little excited in the royal stranger, as I replied — "I am an English woman, seeking fame in the world." — "Ha!" returned he, taking me by the hand, and looking earnestly in my face, "is that your business? Well, we will prosecute our journey together — follow me."

So saying, he turned into a rough and narrow path, which I had great difficulty in traversing, as it was full of fragments of rock, and deep pools of water. Several times I stopped, fearful of proceeding further; but my guide waved me forward, exclaiming, in a lively voice, "Courage! this is the way of the world, persevere to the end, and we shall overcome the world." As he said this, I observed an immense ridge, or bank of earth, rising before us, which bounded the plain in a level line, as far as the eye could reach. The bank appeared sloping, at a distance, and easy of access; but, the nearer we approached, the more tremendous the ascent became, till the ridge seemed rising perpendicularly to the clouds. A deadly fear crept over me — I shuddered, and drew back. "Your path lies over this bank," said the King; "you have gone too far to recede, and must either stay here and perish, or go forward with me."

With trouble and anguish I began to ascend the bank, pausing every moment to take breath. My companion was more fortunate: he continued to proceed, with a slow yet steady pace, and often put back his hand to help me along; but, while I put one step forward, I seemed to slide two or three steps back. At last, stopping, and wringing my hands, I said I could go no farther. "Take time," returned the ex-monarch, "patience will overcome every difficulty. The world will not surely treat you as harshly as it has treated me. — Take this knife," he continued, "and scoop a hole in the bank; and, when you have placed one foot in this artificial step, make another above it, and in time you will reach the top." I followed his advice, laboured indefatigably at the bank, and at last had the satisfaction of seeing my royal guide on the top of the ridge. He stood for a few minutes, and looked earnestly upon me as I toiled up the ascent: then, crying out that his kingdom was won, he disappeared on the other side. With much pain and fatigue, I reached the summit of the bank, anticipating a happy termination of my journey in the Swedish monarch's dominions; but what were my horror and dismay, on beholding, on the other side, a wide and trackless ocean, stretching away into infinity, and bounded on every side, excepting that of the bank on which I stood, by the horizon! Not a sail — not even a floating plank — relieved the dreary monotony of the scene. I turned from the cheerless prospect, bewildered, and sick at heart, to look back upon the fertile plain I had quitted; but there a new object of terror met my eyes. The fields, the houses, the woods and river, all had vanished, and been swallowed up in a vast interminable ocean, like the one on which I had just looked, that seemed rapidly advancing. The bank now shook and tottered beneath the repeated shocks of the boisterous waves. The narrow isthmus at length seemed gradually sinking beneath my feet; and, in the extremity of my despair, I called loudly on heaven to save me. I beheld at my side a giant, whose extended arms were stretched over these two vast oceans, while his head and shoulders seemed to uphold the heavens, and support the massy frame of nature by their own stupendous bulk. I fain would have asked this terrific being, whom he was, but astonishment and fear kept me mute. He seemed to divine my thoughts; and, gazing sternly upon me, said, "I am TIME! Between these two vast oceans, I behold the beginning, and the final accomplishment, of all human events. The ocean behind thee is *Time that is past*; the one from which thou shrinkest with such dismay, is *Time that is still to come*. When this isthmus shall yield to the constant working of their opposing tides, they will both be blended and lost with me in eternity!" The giant touched me with his hand, and I fell forward into the awful abyss which had swallowed up my companion! The moment the waters received me into their icy bosom, I awoke with a loud shriek.

Frequently I returned thanks to the Almighty, that my terrors had been produced only by a dream, and that time had not passed from me for ever!

April 16th, 1828

La Belle Assemblée 3rd ser. 8 (1828): 69–70.

The Pope's Promise

It was St. John's Eve: the summer sun was sinking behind the distant hills, while his last beams glittered on the lofty spires and towers of Marcerata, one of the oldest towns in Italy, and formerly the metropolis of Ancona. The uncommon beauty of the evening had tempted forth most of its younger inhabitants, who were seen in detached groups along the high road, or in the fields, enjoying the fresh air. The wealthier females rode forth, attended by cavaliers well dressed and gallantly mounted, while the happier peasants were dancing on the level plains without the town, to the merry notes of the pipe and tabor. The streets were deserted, the sounds of labour had ceased, and the voice of joy alone mingled with the chiming of the convent bells, which announced the hour of evening prayer. Yet Pietro Ariano was still hard at work at his stall — Pietro, who was reckoned the best singer and the best dancer in Marcerata, and who was withal, though only a poor shoemaker, as handsome and as well grown a young man as any in the Pope's dominions.

Pietro's little domicile stood just without the town, by the road side, and his stall fronted a long low latticed window that commanded a fine view of the adjacent country, and within the shade of which the young follower of St. Crispin was seated, busily plying his awl. His present fit of industry appeared more like an act of imperative duty than choice: his bent brow expressed both impatience and fatigue, and he flung his various implements from side to side with a sullen and dissatisfied air, glancing wistfully from time to time towards the open plains, and muttering imprecations against every fresh party of pleasure that passed his stall.

His wife, a lovely dark-eyed young woman, was earnestly engaged in binding the fellow shoe to that which Ariano held half finished in his hand; and she beguiled the lingering hours by singing, in a sweet voice, an old ditty, to amuse the infant that smiled upon her knee; while from under her long dark eyelashes she watched the perturbed countenance of her husband. As the sun gradually declined in the horizon, Pietro's patience sank with it, and before the glorious luminary had totally disappeared, its last remaining spark was utterly extinguished; and, casting down his implements of labour, he exclaimed, in a hasty tone — "Now, by the mass! not another stitch will I set in slipper or shoe to-night were it to please the Pope! — Ha! 'tis a beautiful evening; and the merry tinkling of that guitar has called forth all my dancing wishes, and my legs, in idea, have been in motion for the last two hours. What say you, my pretty little Francesca," he continued, unconsciously assuming a gayer tone, and slapping his wife briskly on the shoulder, "will you put your boy to bed, and join with me the merry group yonder?"

The young woman shook her head, and looked up into his face with an arch smile — "No, no, Pietro! not till you have performed the promise you made to the handsome young friar last night." — Ariano sullenly resumed his work.

"Ay, keep my promise, forsooth, and be repaid by promises for my labour! Oh, these monks are liberal patrons, who are too spiritual to attend to any temporal wants but their own. To convert neats' leather into shoes and sandals, for their accommodation, is as difficult a task as bringing over so many Turks and heretics to the true faith; and they are more nice to fit withal, than the vainest damsel that ever sported a smart foot and ankle. They live on the general contributions of the public, and take good care to want for nothing that can be obtained by way of extortion. O, 'tis a dainty life!" he continued, plying his awl, in despite of his recent vow, with increasing energy, whilst inveighing against his principal employers, a rich community of Franciscan monks, who belonged to the noble monastery whose august towers formed the leading feature in the beautiful landscape before him, "O, 'tis a dainty life! whose very motto is '*laziness*.' They are the hooded locusts that devour the substance of the land, and receive a patent from the Pope, heaven bless him! to live in idleness. Would that my father had made me a member of this holy community, instead of binding me to his own unprofitable trade!"

"If that had been the case, Pietro, I should never have shared your poverty and your labours," said Francesca, with a glance of reproachful tenderness.

"Il Diavolo!" exclaimed Pietro, laughing; "you would have been much better off. *A monk's mistress*, let me tell you, ever carries her head higher than an honest man's wife."

"Hush! hush! Pietro, is it right for a Christian man to utter such impious invectives against these holy monks?"

"Now, by all the saints and angels whom they pretend to worship!" returned Ariano, "if I live and flourish, the boy you hold upon your knee shall be one of these sleek hypocrites. Who knows what preferment he may arrive at? Several bishops have risen from no higher origin. Ha! what say you to that, my little advocate for celibacy? Have I not well provided for your son?"

"You are very profane to-night, Pietro, and speak more like a swaggering man-at-arms than a poor artizan. Besides, I am sure the handsome young padre is no hypocrite. I never saw such a bright eye glance from beneath a monk's cowl."

"Ha! art thou again thinking of him, Francesca? He is a stranger in Marcerata, but I warrant him a very wolf in lamb's clothing."

The colour mounted to Francesca's brow, and she called out in a hasty voice — "Stint in thy foolish prate, Pietro! the young friar is even now before us!"

Ariano was utterly confounded when he beheld the padre leaning against the stall; and he felt not a doubt that the stranger had heard the whole of his intemperate conversation with his wife: nor was he wrong in his conjecture. The handsome young man, whose noble deportment and graceful figure set off his monastic habit, and whose bright, laughter-loving dark eyes ill accorded with a monk's cowl, had been for some time a silent spectator of the scene. Felix Peretti was highly amused with the abuse that Ariano had so unceremoniously levelled against his holy order, for which he felt little respect himself, and as a child of fortune, from his youth upwards, considered only as a step towards further advancement.

"How now, Signor *Scarpettáro*! is it your ordinary custom to close the labours of the day by abusing your betters? Are the shoes which you promised should be completed for my journey to Loretto, finished?"

"No," returned Pietro; "they yet want a full hour's work for their completion, and I have just made a vow never to pursue my handicraft by candle-light to please any man. So you must e'en perform the journey, reverend padre, as many better and holier men have done before you, barefooted."

"Do you make it a point of conscience, Ariano, to fulfil one promise by breaking another? I cannot commence a long and fatiguing pilgrimage without the aid of the Apostle's horses. Oblige me in this instance, Pietro, and I will put up a private mass for the repose of your evil temper, and the restoration of that goodly virtue in man, *patience*!"

"As to my temper!" returned the *Scarpettáro* fiercely, "no one has any right to complain of that but my wife, and if she speaks truly, she will inform you, father, that, when I am not fatigued with working over hours for *monks* and *friars*, I am the best tempered fellow in Marcerata."

The padre cast a sly glance at the dark eyed Francesca, from beneath his cowl, and something like a provoking smile sat ready to break forth into a hearty laugh, upon his rosy lips. — "Well, friend Pietro, far be it from me, sworn as I am to peace, to rouse the evil spirit into action. 'Resist the devil,' says holy writ, 'and he will flee from you!' But a truce to all further colloquy, I see you are putting the finishing stroke to the disputed articles: tell me how much I stand indebted to you for them?"

"You cannot stand my debtor," said Ariano, recovering his good humour, when he found he had completed his job, "till you have tried on the shoes, and then I fancy you will *stand in* my debt." Father Felix laughed heartily at this sally; and, seating himself carelessly on the edge of the stall, with a very *dégagée* air, proceeded to draw on the shoes.

"By our Lady of Loretto!" said Francesca, who was earnestly watching all his movements, "it were a thousand pities that such a white and well shapen foot should have to contend with the sharp flints and briars."

Pietro's brow contracted into a frown, and, turning abruptly to the padre, he asked him how the shoes fitted him?

"My feet, much better than the price will my purse. What am I to pay you for them?"

"Three testoons. And the cheapest pair of shoes that ever was made for the money."

Father Felix shook his head thoughtfully, and drawing forth a leathern purse from the folds of his monastic gown, calmly took it by one of the tassels of divers colours by which it was ornamented at each end, and emptied the contents on to the board. A few pieces of money rolled, one after the other, on to the stall; and the hollow sound emitted by their coming thus unceremoniously in contact with each other, spoke the very language of poverty. The young friar counted them deliberately over; then, turning to Ariano, without the least embarrassment, explained the state of his finances — "Signor *Scarpettáro*, in these few pieces of money, you behold all my worldly riches: I want one *julio* to make up the sum you demand for the shoes, which luckily will give you an opportunity of performing a good work at a very small expence; for, you perceive, I have not wherewithal to satisfy your exorbitant charge."

"Exorbitant charge!" reiterated Pietro. "Now by St. Crispin! may I suffer the pains of purgatory if I take one *quartrini* less. What! after having worked so many hours over my usual time, to be beaten down in the price of the article. Give me the shoes, thou false friar! and pursue thy way barefooted. A monk! and moneyless, quotha. You have doubtless emptied that capacious pouch at some godless debauch, or poured its contents into a wanton's lap."

"Now, out upon you for a profligate reprobate, and vile *Scarpettáro*!" returned the monk. "Do you think it so difficult a task for a priest to keep his vows? Or do you imagine that we cheat our consciences as easily as you do your customers? My purse contains only eight *julios*, how then can you reasonably expect me to pay you nine? I must, therefore, remain your debtor for the odd coin."

"And when do you propose to pay me?"

"When I am Pope," returned Peretti, laughing, "I will pay you both principal and interest."

"God save your Holiness!" said Pietro. "If I wait for my money till that period arrives, the debt will still be owing at the day of judgment. Or, stop — I will bequeath it to my children of the tenth generation, to buy them an estate in the moon. A Pope! Young father, you must shroud those roguish eyes under a deeper cowl, and assume a more sanctified visage, and carry a heavier purse withal, before you can hope to obtain the *Papal Crown*!"

"When I stoop, Ariano, to pick up St. Peter's keys, I shall not forget to pay my old debts. So fare thee well, thou second Thomas à Didimus, and God be with thee, and with thee, pretty Francesca; and may he render the burthen thou bearest in thy arms the blessing and support of thy future years."

So saying, he stooped, and, pretending to salute the sleeping infant, contrived to imprint a kiss upon the white hand that held him. Francesca blushed all over; and Pietro, bidding his Holiness remember his promise, called Francesca to him, and bade the friar good night. His wife obeyed the summons, but she looked after the handsome Felix till a turning in the road hid him from her sight.

Years glided on in their silent course, and the name of the young friar, and his visit to Marcerata, were forgotten by Pietro Ariano and his wife. Poverty, and the increasing cares of a large family, tamed the vivacity of the *Scarpettáro*'s spirits: he no longer led the dance, or joined in the song, but was forced, by hard necessity, to work both by night and day at his trade, to supply his numerous offspring with bread. Francesca's smooth brow was furrowed by the hand of time, and she had long yielded the palm of beauty to other and younger females. Her son, on whom Father Felix had bestowed his blessing, was early dedicated to a monastic life, and had risen, by transcendent abilities, from the rank of under assistant to the sacristan, to be one of the head members of the monastery of St. Francis. The young Antonio possessed ambition, which made him aspire to the highest ecclesiastical honours; but he had no friends among his wealthier brethren, who beheld in the son of the poor *Scarpettáro* of Marcerata an object of fear and envy. However, he was the pride and delight of his parents, whose poverty he greatly alleviated, but could not wholly remove. One morning, while Pietro was taking the measurement of the smartest little foot in Marcerata, and the pretty village beauty was cautioning him not to make her slippers too large, a sudden exclamation from his wife made him raise his head, as a dignified ecclesiastic entered the house, and demanded if his name were Pietro Ariano? The *Scarpettáro* answered in the affirmative.

"Then, you are the man I seek. Pietro Ariano, I command you, in the name of the Pope, the pious and blessed Sixtus the Fifth, to repair instantly to Rome, and attend his pleasure at the palace of the Vatican."

Pietro was petrified with terror. The implements he had just been using fell from his nerveless grasp, and his limbs were assailed by a universal shivering fit, as if under the influence of an ague. "Alas!" he exclaimed, "what is the nature of my crime?"

"That is best known to your own conscience," returned the stranger.

"Then, the Lord have mercy upon me! I am a sinner, and, what is still worse, a dead man! Like Daniel, I am cast into the lion's den, and there is none to deliver me. Ah, wretch that I am! Why did I live to witness this day?"

"Oh, Pietro! my unhappy husband!" said Francesca, hiding her face in her garments, and weeping bitterly: "I knew long ago into what trouble your intemperate speeches would bring you. Are you not now convinced of the folly of meddling with matters that did not concern you? Did I not tell you, when you would rail at the holy monks, you were casting yourself upon a two-edged sword? You will be sent to the Inquisition, and burnt for a heretic, and I shall lose you for ever!"

"Peace, woman! peace!" returned the tortured Ariano; "reproaches avail not; they cannot save me from the fate which in all probability awaits me. Farewell, my wife — my children!" he cried, alternately taking them in his arms; "cease not to petition heaven to restore me to you!"

The voice of weeping was audible on every side; but Pietro tore himself away, and commenced his long journey on foot to Rome. On the evening of the third day, he arrived at the magnificent city; but his thoughts were too much occupied by his own cares, and his body too much bowed down by fatigue, to notice any of the grand objects which saluted him on every side. He entered Rome as a criminal enters the condemned cell that he never more expects to leave, till the hour which fulfils his sentence. Seeking a small hostlery in the suburbs of the city, he partook of a scanty supper, and retired to bed, dreading, yet anxiously expecting, the ensuing day. In the morning, he learned from his host that the Pope held a public levee in the great hall of the Vatican, to receive the French and German ambassadors; and that if he repaired thither early, and waited patiently till the crowd dispersed, he would be more likely to gain the speech of his Holiness. Unacquainted with the public edifices in Rome, poor Ariano wandered about for some time like a fool in a fair, bewildered in contemplating the august palaces which rose on every side, and imagining each in its turn a fit residence for a king; but, whilst he paused, irresolute how to act, a strange fancy entered his head, and he imagined that the Pope, who was Christ's viceregent on earth, must reside in the grandest church in the city. Accordingly, he stopped on the steps leading to St. Peter's Church, and demanded of an ecclesiastic, who, like himself, seemed bound thither, "If that noble building were the Pope's palace?"

"You must indeed be a stranger in Rome, my friend," returned the priest, with a good-natured smile, "not to know the difference between St. Peter's Church and the Vatican. — What is your name?"

"Pietro Ariano, a poor shoemaker, of Marcerata."

"And your business with his Holiness, the Pope?"

"Alas! reverend padre, with that I am at present unacquainted: his business, it should seem, is with me. I have none with him, unless it be to ask pardon for crimes unintentionally committed."

"Aha!" returned the priest, "you are the very man whom his Holiness wishes to see. He calls himself your debtor; and you will soon know in what coin he means to pay you. But, take heart of grace, Signor *Scarpettáro*; I will introduce you to the Pope."

Trembling from head to foot, Pietro followed his conductor into the great hall of audience. Sixtus was already in his chair, and the ambassadors of various nations were making their obeisance before him; but the splendour of the scene could not induce the terror-stricken Ariano to raise his eyes, and he stood shivering behind the priest, with his head bent down, and his arms folded dejectedly across his breast. At length the crowd gradually dispersed, and the Pope called out to the ecclesiastic, in a facetious tone, very different from the solemnity of manner with which he had addressed the ambassadors — "How now, Father Valentinian! Whom have you got there?"

"Please your Holiness," returned the priest, striving to impel Pietro forward, "the poor shoemaker of Marcerata."

At these words, Pietro uttered a loud groan, and fell prostrate at the feet of the Pope, who, after indulging in a long and hearty laugh, said, in a jocular tone, "Raise thy head, Ariano, that I may be sure of thy identity. By St. Peter! time has nearly worn out thy upper leathers, if it has spared thy *sole*. Is this panic-stricken craven the man who talked so largely, and uttered such bitter invectives against holy mother church? By the mass! I fancy the pains of purgatory will be light when compared with the pangs he now endures!"

"Most holy, most blessed, most incomparable Pope!" groaned forth the prostrate *Scarpettáro*, "I was mad and drunk when I uttered such foul calumnies against your Holiness's brethren. Heaven has justly punished me for my impiety, by revealing my rash speeches to your Excellency."

"It needed no miraculous interposition of saints and angels, Pietro, to inform me of your iniquity; for I heard you with my own ears. But, stand up, man. It was not to call you to an account for your sins, which doubtless are many, that I sent for you hither, but to pay you the debt I owe you. Look me in the face, Signor Ariano. Hast thou forgotten St. John's Eve, and the young friar who called at your stall in his pilgrimage from Ascoli to Loretto?"

For the first time, Pietro ventured to raise his head, when he encountered the glance of the bright dark eyes, whose amorous expression he had so unceremoniously reprobated three-and-twenty years before. That face, once seen, could never be forgotten. Time had given to Felix Peretti a stern and haughty expression; and the eye that, in the heyday of youth, seemed lighted only by the fire of passion, now possessed the glance of an eagle, before which the monarchs of the earth trembled, when it flashed in wrath from beneath a brow that appeared formed to rule the world. "Ha! Ariano, I perceive you recognise the face of an old friend. Have you forgotten the promise I made you, on that memorable night when I prophecied my own future grandeur? What was it, Pietro?"

"Please your Holiness," said Pietro, his eye brightening, and his hopes encreasing in proportion as his fears diminished, "whatever you may think fit to give me."

"Come! Come to the point, Signor *Scarpettáro*," returned Sixtus, in a stern voice, "I will have no interpolations; what is the actual amount of the debt I owe you?"

"One *julio*, please your sublime Excellency; the principal and interest of the said sum, if ever you should come to be Pope, which, God forgive my wickedness for doubting!"

"Amen!" ejaculated Father Valentinian.

"Right, Pietro; the sum shall be faithfully paid," returned Sixtus, drawing a paper from his bosom, on which he had spent some hours the preceding day in calculating the interest of one *julio* for three-and-twenty years. What the sum amounted to, the chronicler of this anecdote does not condescend to inform us, but it was small enough to annihilate all Pietro Ariano's new and highly-raised expectations, and his golden visions melted into air. He received it from the Pope with a vacant stare, and still held open his hand, which disdained to close over so paltry a prize.

"Is not the sum correct?" demanded Sixtus.

Ariano remained immoveable.

"Count it over again, my friend; and if one *quartrini* is wanting, it shall be faithfully paid. What, art thou moon-struck? Hast thou not received that which I owed thee?"

"No," returned Pietro, gathering courage from disappointment; "your Holiness is still my debtor."

"Prove your words," said Sixtus, while a slight flush of anger suffused his face.

"The *julio* I gave your Holiness credit for three-and-twenty years ago, when thou wast only a poor barefooted friar, I should never have walked to Rome to demand at thy hands. — The sum has been faithfully paid, but you have not remunerated me for loss of time — for the expenses I incurred, and the fatigue I suffered, at my years, in undertaking, at your command, so long a journey. The tears my wife and children have shed, and the anguish of mind I have endured, to make sport for your Holiness, are debts of conscience you have still to pay; and, to shew you that a poor shoemaker of Marcerata can exceed the mighty Sixtus in liberality, I absolve the *Pope* of *his promise*!"

Here Pietro made a low reverence, laid the money at the Pope's feet, and was about to depart, when Sixtus called out in a lively tone — "How, Signor *Scarpettáro*! have you the presumption to rival a pope in munificence? Pride has urged you, though a necessitous man, to reject the only sum which you were justly entitled to receive. — It is not for me, as viceregent for heaven, to reward a man for exhibiting to my face one of the seven deadly sins. I therefore transfer my bounty to more deserving objects; give this purse of gold," he continued, "to thy wife, Francesca, and make glad her heart by informing her that her son, Antonio, is Bishop of Marcerata."

Overcome by this unexpected change of fortune, Pietro prostrated himself before his munificent benefactor, and, embracing his feet, called out in an extacy of joy — "Ah, your Holiness! — I am your *debtor* for life!"

La Belle Assemblée 3rd ser. 8 (1828): 245–50. *Victoria Magazine* 1 (1847–48).

Sketches from the Country. No. V. — Old Hannah; or, The Charm

In sooth my tale is built on simple facts,
The actors are no puppets of my will;
I but record what I myself have seen,
And laughed at in my days of youthful glee.

Poor old Hannah! I see her now before me — her short stout figure, framed as it was for labour — her round red face, which long exposure to the weather had so befreckled and betanned, that not one tint of her original complexion was left — her small, deep-seated, merry grey eyes, and the little turned-up impertinent-looking nose, that gave, by its singular elevation, such a grotesque and humorous expression to her countenance. Often have I stolen out into the fields to listen to her odd tales, a pastime which I infinitely preferred to the detested task of conning my lessons. I can see her now before me, as she sat crouched on her three-legged stool, milking her favourite red cow, Strawberry, beneath the shade of the noble old ash in the meadow. They were happy days when I paused delighted by the side of the little white gate, leading into the garden, to catch the snatches of her old songs — to shudder at the treachery of False Anachin, and to enter, heart and soul, into the tragedy of Lord Thomas and fair Ellen.

Hannah first initiated me in ghostly lore. From her I

learned that village-maids had sweethearts, and that men — "heaven save the mark!" — had died for love. Even at that tender age, this last piece of legendary information seemed an inscrutable mystery. But Hannah, for a while, satisfied my doubts, by telling me that "I was young at present; before I died I should know all about it." From Hannah I learned that *gipsies* could actually tell fortunes — that *Fridays* were unlucky days to travel on — and that *charms* were infallible.

I verily believe that the old woman had tried every species of this kind of necromancy, from the age of fifteen to fifty, without obtaining, through the potent influence of magic, the desired effect — a husband! Hannah was a spinster — or, as the country people denominate a single woman, who has to support a family — a grace widow.

Charms were with this antiquated *graceless* damsel, a cure for every complaint that afflicts humanity. For the cramp, she wore the cramp-bone of a sheep, so placed as to touch the part affected; for head-ache, a parcel of mustard seed, sewed up in a small flannel bag, and fixed under her cap on the crown of her head; and, if her teeth pained her, she forthwith proceeded to the orchard, and culled from the oldest codling-tree a small withered apple, which she deposited by moonlight on the gate-post of a distant field, whither she expected chance would never direct her steps again. But for the ague, that terror of the poor, a host of magical remedies were resorted to, with pretty equal success. The *unerring* cure, however, for this cruel disorder, shocked my organ of benevolence, with its selfishness, even when I was a child; but Hannah, though very charitable, felt no such scruples. Here it is: — "Any person afflicted with the ague, and wishing a fair riddance of this evil disorder, must, when the shaking fit is on, go down into a marsh, or low meadow, through which flows a running stream that has a plank over it for the benefit of foot passengers. The person, male or female, must cross the bridge without looking behind, and, standing on the bank, with face to the sun and back to the rivulet, suddenly throw the plank to the opposite shore, chaunting these lines: —

'Ague! Ague! Ague! seize, I pray,
The first living thing that comes this way,
And throws the plank across the river,
But cease to plague me now for ever.
Take them, and shake them — torment them sore,
But, Ague, return to me no more.'

"The afflicted person is then to return home, carefully avoiding the road by which he came; and the first man, woman, or child, who is so unfortunate as to pass that way, and throw the plank over the stream, receives the evil spirit, which, like the hobgoblins of yore, has not the power to cross a running brook."

At Hannah's instigation, as I advanced towards womanhood, I have placed my shoes, "going and coming," when resting in a strange bed, in the vain hope of beholding in my sleep my future spouse. For the same wise purpose, I have picked up a white stone, when passing over ground I had never before trodden, and, on my return home, deposited the prize under my pillow, as a mystic treasure that could reveal to me the secrets of futurity. I have blunted many a good penknife by cutting fern roots aslant, and paring apples, to try for the initials of the favoured swain by waving the parings nine times over my head, and casting them, with a sudden jerk, over my left shoulder. And then, the pips! When seated round a cheerful fire, at the present social season of the year, how often has that potent spell passed from girl to girl, as bright eyes and rosy cheeks bent anxiously over the roaring blaze, expecting, with ill-concealed impatience, the result of their invocation!

"If he loves me, crack and fly!
If he hates me, lie and die."

And I, with whom laughter was almost a disease, have often, out of bravado, reversed the charm, yet listened, with a beating heart, to the snap that annihilated my hopes.

Charms of deeper importance no persuasions from Hannah could ever induce me to try. All her rhetoric, enforced with the true Suffolk whine, and a long pause between every letter, could never prevail on me to eat the apple before the looking-glass at midnight to behold my sweetheart peeping over my left shoulder. The very idea of the thing rendered me nervous. I considered it a crime little short of mother Eve's eating the forbidden fruit in the garden of Eden, and had I seen any reflection in the glass, I should have devoutly taken the apparition for no less a personage than the prince of darkness. However, one new year's eve, a clergyman (an old bachelor to boot) presented me with a piece of bridecake, which had been drawn nine times through the wedding-ring by the bride; proposing, on the whim of the moment, that we should both try the efficacy of the charm by dreaming upon it that very night. I eagerly entered upon the visionary speculation and dreamed — Queen Mab herself must have inspired the dream — that I was married to the King! The donor of the cake was less ambitious, and less fortunate. He imagined that a swarm of wasps maliciously invaded his bed, and devoured the cake from beneath his pillow. This, with the mad levity of sixteen, I treated as a just visitation, and emblematical of the forlorn state, falsely denominated "single blessedness."

But to return to Old Hannah. — The winter had closed in with severe frosts and snow. Every thing wore a cheerless aspect but Hannah's red face, which exhibited unusual signs of hilarity. Her work went briskly off her hands, and you might hear her voice all over the house singing her favourite old catches. No one could divine the reason why Hannah appeared as airy and as gay as a lark, when the inhabitants of the mansion, and even nature herself, had assumed a graver aspect — Hannah was in love! The bailiff who superintended the farm attached to the mansion, was a hale, middle aged man, and a widower withal. Proctor had whispered soft things in Hannah's ear, and she once more resolved to have recourse to one of her most potent charms to learn the sincerity of his intentions. She made me her confidante, and vain were all my efforts to dissuade her from the silly scheme. Hannah was no sceptic: she would have doubted her own existence, as soon as the power of her spells. She slept in a lonely garret, some way apart from the rest of the family, and the charm she had chosen was a very simple one. It consisted only in putting on clean linen on the first Friday in the month, and stepping backwards into bed; repeating, as she did so, the following invocation three times over: —

> "Friday night, Friday night,
> As I lie dressed all in white,
> I pray to heaven that I may see
> The man that my husband is to be;
> In his apparel and his array,
> That he doth appear in every day;
> With the children by his side,
> Which I am to have when I am his bride!"

My brothers, two roguish boys, just escaped from the gloomy precincts of a free school to spend their Christmas holidays at the old mansion house, learned from Mary, the housemaid, Hannah's intention. This knowledge afforded them infinite diversion, and called forth all their mischievous propensities. They sought the enamoured damsel, and, assuming a forced gravity of deportment, they assured her the charm would have no effect unless she took nine black pepper-corns, and shook them nine times in Proctor's boot, and screwed them up in a little piece of paper, and tied them with a bit of green thread round her great toe. Hannah received the information with avidity, and never questioned the source whence her young masters derived their pretended knowledge. She went to bed perfectly satisfied, having smuggled one of Proctor's boots out of his room, to give the nine ominous shakes to the nine black pepper-corns. The process of tying them round her toe would have afforded a subject for Wilkie's pencil; but to these mysteries we were not admitted. The family retired to rest at the usual hour, and before eleven the house was in a state of perfect tranquillity. About midnight, our slumbers were broken by a piercing scream, or rather yell of terror. The sound came from Hannah's garret; and, as it echoed through the long passages of the mansion, all the inhabitants sprang with one consent from the arms of sleep. Before I could reach my wrapping cloak, the door of my apartment was suddenly burst open, and Hannah stood before me — her eyes fixed and staring, and her red face, for the first time, as white as her night dress. Her limbs were convulsed, as if under the influence of an ague fit, and her quivering lips appeared incapable of uttering a single word. There she stood, trembling and shaking before me, the tears rolling down her cheeks, and her hands uplifted in silent horror. Before I could find words to demand the reason of her nocturnal visit, the room was filled with eager and enquiring faces, and the two mischievous imps who had partly been the cause of her terrors were the foremost in the motley group. Anxious to learn the result of their invented charm, they exclaimed in a breath —

"Well, Hannah! — what did you see?"

She answered this abrupt question in a pitiful whine, of such unusual length and emphasis, that I was constrained to turn my back on the afflicted damsel, to hide the painful risibility with which I was irresistibly assailed.

"Oh! Master Thomas, and John, it was all your doings. Instead of Nehemiah Proctor — *Death* came to my bed-side!"

"Death!" repeated the brothers, exchanging a sly glance with each other — "That was rather a strange visitor. I suppose it was old Harry, who, loving hot things, had come to untie the pepper-corns from off your toe."

After much desultory colloquy, the detail of the night's adventure was drawn from old Hannah. She had gone up stairs backwards, and a tiresome job she had had of it; first up one steep flight of stairs, and then another — across Miss Sarah's room, and down the long passage, at the end of which, as ill-luck would have it, the wind blew her candle out, and she dared not go back to light it, for fear of breaking the charm. On she went in the dark, stumbling at every step, till she reached her own door. There she heard such dismal howlings of the wind in the old garrets, and such strange noises, like the rattling of bones, that she stood quaking and shaking with fear. Then the difficulties she encountered, in securing the nine pepper-corns round her toe; and then, jumping backwards into bed, the first spring she gave broke the thread that held the peppercorns, and she heard them go rolling to every corner of the room! "'Tis no use," says I, "seeking for them, I might as well look for a needle in a truss of hay. I contrived at last to get into bed," continued the old woman, in a very sulky tone; "but I was in such a desperate fluster, I made three mistakes in the charm, and that helped to do the mischief. However, after I had made a finish of the conjuration, I lay quite still in the bed, neither looking to the right nor to the left, but with my eyes fixed on the door which was before me, and thinking of Nehemiah Proctor, when I heard a soft low voice say — Mother! mother! — I sprang up in the bed, and the room was no longer dark, but as light as the noon-day. And there stood at the foot of the bed the prettiest pick-a-ninny of a child I ever saw in my life, and I knew the dear babe again — it was my sweet Caleb, whose corpse that wicked old parson —— treated so undecently."

"Hannah," said I, "how was that?"

"My poor babe died in the work-house," continued Hannah, sinking into her usual whine; "and Mr. —— came to bury the child. It was past three o'clock, and he was in a desperate hurry to get home to his dinner. My child's coffin was not brought out quick enough to please him, and he began to read the service over the empty grave, and — in short, it was not a christian burial, and I told him so; but he said, in his blustering way — 'There, there, young woman, it is of no use your making such a bother about the child; you should have been ready before. It is your place to wait for me, not mine to wait for you.'"

Hannah was at length brought to the main point of her story. "Well, as I was telling you when I broke off to give you an account of my dear Caleb's funeral, I was so struck with the beauty of the child's smiling face, that I tried to take him in my arms; but, before I could touch the vision, it turned suddenly into a hideous grinning skeleton, that sprang on to the bed, and, seizing my throat between his long bony fingers, cried, in a hollow voice, 'I am Death! the only husband you will ever have!' It was no dream — it was a struggle for life and death. — I felt his cold bones rattle against me — I saw the blue flames flashing out of the eyeless holes in his skull — his grinning teeth chattered in his fleshless gums, as he tightened the strong gripe on my swelling throat — Oh! oh! I feel him! — I see him still!"

Her face, which had resumed, during her relation, its crimson hue, was again colourless; her lips firmly compressed, and her eyes wild and staring. "How this world is given to fibbing!" cried Tom, with a deliberate laugh; "what a mountain this mole-hill has become!"

I really pitied her distress. "Compose yourself, Hannah," I said; "you have been under the influence of a frightful dream."

"Indeed, Miss, I shall never forget it to my dying day — I was wide awake — I heard it with my own ears — I saw it with my own eyes — I felt its gripe on my flesh. You cannot persuade me out of my senses."

"It was very hard to raise such an outcry against your husband," cried Tom, "I will go and see what has become of him." Before he could leave the room, the door opened, and Master John, who had quietly retired, conducted into our presence a pasteboard skeleton of gigantic dimensions. At the sight of the apparition Hannah gave another frightful scream, and made a hasty retreat behind the bed-curtain, while the manufacturers of the scarecrow exclaimed, in a tone of triumph, "Here, Hannah! here's your husband!"

All my eloquence was vainly spent, when I endeavoured to convince Hannah that she had been deceived; — that my brothers had invented this scheme to cure her of resorting to charms for the future. She turned sullenly away, persisting in the truth of her own story. Tom, the inventor of the scheme, had introduced the pasteboard figure (which was skilfully constructed) into the room after Hannah was asleep, and placed it opposite the bed. Her dream was of the pretty child; but, awakening with the noise which "Death" made on his entrance, her vision was assailed by the frightful apparition, which seemed to grin horribly upon her in the moonlight. Imagination had done all the rest; and the mischievous boys had not a little enjoyed the wonderful and exaggerated account that the love-lorn damsel had given of the spectre. The experiment was not successful. Hannah still continued to practise charms, and still remained a spinster; and the old garret acquired the reputation of being haunted ever after; a calumny which will never be effaced as long as one stone shall remain upon another.

La Belle Assemblée 3rd ser. 9 (1829): 21–24.

My Aunt Dorothy's Legacy. A Tale of the Christmas Hearth

"And is this all the news you have to tell me?" said my cousin, Tom Singleton, drawing his chair closer into the family group which surrounded our cheerful fire last Christmas day. "After a fellow has been absent from home fifteen years, — a great deal more must have happened than you have thought convenient to relate. You tell me of births and marriages, and deaths, some of which formed the nine day's wonder, and were forgotten before I went to sea; but you have never informed me how Aunt Dorothy left her money."

An ill-suppressed fit of laughing passed round the circle. "Not to *you*, Tom," said my brother John, "or you would have heard that felicitous piece of news before."

"I never expected that the old girl would remember that she had a nephew at sea," said Tom, affecting an air of magnanimous indifference; but though he said nothing, he made his disappointment apparent by the violent manner in which he stirred a good fire which required no stirring, and by the sharp ringing sound with which the poker descended to its usual station.

"I never could stoop to flatter the old woman for her money. Cousin Hook had more tact; he understood such matters better, and was always an adept in angling for gold fish. Do you remember how he bowed and smirked old Walcat out of his money? That mean rascal has found the trade of a *sneak* more profitable than I have the profession of a gentleman!"

"Hook threw out his baits to no purpose. Aunt Dorothy left her money to those who knew better how to keep it, than Timothy did to wheedle it out of her," said my brother John.

"If it's a good story, let's have it, Jack," said the sailor, endeavouring to hide his chagrin; for he, like the rest of us, had flattered himself that he was a very great favourite with the old lady. He thought that she would have the sense to appreciate the conscientious manner in which he refrained from ingratiating himself into her good graces. He never brought her monkeys, nor parrots, China-crape shawls, curiously carved fans, shells, nor flowered muslins from the East, for fear Mrs. Dorothy should impute his generosity to a baser motive. For all these delicate omissions, Aunt Dorothy sat in judgment upon him, and this was the verdict she returned — That her nephew, Tom Singleton, was a very avaricious, unpolite young man. That as he did not choose to remember his Aunt Dorothy, she would one day convince him that *she* could forget *him*. And so it was — that when her will was read, Tom's name was never mentioned in the huge sheet of parchment which contained the inventory of her worldly goods and chattels.

John Singleton was highly amused by my cousin Tom's display of indifference. After indulging himself for some time at his cousin's expense, he commenced his relation.

"Tom Singleton, in the presence of so many pretty girls, have you the fortitude to cast a retrospective glance over the lapse of twenty years?"

"'Tis no pleasant affair, that," said the sailor, "to find all your happiest and best days on this side of time, and your hopes for the future, floating at random, without helm or compass, on a stormy sea. It makes one inclined to repay dame Fortune for her evil tricks, by casting anchor in the bay of matrimony with my pretty cousin Martha for life."

My sister Martha blushed and simpered at this sudden declaration of cousin Tom's regard, which for some days past she had more than suspected.

"Come, Tom! this is no direct answer to my question," said John, recalling him from an amatory reverie, by a smart tap on the shoulder. "Can you look back on the past for twenty years?"

"By George! can I not?"

"Do you remember bringing my aunt home, one evening, a cat, when you were a boy of ten years old?"

"Why, Jack, you are making me out an old fellow of thirty," said Tom, interrupting him, and peeping over my shoulder at my sister Martha. "Well, what of that cat? — I found it in a wild cat's nest in the wood at the foot of an old ash tree, and carried it home as a great prize to my aunt."

"That cat," said John, "was the means of destroying the hopes of the house of Singleton."

"Did that cat outlive his mistress? — Pshaw! the beast was venerable when I went to sea, and must have died with repletion long ago. Old Toby — she could not leave her money to him?"

"Aye," said John, "that cat survived to be my aunt's heir. In her last will and testament, Mrs. Dorothy Singleton, spinster, bequeathed to her cat, Toby, 500£. per annum, to be enjoyed by the said animal during the term of his natural life: and the said spinster further declareth Miss Dinah Pinch (an old maid who resided at the next house) the guardian of the said Toby, at whose decease the property was to descend to (one who in common with master Toby, possesses many cat-like propensities) Mr. Timothy Hook."

"And that cat actually choused us out of our share of my aunt's property?" said Tom, in a most discontented tone. "Ha, ha, ha!" from the whole group, was the only answer that Mr. Thomas Singleton, first mate of the noble East India Company's ship the Lady Louisa, received to his interesting interrogatory.

"Well, Tom," said my brother, goodnaturedly, "it cannot be denied that *you* were instrumental to this extraordinary bequeathment."

"But I tell you, John, that cat — and I should know the fellow again anywhere — must have paid the debt of nature long ago."

"Like the great Lama, it never dies!" said John; "it has already outlived its nine lives, and will continue to live as long as Miss Dinah Pinch continues to exist in this mortal sphere."

"How does she contrive to keep the animal alive?"

"I have been let behind the scenes, and I will tell you," said John; "but first you must promise not to betray this most sagacious virgin, for, between ourselves, she has made her will in our favour, and if she should outlive Mr. Hook, 'the king may chance to have his own again.' I am her executor, and to me she confided the important secret of Toby's miraculous longevity. When Toby first came into her possession, Miss Pinch was constantly apprehending his sudden demise. Mr. Hook came daily to see him, and had formed so many atrocious plots for his assassination, that she never suffered him a moment out of her sight. He was fed upon the best of food, and regaled with new milk and chicken broth; but in spite of these luxuries, he daily declined, and grew so thin and consumptive, that Miss Pinch sent, in great perturbation of spirits, for the family doctor, and begged him to write a prescription for him. Dr. K —— condescended to inspect his four footed patient, and declared that no earthly skill could save his life. That Toby was dying of that incurable disease — old age.

"Miss Pinch burst into a flood of tears; and after the man of medicines departed, ordered her carriage, and drove to the Life Insurance Office. A bevy of clerks came bowing to the door to assist her to alight.

"Take care of my cat!" said the cautious Miss Pinch, as Toby poked his head out of the muff into which she had inducted him for fear that the change of atmosphere should affect his lungs. One of the clerks received the muff and its living enclosure with a grin. "Oh yes, Madam, I assure you that I have a very great respect for the feline species, — all sensible people are fond of cats. — Did you ever hear of such an old fool? (whispering to a companion); I verily believe that she has come to insure the life of her cat!"

It was even as the imp of mischief guessed. After a long preliminary speech, Miss Pinch drew Toby from her muff, and asked, with a sigh, "if it were possible to insure the life of a cat?" A peal of laughter shook the room. The gravity of Mr. M., the actuary, was, for once, nearly overturned.

"Indeed, Madam," he replied, "this is the first application of the kind that ever was made to this office; and were there an office for insuring the lives of cats, that poor beast would never obtain a certificate from our attendant surgeon."

"Alas!" said Miss Pinch, "what shall I do?" The actuary, in spite of the gravity of his office, loved fun; and thinking that some mystery was concealed within the antiquated virgin's muff, he dismissed his clerks, and contrived to coax the secret out of her. The case of Toby and his guardian was of so novel a description, that he was both amused and interested by it; and after cautiously patting the wealthy, pampered invalid, he gave Miss Pinch, in a confidential whisper, the following advice.

"If I were in your place, Madam, I would insure his life by procuring another cat exactly like him; and I would, at the same time, take good care that the animal is not too juvenile to awaken the suspicions of the residuary legatee. Toby being a tabby, is so easily matched, that you may prolong his life to the age of Methuselah."

Miss Pinch took the hint. She confessed to me, that she was greatly alarmed lest Toby should expire before she had substituted another Grimalkin in his stead. However, she succeeded in procuring a fine middle-aged cat, the very prototype of master Toby: and though Mr. Hook immediately suspected the fact, so strong was the resemblance between the living and the defunct cat, that he could not get a witness to swear positively to the animal.

"And what became of poor Toby?" said Tom; "she surely was not so ungrateful as to discard him in his old age?"

"He was carried up into the garret, where he peaceably departed this life, and was privately interred in the garden."

My cousin Tom started from his chair and seized his hat. "Where are you going in such a hurry?"

"To congratulate Miss Pinch on her ingenuity in outwitting that sneaking fellow, Hook — and to look at the cat."

Strange are the revolutions that take place in the affairs of men. Before the year has drawn to a close, Miss Pinch, Mr. Hook, and Toby's substitute, have all paid the debt of nature. My aunt Dorothy's property has been equally divided among the members of the Singleton family; and last week I had the pleasure of dancing at the wedding of Mr. Thomas Singleton (now captain of the Lady Louisa) and my pretty sister Martha.

Comic Offering; or Ladies' Melange of Literary Mirth for 1832 (1831): 118–28. As "Tom Singleton; or, How My Aunt Dorothy Left Her Money," *Family Herald* (Montreal) 28 December 1859.

The Vanquished Lion

"Dear mamma, why do you look so very sad?" said Lewis Fenwick to his mother, as she slowly folded together the letter she had just finished reading, and burst into tears. "That letter is from papa — I know his seal. Is he ill?"

"No, my child; he is well, and will be here to-morrow."

"Then why do you cry, mamma?"

"Lewis," said Mrs. Fenwick, with a glance of such tender concern that it brought tears into the eyes of the affectionate boy, "you are too young to enter fully into the cause of my grief. You have only enjoyed the sunshine of life, and at present know nothing of its storms. Yes, my poor children," she continued, as the nurse-maid entered and put little Arthur, her youngest born, an infant eighteen months old, into her arms, "you little know the trials which await you, or the sorrow which at this moment wrings your mother's heart. Listen to me, Lewis — perhaps you may be able to comprehend me. A few weeks ago, your father was a rich man. This fine house, and these beautiful gardens, in which you have played from your infancy, were his own property; and every body looked up to him with respect, and treated him with attention. A great change has taken place. Your father has lost all his fortune. He is now, Lewis, a poor man. This house is no longer his. It has been sold, together with the furniture, to pay his creditors; and these beautiful gardens you will play in no more. The friends who came hither so often, when we could afford to entertain them, have deserted us in our distress; and your father, unable to maintain a genteel appearance in England, has accepted your uncle's invitation to go out to him as a settler to the Cape of Good Hope. We are to accompany him. This letter informs me, that he has already engaged our passage in the Antelope, and to-morrow we are to bid adieu to Hampstead for ever. In another week, Lewis, we shall be upon that vast ocean, of which you have so often read, and which you have so earnestly wished to behold; and we shall see our dear friends and native land no more. It is this thought which pains me, Lewis — which makes me weep. God will give me strength, for your sakes, my dear children, to support this great trial, but at present I feel it very hard to bear."

"And shall I indeed sail in a great ship across the wide sea? and go to that beautiful country, about which papa was reading the other night in Mr. Thompson's Travels? and see the great desert which Mr. Pringle describes in his beautiful poem? and the ostriches and the lions, and all the wild beasts which he saw?" said Lewis, his eyes sparkling with delight. "Is not that the land, mamma, where the oranges, and lemons, and figs, and grapes, grow in the gardens, the same as our pears and apples do here? Do not weep, mamma! — We shall be so happy."

"I have no doubt, Lewis, that you will learn to love the strange land; and perhaps, my boy, I may learn to love it, for your sake. But, Lewis, you cannot tell what it is for persons of my age to part from the country in which they were born; in which the best years of their life have passed calmly away in the bosom of a happy home, and surrounded by dear friends. The Cape will soon become as dear to you as England is now, and the recollections of these pleasant scenes will appear to you like the indistinct outlines of a dream. But, Lewis, I am too old to forget. The love of country is one of the most powerful feelings in the human breast, and the mind ever dwells upon the land of our birth with greater affection, when impressed with the certainty of beholding it no more. But God, my dear child, has appointed the future; and it is weak and sinful in short-sighted mortals like us to murmur at his will. To submit with cheerfulness to the dispensations of Providence is to overcome the world, and to disarm sorrow of its sting."

Here the conversation ended, and Lewis went out to work in his little garden as usual; forgetting that it was for the last time, for his thoughts were entirely taken up with what his mother had told him; and, boy-like, he looked forward with pleasure to the long voyage he was about to take. In the morning, the return of his father, and the bustle and confusion of packing, left Master Lewis no time for castle-building. He was proud of being made useful, and thought himself happy and highly favoured in being allowed to hold string and hand parcels. But, when all was over, and the house was dismantled of the last piece of furniture, and the heavy travelling trunks alone occupied the floor of the once-splendid dining room, Lewis began to think that the scene wore rather a serious aspect. His father stood pensively leaning against the bow-window which fronted the road, anxiously watching for the arrival of the coach, which was to take them away. His mother was seated on a large box, in a dejected attitude, holding her infant on her knee. His venerable grandmother, and his two aunts, were weeping beside her; and Lewis, feeling for the first time the sadness of a final separation from these kind friends, crept to his mother's feet, and, sitting down upon the uncarpeted floor, burst into tears.

The sound of approaching wheels, and the blast of the coachman's horn, roused all parties from their stupor of grief. Then came hurried and passionate adieus — arms were enfolded — and eyes, which had long ceased to hold acquaintance with tears, ran over — and hearts were united in the close embrace which precedes an everlasting separation. "God bless you! God grant you a safe and happy voyage, and protect and prosper you in a foreign land!" burst from pale lips; while some of their friends were too much agitated to express in words their silently eloquent farewell.

"Write to us soon, Edward! and tell us all that happens to you and the dear children on the voyage," said Mrs. Fenwick, tightly pressing the hand of her son. "Think how precious your letters will be when these old eyes must see you no more." — "This is too much," said Mr. Fenwick, pressing his mother more closely to his heart — "These partings are worse than death."

The old servants now crowded round their once dear master and mistress, to take their final farewell. In moments like these, the distinctions of rank are forgotten, and the best feelings of the heart alone prevail; and hands, hardened with labour, are pressed as affectionately as if they had always been accustomed to exchange reciprocal demonstrations of kindness. It was with feelings like these that Mr. Fenwick's family parted from their faithful domestics.

"The coach waits, sir," said the old gardener, as he entered the room, respectfully touching his hat, whilst his tearful eyes were anxiously turned upon his master. Mr. Fenwick understood the old man's look. "Robert," he said, kindly taking him by the hand, "you served my father faithfully for twenty years — do not forget his son."

"Oh, sir! — " The poor fellow could add no more. He turned round to his mistress, to conceal his emotion. "My lady, shall I carry Master Arthur to the coach?" Mrs. Fenwick placed the sleeping infant in the arms of the old man, who hurried off with his precious burden, imprinting, by the way, a kiss on his dimpled hands, and breathing over him a fervent prayer that he might yet return, a rich and worthy gentleman, to his native land.

The last look was given — the last wave of the hand had left the heart silent and the eyes dim — when Mr. Fenwick and his family found themselves rapidly advancing towards the place of their embarkation. When the ocean, with its wide expanse of moving waters, burst upon their sight, Lewis, unable to control his feelings, amused the sadness of the party with exclamations of wonder and delight. The next morning a boat conveyed them on board the Antelope, the noble and swift-sailing vessel, which sat like a sea-bird upon the waters, spreading her broad, white pinions to the fresh breeze. Lewis, captivated with the novelty of his situation, wondered why his mother wept, as she continued to watch, with streaming eyes, the cliffs of her native isle, retreating for ever from her view. "Ah, dear home and country!" she exclaimed; "friends of my youth, farewell, farewell!" The dim veil of approaching night descended slowly upon the waters, and soon hid these beloved objects from her sight.

At that delightful age, when the heart is too tender to retain any lasting impressions of sorrow — when the joy of the present moment drowns the remembrance of yesterday's grief — Lewis Fenwick soon forgot, in the novelty of surrounding objects, the dark features of that painful separation. Their voyage was prosperous; and their fellow-passengers, like themselves, were mostly respectable families, going out as settlers to the Cape. In a few days the party regained their usual cheerfulness.

Mr. Fenwick's family was but small; Lewis, a fine lad of ten years, and Arthur, the little one, to whom my readers have likewise been introduced. Death had thinned the infant band, and left a wide space between the ages of the brothers. Arthur was still designated the baby by his old nurse and mamma; while Lewis began to look about him, to think and act for himself, and to imagine that he was already more than half a man. Dearly did he love little Arthur, who, as a weakly infant, had been made a general nursling and pet; and Mrs. Fenwick regarded him as a treasure, in the possession of which Heaven had bestowed upon her a peculiar blessing.

When the Cape of Storms rose towering, like a crown, above the turbulent billows, which chafe and roar like subdued lions at its majestic feet, Lewis hailed its rocky face with enthusiastic delight. The nearer they approached, the more eloquent he became; and Mr. Fenwick, scarcely less interested than his son, listened with paternal emotion to the outpourings of a heart first keenly awakened to a sense of the sublime and beautiful. The first rays of the sun had scarcely turned the waves into rolling masses of light, on the ensuing morning, before Lewis and his father were upon deck. Struck with the magnificence of the scene, he turned his kindling eyes upon his father, and said, "Papa! this shall be my country. Look at the sea — look at the mountains! Are they not grand? — shooting their tall heads upwards, as though they would pierce the clouds, and bid good-morrow to the sun! What would my school-fellows say, could they stand here, and look upon this glorious scene with me? The hills we thought so high at Greenwich and Hampstead are mere mole-hills, and less, when compared with these lofty mountains."

Mr. Fenwick and his family made but a short stay at Cape Town, where they were met by his uncle, Mr. Clayton, with whom they were to proceed on their journey towards the interior. Mr. Clayton had been for many years settled at the Cape. Heaven had blessed his basket and his store, and he was the envied possessor of one of the finest estates in the colony. But the reward of his industry could not compensate for the loss of those for whom Mr. Clayton had so successfully laboured. In the short space of eighteen months, death had bereft him of an affectionate wife and his son and daughter, and he looked forward to the arrival of his favourite nephew, and his young family, with the greatest interest, hoping to find in their society a mitigation of the grief which had so long preyed upon his spirits. The party left Cape Town, and proceeded towards the eastern frontier in a horse-waggon, accompanied by a party of Hottentots and two faithful domestic slaves. For a few days Lewis felt the prejudices of colour operating very forcibly upon his mind against the natives of the country, which, from this period, he was to consider as his own. Neither his father's arguments, nor the entreaties of his mother, could induce him to go near, or hold any communication with their dark-skinned escort. One of the slaves in particular seemed greatly to excite his aversion. "Mamma," he said one day, while the horses were putting to, "I hate that ugly Charka. I cannot bear to look at him; I feel so afraid of him. I hope he does not always live with my uncle."

"He seems a faithful creature, Lewis," said Mrs. Fenwick; "and it grieves me to see such a cruel trait in your character. Why should you regard with aversion a fellow-creature, whom God has endowed with rational faculties and feelings as keen as your own, merely because his skin is of a different hue. To look upon Charka with such abhorrence, is to reproach your Maker. Your fair face and light hair may excite feelings of a similar nature in the breast of the African. To be black is no disgrace — to be fair is no merit of yours. God has formed you both, and adapted your complexions to the countries in which you were born. The consideration that Charka is a slave should produce in your bosom feelings of compassion and tenderness, instead of hatred and disgust."

"Mamma," said Lewis, thoughtfully, "I am wrong. But what is a slave?"

"A fellow-creature, Lewis, a brother, or sister, in the bonds of Nature, who has been most unjustly and cruelly made the property of his fellow-men. To be torn from their country — to be exposed in the public market-place — to be sold like beasts of burden — to be separated from fathers, and mothers, and brothers, and sisters, and husbands, and wives, and children — to be worked beyond their strength — to have no settled home — to receive no wages for their labour — to be inhumanly punished with a cart-whip for the least offence, and often for no offence at all — to have no one to comfort them when sad, to nurse them when sick, or to feel the least pity for such aggravated sufferings — to pass a childhood, a youth, and a manhood of toil, and an old age of disease and neglect — this, Lewis, is slavery — this, my boy, is to be a slave."

"Then why does such a kind man as my uncle keep slaves?" said Lewis.

"Because, my dear, like many of his countrymen, he has never rightly considered the subject. He is not aware that, in following the customs of the land, he is committing a great national crime. I trust, Lewis, the time is at hand, when your uncle will break the yoke from off the neck of his slaves, and that the British government will restore to the wronged and degraded African his rights as a man."

"Poor Charka! I am sorry for him now," said Lewis. "Mamma, I should not like to be a slave."

With a mind, even at that early age, keenly alive to the beauties of nature, the most barren desert through which they travelled awakened in the breast of young Lewis feelings of interest and pleasure; and, whenever the parties halted to dine, and refresh their weary cattle, Lewis bounded away to explore, as far as he dared, the country round. In these little excursions he was generally attended by two of the Hottentots, armed with guns, for fear of being suddenly attacked by wild beasts. But on one of these occasions he outran his companions, whilst collecting, with childish delight, different specimens of the beautiful heaths that grow wild in these desert places, making the barrenness of nature lovely with their delicate blossoms. As fast as he gathered one piece, another shrub at a distance caught his fancy, and tempted his steps to rove farther into the wilderness, till, unconscious of his danger, he strayed far beyond his party, which, together with the waggon, were no longer in sight. Not in the least terrified by this circumstance, he sat down in the shade of some stunted bushes, and began arranging his nosegay, thinking to please his mother with the beauty of the flowers he had walked so far to procure. Overpowered by the heat of the climate, the bunch of treasures dropped from his hand, and the English boy fell fast asleep. He had not been long in this state, when he dreamed that he had fallen into the sea, and was struggling with the cold waters, which, rolling continually over him, at length deprived him of breath, and rendered him incapable of longer struggling against them. Yielding himself up to his fate, he awoke with a stifled cry, suffering all the horrors of strangulation.

His eyes unclosed, and the glowing heavens flashed once more upon them; but Lewis found himself not only unable to rise, but held down to the earth by a grasp, which appeared to him like the hand of a giant. A shiver of agony ran through his frame, as a large snake, which had wreathed itself about his neck during his slumbers, reared up its arrowy head, and fixed its baleful eyes upon his face. That look blinded the unhappy boy. The earth heaved beneath him — the skies darkened above him — one faint sigh escaped his lips — one spasm of terror convulsed his frame — and he sunk into a state of absolute unconsciousness.

When his senses returned, he found himself supported on the dark breast of Charka, the negro, who was looking at him with a tender and compassionate glance, and his deadly enemy lay extended near them upon the sand. "Oh, Massa Lewis, me tank God you no die," said the black. "Poor missa weep — good massa weep — all weep for young massa if he die."

"Dear Charka," said Lewis, overcome with remorseful feelings for having disliked the generous preserver of his life, and keenly alive to the great service he had rendered him, "what shall I do for you? how shall I thank you for saving my life?"

The eyes of the black glistened with joy as he pressed the fair youth to his dark bosom. "Dear young massa, think no ill of black man — look no dark upon him. Black man have a large heart — black man love all that treat him well."

"Charka," said Lewis, "I did not love you once — but I love you now. I will never speak unkindly to you again. Come, let us go to my mother."

"She afraid you lost, massa — she send me out to find you. Me look a long time in vain — me at last see flowers — then great big snake — and then young massa. Me steal behind the bush — lie down quite flat on the sand, and seize him by the throat, and cut off his head with large knife. Massa quite dead then — no move — no look up. Massa live again, and quite kind to Charka."

When Lewis came up to the waggon, he found all the party in the greatest alarm, occasioned by his absence. Mrs. Fenwick was prepared to chide her son; but, when informed of his miraculous preservation, her angry feelings were turned into joy; and she thanked the negro with tears of gratitude for his prompt assistance.

"Oh, that I could reward Charka for this great kindness!" said Lewis, looking anxiously up in Mr. Clayton's face.

"Well, my boy," said his uncle, taking his hand, "if you had it in your power, what would you do in return?"

"I would make him free!" said Lewis.

Mr. Clayton started, and surveyed his nephew's animated countenance with surprise.

"And why would you do this, Lewis?"

"Because, sir, I feel that it is impossible for any man to be happy whilst he remains a slave!"

Mr. Clayton was struck to the heart. He remained silent for a few minutes, then, turning to Lewis, he said, "You shall have your wish; from this hour your deliverer is free! And not Charka alone — I will emancipate every slave on my location, for that word of yours."

From that hour the most tender and grateful attachment subsisted between the negro and Lewis; and, upon their arrival at his uncle's location, Lewis employed his leisure hours in teaching Charka to read, while the negro, in return, taught him to hunt and to shoot, and the two friends were seldom long apart.

Mr. Clayton had taken great pains in cultivating a beautiful garden round his house, which produced all sorts of fruits indigenous to the climate; and in a sequestered nook of this little paradise he had erected a small urn to the memory of his wife and children. At the base of this little pillar grew the sweetest flowers, nourished by the waters of a clear spring, which had its source only a few yards from the spot. By the margin of this spring Lewis would sit for hours in the cool of the day, with little Arthur upon his knees, conning his tasks; and when he was absent with his father and uncle, Arthur knew the path to the spring, and would play during the greater part of the day among the shrubs and flowers. Though concealed by the trees, the spot was so near at hand, and so close to the house, that Mrs. Fenwick felt no uneasiness at her darling amusing himself in the open air.

One morning, Mr. Fenwick, in great haste, came in, and told his wife that a lion had been seen prowling, late the evening before, near the garden, and that several of his sheep had been carried off; and Mr. Clayton had summoned all the neighbouring boors to track him to his retreat.

"Oh, papa, let me go to the lion-hunt!" said Lewis, springing from his seat, and seizing his little gun. He met his mother's anxious glance. "Dear mamma, I never saw a wild lion — I should like so much to go."

"Let the boy go, Mary," said Mr. Fenwick; "Charka and I will take care that he shall not be hurt."

Mrs. Fenwick gave a reluctant consent, and watched the party leave the garden with a heavy heart. They had been gone about two hours, when she suddenly missed little Arthur. "What has become of baby, Dinah?" she said to her dark female domestic.

"He is playing in the garden, ma'am; I saw him chasing a butterfly not many minutes ago."

"I do not feel easy at his being out to-day," said Mrs. Fenwick. "I will go and fetch him in."

Wishing to gather some figs, she provided herself with a basket for that purpose, and had nearly filled it, when she thought she heard a low growling near the spring. The safety of her child immediately flashed across her mind, and, putting down her basket on the pillar that Mr. Clayton had erected to the memory of his wife and children, she hastened to the spot. But what were her feelings, the terror, the agony, which convulsed her frame, when she beheld the fair child extended senseless on the ground, beneath the very paw of the tremendous monarch of the desert. There was no time for reflection — no time for indulging in selfish fears. Maternal love conquered female timidity. She had not leisure to scan the formidable power of her savage opponent; she only saw the perilous situation of her child; she was only alive to his danger. One brief prayer to the Father of Mercies to protect her from evil, and deliver her boy from the paw of the lion, rose in her heart as she sprang forward, and, flinging herself on her knees before the majestic animal, she snatched the child from the earth, and, pressing it to her beating bosom, continued to look the lion steadily in the face, with eyes brimful of tears, and with an expression of earnest and heart-rending supplication, as though he were endowed with human feelings, and could understand her silently eloquent appeal.

But, if the animal could not comprehend the mother's anguish, there was One who had compassion upon her grief, and restrained his fury. The mother's prayer had been heard; and the lion, who, on her first approach, had fiercely seized in his teeth part of the drapery depending from her shoulders, and already raised one of his tremendous paws to inflict a mortal wound, disarmed by her dauntless courage, appeared, in his turn, to yield to the influence of fear.

At this moment a shot was fired from a steep bank above, and Lewis cried out, in a tone of horror, "The lion, Charka! the lion! — Arthur is dead, and he will kill mamma!"

"God has vanquished him," said Mrs. Fenwick, rising from her knees, as the lordly beast slowly turned round, and walked majestically from the spot. "Let not a shot be fired — I would not act so ungenerously to a noble foe."

In a few minutes she was folded in the arms of her husband, and surrounded by the hunting party, who listened with mingled feelings of wonder and gratitude to the marvellous tale. A handful of water from the spring soon brought the rosy tints of life back to the rescued infant's cheek. Mrs. Fenwick returned to the house, and, carrying her little boy into her own chamber, she sunk once more upon her knees, and returned her heartfelt acknowledgments to the Almighty Power, who had assisted her in the hour of danger, vanquished the lion, and delivered her child from death.

~

Ackermann's Juvenile Forget Me Not: A Christmas, New Year's, and Birth-Day Present for 1832 (1831): 97–115.

The Doctor Distressed. A Sketch from Life

"So, my nephew is returned," said Dr. Beaufort, taking off his spectacles, and laying aside the letter he had been reading. "What will *he* do at home?" This remark was addressed to a stout, rosy, matronly looking woman of fifty, who was seated by the fire knitting, and who acted in the double capacity of companion and housekeeper to the reverend gentleman.

"Humph!" responded Mrs. Orams, without raising her eyes from her work. "Do? why, he will do as most 'young people' do in his circumstances; cut a dash as long as his money lasts, and when it is all gone depend upon his wealthy relations to pay his debts."

"He's an extravagant dog; but I can't think so harshly of poor Harry. No, no, Mary Orams; the half pay of a lieutenant in the army is but a trifle, a mere trifle. I must allow him *something* yearly to keep up his place in society." This was said in a hesitating under tone, and with a timid glance at the housekeeper, whose countenance, now pale, now red, betrayed considerable marks of agitation.

"Oh, your reverence may do as you please with your money, but I am sure, if *I* were in *your* place, I would never deprive myself of my little comforts to encourage a young man in his idle and expensive habits. If his half-pay is not enough to support him, let him do as many better men have done before him, — join Don Pedro at Oporto."

"'Tis a hard alternative," said the doubting but compassionate doctor.

"Not at all, sir," replied the crafty Mrs. Orams. "He's

a fine young man; let him try his fortune in matrimony, and look out for a rich wife."

"Nonsense," said the doctor, whilst a frown drew his gray bushy eyebrows so closely together that they formed a shaggy line across his wrinkled forehead. "The boy would never be so absurd. In his circumstances 'twould be madness. Pshaw! he's too sensible to think of such a thing."

"But young people *will* think of such things," replied Mrs. Orams, frowning in her turn; for well she knew the aversion the doctor had to matrimony.

"And old people *too*," said the doctor, with a bitter smile; "in which *they* show their want of wisdom."

"I hope, sir, you don't mean *me* by *people*. I am not an old woman. It is my own fault that I am single. The foolish respect I entertained for your reverence," she added, adroitly applying her handkerchief to her eyes, "made me reject many advantageous offers. But I thought it better to enjoy the company of a clever man, and contribute to his domestic comforts, than to be the mistress of a house of my own."

"You were a wise woman, Mary Orams," said the doctor, greatly softened by this piece of flattery. "A married life embraces many cares. We are free from them. Our rest is unbroken by the squalling of children and nocturnal lectures. You may bless God that you are what you are."

"Indeed, Dr. Beaufort," said Mrs. Mary, in a sulky tone, "I never trouble the Almighty by blessing him for such small mercies; and since we are upon the subject of marriage, I think it right to inform you that I have received an offer of marriage just now, and to convince you that I am neither old, nor ugly, nor despised, I think I shall accept it."

"What do you mean, Mrs. Orams?" said the astonished old bachelor, sinking back in his chair, and staring the housekeeper full in the face.

"To marry."

"You are not in earnest?"

"Quite serious."

"A woman of your years, Mrs. Orams?"

"Pray, sir, don't mention my years."

"Oh, I forgot; but what in the world can induce *you* to marry?"

"I wish to change my condition; that's all."

"Are you not comfortable here?"

"Why yes, tolerably comfortable; but one gets tired of the same thing forever. Besides I don't choose to be despised."

"Despised! Who despises you?"

"Your nieces, and their mother."

"Mrs. Harford and her daughters?"

"Yes. They are jealous of the good opinion your reverence entertains for your poor servant. There's not one of them will speak a civil word for me; and this fine Mr. Henry, you are so fond of, the last time he was at home, had the impudence to call *me*, a respectable woman, a *toady*, to my face. He might as well have called me a bad woman at once. I have been insulted and ill-treated by the whole family, and rather than be thought to stand in their way, which your reverence well knows is not the case," continued Mrs. Orams, casting a shrewd glance at the alarmed old man, "I will marry and leave you; and then you know, sir, I shall no longer be a servant, but have a house of my own."

"And who is to be your husband?"

"Only Mr. Archer, Squire Talbot's steward," said Mary, simpering, and looking down into her capacious lap. "Your reverence can make no objection to him. He is a regular church-goer, and never falls asleep in the midst of your reverence's sermons, as most of the other parishioners do. 'Tis true he is somewhat advanced in years; but who can attend to an old man's comforts as well as his wife? What hireling can take such an interest in his welfare, and all his domestic concerns? Gray hairs are honorable as Solomon says; and he has plenty of money withal."

Dr. Beaufort groaned aloud during Mary's eloquent harangue on the advantages to be derived from the Archer connexion, which he suddenly cut short by exclaiming, in mournful tones, "And what am I to do when you are gone, Mrs. Orams?" for he perceived with no small alarm, that the affair was likely to prove of a more serious nature than he had at first imagined.

"Do, sir! Oh, sir, there's plenty to be had in my place."

"Ah, Mrs. Orams! for the last twenty years I have

depended solely on you for my little comforts" —

"La, sir, surely 'tis not more than ten?"

"Twenty, Mrs. Orams. Twenty long years you have been the mistress of this house. What can you desire more? Nothing has been withheld from you. Your salary is ample; but if you think it less than your services merit, I will make an addition of ten pounds per annum. I will do anything, make any sacrifice, however painful to my feelings, rather than part with you." Mrs. Orams leaned her head upon her hand, and affected an air of deep commiseration. "I see the idea of leaving me distresses you, Mary."

"True, sir," whined forth Mrs. Orams; "but I cannot loose such an excellent opportunity of bettering my condition."

"But who will cook for me?" said the doctor, in a tone of despair.

"Money will procure good cooks."

"And nurse me when I have the gout?"

"Money will buy attendance."

"It is but a joke," cried the old bachelor, brightening up. "The thing is impossible. You cannot have the heart to leave me."

"Bless me, Dr. Beaufort," said Mary, bustling from her seat; "I am tired of leading a lonely life. Mr. Archer has offered me a comfortable home, and as I see *no* prospect of a better, to-morrow, if you please, we will settle our accounts." She sailed out of the room, and the old man sunk back in his easy chair, and fell into a profound reverie.

For twenty years Mrs. Orams had humoured the doctor, and treated him as a spoiled child, attended to all his whims, and pampered his appetite in the hope of inducing him to pay her disinterested services by making her his wife. But if Mrs. Orams was ambitious, the parson was proud; he saw through her little manoeuvres, and secretly laughed at them. The idea of making such a woman as Mary Orams his wife, was too ridiculous; and not wholly dead to natural affection, the indolent divine looked upon his widowed sister, her son, and her pretty, unpretending daughters, as his future heirs. But what weak mind can long struggle against the force of habit? Mrs. Orams, step by step, insinuated herself into her master's favour, and made herself so subservient to his comforts that he felt wretched without her. Year after year she had threatened to leave him in the expectation of drawing him into making her an offer of his hand. Matrimony was the parson's aversion, and year after year he increased her salary, to induce her to remain in his service. This only stimulated her avarice to enlarge its sphere of action. He was rich, and old, and infirm, and why might she not as well enjoy the whole of his property as a part; and she lost no opportunity of weakening the hold which the distressed Harfords had upon his heart. She hated them, for they were his natural heirs; were pretty and genteel, and young, and disdained to flatter her, in order to get their uncle's property. The return of Lieutenant Harford frightened her. He was, in spite of all her lies and mischief making, a great favourite with his uncle. The frequency of his visits might in time diminish her power, and render her company less indispensable. Mary was resolved to make one last desperate effort on the heart of her obdurate master, and in case of failure abandon his house and services for ever.

Two hours had elapsed since she had quitted the room, but the doctor remained in the same attitude. His head thrown back, and his hands tightly folded over his portly stomach. At length with a desperate effort he put forth his hand, and rung the bell. The footman answered the summons.

"Any thing wanted, sir?"

"John, send up Mrs. Orams."

A few minutes elapsed, the doctor thought them hours, the handle of the door slowly turned, and the comely person of Mrs. Orams projected itself into the room, her countenance flushed to a fiery red by leaning over the kitchen fire.

"Dinner will be ready, sir, in half an hour. If I leave the kitchen just now, that careless Irish hussy, Sally, will be sure to burn the meat."

"Let it burn," said the doctor, with an air of ludicrous

solemnity. "I have no appetite just now."

"La, sir, I hope your reverence is not ill?"

"Not ill, Mrs. Orams, but only a little *queerish*. Sit down, I have something to say to you." Mrs. Orams took a seat. The doctor drew close up to her, and screwing his courage to the pinch, said, in a hurried voice, "You leave me to-morrow?"

"Yes, sir."

"And you wish to be married."

"Yes, sir."

"Have you any objection to marry me?"

"Oh, la, sir, not in the least," replied Mrs. Orams, courtesying to the very ground.

"Then I will marry you myself, Mary; for, to tell the plain truth, I cannot live without you. Now go and send up the dinner."

Mrs. Orams courtesied still lower, and with eyes sparkling with triumph left the room, in obedience to her future lord's commands, without uttering a single word. Avarice, revenge, and pride were alike gratified.

The sequel is curious. After Mary Orams had attained the long-coveted dignity of Mrs. Dr. Beaufort, she attended less to the doctor's gustativeness, and more to her own; she ate more, and cooked less; the consequence was, that fat and indolence increased so rapidly, that before Don Pedro entered Lisbon, the newly promoted Mrs. Dr. Beaufort expired one morning of obesity, in her easy chair, leaving the distressed doctor a widower in the first year of his nuptials. He has lately followed his spouse to the tomb, and, after all, the poor Harfords not only came in for all their uncle's property, but for his wife's savings, a destination certainly little anticipated by herself or any of the young branches of the family.

Lady's Magazine and Museum improved ser. and enlarged 9 (1836): 241–43. As Chapter II, "Of all Fools, Old Fools are the Worst," in "Matrimonial Speculations," *Literary Garland* ns 3 (1845); under original title in *Flowers of Loveliness* for 1852 (1851).

The Sailor's Return; or, Reminiscences of Our Parish

As one of the chroniclers of my parish, it behooves me to act like a faithful and impartial biographer, not merely regarding with interest the memoirs of the rich and great, but condescending to men and women of low estate. Uninfluenced by worldly motives, to put a restraint upon their feelings, the lower classes follow more implicitly the dictates of nature; and their thoughts, words, and actions, in consequence, flow more immediately from the heart. Their affections are stronger, because money, in nine cases out of ten, cannot direct them in their choice of a partner for life. They meet upon equal terms, both having to earn their daily bread by the sweat of their brow; and their courtships generally commence in the field, where necessity, the stern nurse of the hardy, may accidentally have thrown them together. Their friendships are few, and generally confined to those of their own kindred; but, they are sincere and lasting; and I have witnessed with emotion the generous sacrifices which they will make to assist each other, in seasons of distress and difficulty. The peasant's world is contained in the rude hut which shelters his aged parents, and his wife and little ones. And in this little circle he centres and concentrates all the affections and kindly feelings of the heart.

Woodville is a large parish, and it contains many poor families of this description, whose simple histories have often awakened in my bosom the deepest interest and commiseration. It is not exactly of one of these that I am about to speak; for old Caleb Morris had seen better days, and had been reduced by a train of agricultural calamities, to receive wages for working on those lands which he once called his own. I was but a child at the period to which I allude; and my reminiscences of old Caleb are all confined to the pleasant little cottage in which he lived, by the side of the common, with its neat willow enclosures, and the beautiful wallflowers and pinks, and cloves, which grew in his pretty garden; not forgetting the tall sunflowers, that lifted their broad yellow faces over the hedge, as though they were ambitious to attract the observation of the foot passenger, and tempt him by their gorgeous apparel, to stop and ask for a nosegay. And then there was Caleb's pretty daughter Amy, who was the pet and darling of the whole village; the best scholar, and the best sempstress in the Sunday school; and her cousin, Arnold Wallace, a fine rosy cheeked, curly headed, black eyed boy, the orphan son of old Caleb's sister, whom the good man had taken to his fire side, and brought up as his own. Arnold, used to follow Amy like her shadow — he carried her book bag to school for her, and gallantly lifted his little cousin over all the stiles and puddles in their way to the church. I used to call Amy, Arnold's little wife; but the high spirited lad early bade adieu to his fair haired playmate, and went to sea. As the cares of womanhood came on, and mellowed the sunny expression of Amy's brow, her heart received other impressions, and the boy she had ever regarded as a brother, was only remembered with that interest, which generally clings through life, to those with whom we have passed our early years, and who shared with us the hopes and the fears, and the sports of childhood.

I will tell you Amy's simple story as I heard her accidentally relate it to her cousin Arnold. One fine spring evening, I happened to be employed in taking a view of our village church, and its picturesque burial ground. The sketch was for a friend in India, who had been born at Woodville; and he wished to refresh his eyes in that far land, with a simple outline of the quiet secluded spot, where the fathers of his native village slept. My seat was a green bank covered with primroses. A high hawthorn hedge sheltered me behind from the fresh but chilling breezes which generally prevail near the sea at this season of the year; and a little rill, not half a foot wide, ran singing at my feet, discoursing sweet music to the flowers and grass, that crowded about its fairy margin. Enamoured with my employment, I scarcely noticed the entrance of a stranger, till the shadow of Amy Morris fell between me and the light, and I looked impatiently up from the paper. She did not see me, and moved slowly forward to the chancel end of the church, and kneeling down at the head of a high turfed, but stoneless grave, she began planting a young ash tree, which she seemed anxious should serve for a monument for the dead. Poor Amy! sorrow had pursued her hard for the last four years, and stolen the rose from her cheek, and the smile from her lip; and what was far worse, had robbed her of the gay, light heart, she once possessed. Caleb Morris had been dead about eighteen months, and the solitary mourner had been forced to quit their neat pretty cottage, and to gain her living by following the occupations of a clear starcher and mantua-maker. As I saw her approach the grave, I felt inclined to rise up and comfort her. But a feeling of respect for that grief which I might increase, but which I could not mitigate by common-place condolence, fixed me in my seat. Concealed from her observation, by a tall, square monument in front, I continued mechanically to delineate the outlines of the church; and was so much absorbed in my task that the entrance of Amy was forgotten, till a brisk step sounded along the gravelled path of the church-yard, and the poor weeper was joined by a fine young man, in a seaman's dress. Their meeting was of the most tender description. The young man seated himself beside Amy upon the grass; and pointing to the grave, for some time continued to talk to her, in a voice so low and faltering that only half sentences reached my ear. At length the sailor took her hand, and said something to his fair companion, that brought the long banished rose tint into her pale cheek. She rose up hastily from the grave. "Do not talk to me of love, Cousin

Arnold," she said. "My heart is broken. I shall never love again."

Her companion still held her hand, and regarded her with a tenderly reproachful glance. "My uncle has been dead, Amy, eighteen long months. Enough surely has been given to grief?"

"My sorrow is not measured by time," said Amy. "Its empire is in the heart; and I feel that the voice of hope will never gladden mine again. My poor father," she continued looking wistfully upon the grave, "blind — infirm — and old. I no longer weep for him, Arnold; it was not of him I spake."

Tears filled her eyes, and deep sobs convulsed her breast. Arnold Wallace led her gently to the broad, low steps of the church-yard stile. They sat down in silence, which was alone broken by the evening song of the blackbird, and the vainly suppressed sighs of Amy Morris. The young man, who tenderly supported her drooping figure in his arms, was tall and well made, and strikingly handsome. His age did not exceed eight and twenty, but long exposure to the suns of an eastern clime had bronzed, and given a foreign cast to his frank, generous, and truly prepossessing countenance. The spot occupied by the lovers looked down into a deep narrow lane, and was over-arched by the bending branches of a stately ash tree. The attitudes of the youthful pair, and the beautiful landscape which surrounded them, formed a delightful subject for the pencil, and leaving my architectural structure to build itself, I soon transferred the weeping Amy and her manly companion to my paper.

To render Amy's simple narrative more intelligible, I must give my reader a brief sketch of her.

Arnold Wallace had loved his cousin Amy from a boy; but he wanted courage to tell her so, and he went to sea with the important secret locked up in his own bosom; for Amy, accustomed to regard her rosy, dark-eyed playfellow, as her brother, never suspected one word of the matter. But Arnold never forgot his cousin Amy; and after a painful absence of ten years, he returned to his native village, with a heavy purse and a faithful heart, to claim for his bride the object of his early affections; and to comfort and support his uncle through the dark winter of age. Not a little proud of his personal appearance, and improved fortunes, our young sailor bent his steps to the white cottage on the common, where Caleb Morris formerly resided. As he unclosed the gate, which separated the garden from the road, he was struck with the alteration in its once trim appearance. The little plot of ground was no longer conspicuous for its rich gilliflowers, pinks and hyacinths, but overgrown with weeds. The roses, which his own hand had trained over the rural porch, were unbound, and floated mournfully on every breeze! "Amy is not the neat girl she used to be," he said; "but she may have too many things to attend to now, to be able to take care of the garden. I wonder whether she will know me?" he continued, putting back the glossy black curls, which shaded his ample brow, "or the dear old soul who used to dandle me on his knees and call me his own boy?" A sudden chill came over him, and checked his pleasing reveries. "Time may have made sad changes — uncle may be dead; and Amy!" he stifled the sigh which rose to his lips, "and Amy may be married." He rapped at the cottage door with an unsteady hand. It was opened by a stranger. The state of the garden was already explained, and in a hurried manner he enquired for Caleb Morris? The woman answered that he was dead. "It was a great mercy," she said, "that it pleased the lord to take him. He had been a great sufferer, and lost his sight full six years before he died!"

Arnold, who had so warmly anticipated a meeting with his old uncle, thought it no mercy.

"Is his daughter still living?"

"Yes, poor girl, but she looks mortally ill; so thin and so pale, she is but the shadow of what she was. It's enough to make a body melancholy to look at her. But, well a day sir, she has suffered enough to break a young and tender heart!"

"Is she married," asked Arnold, with an air of affected indifference, which only rendered his emotion more apparent.

"Married! good lack! and never will be. It is an old prophecy in our village that Amy will die a maid."

Arnold smiled to himself, and enquiring of the loquacious dame the way to Amy's new place of abode, he pursued his walk towards the village. Wishing to visit the graves of his parents, to see that the sexton had properly kept them up, he took the path that led through the church lane.

"So my poor uncle Caleb is gone at last," he said, wiping his eyes with the corner of his black-silk cravat, as if ashamed of the unusual mist that dimmed his sight. But none of his gay mess-mates were near to laugh at his weakness, and the tribute to nature was freely paid.

"Amy has had a hard trial, it seems, but the task is ended, perhaps," and he glanced with secret satisfaction on the smart uniform, which set off to great advantage his manly figure. "The return of her old play-mate may dry her tears." He was now opposite the church, a low picturesque edifice, embosomed in fine old elm trees; its elevated burial ground divided from the lane by a high and neatly trimmed hawthorn hedge. It was a spirit-stirring evening and the blackbird was trilling his merry lay from a bower of May-blossoms, and green banks, on either side of the narrow road, were gemmed with flowers. Arnold felt his heart expand with many long forgotten emotions, as he ascended the rugged flight of wooden steps, which led to the church-yard. He thought how many strange changes had taken place since he was last there. How many lands he had visited, and how many dangers he had dared, since he and his pretty cousin used to seek that spot, hand in hand, to look for the first violets. "Nature," he thought, "does not change like man. The church-yard wears the same aspect which it wore ten years ago. The primroses appear the same, and the blackbird speaks the welcome of an old friend. And shall I cast anchor here at last?" he continued, unconsciously aloud; "would it not be sweeter to sleep under this emerald sward, than to be tossed constantly to and fro by the turbulent waters of the ocean?"

His voice startled Amy. She looked up from her task,

and the level beams of the setting sun glanced full upon her pale fair face. Prepared for this change in her personal charms, Arnold instantly recognised the stranger, Amy Morris. The discovery was mutual. Amy flung her arms about his neck, and wept upon his bosom, returning, with sisterly affection, the fond kisses he imprinted on her cheek. Seating himself beside her on the turf, he listened with untired interest, while she recounted the events which had taken place during his absence.

When she had closed the sad tale of domestic misfortunes, Arnold urged his suit with all the earnestness of a genuine and long cherished passion. His declaration carried a pang to Amy's heart, and her answer, though it did not entirely annihilate hopes which had been so fondly nursed, threw a deep shade of gloom over the joyful feelings of return. The first wish of his heart, to find Amy unmarried, had been realised; but, during their conversation, she had alluded to a prior engagement, and Arnold was lost in a thousand painful doubts and conjectures.

"Cousin Amy," he said, "I have loved you from a boy. I have worked hard, and ploughed the salt seas, in the hope of making you rich, and my poor uncle comfortable in his old age. I have so long considered you as my future wife, that it would break my heart to see you married to another."

"You will be spared that trial, Arnold; your rival is in heaven."

Something like a smile passed over Arnold's face. He was not sorry to find that his rival was dead, and that Amy was free from any living tie. Hope revived again in his breast, and brightened the expression of his dark and spirited eyes. "If you cannot love me, Amy, as you loved him, grant me your esteem and sympathy, and in the possession of these I will be happy. But is your heart so wholly buried in your lover's grave that it cannot receive a second attachment?"

"Arnold, I suffered too much for his sake, to transfer my affections lightly to another. The heart is incapable of feeling a second passion. The woman who has truly loved can never — no never — love again."

There was a very long pause; at length it was broken by Amy.

"Mine is a sad tale, cousin Arnold," she said, "but I need not blush to tell it, and I will tell it, for it will be a satisfaction to us both."

She passed her hand thoughtfully across her brow, looked sadly up in her cousin's face, and then commenced her simple narrative in a livelier tone.

"Four years after you went to sea, Arnold, my father was attacked with the typhus fever. I nursed him with the greatest care, and it pleased God to listen to my prayer, and prolong his life. The fever abated, and his senses returned; but he never more beheld the face of his child. I shall never forget that melancholy day, or the painful emotions which it occasioned. I had watched beside him during the night — the long night, whose solitary hours were alone marked by my own gloomy forebodings, and the delirious ravings of the poor sufferer. At length the day dawned. The sun rose brightly, and the birds were singing sweetly, in the little copse at the edge of the common. Nature rejoiced beneath the effulgence of her Maker's smile, and her wild tribes united their feeble voices in a universal burst of thanksgiving and praise. My father had fallen into a heavy stupor. I could scarcely call it sleep, but it was cessation from suffering; and when he recovered the fever was greatly abated, his mind was more tranquil, and for the first time for many days, he recognised my voice.

"'Amy,' he said, 'do the birds sing at midnight? Draw back the curtains — it is very dark.'

"I instantly complied with his request, and the red beams of the newly risen sun flashed full upon his pale and emaciated face.

"'It is enough my child, I feel the warmth of his beams, but I shall never behold them in this world again.'

"He folded his hands together and bowed himself upon the bed, while his pale lips moved for some time, apparently in earnest prayer. He could not behold my tears, and I hid my grief from him, for I perceived that it would increase the weight of his calamity. He slowly recovered, and his helplessness rendered him an object of tenfold interest, and strengthened the tender tie which bound him to my heart. He could no longer labour for his own support; and, roused by the imperious call of duty, I worked hard to procure for him the necessaries of life. My exertions far exceeded my strength, and I should have sunk under the complicated fatigues of mind and body, when it pleased the Almighty being, who had called me to endure these trials, to raise me up a friend, at the period when I most doubted the all-sufficiency of his protecting arm.

"Mr. Jones, our old neighbour, left his farm on the common, and a Mr. Ashford hired it of Squire Hurdlestone. He was a native of one of the midland counties. His family consisted of one son, and a daughter about my own age. I offered my services to the new comers, and assisted them to arrange and unpack their furniture. I could not wholly forget, whilst talking to Miss Ashford, that I had been a farmer's daughter myself, and though reduced by misfortunes, which could neither be foreseen nor avoided, to my present condition, I still enjoyed the benefits arising from a respectable education. My manners ill accorded with the meanness of my apparel. Mr. Ashford remarked this, and made himself acquainted with our history, and from that time I became a frequent visitor at his house; and my poor father wanted no comfort which his bounty could supply. The generous interest which this benevolent man took in our welfare was acknowledged by us with gratitude, which was more deeply felt than expressed in words.

"Emma and James Ashford were my constant companions, and a day seldom passed without some friendly intercourse between us. My father was as often led to his favourite seat, beneath the old maple tree in the garden, by the young Ashfords as he was by me; and James seemed to feel a peculiar pleasure in reading to his aged and sightless friend, when he returned at evening or noon from the labours of the field. The attention which was paid to me by this clever and amiable young man, did not escape my father's notice; and he mentioned the circumstance to me, with all the fond and excusable pride of a parent, contemplating the future happiness of a beloved and only child. The discovery gave me great pain; for though on analyzing my feelings, I found them equally inclined to favour his suit, a sense of gratitude to the father, forbade me to encourage the addresses of the son. I avoided his society, went less frequently to Mr. Ashford's, and always contrived to be absent when James called at the cottage, which was daily, to enquire after my father's health. It was then, and not till then, that I became acquainted with the real state of my heart, and the impression which young Ashford's attentions had made upon it. These acts of self denial robbed my cheek of its bloom, and my bosom of peace. I was no longer the gay, happy Amy Morris, but a melancholy, hopeless creature, cherishing a passion, which I considered myself bound in duty to conceal. Emma remarked the great change which had taken place in my manners and appearance, and Mr. Ashford called at the cottage one morning to learn of my father the cause of my estrangement. They were shut up for some time together, and during their conference I felt a restless desire to know the meaning of Mr. Ashford's long visit. At length the door opened, and he came out to me. I was in the garden pretending to fasten up a branch of one of the rose-trees, which the wind had loosened from the wall; but, in reality, it was only an excuse to conceal my anxiety. Mr. Ashford called me to him, his benevolent face was irradiated by a smile of inward satisfaction. An unusual degree of timidity kept me aloof. He took my hand, and kissing my cheek, said:

"'How now, little trembler, have you learned to fear me?'

"My eyes were full of tears, I could make no reply; and I suffered him to lead me passively into the house. My dear father was sitting in his high-backed arm chair, his head bent upon the clasped hands that rested on the top of his stick; and standing beside him, with a face sparkling with joyful animation, I beheld James Ashford; his manly upright figure, and healthy complexion, forming a striking contrast to the white locks, and feeble drooping attitude of age. My father raised his sightless eyes as I approached; but when I encountered the glance of my delighted lover, I coloured deeply, and drew involuntarily back. He sprang forward to meet me, and whispered in my ear: — 'Amy, you can make me so happy.'

"My hand trembled in his; a thick mist floated before my eyes, as Mr. Ashford, stepping forward, joined our hands and bade us be happy in each other's love. Seeing me about to speak, he playfully interrupted me. 'We will take no refusal, Amy; your worthy father and I have settled the business, and disposed of you as we think for the best. The only alternative now left to you, is to be a good and dutiful child, and anticipate our wishes.'

"'Dear, generous Mr. Ashford,' I faltered out at last; 'you have indeed, anticipated mine.'

"James looked his thanks, as he led me to my father. The dear old man blessed us with tears in his eyes; and in spite of his poverty and many infirmities, he declared that moment to be the happiest in his life. From that blissful hour, I considered James Ashford as my future husband; and we loved each other, Arnold, with a tenderness and confidence which can only be felt once. The heart cannot receive such a faithful and lasting impression a second time. We took sweet counsel together, and enjoyed that communion of spirit which can only exist between kindred minds." Arnold sighed deeply as Amy continued.

"Every preparation was made for our approaching marriage. Mr. Ashford agreed to resign his farm to his son, that we might begin the world under fair auspices. The current of our happiness had hitherto run so smoothly that it appeared almost impossible that we should experience an alloy. But the storm was even then at hand, which burst suddenly upon us, and overthrew all our highly raised expectations. A large county bank, in which Mr. Ashford's property was principally vested, unexpectedly failed; and reduced this worthy man from a state in which though humble, he enjoyed all the comforts of life, to one of comparative poverty. The bills which he had contracted with various tradesmen, in the village, when he took and stocked the farm, were still unpaid, and nearly half a year's rent was due to his landlord. This the squire generously forgave, and with his usual benevolence, enclosed with his letter, a draft on his banker for twenty pounds to supply Mr. Ashford's immediate wants. After the crops in the ground, and the stock upon the farm, were sold, and the creditors faithfully discharged, Mr. Ashford and his family were cast penniless upon the world.

"Alas, this was no time for marrying or being given in marriage; and whenever James and I met, it was only to talk over our blighted hopes, and form fresh plans for the future. Whilst Mr. Ashford's affairs were at this desperate crisis, a brother, who had settled some years before in Upper Canada, wrote to him, inviting him to come out with his family, and he would put them into a good grant of land, and render them all the assistance he could. This offer was too advantageous to be refused, and the Ashfords, grateful to Providence for this interposition in their favour, prepared to bid adieu to their native land. I contemplated the departure of my friends, with feelings of regret which almost amounted to despair. James, on the contrary, was full of hope; and urged me continually to fulfil my engagement, and accompany them across the Atlantic. My heart for one selfish moment yielded to his solicitations; but when I turned to my father, my dear, infirm, blind, old father, I instantly abandoned the unworthy thought. Could I leave him in his old age to the care of strangers, or suffer him to terminate his virtuous life in a work-house? But he, only alive to my happiness, in the most pathetic manner urged me to accept young Ashford's offer, assuring me that even in the work-house, he should die contented in the thought that his child was the happy wife of the man she loved, and beyond the reach of poverty's heart-withering gripe. James, at length, yielded to my reasoning, and pressing me to his generous heart, told me to keep up my spirits and to be good and cheerful; and as soon as they were comfortably settled in Canada, he would return and take me out as his wife.

"The day of their final departure came too soon, for

those who apprehended that the friends whom they then saw, they should behold no more. The Ashfords were to take the coach for London, at the end of this lane. I accompanied them hither. My father tottered to the garden gate, and held up his hands as long as we could distinguish his venerable figure in token of farewell. Mr. Ashford was calm; he even chided me gently for my want of confidence in the wise dispensations of an over-ruling Providence. James was silent, but his silence was more eloquent than words. Emma had left us some days before, and was waiting in town, at the house of a friend, the arrival of her father and brother, so that my heart was spared at that moment, an additional pang.

"Yes, Arnold," continued Amy, with increasing agitation, "it was on this very spot — beneath the shadow of this very tree that we parted. When we arrived in front of the church, the coach was not yet in sight. It was a fine evening in June. The sun had sunk beneath a canopy of crimson and golden clouds; and the low, gothic windows of the church, were illuminated with the reflection of the splendid light. The gorgeous sunset seemed to mock the darkness of my mind. Mr. Ashford sat down on the step of the stile beneath this beautiful ash tree. He was cheerful, and tried to render our separation less painful, by the liveliness of his conversation. But his tenderness failed to produce the desired effect. My heart was bursting, and the tears flowed incessantly from my eyes. Mr. Ashford took off his hat and looked from my pale and agitated face, up to the glaring heavens, as if to implore the father of lights to comfort and restore peace to his afflicted child. The breeze lifted his grey hair from his temples, and the most beautiful and resigned expression pervaded his countenance. He did not speak, but his thoughts were easily read; his face, like a mirror, reflected the objects which were passing through his mind. At length he drew me towards him, and said: 'My child, we must part — perhaps for ever. This is the last time we may be permitted to admire this glorious scene together.'

"I sunk weeping into his arms, he folded me to his

heart, and our tears were mingled in deep and silent sorrow. The rapid approach of the mail tore us apart. 'Amy,' he said, 'If we meet no more here we shall meet again in that country where the voice of sorrow is unknown, and where there will be no more sighing and tears. May God bless and protect my child.'

"I was encircled in the arms of my betrothed husband; I felt his tears upon my cheek, and his lips trembled upon mine, as he murmured in accents scarcely audible. 'Amy — my own Amy. Farewell!' We parted. But, it was not till the last sound of the wheels died away, that I found myself completely alone. I looked at the stile — but the seat was vacant. I looked up to the heavens — but the glorious light had faded away. I have never seen my dear friends since. I shall never see them again. But I love to frequent this spot, for I never look at the stile or the weeping ash, but I fancy I still see them there. Mr. Ashford's last words ring in my ear. I turn away, with a quick step, and a beating heart. It is too true that my adopted father and sister, and my betrothed husband, have filled the same watery grave."

Here poor Amy concealed her face with her hands and sighed as though her heart would break. It was, however, but a momentary pang, inflicted by a too tenacious memory, and she continued: "The ship was lost in her passage out, and all hands on board perished. The fatal news reached our village too soon; and for some months after, the world was to me a blank, and the flight of time unheeded. They tell me, Arnold, that I was mad — but I cannot remember anything, but the grief I felt for the loss of my friends, during that calamitous period. When I awoke from this horrible stupor, and the memory of the past returned, the increasing debility of my poor father demanded my constant care, and urged upon me the necessity of moderating my grief. My father did not long survive the wreck of his daughter's peace. He died in my arms. We buried him here, and I was left alone in the world, without a comforter. Ah, dear friends, why do I continue to mourn for you as one without hope? Why do my tears flow unceasingly? Dear James and Emma! Ye went from among us in the season of youth, while life was in its first lovely bloom. Your hearts felt but one bitter pang, and death was swallowed up in victory. Why do I mourn for you?"

Amy rose up, and walked hastily away! Arnold respected her sorrow too much to follow her.

"And did Amy Morris marry her cousin?"

Yes, gentle reader, she did. Only two years after this interview, which I witnessed in the church-yard, I passed a beautiful young matron in the church lane, guiding the tottering steps of a lovely infant, to whose innocent prattle she was listening with intense delight. Her rosy cheek, light steps, and blithesome glance, forming a strong contrast with the then pale and woe begone looking Amy Morris. Yet it was Amy, the loving and the loved; the happy wife of Arnold Wallace. She had proved the fallacy of that theory which asserts that the warm and devoted heart of woman is incapable of receiving a second attachment; that her first love is her last. Whilst the cup of domestic happiness flowed to the brim, and she met the fond glance of her affectionate husband; she wondered that another man had ever appeared more pleasing in her eyes; that she had ever loved James Ashford better than her cousin Arnold.

Literary Garland 4 (1841): 13–18.

The Broken Mirror. A True Tale

Chapter I

Providence is always true to those
who remain true to themselves.

"Dry your tears, dear mother. This violent grief destroys your health, without altering in the smallest degree our present circumstances. Look forward with hope to the future. Better days are in store for us."

"Robert Harden, you speak like a boy perfectly unacquainted with the trials of life," said the widow, in no very gentle voice, for sorrow and disappointment had soured a hitherto even temper, and rendered her peevish and irritable. "What prospect have we of bettering our condition? Who is there amongst all our summer friends who would put themselves to the least inconvenience to help us? Have they not all deserted us in our distress? All — all," and here she buried her face in her handkerchief, and wept afresh.

"There is One, mother, who never deserts His children in distress; who, when the world forsakes them, has promised to hold them up. Trust in Him, and all will be well."

The poor widow looked up into the face of her fine boy, and smiled through her tears:

"Robert, where did you learn this lesson of faith?"

"Of you, mother. Who else taught me to love God, and to trust in His divine providence, but you?"

"Ah, my son! these heavy afflictions have made me forgetful of my duty. In the hour of trial I have forgotten God. Pray for me, Robert. I have often prayed and wept for you. Pray that strength may be given to me, to bear with resignation my present grief."

Her head sunk upon the bosom of the tall lad, whose willing arms fondly encircled her drooping figure, as, after some moments, their tears flowed silently together. Youth, especially virtuous youth, is ever hopeful; and Robert Harden possessed a mind too active and independent to waste its energies in unavailing regret. He and a brother, two years younger, were the only children of a wealthy merchant in Edinburgh. During their father's lifetime, they had enjoyed all the comforts and luxuries which competence can bestow. Their education had been conducted on a liberal scale; and the boys were just beginning to profit by their advantages, when the head of the family was suddenly called away by death. This was a dreadful blow to his widow and young sons. It was so unlooked for — so unexpected. He had been taken from them, at a moment's warning, in the very prime of life. The affectionate, loving husband — the fond, indulgent father: could any grief equal this? was a question which they often asked themselves, in the first sad days of their melancholy bereavement. The friends and neighbours who called upon Mrs. Harden after the funeral, attempted to console her, by representing to her the independent circumstances in which she had been left. Mr. Harden had been a man of property — she and her children would want for no comfort — there were thousands in worse circumstances — this thought should be enough to console and mitigate her grief. Poor Mrs. Harden loved her husband tenderly, and these worldly considerations had never entered her mind since the dark moment in which she found herself for ever deprived of her bosom friend and companion. Could she have derived any satisfaction from these circumstances, she was doomed to undergo a still further trial — a still deeper disappointment.

To the surprise of his friends and family, when they came to look into Mr. Harden's affairs — for he had died without a will — they discovered that he had died a poor man; that when all his creditors were paid, there would be no provision left for his family. He had entered into speculations of a very doubtful nature — whether deceived by himself or others, none could tell — and his losses had been so extensive, that it was supposed that the sudden reverse in his fortune, which he had not had courage to declare to his wife, had pressed so heavily upon his mind, that it had led to his premature death.

The loss of her husband had been severely felt by Mrs. Harden; but when the loss of all his property left her entirely dependent for support upon the charity of others, the poor widow lacked fortitude to bear up against the blow. She wept unceasingly — refused all sustenance — and sunk into a stupor, from which the commonplace condolence of friends, who offered no other than verbal assistance, failed to arouse her. The return of her sons from school, and the bitter consciousness of all they had lost by their father's death, served for a time to renew her grief. Their presence, however, was a great comfort; and the manly and affectionate conduct of the elder, in some measure reconciled her to the mournful change.

Robert Harden, although a mere boy of sixteen, immediately comprehended their situation, and saw that something must be done to enable them to provide for the future. He had endeavoured to prepare his mother's mind for the alteration in their circumstances. He tried to convince her that poverty, although an evil, was an evil which, if borne with becoming fortitude, might be subdued, or, at any rate, softened; and that he was able and willing to work for a parent whom he dearly loved. But poor Mrs. Harden was not willing that her fine boys, who had been educated as the sons of gentlemen, should work; and the most severe trial she was called to endure, was seeing them forced to leave their studies, and give up the prospect of honourable advancement, to toil in some menial capacity, to obtain bread.

The mother and son were still locked in each other's arms, when a little round-faced man, in a broad-brimmed hat, with spectacles on his nose, peered into the room, and, seeing the widow and her son in tears, hurried forward, and commenced a conversation in the following abrupt manner:

"Hout woman! wilt thee never cease greeting? Have mair trust in God. I bring thee glad tidings!"

"What is it, Mr. Sylvester?" said Robert, advancing to meet the old Quaker, who shook him cordially by the hand. "Good news could never come at a more acceptable time."

"Can'st thee bear a little hardship, young man, for thy mother's sake?"

"Any thing, my dear sir. I will work for her — beg for her — do any thing, but steal, for her."

"Be not too confident, Robert Harden. Better men than thee have broken God's commandments to satisfy the wants of nature. Necessity, Robert Harden, knows no law. Hunger teaches men strange secrets. Albeit I am no advocate for theft; and I like to see thee so forward in spirit to help thy mother. The news I have for thee is simply this: thy uncle William and his family are about to leave Glasgow, and emigrate to the Cape of Good Hope. He and thy father were both engaged in the same speculations, which have proved their ruin. I do not wonder at thy father entering into such vain schemes, for he was a dreamer. But that thy hard, money-getting, worldly-minded, shrewd uncle, should be so deceived, doth surprise me not a little. Well, well, some men grow rich with little pains, and others take as much trouble to make themselves poor. But this has nothing to do with that which I came to tell. Several respectable families have joined themselves to thy uncle's party; and if thee and thy mother and brother art willing to accompany the expedition, and try your fortunes in the strange land, I will, out of respect to thy father's memory, pay the expenses of the voyage. More than this, though willing to befriend thee, I cannot do. I have a family, friend Robert — a large young family — and children must be fed."

"Ah, sir! how can I express my thanks?" cried the eager Robert, warmly grasping the old man's hand, and a prophetic glance into the far-off future flashed upon his mind. "Gladly do I accept your kind offer, and here faithfully promise to repay you any sum of money advanced for our benefit, when God shall have blessed my honest endeavours to provide for the wants of my family."

"Softly, softly, friend Robert; many difficulties have to be met and overcome before we can talk of that. Be contented with the present: leave the future to Him, who has promised to provide for the fatherless, and has bade the widow trust in Him. We will talk of remuneration when thou art an independent man, which I one day hope thee to be. Dost thou think that thy mother and brother will be willing to accompany thee?"

Robert turned an enquiring eye upon his mother, and was not a little mortified and surprised to mark the anxious and alarmed manner in which she returned his glance.

"And what in the world should we do at the Cape?"

"As others have done before us, dear mother: learn to work."

"I cannot work, Robert. My constitution is broken: I am growing old and feeble."

"No one thinks of your working. William and I are young and strong. We will work for you — "

"In that weary land!"

"The climate is beautiful!"

"And the wild beasts!"

"Will not harm you, while the hunting of them will form delightful amusement for a leisure hour."

"And the dreadful heat!" cried the reluctant widow, heaping objection upon objection.

"Is not so great as you imagine it to be. I heard a gentleman, who had spent many years at the Cape, tell my master that it was far pleasanter than the hot season in Britain; that the sea breeze, which blows steadily on the shore all day, tempered, and rendered it far from oppressive, — "

"Say no more about it, Robert; I cannot consent to go."

"Anne Harden, thee wilt think better of it," said the Quaker, who had been attentively listening to the dialogue between the mother and son. "Robert is willing to sacrifice all for thee: wilt thou do nothing for him in return?"

The widow was struck with the old man's last observation. She looked down, and was silent.

"I have taken thee by surprise. The question I have put to thee requires mature consideration. I will call again tomorrow, for when once thy resolution is taken little time can be lost. By the bye," he continued, with a lively air, "when does the sale take place? This splendid furniture, if it goes off well, will nearly satisfy all the creditors that remain unpaid."

"On Monday, I believe, sir," said Robert, glancing mournfully round the handsomely furnished apartment, which they could no longer call their own. "You, sir, are one of the principal of these creditors; will you grant my dear mother a small favour?"

"Let me hear it, friend?"

"You see that large Italian mirror: it was a present from my grandfather to my mother; it had been many years in his family, and she prizes it very highly; she cannot bear to part with it."

"A useless piece of vanity, friend Robert. Ask something more profitable than the looking-glass."

"My poor mother has set her heart upon it."

"Nonsense, Robert Harden! The brook must serve thee for a mirror. I will not consent to part with this vain toy."

"There will be enough to pay the creditors without it," said Mrs. Harden; "at least so Mr. Munroe informed me. If we are obliged to go to South Africa, it might sell well at Cape Town — perhaps for double its value. It cost, I believe, a hundred guineas."

"Fools and their money are soon parted," returned the Quaker. "Friend Anne, there is more sense in thy last observation than has proceeded out of thy mouth the whole morning. If thee wantest the glass to sell, it is thine; but if it be only with the view of continuing a certain idol worship, which, at thy years, thou should'st long ere this have lain aside, I should consider it an act of duty to deny thy request. Is there any other article thou wishest reserved for thyself?"

"The drawing-room carpet," said Mrs. Harden. "It

was the gift of my dear uncle when I first went house-keeping — now eighteen years ago."

"Humph!" said the Quaker. "It has worn well, and seen good service. A real Turkey. We have no such carpets manufactured now. Well, thee shall have the carpet; but I can grant no more on my own responsibility. If thee wishest to retain all the gifts of thy kindred, we shall have but a poor sale."

"I am contented to part with all the rest," said Mrs. Harden, with a sigh. "Who knows but that this little may be the means of restoring to us the wealth we have lost? I feel something whisper to my heart that we shall have luck with it."

"Be not too sanguine, friend; winds and waves often disappoint our best hopes; hold all things here with a loose hand. Thee hast already experienced the instability of earthly riches. Seek for treasures in Heaven, Anne Harden; treasures of which no hungry creditor can deprive thee."

So saying, the worthy man withdrew, leaving the mother and her two sons to consult over their future plans.

"Perhaps there will be something over for us, mother," said William, who had just joined them, "after all things are sold. You know the sale of the landed property paid most of the heavy debts."

"I am sure there ought to be," returned Mrs. Harden, glancing with an eye in which pride still lingered, around the room. "The furniture is very handsome, and, if it sells for its real value, there must be a large sum to spare. The side-board alone is worth twenty pounds — the sofas as much more — and as to the dining-table, there is not one so handsome in any merchant's house in the city. It ought to sell for forty pounds at least." This was, however, valuing every article at the price it originally cost; for the poor widow, like many other elderly ladies, considered that years greatly increased the value of every thing belonging to them.

Chapter II
The Sale

Monday came at last, and all the world went to the sale of Mrs. Harden's effects — that is, all the good people which composed the world of the large street in which Mr. Harden had for years carried on an extensive business, and had been looked upon by his neighbours as one of the richest men in the place. How condescending they all were to the poor widow on that day; how they commented upon and pitied the unfortunate circumstances which had placed her in her present mortifying situation; and that without any regard to the feelings of the poor sufferer, whose presence was deemed necessary by her friends, on this trying occasion. Whilst discussing the value of the beautiful mahogany dining-table, a group of these sympathizers quite forgot how often they had partaken from it of a sumptuous meal. But times were altered now. The widow of John Harden was poor, and they were rich. It was quite right that pride should have a fall, and her acquaintance was valued accordingly.

"What have you done with the fine mirror, Mrs. Harden?" asked one of the lady inspectors of the furniture. "If it went *very* cheap, I should like to buy it for my drawing-room."

"It will not be sold, ma'am," returned Robert. "My mother will take it with her to the Cape."

"Bless me! Mrs. Harden! what use will you find for such a costly mirror as that amongst the Caffres and Hottentots? One would imagine that it is one of the last things upon earth that you would require," said the disappointed applicant.

"The old fool!" whispered another kind neighbour. "I always told you, Mrs. Hutton, that Mrs. Harden was the vainest woman in town. You will believe me now."

"Does Mr. Sylvester know, ma'am, that the mirror has been kept back?" asked the aforesaid Mrs. Hutton, with a spiteful twinkle of her envious black eyes. "It will spoil the sale. For my part, it was the only thing that I thought worth coming so far to purchase. The rest of the articles," she muttered, in an under tone, to Mrs. Barry, "are old-fashioned trash — not worth looking at."

How the heart of the poor widow swelled at this affront to her household gods and goddesses. These Lares, that, for eighteen years, she had been accustomed to regard with such silent homage; in the keeping in good order of which, she and her numerous Abigails had bestowed so many hours of time, which might have been better employed, in the rubbing and polishing, and which she justly considered had been objects of envy and admiration to her less wealthy neighbours. And had it come to this? was she doomed to hear them openly despised by a vulgar, low-bred woman, who had never been able to purchase any thing half so costly? A philosopher would laugh at such a ridiculous cause for grief. But Mrs. Harden was no philosopher; she was a weak, erring woman, still too much in love with the world, and the world's paltry prejudices, not to feel these things very keenly. How often must our hopes be disappointed — our warm affections crushed — and our generous confidence abused, before the mind rises superior to the selfish usages of society, and, leaving the friendships of earth, seeks the approbation of conscience, the confidence and love of God! Glorious adversity! despised as thou art by the sons of men, from thee all that is great and noble in our nature emanates. It is only thou which teachest us a knowledge of self, and the insufficiency of human means to satisfy the heart.

The sale went on without the mirror, and the furniture sold better than Mr. Sylvester expected; nay, such was the eagerness of people to buy bargains, that old, worn-out carpets and curtains sold for as much as they cost when new, while things of real value were purchased for a trifle.

"Is it not vexing," whispered the widow to Mr. Sylvester, as he bustled amongst the crowd, encouraging purchasers, or judiciously bidding on any article which he thought was going too low, "to see the good articles given away in this manner?"

"Never mind, friend," said the Quaker, rubbing his

hands with a satisfied air; "the sale's a good sale after all. If the drawing-room brings but small returns, the kitchen and pantry do wonders. Why, friend, I saw a man, who should be a better judge of the value of such articles, buy an iron pot, with a crack across the bottom, for as much as it cost new. So cheer up, and set one thing against another."

The auction at last closed. The non-bidders were dissatisfied with their over caution, and the purchasers went away, rejoicing in their bargains. The more unprofitably they had laid out their money, the greater boast they made of their own sagacity. Mrs. Harden and her sons sat down to rest themselves in one of the unfurnished rooms, to partake of some ham sandwiches, which the good Quaker had provided before they bade adieu for ever to the home of years. Nothing of their former grandeur now remained to console them, but the large mirror, (which still hung suspended from the wall, reflecting soiled clothes and careworn visages), and the drawing-room carpet, which, rolled up at the end of the room, afforded them a seat.

The change seemed to strike painfully on every heart. The widow wept; and the boys, though really hungry, scarcely tasted the food in the basket at their feet. Robert was the first to break silence:

"Well, dear mother, it's all over now," he said, affectionately kissing her pale cheek. "For your sake, I am glad that it is over. While we continued to live in this fine house, we could never convince ourselves that it had ceased to belong to us, and that we were poor and destitute. We know it now, and my mind is braced to bear it. The only thing which remains to trouble us is this large mirror. I almost wish that it had been sold with the rest."

"And so do I," said William; "but 'tis a whim of mamma's, and we must try to please her. Mr. Sylvester has sent a large case to pack it up in. You will find it in the next room."

"Well boys, you laugh at my venture," said Mrs. Harden; "but I trust, with the blessing of God, it may be the means of obtaining for us the necessaries of life in the strange land in which we are destined to sojourn."

"We will be very careful in packing it up, then," said William, with a sly glance at his brother; "for you seem, mamma, to think that it contains as many magical properties as Aladdin's far-famed lamp."

"We will wrap it up in the carpet first; it will protect it from injury," returned Robert, springing to the task.

It took the mother and sons about an hour to pack up the beautiful mirror to their own satisfaction, and when this important affair was adjusted to their mutual liking, it was carefully deposited in the hand-barrow, which the old Quaker had provided for the occasion, and, after many fears for its safety, and much fussing, conveyed to uncle William's lodgings, preparatory to being sent on ship board.

Uncle William was not a bad man, nor a hard-hearted man, but he was a commonplace, matter of fact man of business, and of the world. He was never known to do a wilfully unkind action; but he never attempted to put himself out of the way to do a kind one. He was a blunt man; that is, a man who loved contradiction for its own dear sake; who said and did rude things, to shew his own superior wit and sagacity, without reflecting what the effect might be which such conduct generally produces upon others. Blunt people are always great egotists, and not always sincere. Their aim is to appear clever at the expense of their neighbours; and the wanton disregard which they shew for wounding their feelings, betrays the selfishness and insensibility of their own.

"Well, Anne," said Mr. William Harden, regarding the huge package which contained the poor widow's worldly treasures, with no very friendly eye, "that's what I call a useless package. You had better have sold it at the auction, and laid the money out in necessary articles for yourself and the lads, than encumbered us with it on the voyage. But silly women are hard to be persuaded. I am very sure that it will be smashed to pieces in the hold of the ship."

"Not a bit of it, uncle," said his namesake, William. "It is well packed, I assure you."

"Well, we shall see," said Mr. Harden, "who is the

true prophet," and secretly in his heart he wished it might be broken, that his words might prove true; not that he really wished any ill to befall his poor widowed sister, but because he had said that it would be so, and his sagacity and powers of forethought were involved in the fulfilment of the prediction.

The mirror was safely got on board, and the emigrants, after breathing their last sighs and prayers for the dear land they were leaving, found themselves one morning steering their course across the wide Atlantic, under full sail, and driven onward by a spanking breeze.

Chapter III
What Befel the Mirror and its Owners

For the first three weeks of their voyage, the whole party felt too much indisposed, from the effects of their trip to sea, to indulge in speculations for the future. The present was sufficiently burdensome, without anticipating remote contingencies; and often, amidst the paroxysms of that most painful, but least compassionated of all acquatic ills, sea-sickness, they wished themselves at the bottom of the ocean, as the only means of terminating their sufferings. But, as this would not have been considered a legal method of curing the evil of which they bitterly complained, they were told by the initiated to take patience, in the shape of plenty of brandy and water, and to eat as much as they could, and the disorder would soon cure itself. The temperance pledge was not then in fashion, for the events of our tale really occurred in the year of our Lord 1817, and the improvement in morals and manners has greatly progressed since that remote period, or the suffocating smell of this universal panacea would have overcome the widow's scruples, and made her a teetotaller for life. But sea-sickness, like all other miseries, has an end; and Mrs. Harden and her sons, no sooner found themselves able to look upon the waves without changing colour, than they began to speculate upon the future.

"We shall obtain, through your uncle's interest with

the governor's private secretary, a grant of land," said the widow; "and the money that the sale of the carpet and the mirror will procure will stock it with sheep and cattle; and, with industry and prudence, my dear boys, we shall soon be as well off as our neighbours."

"That you will, sister," said Janet Harden, the meekest and most amiable of old maids, who bore the reproach of celibacy with the best grace imaginable; who, when tormented by one of uncle William's children, to tell him what an old maid was — for papa said that she, aunt Janet, was an old maid — answered the child, with a benevolent smile, instead of resenting the implied insult from her blunt brother — "A wise woman, child."

Aunt Janet, or Jessy, as the children called her, had kindly consented to accompany her brother William in his emigration; generously giving up a school, from the proceeds of which she obtained a comfortable living, to assist them in their first settlement, and superintend the education of their family. "You have no cause for despondency," continued this truly devoted woman. "The boys are healthy and strong; and even if you should be disappointed in the sale of these things, if they consent to work out for a few years, they will soon earn for you flocks and herds."

"Now, Jessy, don't go to break my heart, by talking of their working out as servants. Could you bear to see your own brother John's children brought so low? Is there one of William's sons to compare with them?"

"I hate comparisons among friends," returned Janet, without noticing her sister-in-law's splenetic speech. "The children are all equally dear to me; and if God has given to some fairer faces and better talents than the rest, pray whose fault is that? Not the bairns; and to find fault with the all-wise Disposer would be to commit sin. As to work — to employ the hands in an honest endeavour to provide for the wants of a family, is no disgrace, but a virtue. If Providence has placed the means of living at ease beyond our reach, it is our duty to work, in order that we may not be a burden to others. Besides, sister Anne, to work faithfully for another, teaches us to work profitably for ourselves."

"It is very well for you to preach, Jessy, who are so much better off yourself; but were you in my situation, the case would be different," murmured the widow, who had not yet learned to rest her burden upon the Lord.

"Do you suppose, sister, that because I have two or three hundred pounds of my own, that I mean to be idle?" said Janet. "To tell you the truth, I have already forestalled the larger part of this sum in paying the poor Giffords' passage out. And as it may be years before they are able to repay me, if ever, I must work hard to make it up."

"I always knew that your sister Margaret was your favourite," said the widow. "For my part, I never could ask favours of any one, although I have conferred many in my time." And here she wiped away the tear, which, naturally enough, obtruded itself upon her cheek, as vain recollections of her former affluence crowded upon her mind.

"My dear Anne, I could not help you both at the same time," said the kind old maid. "Margaret has a sick husband, and four small children. The change of climate was recommended for his health, and I was only too happy to contribute my mite to effect this important object; for Gifford, you know, is an excellent man, and his valuable life of the utmost consequence to us all. It is little I want for myself; and if I live a couple of years longer, I hope I shall be able to assist my dear nephews, Robert and William, to settle in life."

"If the mirror sells for what it ought to fetch," said Mrs. Harden, proudly, "we shall not require any assistance."

"Confound that useless piece of trumpery!" cried Mr. William Harden, who had been listening unobserved to the conversation of the ladies; "I am sick of hearing about it. You had better not reckon too much upon the sale of it. You know what I have told you on that head before."

"I know you delight to vex me," said the widow, "and say these illnatured things on purpose to wound my feelings; but, in spite of your ugly prophesies, I feel assured that the mirror will make our fortunes."

"You forget the old carpet?" said Mr. Harden, with a provoking laugh. "Is that to perform no part in this important object? But we shall see — "

"Yes, we shall see," responded the widow. "Why should not I be as good a prophet as you?"

"I have probability on my side."

"The most probable events are not those which most frequently come to pass," said the widow, "or most of the schemes of human forethought would be successful, whilst we constantly see them overthrown by circumstances, which no prudence could have foreseen. A few months ago, what would have appeared more improbable than my present situation? Who could have imagined that I should be forced to leave my comfortable home, houseless and penniless, to wander over the great deep, with my orphan boys, in search of bread." And here Mrs. Harden burst into tears, and her relatives felt grieved that they had said any thing to wound her feelings. Even the rude William Harden took her hand, and promised that she should never want a home while he had one to offer her.

A succession of violent storms put an end to family disputes. For many days the vessel was in imminent danger of sinking, and all minor considerations were forgotten, in the all absorbing thoughts of self preservation. At length it pleased the Almighty Mover of the elements to calm the winds and waves, and bring the poor wanderers in safety to the desired haven. On their first landing, all was bustle and excitement. With exaggerated feelings of pleasure, they trod, for the first time, the promised land. Its skies appeared clearer, its suns brighter, its mountains more lofty, and its scenery more magnificent, than aught they had ever witnessed. But these feelings gradually subsided, and, before they had secured lodgings for the night, the first painful symptoms of that deep heart-ache, which has been so pathetically designated home-sickness, was experienced alike in the rudest and most sensitive bosom.

"Ah, this is not like our ain land!" sighed one.

"This will never be Scotland to me!" said another.

"I've a sair heart the night, sir," said a third; "but there's no help for it now. We must a' make the best o' a bad bargain."

And thus the poor emigrants complained and consoled each other for their mutual sorrow. None felt that deep depression of heart and spirits more keenly than Mrs. Harden; none looked forward with more eager hope into the veiled future than her portionless sons.

Several days were employed in getting their luggage on shore. To several persons who had called upon the strangers on their first arrival, Mrs. Harden had mentioned the mirror and carpet; and one wealthy Dutch merchant was desirous of becoming a purchaser of both articles. Mrs. Harden was delighted with her success. Nothing could equal her impatience for the arrival from ship board of this, to her invaluable, portion of the cargo. Mr. W. Harden alternately joked and sneered at his poor sister-in-law, assuring her that it would come time enough to make or mar her fortune. At last it did arrive; and, with eager haste, she and her sons and aunt Jessy commenced to unpack it.

"Do be careful, boys. William, don't shake the box so roughly. Jessy, give me leave — I understand these things much better than you," were expressions which burst continually from Mrs. Harden's lips.

"The salt water has penetrated the case, mamma," said William, lifting from it a mass of wet tow. "I hope it has not spoiled the mirror!"

"Nonsense, child! it could never soak through that immense carpet."

"Indeed it has, mamma! The carpet is wet through!" The boy paused — looked at his mother — and turned very pale. Then holding up a piece of broken glass, he said: "Ah, aunt Jessy! look at this!"

The widow gave a faint cry, and sunk back on her chair. The mirror was broken into a thousand pieces.

"I was afraid of that storm," sighed Robert.

"Here end the hopes of a family!" said Mrs. Harden.

"Well, Anne, who was right?" said Mr. Harden; "I told you it would be so. You had better have sold it. But, like all obstinate women, you would not listen to reason."

"It's of no use reproaching me now," said poor Mrs. Harden. "The carpet is spoiled — the mirror is broken —

and we are beggars!"

"Not so bad as that, mother," said Robert. "Come, William, help me to pack up these pieces of glass; they may turn to some account."

"You may throw them away," said Mrs. Harden.

"I can pack them in a small box, with some of this tow," returned Robert. "Who knows what they may turn to yet?"

"Why, Bob, you are as bad as your mother," said his uncle; "a greater simpleton, still. Her hopes were founded upon glass; yours are built upon fragments of the same brittle ware, already washed by the waves."

"You make light of our misfortune, sir," said Robert, gravely. "My poor mother feels it severely. In pity to her, say no more upon the subject; and leave me to do as I think best with the wreck of our little property. Such is my trust in God, that I believe that He is able to turn these broken fragments, that you despise, to a good account."

"You are a good boy, Robert, though rather credulous, and I have no doubt that you will soon be able to support your mother by your own industry. But as to the broken glass — hout, lad! — the very idea of the thing provokes mirth."

Robert did not listen to his uncle's last speech; he was busily employed in collecting and packing into a small compass the pieces of the splendid mirror, many of which he knew would cut into small dressing-glasses, which, if fitted into neat frames, might sell for something. The carpet he rinsed well in fresh water, and, with his brother's assistance, hung out to dry. This latter article was very much cut with the sharp ends of the broken glass, and the colours were all run into each other. It was perfectly unsaleable.

"My poor mother!" said Robert, "we should never reckon too much upon any thing. Such is the end of most of our earthly hopes."

Chapter IV
In Conclusion —
What Became of the Broken Mirror

After some necessary delay at Cape Town, the emigrants obtained a grant of land for their general location, on the frontier; and Mr. W. Harden engaged the services of his nephews, for the two ensuing years, promising, by way of remuneration, to provide for their wants and those of their widowed parent. This arrangement proved highly satisfactory to all parties; and, full of hope and happy anticipations of success, the emigrants commenced their long journey to the frontier. The sublime and romantic scenery, through which they had to travel for many hundred miles, in a great measure atoned for the length of the journey. The young people found objects to excite their interest and admiration at every step, and the spirits of the elder part of the community rose in proportion.

A beautiful fertile valley, between two lofty mountain ranges, had been granted for their location. A fine clear stream of water travelled the whole length of the glen, its devious windings marked by the fringe of Babylonian willows that shaded its rocky banks. A more delightful spot could scarcely have been chosen by the most enthusiastic lover of nature, than chance had thus provided them. The valley contained several thousand acres of excellent land, which was surveyed and equally divided among the males of the party. The lots which fell to the young Hardens stretched in opposite directions quite across the valley — the stream dividing them in front — the lofty mountains enclosing them in the rear; and the young possessors of this wild domain often sighed in vain for the necessary funds to enable them to make a settlement upon their useless lands. A situation of entire dependence is seldom to be coveted; and their willingness and strength were taxed to the uttermost by their hard, griping uncle, who, if he did not treat them with actual unkindness, yet was a stern, exacting master, who made them feel that the bread they earned was not their own. For his mother's sake, Robert never complained of his uncle's harshness, although he confided to aunt Jessy his sorrows, and often consulted her on the most probable means of bettering their condition. Miss Janet deeply sympathized with the lads, and often remonstrated with her brother on his over-bearing conduct. Her appeals to his better feelings were generally treated with contempt. "Women," he said, "were weak fools, who knew nothing about business, or the management of boys, whom they always spoiled with indulgence. To them he might seem a hard task-master; but he was only doing his duty, by making the lads attend to their work."

"But, brother! by exacting too much, you may lose their services altogether."

"Pshaw!" muttered Mr. Harden, in reply. "Who is to support their mother if they quit my service?"

"I will do that," said Miss Jessy, reddening, "rather than see my poor sister and her orphan boys imposed upon."

"I wish you would mind your own business," said Mr. Harden, tartly. "The boys would be quite contented if you would let them alone. It is a pity that old maids are such busy bodies."

"Brother William! you have sons of your own. If they were so situated, would you like them to be so treated?"

"I should be thankful to their employers if they made them attend to their business, and very much displeased with any meddling, mischief-making old body, who tried to render them discontented."

Miss Janet turned away with the tears in her eyes, while Mr. William Harden, who considered himself the injured party, walked off with great dignity, to inspect his flocks and herds, of which he already possessed a considerable number.

The two years of servitude were fast drawing to a close. The little settlement was in the most flourishing condition. Bee-hive cottages arose on every side, and the green valley was dotted over with sheep and cattle; every location had its primitive dwelling, and was possessed by a thriving family. All, but the pretty lots of the young Hardens, looked well and flourishing.

"Oh, that we possessed the means of purchasing a few agricultural implements, and a dozen head of sheep and cows," said Robert, with a sigh. "We would soon put up a cabin for my dear mother, and be as well off as the rest."

"If we had had the good luck to save the mirror," said Mrs. Harden, with a sigh. It was the first time his mother had made any allusion to the loss for many months.

Robert started, and looked musingly at her: "The mirror — yes; I had forgotten the mirror. By the bye, aunt Jessy, I wanted a bit of the glass to shew my favourite old Caffre, Gaika, the reflection of his own face. Do you know what I did with the box containing the pieces?"

"You will find it in the outhouse," said aunt Jessy. "I wish you could frame us a small dressing-glass out of the fragments."

"I will try," said Robert; and, finding the box, he selected several square pieces of glass, and put them into plain wooden frames, which he fashioned tolerably well with what tools he could collect. He was still busy at his task, when the settlement was visited by several leading men among the frontier tribes, who often visited the glen, to make a friendly exchange of their native commodities, for knives and beads, and other trifles of the same nature. The sight of a mirror was new to them all. It seems a species of vanity inherent in man, to be delighted with the reflection of his own image. For hours the savage chiefs amused themselves with examining their features in these wonderful pieces of glass. They looked and looked again, and the more familiar they became with their own faces, the more enamoured they seemed with their sable visages. Nothing would satisfy them but the actual possession of these magic glasses; and, before they left the valley, they had bartered with Robert Harden flocks of sheep and herds of cattle for these once despised fragments of broken glass.*

---

* This circumstance is a fact. The widow and her sons owe their present wealth to the sale of these pieces of broken glass.

"Mother, dear mother! is it possible," exclaimed Robert, as he flung his arms about her neck, and kissed her, in an ecstacy of delight, "that these flocks can be ours? See what God has sent us. He has restored to us the value of the mirror seven-fold! Who, who will ever doubt his providential care, who listens to the tale of our Broken Mirror?"

But this happy change in the fortunes of the Hardens did not end here. The old carpet, likewise, played its part in this strange drama. Aunt Jessy cut out all the soiled and torn parts, and made up the remainder into aprons, such as are worn by the native women; and these had as great a sale as the pieces of glass. Not a fragment of either article but turned to account; and from being the poorest and most dependent settlers in the glen, the widow and her sons became the most wealthy and independent.

"What will you say to my venture now, brother?" said Mrs. Harden, the first time she received her brother into a comfortable stone house, which her sons had erected, some five years after this, upon Robert's farm — previous to his bringing home one of his cousin Giffords, as his wife. "The broken mirror and the old carpet have made our fortune after all."

"The boys have been confoundedly lucky," said the old man, casting rather an envious glance round the neatly furnished apartment.

"Rather say, uncle, that God has been very good to us," returned Robert. "The means He has used in this instance to place us above want appear to me quite miraculous. I hope I shall ever retain a grateful sense of His mercies."

"Who could have imagined," said his brother, "that the very circumstance which was the death-blow to our hopes, should be the means of procuring those advantages which we considered lost for ever?"

"And have you paid Mr. Sylvester the money he advanced for your passage out?" asked Mr. Harden, in his usual rude way.

"Two years ago," said Robert, proudly. "Thank God, we do not owe a debt in the world."

"You have been very lucky," again responded the

disappointed interrogator. "And when is the marriage to take place?"

"In our new church, on Sunday next."

"Hout, man! Sunday is no day to get married upon. Are there not six days in the week to pursue your worldly matters, without your pitching upon the Lord's day?"

"It will be the first time that public worship will be performed in our valley, by a minister of God," said Robert; "and I wished the happiest event of my life to be celebrated on this joyful occasion."

The old man had nothing further to say on that subject, but he indulged his contradictory humour in a thousand other subjects, rendering his company as disagreeable as he possibly could to his kind entertainers.

The brothers had assisted, both with money and their own labour, to the erection of the neat presbyterian church, which formed a most picturesque addition to the lovely scenery of the pastoral valley. A good man had been appointed from home to take charge of this flock in the wilderness; and the congregation, consisting of about forty-eight families, had welcomed their minister with every demonstration of affection and esteem, to his new abode.

The Sunday following the little church was crowded with happy faces, and the happiest and the proudest man there was Robert Harden, as he led into the sanctuary he had contributed so largely to raise, his widowed mother and his young blooming bride. He felt that he owed all to God, and his heart overflowed with gratitude to his great benefactor.

After the disuse of years, how solemnly the public service of God appeals to every heart. It is as if a voice from Heaven spoke to man, reproving him for his past sins, and admonishing him for his future and eternal welfare. During the first impressive address, many eyes filled involuntarily with tears, but when Mr. Gordon gave out the favourite and well-known paraphrase,

> O God of Bethel, by whose hand
>   Thy children still are fed,
> Who through this barren wilderness
>   Hast all our fathers led.

The voice of weeping, which could no longer be suppressed, was heard from one end of the church to the other. It was the simple voice of nature, which, unrestrained by the cold formal etiquette of society, poured forth its own plaintive language to the throne of God.

"Don't be ashamed of your tears, sister Jessy," whispered Mrs. Harden to her sister, who was struggling to conceal her emotion; "ye may be proud that ye are permitted this day to weep before the Lord."

The rest of the day was spent in the solemn services of religion. The following morning the inhabitants of the valley assembled in their best attire, to celebrate the marriage of their favourite, Robert Harden, and his cousin Anne Gifford.

Literary Garland ns 1 (1843): 145–54.

The Well in the Wilderness; A Tale of the Prairie. — Founded Upon Facts

In vain you urge me to forget —
That fearful night — it haunts me yet;
And stampt into my heart and brain,
The awful memory will remain;
Yea, e'en in sleep, that ghastly sight,
Returns to shake my soul each night. — *Author.*

Richard Steele, was the son of one of those small landholders, who are fast disappearing in merry Old England. His father left him the sole possessor of twenty-five acres of excellent arable land and a snug little cottage, which had descended from father to son, through many generations.

The ground plot, which had been sufficient to maintain his honest progenitors for several ages, in the palmy days of Britain's glory and independence, e'er her vast resources past into the hands of the few and left the many to starve, was not enough to provide for the wants of our stout yeoman, and his wife and family; which consisted at that period, of three sons, and one daughter, a lovely blooming girl of ten years, or thereabouts. Richard and his boys toiled with unceasing diligence — the wife was up late and early, and not one moment was left unemployed; and yet they made no headway, but, every succeeding year, found them in arrears.

"Jane," said the yeoman, one evening, thoughtfully, to

his wife, after having blessed his homely meal of skimmed milk and brown bread, "Couldst thee not have given us a little treat to-night. Hast thee forgotten, that it is our dear Annie's birth-night?"

"No Richard, I have not forgotten, how could I forget the anniversary of the day, that made us all so happy. But times are bad. I could not spare the money to buy sugar and plums for the cake; and I wanted to sell all the butter, in order to scrape enough together, to pay the shoemaker for making our darling's shoes. Annie, knows that she is infinitely dear to us all, though we cannot give her luxuries to prove it."

"It wants no proof, dear Mother," said the young girl, flinging her round, but sunburnt arms, about her worthy parent's neck, "Your precious love, is worth the wealth of the whole world to me. I know how fond you, and the dear father, are of me, and I am more than satisfied."

"Annie is right," said Steele, dropping his knife and holding out his arms for a caress. "The world could not purchase such love as we feel for her, and let us bless God, that poor though we be, we are all here to night, well and strong, aye, and rich, in spite of our homely fare, in each others affections. What say you my boys?" and he glanced with parental pride, on the three fine lads, whose healthy and honest countenances, might well be contemplated with pleasure, and afford subjects for hopeful anticipation for the future.

"We are happy father," said the eldest cheerfully.

"The cakes, and the spiced ale would have made us happier," said the second, "Mother makes such nice cakes." "So she does," cried the third. "It seems so dull to have nothing nice on Annie's birth-day. I should not care a fig, if it were Dick's birth-day, or Owen's, or mine, but not to drink Annie's health, seems unlucky."

"You shall drink it yet," said Annie laughing.

"In what?" asked both the boys in a breath.

"In fine spring water," and she filled their mugs, "Better God never gave to his creatures. How bright it is — how it sparkles. I will never from this day, ask a finer drink. Here is health to you my brothers, and may we never know what it is to lack a draught of pure water." Annie, nodded to her brothers, and drank off her mug of water; and the good-natured fellows, who dearly loved her, followed her example. Oh little did the gay hearted girl, think in that moment of playful glee, of the price she was one day destined to pay for a drink of water.

The crops that year were a failure and the heart of the strong man, began to droop. He felt that labor in his native land, could no longer give his children bread, and unwilling to sink into the lowest class, he wisely resolved while he retained the means of doing so, to emigrate to America. His wife made no opposition to his wishes, his sons were delighted with the prospect of any change for the better; and if Annie felt a passing pang, at leaving the daisied fields, and her pretty playmates the lambs, she hid it from her parents. The dear homestead, with its quiet rural orchard, and trim hedge-rows, fell to the hammer; nor was the sunburnt cheek of the honest yeoman, unmoistened with a tear, when he saw it added to the enormous possessions of the Lord of the Manor.

"Jane," he said, grasping his wife's trembling hand, hard between his own, "courage my woman; the sooner we go now the better. We have no longer a home in England." "I was born here Richard," said the poor creature, in a broken voice and with her eyes streaming with tears, "and it is so hard, to tear one's self away."

"So was my father, Jane, and my father's father," returned the husband, "and 'tis riving my heart assunder, to part with the roof which sheltered an honest race for so many years; but duty demands it of me, and now the debt is paid."

"Oh, father, shall we ever love another place like this?" said Richard, the eldest boy. "I did not think, that I should feel so bad at going away. Every thing looks mournfully to-day; and my heart is so full, I can scarcely speak without feeling the tears come into my eyes. The dumb animals seem to know that something is wrong with us, as we pass to and fro, in a sort of stupid amazement. The very house, if it could speak, would tell us, that it was sorry to change owners."

"Don't mention it, Dick. I feel low enough myself. Keep up your spirits. Strive to be cheerful, it will comfort your poor mother, under this severe trial. Women, my lad, feel parting with the old familiar places and faces, more keenly than men."

The Yeoman was right. His wife, who had been born and brought up on the farm, and had never known any other home, (for she was first cousin to her husband; an orphan child whom his mother had adopted,) was dreadfully cast down, and it required the united efforts of the whole family, to reconcile her to the change that awaited her.

After the sale was completed, and the money it brought duly paid, Steele lost no time, in preparing for his emigration. In less than a fortnight, he had secured their passage to New York, and they were already on their voyage across the Atlantic. Favored by wind and weather, after the first effects of the sea had worn off, they were comfortable enough. The steerage passengers were poor but respectable English emigrants, and they made several pleasant acquaintances among them. One family especially attracted their attention, and so far engaged their affections during the tedious voyage, that they entered into an agreement to settle in the same neighborhood. Mr. Atkins, was a widower, with two sons, the age of Richard and Owen, and an elder sister — a primitive gentle old woman, who had been once, both wife and mother but had outlived all her family. Abigail Winchester, for so she was called, took an especial fancy to our Annie, in whom she recognised a strong resemblance to a daughter whom she had lost. Her affection was warmly returned by the kind girl, who by a thousand little attentions, strove to evince her gratitude to Abigail, for her good opinion.

They had not completed half their voyage, before the Scarlet Fever broke out among the passengers, and made dreadful havoc among the younger portion. Steele's whole family were down with it at the same time; and in spite of the constant nursing of himself and his devoted partner;

and the unremitting attentions of Abigail Winchester, who never left the sick ward for several nights and days; the two youngest boys died and were committed to the waters of the great deep, before Annie and Richard recovered to a consciousness of their dreadful loss. This threw a sad gloom over the whole party. Steele said nothing, but he often retired to some corner of the ship to bewail his loss in secret. His wife was wasted and worn to a shadow, and poor Annie, looked the ghost of her former self.

"Had we never left England," she thought, "my brothers had not died!" but she was wrong. God who watches with parental love over all his creatures, knows the best season in which to reclaim His own. But human love in its blind yearning, is slow in receiving this great truth. It lives in the present, lingers over the past, and cannot bear to give up, that which now is, for the promise of that which shall be. The future, separated from the things of time, has always an awful aspect. A perfect and childlike reliance upon God, can alone divest it of those chilling doubts and fears, which at times shake the firmest mind, and urge the proud unyielding spirit of man to cleave so strongly to kindred dust.

The sight of the American shores, that the poor lads had desired so eagerly to see, seemed to renew their grief, and a sadder party, never set foot upon a foreign strand, than our emigrant and his family.

Steele had brought letters of introduction to a respectable merchant in the city, who advised him to purchase a tract of land in the then new State of Illinois. The beauty of the country, the fine climate, and fruitful soil, were urged upon him in the strongest manner. The merchant had scrip to dispose of in that remote settlement, and as is usual in such cases, he only consulted his own interest in the matter. Strangers are too easily persuaded. Steele thought the merchant, who was a native of the country, must know best, what would suit him, and he not only became a purchaser of land in Illinois, but induced his new friends to follow his example.

We will pass over their journey to the far west. The

novelty and beauty of the scenes through which they passed, contributed not a little to revive their drooping spirits. Richard had recovered his health, and amused the party by his lively anticipations of the future. They were to have the most comfortable log house, and the neatest farm in the district. He would raise the finest cattle, the finest crops, and the best garden stuff, in the neighborhood. Frugal and industrious habits, would soon render them wealthy and independent. His Mother listened to these sallies with a delighted smile, and even the grave Yeoman's brow, relaxed from its habitual frown. Annie entered warmly into all her brother's plans; and if he laid the foundation of this fine castle in the air, she certainly provided the cement, and all the lighter materials.

As their long route led them farther from the habitations of man, and deeper and deeper into the wilderness, the stern realities of their solitary locality, became hourly more apparent to the poor emigrants. They began to think, that they had acted too precipitately in going so far back into the woods, unacquainted as they were with the usages of the country. But repentance came too late; and when at length, they reached their destination, they found themselves at the edge of a vast forest, with a noble open prairie stretching away as far as the eye could reach in front of them, and no human habitation in sight, or indeed existing for miles around them.

In a moment the farmer comprehended all the difficulties and dangers of his situation; but his was a stout heart, not easily daunted by circumstances. He possessed a vigorous constitution, and a strong arm; and he was not alone. Richard was an active energetic lad, and his friend Atkins, and his two sons, were a host in themselves. Having settled with his guides, and ascertained by the maps which he had been given at Mr. —— 's office the extent and situation of his new estate, he set about unyoking the cattle which he had purchased, and securing them, while Atkins and his sons, pitched a tent for the night, and collected wood for their fire. The young people were in raptures with the ocean of verdure redolent with blossoms, that lay smiling in the last rays of the sun before them. Never did garden appear to them so lovely, as that vast wilderness of sweets planted by the munificent hand of nature, with such profuse magnificence. Annie, could scarcely tear herself away from the enchanting scene, to assist her mother in preparing their evening meal.

"Mother where shall we get water?" asked Annie, glancing wistfully towards their empty cask. "I have seen no indication of water for the last three miles."

"Annie, has raised a startling doubt," said Steele, "I can perceive no appearance of stream or creek, in any direction."

"Hist, Father!" cried Richard, "do you hear that? The croaking of those hateful frogs is music to me just now, for I am dying with thirst," and seizing the can he ran off, in the direction of the discordant sounds.

It was near dark, when he returned with his pail full of clear cold water, at which the whole party slaked their thirst, before asking any questions.

"What delicious water — as clear as crystal — as cold as ice. How fortunate to obtain it so near at hand," exclaimed several in a breath.

"Aye, but 'tis an ugly place," said Richard thoughtfully. "I should not like to go to that well, at early day, or after night-fall."

"Why not my boy?"

"'Tis in the heart of a dark swamp, just about a hundred yards within the forest, and the water trickles from beneath the roots of an old tree, into a natural stone tank; but all around is involved in frightful gloom. I fancied that I heard a low growl, as I stooped to fill my pail, while a horrid speckled snake glided from between my feet, and darted hissing and rattling its tail into the brake. Father you must never let any of the women go alone to that well."

The yeoman laughed at his son's fears, and shortly after the party retired into the tent and overcome with fatigue were soon asleep.

The first thing which engaged the attention of our

emigrants, was the erection of a log shanty for the reception of their respective families. This important task was soon accomplished. Atkins prefered for the site of his, the open prairie; but Steele, for the nearer proximity of wood and water, chose the edge of the forest, but the habitations of the pioneers, were so near, that they were within call of each other.

To fence in a piece of land for their cattle, and prepare a plot for wheat and corn, for the ensuing year, was the next thing to be accomplished, and by the time these preparations were completed, the long bright summer had passed away, and the fall was at hand. Up to this period, both families had enjoyed excellent health, but in the month of September, Annie, and then Richard, fell sick with the intermittent fever, and Old Abigail, kindly came across, to help Mrs. Steele nurse her suffering children. Medical aid was not to be had in that remote place, and beyond simple remedies which were perfectly inefficacious in their situation, the poor children's only chance for life, was their youth, a good sound constitution, and the merciful interposition of a benevolent and overruling Providence.

It was towards the close of a sultry day, that Annie burning with fever, implored the faithful Abigail, to give her a drink of cold water. Hastening to the water cask, the old woman was disappointed in finding it exhausted. Richard having drank the last drop, and was still raving in the delirium of fever for more drink.

"My dear child, there is no water."

"Oh I am burning, dying with thirst. Give me but one drop, dear Abigail — one drop of cold water!"

Just then Mrs. Steele, returned from milking the cows, and Abigail proffered to the lips of the child, a bowl of new milk, but she shrunk from it with disgust, and sinking back upon her pillow, murmured, "water, water, for the love of God, give me a drink of water."

"Where is the pail," said Mrs. Steele, "I don't much like going alone to that well, but it is still broad day, and I know that in reality there is nothing to fear. I cannot bear to hear the child moan for drink in that terrible way."

"Dear Mother," said Richard faintly, "don't go. Father will be in soon, we can wait till then."

"Oh, the poor dear child, is burning," cried Abigail, "she cannot wait till then, do neighbor go for the water. I will stay with the children, and put out the milk, while you are away."

Mrs. Steele left the shanty, and a few minutes after, the patients exhausted by suffering fell into a profound sleep.

Abigail busied herself in scalding the milk pans, and in her joy at the young people's cessation from suffering forgot the mother altogether. About half an hour had elapsed, and the mellow light of evening had faded into night, when Steele returned with his oxen from the field.

The moment he entered the shanty, he went up to the beds which contained his sick children, and satisfied that the fever was abating, he looked round for his supper, surprised that it was not as usual ready for him upon the table.

"No water," he cried "in the cask, and supper not ready. After working all day in the burning sun, a man wants to have things made comfortable for him at night. Mrs. Winchester are you here. Where is my wife?"

"Merciful goodness!" exclaimed the old woman turning as pale as death. "Is she not back from the well?"

"The well!" cried Steele grasping her arm, "How long has she been gone?"

"This half hour, or more."

Steele made no answer. His cheek was as pale as her own; and taking his gun from the beam to which it was slung, he carefully loaded it with ball, and without uttering a word rushed from the house.

Day still lingered on the open prairie, but the moment he entered the bush it was deep night. He had crossed the plain with rapid strides, but as he approached the swamp his step became slow and cautious. The well was in the centre of a jungle, from the front of which, Richard had cleared away the brush to facilitate their access to the water; and as he drew near the spot, his ears were chilled with a low deep growling, and the crunching of teeth, as if some wild animal was devouring the bones of its prey.

The dreadful truth with all its shocking heart-revolting reality, flashed upon the mind of the yeoman, and for a moment paralized him. The precincts of the well, were within range of his rifle, and dropping down upon his hands and knees, and nerving his arm for a clear aim, he directed his gaze to the spot from whence the fatal sounds proceeded. A little on one side of the well, a pair of luminous eyes glared like green lamps at the edge of the dark wood; and the horrid sounds which curdled the blood of the yeoman, became more distinctly audible.

Slowly Steele raised the rifle to his shoulder, and setting his teeth, and holding his breath, steadily aimed at the space between those glaring balls of fire. The sharp report of the rifle, awoke the far echoes of the forest. The deer leaped up from his lair. The wolf howled and fled into the depths of the wood, and the panther, for such it was, uttering a hoarse growl, sprang several feet into the air, then fell across the mangled remains of his victim.

Richard Steele rose up from the ground. The perspiration was streaming from his brow; his limbs trembled and shook, his lips moved convulsively, and he pressed his hands over his heaving breast, to keep down the violent throbbing of his agitated heart. It was not fear that chained him to the spot, and hindered him from approaching his dead enemy. It was horror. He dared not look upon the mangled remains of his wife — the dear partner of all his joys and sorrows — the companion of his boyhood — the love of his youth — the friend and counsellor of his middle age — the beloved mother of his children. How could he recognize in that crushed and defiled heap, his poor Jane. The pang was too great for his agonized mind to bear. Sense and sight alike forsook him, and staggering a few paces forward, he fell insensible across the path.

Alarmed by the report of the rifle, Atkins and his sons proceeded with torches to the spot, followed by Abigail, who unconscious of the extent of the calamity, was yet sufficiently convinced that something dreadful had occurred.

When the full horrors of the scene were presented to the sight of the terror-stricken group; their grief burst forth in tears and lamentations. Atkins alone retained his presence of mind. Dragging the panther from the remains of the unfortunate Mrs. Steele, he beckoned to one of his sons, and suggested to him the propriety of instantly burying the disfigured and mutilated body, before the feelings of her husband and children, were agonized by the appalling sight. First removing the insensible husband to his own dwelling, Atkins and his sons returned to the fatal spot, and conveying the body to the edge of the prairie, they selected a quiet lovely spot beneath a wide spreading chestnut tree; and wrapping all that remained of the wife of Richard Steele in a sheet, they committed it to the earth in solemn silence; nor were tears or prayers wanting in that lonely hour, to consecrate the nameless grave where the English mother slept.

Annie and Richard recovered to mourn their irreparable loss, to feel that their mother's life had been sacrificed to her maternal love. Time as it ever does, softened the deep anguish of the bereaved husband. During the ensuing summer, their little colony was joined by a hardy band of British and American pioneers. The little settlement grew into a prosperous village, and Richard Steele died a wealthy man, and was buried by the side of his wife in the center of the village church-yard, that spot having been chosen for the first temple in which the emigrants met to worship in his own house, the God of their fathers.

Victoria Magazine 1 (1847): 54–58. *The Odd-Fellow's Offering* for 1852 (1851); *Bentley's Miscellany* (1853).

Rachel Wilde, or, Trifles from the Burthen of a Life

Chapter I

Fiction, however wild and fanciful,
Is but the copy memory draws from truth;
'Tis not in human genius *to create*;
The mind is but a mirror, which reflects
Realities that are; or the dim shadows
Left by the past upon its placid surface,
Recalled again to life.

S.M.

We are all more or less, the creatures of circumstance. Human vanity may rise up in arms and contradict this assertion; but it is nevertheless true. Others have formed links in our destiny; and we in our turn, form links in the destiny of others. No one ever did, or could live for himself alone. We talk of originality of thought. Can such a thing in this stage of the world's history exist? Our very thoughts are not our own: they have swayed the minds of thousands and millions before us; and have taken a coloring from the location in which we were born, and from the opinions of those with whom the first years of our existence were passed.

The quiet rural beauties of a rich agricultural district; or the bold rugged grandeur of a mountain land, leave their abiding traces upon the ductile heart of youth, and often determine the future character of the individuals, born and educated amid such scenes. A taste for peaceful and elegant pursuits, will mark the one, while a spirit of enterprize, and a stern desire for military glory will predominate in the other.

The unconquerable love of freedom which has marked the mountaineer of all ages and countries, is doubtless derived from the sublime objects which surrounded him in childhood. The difficulties and dangers which beset his path, and the boyish pride he felt in surmounting them, mingles with all the after contingencies of life, supplying him with that energy and coolness in the hour of peril, which constitutes true courage. The image of the lofty mountain still remains upon his mind; and he owes to his early association with the hills, greatness of mind and energy of action. In like manner, the pursuits, mode of thinking, nay, even the prejudices of those with whom we pass our early years, mingles with, and often forms a part of our own character.

Thus it was with Rachel Wilde. She was the youngest of a very large family, mostly composed of females. This sisterhood, were girls of extraordinary capacity; and like most children of this class, brought up in solitude, and educated at home, their amusements and pursuits were chiefly of a mental cast. They told stories, wrote poems, and acted plays, for the mutual benefit; and the infant Rachel soon imbibed a strong taste for these literary pursuits, which displayed itself in a thousand vagaries.

The father of Rachel was a man of great scientific and literary acquirements. He was a vigorous and independent thinker, and paid little regard to the received prejudices and opinions of the world. He acted from conscience, and the dictates of a powerful mind; was an excellent husband and father — a generous master, and a kind neighbor. The poor loved him, and the rich, whom he could not flatter, respected him; to be brief, he was a good and just man, and his family regarded him with a reverence only one degree less than that which they owed to their Creator. The memory of such a parent never dies; it lives for ever in the heart of his children. In after-life they are proud to echo his words, and maintain his opinions.

Mr. Wilde had lost a large fortune in entering too deeply into commercial speculations; and retiring from the city, he purchased a small estate in the country, determined to spend the rest of his days in rural occupations, and devote all his spare time to the education of his large family.

Mr. Wilde held all public schools in abhorrence, and his mode of tuition was the very opposite to that pursued in the seminary. Lessons were seldom committed to memory. He read, — he explained, — he argued with his children. He called their attention to the subjects which he selected for their information, and set them thinking. They were allowed freedom of discussion; and they were never suffered to abandon a point until they understood its meaning. History, which is rendered so dull and distasteful to the young, by being dunned into them as a task, was a delightful recreation to the little Wildes; and they ransacked every book in a well-furnished library, to make themselves masters of all the histories, and biographies which it contained. From this source they drew all the impromptu subjects for their poems, and heroes for their dramas. They lived with the mighty dead of all ages, in a world of history and romance. The little Rachel listened with eagerness to every word which fell from the lips of her elder sisters. The jumble of history, travels, biography, and poetry, mixed up in her infant mind, produced a strange combination of ideas, and made her see visions and dream dreams — which greatly amused the good father and the young sisterhood. Every morning she related her adventures of the night, to her father, as she sat upon his knee at breakfast.

Her novel descriptions of what she had seen, in the realms of fancy, were received with peals of mirth; and the little creature was encouraged in her fancies, by the applause with which they were greeted.

As she grew older, and learned to read, she fell in love with all the heroes of antiquity. At seven years old, she had read Shakespere, and knew most of the Iliad of Homer by heart, and was ready to do battle for Achilles and his favourite, in opposition to her sister Ann, who always espoused the Trojan cause.

Her first essay in the gentle art of rhyming, was so ludicrous, that I cannot refrain from mentioning it here.

Her father, who loved to see his little girls innocently employed, had given to Rachel, and her sister Dorothea, two rather extensive flower borders, which were separated by a broad gravel walk. — These, they were enjoined to keep in good order, and to strive which could produce the prettiest shrubs, and flowers.

The little girls received their charge with delight, and all their spare time was devoted to the care and culture of their gardens.

The first song of the birds, awakened them to their task, and they sang and worked away at their borders with joy in their eyes, and health upon their cheeks. Their shoes were saturated with the morning dews; but they were too happy to feel the least inconvenience. Those were the days in which love, hope, and innocence, formed the prism in the rainbow of life.

One morning Rachel communicated to Dorothea, who was scarcely two years her senior, the bold scheme she had formed of writing a poem in praise of their favorite flowers, which she intended to suspend round the neck of each, in order to draw the attention of the family to the merits of her *proteges*. "It would be beautiful," she said, "to see how Lodge, the gardener, would stare; and to hear how papa would laugh, at all the fine things she meant to write." Dorothea entered with heart and hand into the scheme; and to work went the happy pair; and as they were too young to write a readable hand, they printed their doggrels with a pen, upon some old parchment, which had long been consigned to a lumber room, in company with all the musty magazines of the last century.

Mid hearty bursts of laughter, with flushed cheeks and sparkling eyes, the children produced their first attempts at poetry. When a lap full of these stray leaves from the "*Mount Divine*," were committed to the yellow parchment strips, upon which they were destined to figure, the little girls ran down to the garden, surrounding the delicate stems of their victimized flowers with huge halters of the unpliable material which contained their highly prized verses.

I will give my readers a specimen or two, from this joint-stock company of bad rhymes: —

On a double scarlet catchfly:

Of the flowers of yore
I can tell nothing more,
But that I
Am a catchfly!

On a choice young apple-tree, and as if addressed to unwelcome visitors:

If you touch a single apple,
You and I shall surely grapple.

Two double red stocks stood boldly forth, presenting to the astonished reader, the following ridiculous announcement:

Here stand two famous scarlet stocks,
So pray good people move your *hocks*!

This by the way, was a composition of Dorothea's, and both the children thought it excellent. They knew not, poor light-hearted little ones, that such a word as *hocks*, was unknown in the vocabulary of Apollo, if his Godship of the lyre, needed such a useful article.

A primrose and a pansy,
  Growing side by side;
Of all the buds that blosom,
  The glory and the pride.

And

My pretty, modest, pink-edged daisy,
Your beauty sure will drive me crazy.

Tulips were no favourites with the children, and were thus apostrophized: —

Oh tulips! you look proud and bold,
Your streaks have more of brass than gold.

Then to the wind-flower, that beautiful child of April's varied skies, the very recollection of which, brings the tears to my eyes; and recals the lovely gardens of England, in all their rich array of evergreens, and gay parterres.

Anenomies, red, white, and blue,
The rose alone, surpasses you.

Dear rose, we love you best of all the flowers,
Our chief delight, to tend, and call you ours.

The lily is so graceful, tall and white,
We love her, as the fairies love moonlight!

Oh, *that* the sister florists thought so pretty, and themselves so clever for having invented; that we will leave them here, and merely tell, how the gardener Lodge, discovered the huge labels, hanging from the stems of the poor drooping flowers; crushed beneath the weight of flattery, which bowed their simple beauties to the earth; and which like the human flowers to whom the same treatment is applied, sadly marred their native charms. How he ran with his hands full of these curious tickets, as he called them; to his master; and how the good father laughed at the whimsies of his eccentric children: and at his death, which happened some years after; these papers were found carefully tied up, and labelled in a corner of his desk. Ah, human love! parental love! how dost thou treasure up in thy inexhaustible store-house trifles like these. Ridiculous as this beginning was in the art, "unteachable untaught," there was now, no end to Rachel's attempts at rhyming; all her thoughts whether grave or gay, ran lilting into verse; and burst forth extemporaneously, to the great edification of her playmates, who generally called upon her to invent plays, and tell stories. — One of these impromptu dramas, met with rather a melancholy termination for the juvenile author and manager; and for a time, checked the vivacity of the little Rachel's genius. It was an interlude in one act, to be called the "*wood Demon.*" The scene, a beautiful meadow, which opened into the flower garden; and which said meadow, terminated in a deep, romantic dell, planted with flowering shrubs and overhung on all sides by tall forest trees. The characters in the piece, a brave knight and his lady, personated by Dorothea, and her eldest brother. This knight and lady fair, were the parents of one lovely child, a little boy on whom they doated, as all fond parents always do, and whose part fell to the share of Rachel's youngest brother, a fat, rosy, peaceable little fellow in frocks and trowsers. This child, the wood Demon, (Rachel herself) was to carry off and hide up in his den, a sand-pit in the afore mentioned dell, where a gallant page, belonging to the lady, was to find him, kill the "*wood demon*," and restore the child to his distracted parents.

Now, this in Rachel's opinion, was a glorious plot. The acting commenced under the most happy auspices. The month was June, the day, one in which nature appears conscious of her own beauty and revels in the excess of light and loveliness. — The air was full of the warblings of birds, of the scent of flowers, and the music of gentle breezes. The lady led her little boy into the centre of the meadow, and bade him amuse himself among the flowers. The boy was busy filling his cap with "daisies pied, and hare bells blue" — when a yell from the dark grove, made him start and look up; and lo the *wood demon*, crowned with bits of yew, and poisonous briony, rushed from his hiding place, and with frightful yells, seized upon the terrified child. But, just as he is carrying him off in triumph, Miss Wilde, alarmed by the outcries, issues from the house, and shocked at seeing a carriage drawn up by the meadow paling, and a gentle man and lady enjoying the pastime as much as the poor actors, gives a cuff to one, and a shake to another; and the poor wood demon, vanquished in the very moment of victory, returns weeping to the house.

Chapter II

Rachel was yet a child, when a lady came on a visit to the family. Miss Long, was the daughter of a very old friend of the father's; and she was treated in every respect like a friend of his own. — During her long stay, a great attachment sprang up between her and the little Rachel; and when the time of her departure drew near, she begged as a great favour, that the little girl might be allowed to accompany her, to her distant home.

Rachel was a sickly, consumptive child; and it was agreed upon, on all hands, that the change would be beneficial to her health. Rachel heard the decision with unmixed delight; and listened with eager attention, to the many consultations held upon this important subject; and stood still and patiently, to be fitted with the few additions which were necessary for her equipment; and thought herself as rich as a queen, in the possession of two new frocks, a gay scarlet pelisse, a cap of the same material, with a gold band and tassels. Such a theatrical costume, was fashionable in those days; and poor Rachel, who was not the first of her sex, whose head had been turned by a scarlet coat and a gay feather, felt as proud as a peacock, as she strutted about in all the dignity of her new finery.

At last, the preparations come to a happy termination. Our little one had received the last kiss, and the last blessing, from her kind parents; had been hugged and kissed, and wept over, by the young sisterhood, who individually charged her, not to forget them; and in a few minutes after, she found herself seated beside her friend, Miss Long; and rolling along the London road, in a neat post-chaise.

It was the first time Rachel had ever lost sight of her home, and she wondered why her heart swelled; and tears blinded her eyes. It was the hand of nature knocking at her unsophisticated heart, and demanding the sympathies, which had been planted and fostered, by the divine mother, unknown albeit, to her thoughtless offspring. The tears of childhood are holy things; showers from heaven, which fall from angel eyes, to refresh and vivify the souls of the children of earth. A thousand mental graces spring up and flourish under their influence. There is no sorrow in such tender emotions, they may truly be termed, the joy of grief.

Rachel wept silently for a few moments, but, hope and expectation, soon dried her tears. The *present*, to children is the only period of enjoyment. They are too young, too unacquainted with care, to anticipate the future; and the past, however sorrowful, is quickly obliterated from their memory. The moment which dries their tears, spreads a blissful veil of oblivion over the cause from whence they flowed; and Rachel, when she recovered her spirits, marvelled to find Miss Long, still sad and dejected.

Miss Long was in love, and had just parted with her sweetheart; but Rachel, poor child, was ignorant of all this. She knew of no love, beyond the love which a child feels for its parents, and brothers and sisters; and the friends who are kind to it. She would have esteemed the love she bore for her cat and dog, as a superior sentiment, to the passion Miss Long felt for her lover. She thought that her dear Lucy was cross and sulky, because she would not tell her stories, and talk and play with her, as usual. All the observations she could draw from her companion, were as uninteresting as the following:

"Bless me, child! how you tease! Can't you sit still and be quiet. Will your tongue never tire. You will be out of the carriage window and break your neck."

"Dear Lucy," said the incorrigible Rachel, lolling across her lap, and looking beseechingly in her face. "How cross you are to day."

"You are a spoilt little girl," she returned, kissing her. "There, you may stand at the window, and look at the Highlanders."

Oh what a grand spectacle was that for a child of six years of age. The gallant —— Highland regiment was marching past to embark for the continent. Rachel screamed with delight at their waring plumes, gay tartans and rich accoutriments, until the sight of their naked knees, threw the volatile child into convulsions of laughter.

"Look, Lucy, look! Their stockings are all too short

for them. How cold they must be with their knees bare!"

As the carriage drove slowly through Chelmsford, Rachel's excitement was increased, by a curious incident. The officer who commanded the detachment, was a remarkably handsome, dignified looking man. His stately figure and soldier-like bearing, impressed her with a species of awe; and she insisted that he must be the king, and refused to be undeceived by Miss Long. As the regiment was marching past a range of mean-looking houses in the suburbs of the town, an old woman rushed suddenly from the door of one of them; and flinging herself upon her knees before the gallant officer, she cast her withered arms about him, kissing his knees with the utmost devotion, between broken exclamations in her native tongue, sobs and tears.

The officer smiled good-humouredly, and raising the venerable dame from the ground, shook her heartily by the hand, into which he slipped several bright looking pieces of money, answering her passionate appeal to him in the same strange dialect.

The regiment marched forward, but the old woman remained standing upon the same spot till it was out of sight. Her white hair streaming from beneath her coarse cap, her eyes shaded by her withered hand, and the tears rolling fast down her furrowed cheeks. For years, that picture of humble attachment haunted the memory of Rachel Wilde; and she longed with intense curiosity, to know something of the history of these passing actors in the great drama of life. Perhaps that ancient woman had been foster mother to the princely-looking warrior.

At Chelmsford, our travellers put up for the night. The window of the little back parlour of the Inn which for the time being, they were to consider their own, looked out into a spacious yard, which was fast filling with a party of Dragoons, who were leading out their horses from the stables that surrounded the court, preparatory to their departure for the seat of war. Seated upon the table by the window, which commanded a view of the Inn-yard; Rachel was soon deeply engaged in watching the movements of the soldiers with eager curiosity. She did not admire them so much as the Highlanders; but, to a child, there was something wonderfully imposing in the high fur caps, and scarlet coats, of the dragoons — and then their horses; from her cradle, Rachel had always admired those noble animals, and these were so sleek, so handsomely caparisoned, that they looked worthy to be the bearers of the brave fellows who bestrode them so gallantly.

Just opposite to the window where Rachel was perched, a tall, pale young man, mounted upon a splendid black charger, was stooping from his saddle, holding by the hand, the pretty waiting maid. His voice trembled, as he said, "Eliza you will forget me, when I am gone."

"Oh, never, never!" returned the fair girl, looking demurely down. "If you should be killed in the wars, it would break my heart, I know it would," and she hid her face in her apron and appeared to weep, for her frame shook and trembled; but we, the chroniclers of this event, much fear that the jade was only laughing.

The tear was in the young soldier's eye, as he pressed her hand devoutly to his lips and heart. — "Adieu dear, dear Eliza, if ever I live to return, I shall claim you as my wife."

"And we shall be so happy," murmured the chamber maid. The word to march was given by the officer in command. The lovers parted, and the Highland regiment filed into the spacious yard in an opposite direction.

"Is it possible!" cried Miss Long, who like Rachel, had witnessed the parting scene from the window. "Can that be Eliza, who is flirting away with the handsome Highland serjeant, with sparkling eyes, and cheeks glowing with blushes. The poor young Dragoon! She has verified the old saying: 'Out of sight, out of mind.' The street has scarcely ceased to echo the trampling of his horses hoofs, and he is already forgotten."

Rachel was too young to moralize upon these scenes then; but they formed themes for after reflection. Yet, it was at that window, and while witnessing the parting of that soldier and his betrothed, that she first learned the meaning of the word, *love*!

"Why did the poor soldier cry, Lucy, when he bade the girl good bye?" she asked of Miss Long.

"The young man is in love with her," was the reply, "and that occasions the grief he feels at parting with her."

"And does she love him Lucy?" said Rachel, not exactly satisfied with the flirtations of Eliza.

"I should hope so."

"Ah, no, she does not love him," said Rachel, thoughtfully, "or she would not be laughing with the Highlander yonder. How vexed the poor redcoat would be, if he could see her."

Miss Long glanced at the window, and shrugging her shoulders muttered, "yes a true woman."

"Do all women behave so to their lovers?" asked the innocent Rachel. Miss Long laughed, pushed her from her, and told her, "that little girls should not ask such questions." But though little girls are forbidden by their elders, to ask such questions; when once their curiosity is aroused, they will think upon the subject of their enquiry with more intensity from the very prohibition; and they generally contrive to puzzle it out of their own heads at last. This is human nature, and Rachel, at that period, was a child of nature, and listened to no other teacher.

The home to which our travellers were journeying, was the pretty village of S ——, in Kent, about six miles from the old town of Rochester. London lay in their route. They entered the metropolis after dark; and the long line of lamps, and the splendidly illuminated shops, reminded Rachel of the fairy tales told her by her nurse; and Miss Long laughed heartily when the little girl demanded of her, "if she were awake, for it looked just like a dream?"

"We shall stay here a week," said that lady, "with my uncle, and I will take you Rachel, to see the play, and many other fine sights."

Now, be it known unto our readers, that Miss Long's uncle, kept a tallow chandler's shop on Ludgate Hill; was a wealthy Alderman of the great city of London, kept his carriage and had a fine country house at Clapham, and looked upon himself as a very respectable and substantial personage, as in truth he was. But Rachel was the daughter of a poor gentleman, had been brought up with very aristocratic notions, and the sight of the shop, called all her pride into active operation. She drew stiffly back from the entrance, and with a curl of her lips, exclaimed: "I don't mean to stop here. Papa never visits with tradespeople."

"Nonsense child! none of these airs if you please," said her wiser friend, pushing her forward, and accompanying the action with a smart box on the ear. "My uncle is rich enough to buy your father's estate with one year's income."

"But he is not a gentleman," said Rachel, stoutly resisting.

"Phoo! you know nothing about it. If you do not behave yourself, I will whip you, and put you to bed without your supper."

Such conduct from Miss Long, appeared outrageous. She who had been all smiles and good humor at —— hall. Rachel could scarcely believe her own senses, as she doggedly remained in the half open door, without advancing a step. It was now thrown wide open, and the dazzling light which streamed forth from the colored wax-lights which adorned the spacious shop, almost blinded her, and a good natured old man took her by the hand. "Is this your young friend Lucy — a nice child — will you give me a kiss little one?"

"No," muttered Rachel, sullenly struggling in his embrace, "you keep a shop."

"Ha, ha, ha," burst from the old gentleman, like the explosion of a gun. "A sprightly lass this. — Yes my dear, I do keep a shop; and you and I, will have fine fun together in the shop yet," and snatching her up in his arms, he bore her in spite of her kicking and screaming, into a handsomely furnished apartment, where two fine young women, (his daughters,) were waiting tea for the travellers.

Now though Rachel felt very sulky and angry, she happened to be very hungry, and the sight of the hot toast and nice plum cake, which graced the table, went very far to reconcile her to the shop. Mr. Pearce took her upon his knee, and supplied her plentifully with these dainties; and Rachel began to feel half ashamed of her ungentle conduct; but, soon dropping to sleep, she forgot all about the insult which her dignity had received, until the morning.

Chapter III

The next day, Miss Long and her cousins went out shopping, and not wishing to be bothered with the company of a child; they left Rachel in charge with the housekeeper. The old woman was kind enough; but she was very ugly, and very deaf. Rachel could not bear to come near her. Instead of trying to amuse her, by telling her nice stories, the little girl had to bawl in her ears at the very top of her shrill treble, to make her comprehend her wants; and even then, her utmost exertions, often produced no effect; and the provoking old creature, only put up her withered hand to her ear, and with a most abominable squint, exclaimed, "Eh! Bless my soul! I'm so deaf, I can't hear." Rachel wondered, what use she could be in the house, and ran away from her into the parlor, to seek for amusement.

The book-case was locked — the pictures that loaded the walls, were beyond her reach; and there was neither cat nor dog to play with, or to help dissipate the intolerable weariness of having nothing to do. Rachel felt horribly dull, and had wished herself at home with her brothers and sisters for the hundredth time, when she perceived a door which she had not noticed on the preceding evening.

With a cry of delight, she sprang from the floor, and peeped into a long passage, at the end of which she discovered another door, which some one, had neglected to fasten. On the *que vive* for adventure, Rachel softly stole out of the room, determined to explore the unknown regions which lay beyond. Walked boldly down the passage, and reconnoitered the premises through the aperture. It was the shop. She drew back in disgust. "What a greasy smell." (They were boiling fat in some of the outhouses.) "The nasty shop!"

"Who's there?" asked a kind voice. Rachel slunk

behind the door, but not in time to escape observation. Mr. Pearce ran forward, and caught her by her hand.

"So, so, you have come to see me, after all?"

"No, no, let me go."

"I have caught you on Tom Tickler's ground, and you can't get away. Besides, I will give you such pretty wax flowers and a doll, half as big as yourself."

"Are you sure," said Rachel, beginning to feel interest getting the better of inclination.

"Yes, quite sure — come and see."

Rachel was soon perched on the large counter, admiring the fine ornaments for the gay wax candles, while the good old gentleman sent one of his people, to buy a large doll. Rachel was transported into a paradise. The shop suddenly lost all its terrors. The wax trees and flowers, appeared to her, as beautiful as the wondrous fruit trees in Aladdin's magic garden.

"Well, what do you think of the shop now?"

"I don't know."

"Oh yes you do — you think it a very nice place."

"It is better than the parlor, or shouting to old Sarah. But I am going to the play to night. Oh, that will be grand."

"Humph!" said the old gentleman — "not a very proper place for a child. But my niece is a goose."

Just at that moment, a handsome lad of sixteen, stepped up to the counter.

"Good morning Lewis," said Mr. Pearce, shaking the new comer cordially by the hand. "How is your mamma, your sisters, and your grand father?"

"All quite well. But what a dear little girl you have here. Is she, your grandchild?"

"No," returned Rachel, drawing herself up with a pretty air of disdain, and answering for herself — "I do not belong to the shop." This sally, was received with a burst of merriment; even the shopmen laughed at Rachel.

"And who *do* you belong to, my little dear?"

"My papa, is a gentleman. He has a fine house in the country, and such beautiful gardens."

"And what brought you to the shop?"

"To see the play," said Rachel; whispering to him confidentially, "Papa don't know of my being here, or he'd soon send for me back again."

"Will you come and see me?"

"Yes — if you don't keep a shop."

"I am too young for that. But I have two dear little sisters, who will be so glad to see you; and if you will come and play with them, I will call for you at six o'clock. I will shew you such beautiful pictures: and we will have a good game of romps together."

Forgetting all about the play, Rachel exclaimed in an extacy of delight, "I will go — I will go. But may I take the doll?"

"Yes Dolly shall go too. I will carry her."

Thus had Rachel made an appointment with some person of whom she knew nothing; but as Mr. Pearce seemed very willing to recognize the engagement, we will suppose, that the young gentleman was not unknown to him.

The rest of the day, passed heavily along. At four o'clock, the ladies returned to dinner, and Rachel was lifted upon the table, to give her opinion of lots of ribbons and artificial flowers, which had made a part of their purchases.

"This pretty sash, is for you Rachel," said Miss Long. "It will fasten your frock when you go to the play with us to-night." Rachel had forgotten the play.

"Rachel is going to drink tea, with Lewis and his sisters, to night," said Mr. Pearce.

"How fortunate!" exclaimed the three ladies, in a breath. "We shall not be bothered with her."

"I will go to the play," cried Rachel, bursting into tears. "I will not go with that strange boy."

"You must not break your word, Miss. It was your own doing. You shall go!" said the unkind Lucy. A sullen, "I won't," was all the answer given by the indignant Rachel, to this speech; and she cried and screamed until she was hoarse; but all she got by her violence, was a sound whipping and a corner of the dark passage, until her unknown friend called for her. His entreaties to get her to stir one inch from her position, were all in vain. The spirit of resistance had been aroused in the little creature, and she absolutely determined to remain where her friends had placed her. Lewis gave her a large paper of sweeties. She flung them upon the ground. He took her in his arms and kissed her. Oh, horrible ingratitude — she returned his caresses with a *bite*.

"I have it now," he cried; "the doll shall go with me, instead of you." He seized the doll, which had never quitted Rachel's grasp, since the morning, and hurried off with her. With one bound, Rachel overtook, and caught him by the leg.

"Give me my doll!"

"She was invited to tea with you. She is a good girl. She shall go."

"Put on my bonnet, and I will go too."

"I don't know that I will take you. I don't like naughty girls that will bite." But as he said this, the good-natured fellow tied on her bonnet, which one of the ladies supplied, and in a few minutes, Rachel was alone with her young protector, in the wide street. But turning to Rachel's manuscript, which is now before us; we will cease to play the editor, and give her recollections of this lad, in her own words.

"Friendly reminiscences of that handsome boy, have haunted me all my life. He must have been the most good-natured of good fellows, to put up with all my wayward caprices, my petty tyrannies. His name Lewis, is all I know of him. — Who, or what he was, I never learned; and the adventures of that evening spent in his charming family, is still hoarded amongst the most pleasing recollections of my early years.

"I still smile at the mysterious awe, which crept over me at finding myself, young as I was, alone with him, in the vast crowded streets of London. The rattling of the carriages frightened me, and he carried me in his arms. He stopped at length, in a less busy street, before a large store house; we ascended several steps and were admitted by a servant in livery, into a large hall, and my young friend led me up stairs into a handsome drawing room, in which I found a mild-looking, middle-aged lady, in a widow's dress; two fair young girls, of nine and ten — in dress mourning, and a dear venerable white haired old man in a uniform coat, which in after years, I knew to be the dress of a Naval officer.

"The old gentleman received me with a smile, and lifted me onto his knee. He had lost a leg, and he was greatly amused by all my questions respecting his wooden one.

"'Could it feel? Did it go to sleep when he went to sleep — and how did he come by such a queer thing?'

"Then he gave me an account of the battle in which he lost his real leg, and shewed me a large picture which hung against the wall, of the death of Nelson, and the battle of Trafalgar. Vague ideas of death and destruction flashed into my mind; and I thought what a horrible thing it must be, to go to battle and lose our legs.

"With what patience that dear old man, turned over vast volumes of his library, to shew me the prints; and after ten, Lewis frightened me out of my wits, by playing off an electrical machine, and conjuring up phantoms with his magic lantern. I no longer regretted the play, while amusing myself at blindman's buff, and puss in the corner, with Lewis and his pretty sisters Lucretia and Maria, who loaded me with pieces of silk and velvet for my doll; and gave me all sorts of treasures, beads, flowers and toys. It was twelve o'clock when Lewis carried me home. I kissed him at parting and told him to come and see me again. The next day, we pursued our journey into Kent, and I never saw my young friend, or heard of him again."

Chapter IV

"It was the noon of a November day, when the coach set us down at the head of the romantic lane, which led to Mr. Long's estate. The air was raw, and a dense fog hung on the leafless bushes. I was chilled with the cold and cried bitterly.

"Miss Long's father, an old man of eighty, received us at the door of a pretty white house. He had not an agreeable physiognomy. His features were thick, and expressed violent passions. His head was quite bald, and his face very red. I did not like him at all, and I shrunk behind his daughter.

"He led the way into the sitting room, and I was presented to two of the fattest women, I ever beheld. They were really mountains of flesh. These ladies were the daughters by a former marriage, and either of them, old enough to be Long's mother. Miss Betsy, the elder, was considerably turned of fifty, and like her father, possessed a repulsive countenance. She had the same thick features. — The same red face; but was shockingly marked by the small pox. The second daughter, Miss Sally, had fine dark eyes, and a very handsome face; but the enormous proportions of her full blown figure, spoilt all. Among flowers, she would have been a piony. 'So Lucy,' said the elder, 'we are to be pestered with this child, for the next twelve months. That is what we get by your long visits from home.'

"'She will be no trouble,' said the old man, patting my head; 'she will help to amuse me.' From that hour I nestled up to the old man; and Miss Betsy was my horror.

"I have visited many a lovely spot that has faded from my memory; but time can never efface from my recollection the localities of that place.

"Thirty-eight years have passed over me since I was there; yet, I could find my way back to that spot.

"The green lawn in front of the house — the large pond overhung with willows — the orchard that opened out of the vegetable garden, with its green banks and tufts of violets and primroses — all came as vividly back to my mind, as if it were but yesterday that I sat among the primroses, and played with the young lambs. But what have I to do with flowery banks just now. It was winter, chilly winter, when I arrived; and I felt myself very lonely among grown up persons, with no child to play with. Youth is fertile in invention. I soon made companions and playmates, from the living creatures around me.

"Mr. Long kept a pack of fox-hounds, which were a partnership concern between him and a rich old fox-hunting squire, whose fine hall, with its tall chimnies and ancient gables, rose towering from among the giant oaks and elms which surrounded it. The dogs were kept in a paved court behind the house, with kennels on three sides, for their accommodation, and a cistern of clear water in the centre, overshadowed by a tall ash tree. That cistern, the old tree, and those dogs, were my delight. Many a whipping I got for soiling my white frocks and trowsers, by dabbling with sticks in the water, and rolling over and over upon the pavement with the dear dogs — Rover, Ringwood, Lightfoot: how I loved them all: and one, a beautiful spotted dog, called Clio, with a whole litter of mischievous pups, that bit my fingers and gnawed the hem of my frock into tatters.

"No state of existence is free from trouble; even this sacred spot contained an adversary to my peace, in the shape of a large turkey-cock, which sometimes invaded the dog-yard, and strutted and fretted his brief day of power among its tenants — biting some, and flapping others with his strong wings. The turkey-cock was decidedly very unpopular among the dogs; and, as for poor me, I fled like a coward at the mere sound of his hoarse voice; and, for days after, never dared to poke my nose into the dog-yard, without first being certain that Mr. Gobbler was gone. The turkey-cock greatly resembled some purse-proud ostentatious fool, thrusting himself, uninvited, among persons vastly his superiors, and thinking by his noise and fluster, to impress them with an idea of his own importance.

"Besides my friends, the hounds, I had established a most intimate acquaintance with a large tame raven, who hopped about the garden, and went by the familiar name of Jack. I never failed to save half of my cakes and bread and butter for Jack. Every warm sun-shining day, I found him standing at the root of the old willow, nodding and winking in the sun. To fling myself beside him, to kiss his shiny black head, and pat his glossy back, and to feel him knabbling my fingers in return was my delight. Then I ran races up and down the neat box-edged walks.

"How freshly they smelt in the first days of spring, and laughed to see Jack hopping quickly at my heels, calling aloud his own name, to increase the sport—Jack, Jack. I verily believe that he used to laugh too. Then, there was Gipsy and Rose, the two large shepherd dogs, who were not the least beloved among my pets; — the great tortoise-shell cat and her two kittens, who lived in the barn, and helped to amuse me on a rainy day; — to say nothing of the pigeons, who inhabited a large dove-cot near, and whom I went with the maid, Anne, every morning to feed.

"When I was away from the parlor and cross Miss Betsy, I was as happy as a queen with all my subjects round me.

"Unfortunately for me, Miss Lucy Long was a great favorite in the neighborhood, and was seldom at home, and I was left almost entirely to the tender mercies of Miss Betsy, who privately kept a rod behind her father's bureau for my especial benefit.

"How I longed to shew the old gentleman this instrument of torture; but, she threatened me, that if I did, she would flay me alive. Silly child that I was, to believe this threat. But so it was. I thought it would be a dreadful thing to lose my skin; and I felt sure that the cruel old maid would not scruple to keep her word. Mr. Long, on the other hand, spoilt and humored me to my heart's content; but he was a violently passionate man, and used to storm at his daughters and servants in a way which made my flesh creep."

Chapter V

One bright sunny day in the beginning of March, Miss Betsy dispatched Nancy the parish apprenticed girl, to the village of S——, to buy some treacle for the farming men employed upon the estate, to eat with their apple dumplings; and as Rachel had been a good girl, and said her lessons without blundering, she was to accompany her. Rachel was delighted, for no one loved praise, or enjoyed recreation, more than did the little girl; and she anticipated a pleasant stroll by the banks of S —— wood; and lots of violets and primroses, treasures incalculable to the young heart overflowing with the love of nature. Besides — had not Miss Betsy bestowed upon her a penny — wonder of wonders — for she was the most parsimonious of human beings. A penny to Miss Betsy, was of more value than a crown to others; and she had really opened her heart, and her purse strings, at the same time, and given the child a penny, charging her to lay it out discreetly in a book or toy, and not to buy sweeties with it, for when once eaten, it was gone for ever.

As Rachel kissed and thanked Miss Betsy, for her munificence, she wondered what had made her so good natured all of a sudden. Perhaps, the donor could not have solved her doubts. It was one of fortune's caprices, and it made Rachel the happiest of children, as she trotted off, dressed out in her gay pelisse, and holding Nancy by the hand.

The village was about a mile distant, and the path lay by the side of a noble wood, where giant oaks and elms cast fantastic shadows upon the grassy road. The mavis and black bird, those loving heralds of spring, carrolled their sweet loud notes, high up among the budding branches; and the lark whistled his clear lay at the edge of the white fleecy clouds, as they sailed along in the deep blue ocean of heaven. Rachel clapped her hands, and laughed and sung, in the sheer joy of her heart. The birds were her birds, the trees were her trees, and the flowers were her flowers. She was a queen in the green dominions of nature; and her mind reigned without a rival over the fair and beautiful.

Ah, blessed, thrice blessed season of youth and innocence — when earth is still the paradise of God, and its crimes and sorrows are veiled from the eyes of the undefiled by the bright angel of His presence. They see not the flaming sword, they hear not the doom of the exile; but wander hand in hand with pitying spirits through that region of bliss.

Who would not gladly be a child again, to sit among the grass and weave daisy chains, to build grottos with twigs, and decorate them with snail shells; to hear mysterious music in the breeze as it wanders amid the tops of the lofty pine trees, or impels forward the small wavelets of the brook — to have no knowledge of sin — no fear of death — no agonizing doubts as to the future. Well has the bard of nature exclaimed, when these holy recollections of his infant years thronged fast around him:

"Heaven lies about us in our infancy" —

And Rachel while filling her little basket with primroses, was richer than the miser doating over his useless hoards.

At length the village was gained; and Nancy led the way to the only shop it contained. Well did it deserve the name of *general* — for it was the depot of every article in common use which could be enumerated. It was a bakery, a grocery, and a hardware establishment — while the owner luxuriated in the titles of silk, mercer, linen draper, and hosier, and yet, it was but a sorry affair after all. His silks occupied a very small portion of a very small shelf. His linen, was tied up in one old cove; and his hosiery consisted in a few pairs of white and colored stockings, dangling in the windows, between jars of gingerbread, nuts, and peppermint drops.

Then, he had books for the old and young. Histories of Goody two shoes, and Cinderella, bound in gilt for one penny, and Tom Thumb, and Jack the Giant killer, for two pence. This department of the shop, was decidedly the one that Rachel meant to patronize; and when she first entered it, she thought her single penny, made her a person of such consequence that, with it, she might command the best things it contained. Older heads than Rachel's, have been as easily deceived.

Mr. Blake, the master of the establishment, was a little, tidy, dapper old batchelor. Fond of money, but fonder still of that, which money could not buy — little children. He took Rachel up in his arms, begged a kiss, which she would not give without a struggle, and seated her on his counter. He asked who she was? and she frankly gave her whole history — and he gave her a gingerbread husband in return —

for which the little girl offered to pay him in primroses, for she wanted to lay out her penny, in the history of her of the glass slipper. He good-naturedly accepted the primroses, and picked her out the gayest copy of the much abused fair one, he could find; and Rachel, the happy Rachel, departed pleased with Mr. Blake, pleased with her pretty book, and doubly pleased with herself — for she justly argued, "He must have thought me a nice little girl, or he never would have given me the ginger bread husband."

They had walked nearly half a mile on their homeward path, before Rachel noticed the four pounds of treacle that Nancy was carrying, in a red pipkin. "What nasty black looking stuff" said she. "Do the men eat that with their dumplings?"

"Ah, 'tis very good Miss Rachel," said the artful girl, dipping her fingers into the pan, and drawing them through her mouth, with great relish. "Come here, and taste it for yourself."

"No that would be stealing," said Rachel, drawing back. "What would Miss Betsy say?"

"Nonsense, she could not see you, and I would not tell of you."

"But God would," said the child, who had been brought up in the wholesome fear of his laws. — "If you did not tell of me, if she asked me, I could not tell a lie," and jumping into the green bank, where she had just discovered a delicious nest of white, fragrant violets, Rachel forgot the treacle and the temptation.

While busy in securing her treasures, a friendly voice called her by name; and on looking up, she beheld Squire C ——, surrounded by the hounds, for he was out hunting.

"You are a good child," he said, "not to do what that naughty girl bade you. I feel proud of you."

Rachel dearly loved Squire C ——, and she had reason, for he was an excellent man, and a kind friend to the little girl. He was lord of the manor, and lived in a noble old hall which stood in a stately park, beyond the village which they had just left; and he was beloved and respected by the whole parish. He had taken a fancy to Rachel, and he came over to Mr. Long's almost every day to see her; and was anxious to adopt her for his own child; but Mr. Wilde, would not part with his eccentric little girl, to her rich friend.

His visits were not merely for amusement. He taught Rachel to read, heard her the catechism, and to him, she generally said her prayers, kneeling reverently upon his knees, while he held her clasped hands in his. He was to Rachel in the place of the father she had left; and she knew his military step, for he had been a colonel in the army, and she ran to meet him, when he approached the house, and she knew the pocket, in which he always had stores of sweeties for his dear little girl, when she had said her task. And she loved to ride before him on his white mare Susan, back to the old hall; and to ramble about the beautiful gardens with his good old house-keeper. And there was a beautiful little brown pony, he called her's, and a troop of splendid peacocks, and a monkey chained up in the hall, that played all sorts of droll tricks, and when Rachel was naughty, the colonel threatened to chain her up with the monkey, and she had a wholesome fear of master pug and his chain, to the great amusement of her friends.

Now Rachel scarcely knew why Squire C ——, called her a good girl that morning; and when he rode off, she went on picking the violets, while Nancy went on eating — and the treacle was diminished in the pipkin to such a degree, that Miss Betsy very angrily demanded, who had stolen it?

"Oh," said this truly wicked girl. "It was Miss Wilde. I told her not, ma'arm, but she would do it, in spite of me."

Imagine the astonishment of poor Rachel, thus falsely, and cruelly accused. Her face flushed to scarlet, as with tears in her eyes, she denied the infamous charge.

"I see it is *you*, Miss. I know it by your tell-tale face. You cannot deceive me," cried the angry Miss Long, seizing her by the arm, and dragging her into a dark room. "It is my duty to punish you for theft, lying, and bearing false witness."

All expostulations and explanations upon Rachel's

part, were vain; and then came the horrid rod, and the debasing punishment, and Rachel would not cry; she bore her chastisement with Spartan firmness, for her heart felt bursting with the sense of intolerable wrong, and her indignation was called wicked obstinacy, and her punishment was doubly severe; and this was on false evidence — which has sent to the gallows and the hulks, its countless victims.

Rachel lay upon the floor of the dark drawing-room, from noon-day until night. She neither moved nor cried. She only felt that she had been deeply injured, and every other feeling was hushed under the mighty pressure of undeserved punishment.

And how felt her miserable accuser, Rachel never knew, and never asked; but, we can believe from the character of the girl, that it gave her no concern. She was a domestic slave, and the hard treatment she had received from others, had made her callous to praise or blame. If she was an artful, dishonest creature, she had been rendered so by circumstances over which she had no control.

Her birth was one of infamy; and her education in a country work-house, forty years ago, had been for evil, not good. The hand of every one was against her; mankind seemed her general enemy — for she had received naught from her fellow-creatures but ill-usage, and mental debasement. Such neglected beings are more objects of deep compassion, than of thoughtless blame: — while contemplating their unmitigated wretchedness, we strive in vain to solve the great riddle of life.

Some, from the first dawn of existence, appear the sport of an untoward destiny — vessels of dishonor fitted for destruction; while others occupy the high places of the earth, and revel in its luxuries to satiety. Alas! for the sinful pride of man, for to it, and it alone, must we trace this fearful incongruity. Pride must have broken the ancient bond of unity, which, at some remote period of the world's history, existed between its children. Yet, God, in his infinite mercy, has provided a link which shall yet bind into one, the dissevered chain, and through the mediation of his blessed son, unite into one loving family, the severed kindreds of the earth; and the holy precepts that Jesus taught, practically borne out, shall produce the great moral reformation, that shall banish poverty and misery from among us: —

> "That man to man, the world o'er,
> Shall brothers be for a' that."

But, to return to Nancy. She was the worst fed, the worst clothed, and the worst lodged, of any person in the establishment. All the coarse dirty work, fell to her share. She fed the dogs, cleaned the kennels, carried water and fuel, scoured the knives and pots, blacked the shoes, and ran all the errands. These were but a few out of the many jobs that fell to her daily lot. She was under-drudge to the cook, who beat and kicked her in a cruel manner, if she disobeyed her orders. She was fag to the house-maid, who regarded her with as much contempt, as she did the dust she swept from beneath her feet.

Poor Nancy, unhappy child of guilt and misery, her whole existence was a life-long agony. She never got a kind word from any one; and was the general butt at which the farm servants threw all their coarse jokes. To live at peace with the other members of the family, she had to fawn and flatter, and sneak, to act the spy for one, and to conceal, with unblushing falsehoods, the misdemeanors of another. Her life was made up of a tissue of lies and subterfuges; and can we wonder, that to secure herself from blame, she falsely accused an innocent child.

Rachel scarcely knew how the day went away; time seemed to have come to a stand still with her. One thought alone possessed her mind — the deep sense of undeserved injury. At length the door of her prison was unlocked, and Miss Lucy Long lifted her from the ground.

"Rachel, are you asleep?" No answer. — "Dear Rachel, that wicked girl told a cruel story about you. Colonel C —— is here: he has told us all about it."

Rachel was alive in a moment. Her heart bounded — the tear was arrested on her eye-lash, as she exclaimed, clasping her little hands fervently together — "I never did it — God knows! I never did it! Miss Betsy had no right to beat me. I hate her: I will never speak to her again!"

"My dear child, she was deceived: she was right to punish you while she thought you guilty," said Colonel C ——, now entering. "You must forgive her for my sake, whom God sent to prove your innocence. You owe Him a great debt of gratitude, Rachel, for it is not always that the innocent are cleared from the false accusations of the guilty. Come with me to Miss Betsy, she is very sorry for you, and is anxious to be friends."

Rachel went, but I fear with a very ill grace, for her back still smarted from the strokes of the rod; and the sight of Miss Betsy seemed to renew the pain. The reconciliation took place, and in a few moments Rachel was nestled in the bosom of the good Colonel, and wearied with over excitement, soon fell asleep in his arms.

Miss Betsy was very kind for some days, and Rachel had almost forgotten the wrong, when an untoward accident again called forth all her vindictive feelings, and involved her in an adventure which might have terminated in a very serious manner.

The parlor window frames had been recently painted, and Rachel, who had nothing to do, was standing in a chair, looking out of the window, with a small pair of pointed scissors in her hand, and she began drawing with the points, houses and dogs and cats, upon the fresh paint, disfiguring it sadly. Still the child was not aware that she was doing wrong. Mr. Long had laughed heartily at some of her rude attempts in white chalk, traced all over the barn walls, as high as she could reach; and Rachel thought that he would be as well pleased with her designs drawn upon the window sill.

Just as she had finished a house, greatly to her own satisfaction, Miss Long entered, and without explaining to the child the unintentional mischief she had done, she seized the rod from its hiding place, behind the bureau, and throwing Rachel rudely upon the floor, gave her a severe whipping, accompanied with very violent language. She had scarcely taken summary vengeance on the child, before a Mr. Albany drove up in his tandem to the door, and she had to leave her indignant victim to receive the visitor.

With a heart bursting with rage, Rachel sprang from the floor, and glancing rapidly round the room, to see that no one was near, her resolution was taken in a moment, and while Miss Betsy was ushering her guest to the drawing-room, she darted, unobserved, through the open door, crossed the garden, and the road in front, and paused for one second beside the stile that led to a path which crossed a large field opposite.

"Which road should she take?" The field was the least likely to awaken suspicion, — would be the least likely to be explored: she mounted the stile, and in a few moments was out of sight.

And what did this mad child in her delirium of anger, mean to do? Reader, to run away. You know not what great thoughts were swelling that proud little heart. In fancy she had already traversed the hundred and forty-eight long miles, that lay between her and home. It seemed but a step in that moment of deep excitement. She would be ill-treated by Miss Betsy no longer: she would return home.

The day was cold and bright, as days in March often are. She had no hat upon her head: her neck and arms were bare: her white frock and trowsers, and red morocco shoes, a poor protection against the keen wind that rustled the dry stubble of the wide field before her. Rachel did not care, and she ran on as fast as she could. The path she was pursuing led to Gravesend, over the fields — the latter place being four miles distant. — She passed over S —— common, with all its rugged dingles and pools of water, and fearing lest she should be found, if she kept the path, she turned off to the left, and wandered on until she gained a steep bank some miles distant from the home she had quitted.

Her trowsers were torn with the brambles; she had lost one of her shoes in a mud-hole, and she was foot-sore, hungry, and weary. Fortunately for our young runaway, there was a gap in the hedge, which crowned the steep bank, and after many unsuccessful efforts, she succeeded in scrambling to the top. On the other side, a bare, brown, newly-harrowed field, stretched far before her, on which the shadows of several forest trees extended their giant proportions in the setting sun.

Rachel cautiously descended the bank on the other side, but uttered a cry of fear and astonishment, as a girl about fourteen years of age, dressed in a quilted green stuff petticoat, and a man's jacket, approached to offer her assistance in affecting the descent.

Now the girl knew Rachel, although Rachel to her knowledge, had never seen the girl; and she marvelled greatly what had brought Miss Wilde there.

Speaking kindly to the child, soon drew from her the tale of wrongs: — how she had been cruelly beaten, and was on her way home, — that she was very tired, and very hungry, — that she did not know where to sleep that night, for she had not passed a single house since she set out in the morning.

The kind girl pitied the poor young stranger, and taking off the man's jacket, wrapped it, like a good Samaritan, about the little creature's shivering form. Then seating her by a fire she had in the bank, for she was employed in keeping the crows off the newly sown barley, she drew the remains of a very brown loaf from a small weather-beaten, brown basket.

"Here is bread for you, but it is very coarse."

Rachel had never seen such bread in her life, but plum cake would have been less delicious than that coarse fare. She was so hungry that she literally devoured it, and the good-natured girl laughed to see her eating it so fast. Putting an old sack over her own shoulders, she took Rachel into her lap, and held her feet near the embers of the fire.

"Poor little soul," she said "you are very cold: stay here a few minutes, while I go and look for your shoe."

"No, no, you cannot find it; it is a great way off; and it would be all wet and spoilt with the mud," said Rachel, clinging to her new friend. "May I live with you, and help you to keep the crows away?"

"Yes, and I will take you home to sleep with me

to-night; but my bed is very hard."

"And you won't beat me with a rod?"

"Oh, no: you shall do just as you please."

Rachel was happy, and she nestled closer to her new friend, when the sudden appearance of a man and two dogs, in the gateway on the other side of the field, filled her with fearful apprehensions.

"Do you see those dogs?"

"Yes. What of them?"

"They know me," said Rachel. "They are Mr. Long's shepherd's dogs; and that man is the shepherd. Oh, cover me up with the sack, and hide me in the hedge, or those dogs will find me out."

The girl did as she was bid, at the same time she beckoned the shepherd, unknown to Rachel, to advance.

Poor Rachel, how her little heart beat, as she lay cowering under the sack. Her old friends, Gipsy and Rose, ran hither and thither: at last they came upon her hiding place, and gave a joyous bark.

"What have the dogs got here?" said the shepherd, winking to the girl, who was no other than his daughter, and the next moment he lifted Rachel, pale as death, and trembling with fear, from the ground.

"So, my little lady, I have found you at last?"

"I won't go home," said Rachel, clinging to the bushes. "I will die first!"

"Then I must leave you to the gipsies in the lane. They know how to make little girls behave themselves."

Rachel was dreadfully afraid of the gipsies. — "Well," she said, "I will go with you, if you will promise me that I will not be beaten when I get home, and that you will carry me every step of the way, for I am too tired to walk."

To this the good shepherd readily agreed, and seating Miss Rachel on his shoulder, he walked off with her at a round pace. — Informing her that his old master had been nigh distracted for her loss, — that he had been all over the country in search of her, — that the Colonel had spoken very angrily to Miss Betsy, and burnt the rod, and sent his servants in all directions to find the runaway. Rachel had wandered more than four miles from home; and it was dark when the shepherd deposited her safely by the fire-side in the parlor.

Chapter VI

Rachel expected a severe reprimand for her late conduct, and a whipping as a matter of *course*. She was agreeably disappointed. Her kind friend, Colonel C ——, had burnt the rod, and Mr. Long was so fearful of her running away again, that not a word was said to her on the subject that night. In the morning, the old gentleman called her to him, and taking her up on his knee, said to her:

"Was it to keep crows with Annie Herd, that you ran away yesterday, Rachel, and made us suffer so much uneasiness on your account?"

"No," whispered Rachel, who surely thought that the anticipated punishment was at hand. "I ran away because I was beat with the rod."

"Do not you think that you deserve some punishment for your bad conduct?" Rachel hung her head. She thought Miss Long deserved to be whipped for her conduct to *her*, but she said nothing. "Rachel, I should not be your friend, if I did not punish you," said the old gentleman. "You chose to keep crows yesterday with my shepherd's daughter, to please yourself, and to day I mean you to keep sheep with another daughter of his, on S —— Common, to please me. Now get your breakfast and eat heartily for you will be away all day." Rachel did not understand the nature of her sentence, but she supposed, that it must be very dreadful; and she could not eat her bread and milk with any appetite for thinking about it.

After breakfast Miss Lucy put on the little girl's pelisse and hat, and the man servant led Mr. Long's favorite brown pony, Punch, to the front door. Mr. Long mounted, and ordered the man, to put Rachel before him on the horse; and off they jogged at a round trot down the lane. The sun was shining brightly, and the birds were singing in the budding hedge-rows; and the smell of the golden furze bushes, then in full blossom, was delicious. The air was sharp and keen, but the country looked so beautiful, and Rachel enjoyed her ride so much, that to have seen the little girl, smiling and gazing around her with animated delight, no one could have imagined that she was a culprit, going forward to receive punishment for a very serious offence.

The lane terminated on the Common, which, gay with furze bushes, and knots of daisies and primroses, was speckled over with sheep and their young lambs. The lambs were gamboling hither and thither, and cutting a thousand graceful antics on the green sward. A girl about two years older than Rachel's friend of the proceeding day, was the presiding genius of the scene. She was seated upon a sunny knoll, sheltered from the wind by a low range of bushes, the two dogs, Gipsey and Rose, crouching at her feet, while their young mistress was employed in knitting.

"Susan," said Mr. Long, riding briskly up, "I shall leave Miss Wilde with you to-day. She was very naughty yesterday, and ran away from me to help your sister Annie keep crows. Pray make her help you keep the sheep, and see that she is not idle; for idleness you know is the root of all evil."

Susan came forward and lifted Rachel from the pony. She seemed surprised that the little girl made no resistance, but looked up to her with a smiling countenance; and Susan promising Mr. Long that she would take great care of her, the old gentleman rode off, saying "that he would come to the cottage for her in the evening."

"Oh, how happy we shall be, playing with the dear lambs and gathering flowers," cried Rachel, clapping her hands and frisking about as blythely as any lamb in the flock. "I wish they would send me here every day." Susan laughed at her companion's vivacity, and found her a nice seat among the primroses, and in ten minutes they were the best friends in the world. Susan taught her how to make chains of daisies and dandelions, and to weave the primroses and butter cups with the long slender branches of the green broom, to make garlands for the lambs. Then they ran races up and down the verdant slopes of the common, trying their speed to the utmost, and laughing and shouting in their uncontrollable glee. The dogs entered fully into their sport, and ran round them in circles, leaping and barking with all their might.

Rachel's cup ran over with the nectar of happiness. Free, and surrounded by beautiful objects she revelled in the mere consciousness of existence: and her heart expanded and grew light as the air she breathed.

"Why do people remain half the day cooped up in dark, dull houses," she cried. "Is it not better to be here with the lambs. To hear the birds sing, and to see the sun shine?" "But birds do not always sing, and the sun does not always shine," said the girl. "There be dark, rainy, foggy days, when 'tis not so pleasant to remain on an open exposed place like this. How would you like to be drenched with the rain, and chilled with the cold, as I often am. No, no, the gentlemen in their fine houses, know little about the sufferings of the poor. It is not *all* play like this."

Rachel felt the shadow of the rainy day descend upon her soul. "Why are some people poor and others rich?"

"I don't know," said the girl; "'tis God's will, and it must be right; but it seems hard to us who are poor. Maybe we shall be rich in the next world."

"I hope so," said Rachel. "If we are good, Mr. C —— says, we shall be happy there."

"I often wish myself one of the lambs," said the girl; "they do seem to enjoy their life so much, and they have not the dread of the butcher, though he will surely one day come for them, and in a day when they least expect it, when the sun is bright, and the air is warm, and the grass is fresh and green, and they are full of frolic and play, as they are at this moment. But God provides them with a good warm coat, and they never know what it is to be hungry like us, or to see their fleece worn out, without knowing where to get money to buy a new one. Oh, it would be so nice, to sport about in the fields all day, without work and without care, like the lambs."

"And never to be beaten with a rod, and called harsh

names," said Rachel, whose thoughts kept turning continually upon that hateful flagelation. "Yes, I should like to be a little lamb." And thus the two friends conversed together, until noon reminded them that it was dinner time. Susan produced her little basket of coarse bread and cheese which was duly shared with Rachel, and the two dogs, who gratefully licked the hands of their benefactors. Exercise, and the free, fresh, bracing air, had given our little one, a sharp appetite; and the dinner that had been provided for *one*, seemed very scanty for *four*.

"Never mind Miss Rachel, you shall have a good supper at night, of warm bread and milk, and my dear old granny shall tell you a pretty story; she knows hundreds of them."

"I love stories," said Rachel. "I wish it were night."

"Are you tired of the lambs already?"

"No but I want to hear your granny's stories."

"But you will tire of granny and her stories and want to go home?"

"Not while you are kind to me. We will keep the sheep to-morrow and make garlands of flowers, and be as happy as we have been to day."

A long day of play is very tiresome, even though spent among the flowers. The mind that lacks occupation must have change, or pleasure becomes satiety, and that which produced excitement whilst new to it, ends in weariness. Rachel grew tired with excess of freedom. The flowers she had gathered withered at her feet, and the day before so sunny and bright, grew dull and cloudy. The wind whistled shrilly through the furze bushes, and Susan, experienced in the changes of the weather, said there would be rain before morning.

The sun at length descended in the west, although hidden in a thick mist. The dogs scoured the common, and gathered the sheep together into the fold; and after Susan had shut them in for the night, she took Rachel by the hand, and raising her voice into a glad song, they turned their steps homeward. They left the broad common, and entered a narrow sandy lane, girt on either side by furze hedges. Among a shower of golden blossoms, Susan shewed Rachel a robin's nest with five speckled eggs in it.

"Oh, give me one of those beautiful eggs."

"It is unlucky," said Susan, shaking her head.

> "The robin and the titty wren,
> Are God Almighty's cock and hen."

"God would be angry with me, if I robbed the nest of his favourite bird; I have heard," and the girl bent down lower to her companion, and her countenance grew dark, and mysterious, — "I have heard granny say, that when the wicked Jews raised the cross on which our blessed Lord was crucified, that a little robin lighted upon the top of it, and sang so sweetly, that his murderers stopped to listen to it, and Christ blessed the bird, and his breast became blood-red from that day. I don't know whether it be true; but this I do know, that if you bereave a robin of her young, no good ever happens to you again. You are sure to break a limb, or meet with some dreadful accident. We are told in the bible, that God takes care of sparrows, who are but a bold, thievish crew; then how much more likely it is for him, to protect his own pretty robin."

"I always loved the robin," said Rachel, "but I will love it still more now."

At the end of the lane, they crossed a little brook by a rude plank thrown across it; over this rustic bridge, a tall willow threw its long pendant branches. Having crossed the bridge, they entered a neat little garden, surrounded by a hedge of sweet-briar whose thick buds, half expanded into leaf, threw out a most grateful odour. The shepherd who had just returned from folding the rest of Mr. Long's numerous flock of sheep, was standing in the doorway of a snug mud cottage, whose white-washed walls, and green moss grown thatch, gave it a peculiarly rural appearance.

"Susan, thee be'est just in time for supper," he cried. "Bring in the little lady, she looks cold and hungry."

Rachel was soon divested of her gay pelisse, and perched upon the knee of granny Herd, by the side of a cheerful fire on the hearth. A low oak table was covered with a coarse cloth, on which was placed several wooden bowls and platters — some very brown bread, part of a skim-milk cheese, a plate of onions, and a saucer with salt. A red pipkin of milk, was simmering upon the hearth stone, and two sturdy boys, were sitting upon a rude bench watching its progress with evident satisfaction. Granny Herd cut some of the brown bread into each of the wooden bowls, and the milk was poured over it, and duly distributed. Rachel was so hungry, that she thought it excellent, and made amends for her scanty dinner by eating heartily of the plain fare before her. After the things had been removed, and her friend of the day before, had washed them away, Rachel nestled up to the old woman, and begged her to tell her a story.

"A dozen if you like," said the old dame. "What shall it be. About fairies, or hobgobblins, or ghosts."

"I don't care which," said the little girl. "I have heard of fairies; they are pretty little men and women, who live in the flowers, and dance by moonlight in the green rings in the meadows. I should like to see a fairy very much, but I am afraid that they would never let me catch them."

"Bless me! the child talks of fairies as if they were butterflies and beetles," said the old woman.

"But ghosts, and those things you were talking about with the hard name," said Rachel, "I never heard of them before."

"Never heard of ghosts?" screamed the old dame.

"Hush, mother! don't go to frighten the child, with your ugly tales," said the shepherd.

Rachel's curiosity was excited; she sat bolt upright upon the old woman's knees, and her eyes grew round as she gazed intently in her face.

"Tell me, what are ghosts?"

"Nothing, my child, nothing, only the spirits of dead folk who cannot rest in their graves; persons who have been murdered, or have murdered others, who walk the earth of a night and frighten people in lonesome places. I have seen a ghost myself."

"Oh do tell me all about it," said Rachel, while she

felt her blood trickling back in a cold stream to her heart; and her teeth chattered, and her rosy cheek grew white as ashes.

"Hold your tongue Mother," cried the good shepherd, "don't you see how you are scaring the child?" But the old woman was in for the story, and in spite of her son's admonitions, she was determined to have her talk out.

"When I was a young gall," she commenced, "and was in service at S —— Hall, with Squire C —— 's mother." Here a shout from the bridge, made the narrator start and look up. "By jolly!" cried the shepherd springing from his seat, "that is the master's voice. Come little miss, be quick, and put on your coat; the night is dark, and he will not like to wait in the cold."

"Oh, but the story. I want to hear the story."

"You must wait until some other time," whispered Susan, kneeling on the ground and slipping the little girl's pelisse over her head, "Hark? Mr. Long is calling again. If you keep sheep with me to-morrow, I will tell you the story, for I know it by heart." This promise pacified Rachel, and in a few minutes she was in the saddle before Mr. Long, who bidding the shepherd good night, set off home at a round pace.

"Why do you cry Rachel?"

"I don't want to leave the cottage. I should like to live there always. Do let me keep sheep to-morrow with Susan."

"Are you happier there than with us?"

"Oh, yes, a thousand times happier."

Mr. Long felt hurt at the enthusiasm with which his little visitor proclaimed her sentiments. He forgot that she was only a child. That the day spent with nature, free from the artificial restraints that wealth imposes upon its children, was more highly prized by the unsophisticated Rachel, than all the luxuries of his comfortable home. He considered Rachel an ungrateful little baggage to prefer the shepherd's cottage to his own handsome house; but the young creature he thoughtlessly blamed, was true to herself — to the best feelings of humanity. She lived in a world of poetic liberty — a world of her own — a world peopled by bright thoughts and natural objects, and unacquainted with the philosophy of human institutions, she was still in blissful ignorance of the hard names that human pride had invented to separate into two distinct species, the rich and the poor. To Rachel, the shepherd and his family were as worthy of love and respect, as the wealthy Mr. Long. They had been as kind to her, and she knew no difference. The first worst lesson of humanity, was taught her from that hour.

When Rachel entered the parlor, a strange gentleman and lady rose to meet her. Rachel looked into the gentleman's face enquiringly: a cry of delight burst from her lips. It was her father! — the young lady, her eldest sister. They had come to take home their little absentee.

Chapter VII

A lapse of five years occurs in Rachel's reminiscences of her early childhood; and from the tear-stained pages of the growing girl, we shall extract a few trifles which may amuse our readers.

At nine years of age, we find her battling with a governess, who unable to discern the light, bright tints in her character, pronounces her entirely bad; a stubborn, self-willed, crazy-pated creature, to whom it was impossible to impart a rational idea; and the poor girl like many an unfortunate, misunderstood child of genius, remains unteachable, untaught. Keenly sensible of the unjust prejudice which had pronounced the ban against her; and too proud to conciliate the favor of the tyrannical mistress she despised, Rachel obstinately refused instruction. Her father rebuked, her mother scolded, her elder sisters blamed, and Miss —— threatened, but Rachel, firm to her promise, bore it all without yielding an inch. This was wrong, Rachel felt that it was so, but had she been treated with the least kindness or consideration; had the tenderness of love been tried, instead of the stern brutalizing force of blows, and the insulting abuse of power; the child, who stood aloof, invincible in her wounded pride, had bent to instruction and received the chastisement of her faults, with tears of penitence. Poor Rachel, her heart was full of affection, full of deep, abiding love — love strong as death, but those around her, knew not how to call forth all its energy and tenderness. In all her sorrows, and they were many, she found one faithful friend and counsellor, in her sister Dorothea.

Dorothea, was nearly two years her senior; was a gentle, loving, lamb-like creature, full of sincerity and truth. Her talents were equal, perhaps superior to those of her impetuous, irascible sister: but she had a perfect controll over her passions. Her temper by nature was placid and kind, she could not bear to see Rachel suffer; and she did all in her power to soften and heal the wounds which the daily friction of uncongenial minds, stamped into the unfortunate girl's too sensitive heart.

Oh how devotedly Rachel loved this kind sister. Her affection for her, fell little short of idolatry; untractable to others, she was tractable to Dorothea. To lay her aching head in her lap, to sob out her full heart upon her bosom, to feel her hand wipe away the tears, she was too proud to shed before those by whom she was insulted, and reviled, was the only comfort the young girl knew. Had she possessed any knowledge of the human heart, could she have seen, that her own perverseness drew down upon herself, much of the misery, which shed a doleful gloom upon her mind and character, and darkened the days of her future years, she had turned with meekness to those who knew as little of her mind, with all its lofty aspirations, and poetic images, as she did herself, and sought their sympathy and regard with the same earnestness, that she did the esteem of her beloved Dorothea.

But Rachel had yet to learn by bitter experience, the philosophy of life. To force a strong will, instead of battling with others, to make successful war against the imperfections of her own faulty temper, and those head-strong passions, which at this period of her history, bid fair to destroy a fragile body, and a sensitive and highly imaginative mind.

Rachel was a solitary child. Other children felt no sympathy with her — they could not comprehend her fantastic notions. She talked of things they understood not, and asked questions which they could not answer. Full of vague and undefined thoughts, with a mysterious consciousness of the great mystery of life, overshadowing her like a cloud, from the midst of whose darkness, gleams of that far off eternity, flashed from time to time, like lightning through her brain; Rachel lived in a world of her own creations. She felt that some great unknown power had called her into existence, dream-like as that existence appeared to her; and her young soul stretched forth its longing arms towards God. An intent desire to know, what to her, was buried in impenetrable mystery, conquered even the fear of death. She longed to die — if death could answer her questions, and solve her doubts; and day after day, she sought a deep dell in a beautiful grove upon the estate, to sit alone with nature, and ponder over these awful dread sublimities.

From constantly brooding on such themes, her character took a sadder, sterner tone, and she loved those objects best, that best assimilated with her thoughts. The lofty trees tossed into furious motion by the winds — the deep surging of ocean rolling in terrible grandeur to the shore — the black embattled thunder clouds — the solemn roar of the earth shaking thunder — the sweeping rush of the devastating rain, was music to her ears. Her spirit rode sublimely above the warring elements, and gloried in the majesty of the storm.

There was no fear in her heart, no quailing of her eye, when God agitated the mighty fabric of his creation, and the world trembled at the manifestations of his power. Then would the tumultuous thoughts, cribbed and confined within the narrow circle of a human heart, expand and break forth in words of fire; and the young improvitrice, forgot all her sorrows in the extatic joy of her wild unmeasured, unwritten, spontaneous bursts of song.

The consciousness of this gift, formed a new era in the life of Rachel, and imparted a dignity to her nature, which atoned in her own eyes, for all the reproaches daily poured against her ignorance and want of sense. She began to feel faith in herself, to believe that the lofty visions that amused and soothed her solitary hours, were inspirations direct from heaven. If not from above, from whence came those electric flashes of mind — those sudden revelations of the spirit world within and around her. They came unbidden, and they departed as suddenly, leaving the young visionary intoxicated with a sweet delirious extacy.

Then came the tempting fiend, and whispered,

"Oh, that I could give life and reality to those visions that so charm me — that I could convey in words, the bright pictures in my mind — that I could leave behind me when I die, some memorial that I once lived — that my name might be mentioned with respect by the wise and good when I am dust." Oh, who can fathom all the vanity of the human heart. Fancy can so clothe its littleness in the sublime language of poetry; and cover with a shield of light, all its imperfections.

Youth blind to the faults of others, is as blind to its own! It is the age of love, and trust — it hopes for all things — believes in all things — and in the simplicity of its reliance, finds all things true. Rachel sitting among the grass, and discoursing poetry to the flowers, felt not the darkening influence of the dust and rubbish of the world. Her wealth was the abundance of nature, the garniture of fields and woods. To have been undeceived would have robbed her of the beautiful, to have driven her forth from paradise with the flaming sword. When goaded into pain by the sneers and scoffs of those who knew not of her hidden Eden, Rachel sought the "Divine Mother," and on her verdant ever fragrant bosom, dried her tears. It was in one of these moods, that she exclaimed in the bitterness of her soul, —

"Oh nature though the blast is yelling,
Loud roaring through the bending tree —
There's sorrow in man's darksome dwelling,
There's rapture still with thee."

"From the sublime to the ridiculous," said the great conqueror "is but a step;" and the child who revelled in grand conceptions alone with nature, and the solitude of her own soul, was the strangest, most eccentric impersonification of a feminine humanity, that could well be imagined, when among her young compeers. We have alluded to the mighty devastator of the nineteenth century, the great Napoleon, and linked with his name, are woven some of the absurdities and oddities, of Rachel's desultory childhood.

Napoleon had just commenced his unfortunate Russian campaign; and the whole world rang with the fame of his exploits. In England, he was belied and abused, and his name made a bugbear to frighten refractory children; but whether from a contradiction in human nature, or from an inherent admiration of genius, Rachel had conceived a romantic love for the detested Bonaparte. In him, she saw realized all the greatness of her favourite heroes; and she pursued his victorious career with an enthusiasm unsurpassed by his most devoted followers. He was the idol of her imagination, whom she worshipped to the exclusion of all others. She triumphed in his success, and gave herself up to despair, when fortune ceased to favor his arms. He was the hero of all her tales and impromptu poems; and once she got a beating from her mother, who had set her to write some lines on her sister Janet's birth-day, when instead of commemorating the happy day in gentle, affectionate milk and water rhymes, she composed an ode to the great Napoleon, whose early victories had occurred about the same period, and thus was poor Janet merged in the illustrious conqueror; and the only compliment paid to her, was that she had received her existence at this important era. To punish the child, for such an extraordinary fault, appears ridiculous to Rachel now, and is only remembered by her, as a matter of mirth; but it pained her exceedingly at the time; and she committed her ode to the flames, secretly vowing never to degrade her mind, by writing birth-day odes again. A promise which she religiously adhered to all her life.

An old friend of her father's, whom we shall call Mentor, was exceedingly amused by this anecdote of Rachel, whom he loved in spite of all her eccentricities, and tried to convince her father that the germs of future excellence, might be contained within this rude shell.

Mr. Wilde was very sceptical. He did not comprehend Rachel, and he was really displeased with her, for the mad love she evinced for the enemy of her country.

"She is a strange girl," he said, "she fills my mind with painful doubts."

"Ah let her alone," would the good Mentor say, "My pet lion's heart is in the right place. — I love to see her ruffle up her mane. — She is a mountain torrent which restraint would render more impetuous. — I will try what I can do with her."

And much, did this truly excellent man do for his little friend, who loved him with a zeal only one degree less, than that she bore for Napoleon. He entered into correspondence with her, and endeavored to call out all the powers of her mind. He stimulated her to study — he taught her to think. He sent her books to read, and made her write her opinions to him of their contents — to mark down the impression they made upon her mind, and the reflections they called forth. Rachel was proud of this correspondence — she entered into it with all her heart and soul; and learned more in one month by pursuing Mentor's system, than she had done for many years.

Wishing to cure her of the Bonaparte mania, which had so strangely possessed her, Mentor sent her the present of a large bust of Lord Wellington. Living entirely in the country, Rachel had never seen a picture of either, and therefore readily mistook the high stern features of the one, for the classical face of her heart's idol. The poor child received this gift with rapture. The bust was never out of her sight. Every day she crowned it with fresh laurels, and at night it lay upon her pillow. It possessed in her eyes, the perfection of beauty. It was the effigy of a hero. Alas for love and faith, a cynical sort of a Diogenes, a doctor in the neighbourhood, who was very intimate at the house, came one afternoon to visit Rachel's father. He used to tease Rachel not a little, and she had christened him Diogenes. In the pride of her heart, she displayed the bust of her hero, and he burst into a long, continuous roar of laughter. Rachel heard him with indignation and astonishment. She always thought him a rude fellow — had often told him so — but he appeared ruder and more intolerable than usual.

"Ho, ho, Miss Rachel, and so you worship that image as the head of old Bony, they may well say that love is blind — it is the head of Lord Wellington!"

Had a thunderbolt fallen upon her idol and shivered it to atoms, its destruction could not have been more complete — enraged at having been cheated into paying adoration to a false God, Rachel dashed the bust to the ground, and trampled it to pieces beneath her feet, then fled to her own chamber, to conceal the tears of mortified pride, shame and regret. It was some time before she could forgive Mentor, for what she considered his illnatured trick.

A few weeks after, she went to visit her father, who was staying at the city of ——, to transact some important business. Mentor resided at —— and he soon made his peace with his little friend, and presented her with a crown to buy a Napoleon for herself.

There was an Italian boy who sold images daily in the market place; and elated with her prize Rachel hastened hither. She found the swarthy lad standing silent and solemn as an image among the crowd, bearing the modern conquerors, monarchs, great authors and statesmen, upon his head, which like a second Atlas, bent not beneath their ponderous weight.

"I want to buy the head of Napoleon," cried the impatient Rachel, holding up the crown piece. "Now you must *be sure*, to give me the right one?" The boy must have marvelled at the doubt — but a tall soldier of the German legion, then stationed in the city, anticipated him, and lifting down from his elevated perch, a large bronze bust of the Emperor, he exclaimed.

"Little maid, dis is him, I know Napoleon, by his sulky look."

Rachel's eyes flashed, she could have beat the soldier for the insult offered to her darling. She however, restrained her anger, paid the crown, and hugging the emperor to her bosom hurried homeward, anxious to display her treasure. In St. —— street, she met the son, of a Captain Thompson, who had fought and bled at the battles of Barossa and Vittoria. Fred was very loyal, and for his father's sake, a great hater of old Bony, as he sacrilegiously termed the master spirit of the age — and as he passed Rachel, he dexterously fractured the skull of her image with a stone. Rachel pursued the culprit with tears in her eyes, but he laughed at her and fled — and to make bad worse, her misfortune was greeted with peals of mirth, when she told to her father and sisters, and Mentor, the tale of her wrongs.

"Never mind Rachel," said Mentor. "Many a great hero has passed through a long life, with a cracked head. Bring me a piece of black sealing-wax, and a lighted candle; and I will restore to the Emperor a sound cranium."

The fracture was dexterously healed, and Rachel dried her tears, and for many long years, the bust of Napoleon adorned her writing table.

It cannot be denied, that this infatuation with regard to Napoleon, led her into the commission of many absurdities. At church for instance — instead of praying for the King and the Royal family, she substituted Napoleon's name, and that of the young King of Rome. Being very vehement in her prayers in their behalf, she was overheard by the wife of an old Captain in the Navy, who thought it incumbent upon her, as a matter of duty, to inform Miss Rachel's Mamma of this act of treason.

"Really Mrs. Wilde, you should punish Miss Rachel — it is very wicked — very wicked indeed, for any one to go to church and pray for our enemies. 'Tis a shame and a scandalous shame — and Miss Rachel, is old enough to know better."

Thus spake the wise woman of Gotham, and Rachel was punished accordingly.

At length the fate of the Emperor was decided, the

allied armies entered Paris, and he was banished to Elba. Oh, how Rachel wept his fall — how she longed to share his exile — while the cloud of defeat hung over him, little minds triumphed in his misfortunes, and reviled his name. Rachel fought for him like a lion, could she have cleared his name from reproach and calumny, she would have done so with her heart's blood. Almost forbidden to mention him, she brooded over his captivity in secret, and lost no opportunity of learning any news respecting him.

It was in the spring just preceding the battle of Waterloo; that Rachel, was busy writing with her sisters and brothers, at a long dining table the usual copy daily set them by their father, when an old Yorkshire pedling merchant, who travelled the country with broadcloths and blankets, with whom Mr. Wilde often dealt, entered the room.

"Oh sir," he cried "have you heard the terrible news?"

"What news?" quoth Mr. Wilde.

"Bony has escaped from Elbow!"

"Thank God!" exclaimed Rachel flinging down her pen, and starting up with a scream of delight. "He will be Emperor of France again!"

"Send that girl to bed," said Mr. Wilde, with a frown, "she is a traitor to her country."

Rachel longed to hear the news, but to remonstrate with her father was useless; and she left the room, but lingered on the last step of the back staircase, till the old Pedlar, his gossip and trading completed, passed through the kitchen on his way out. Then springing from her hiding place, she implored the good man, to tell her all he knew about the escape of Napoleon. This he very good naturedly did, and Rachel retired to spend a long spring day in bed, and fasting, on the tip toe of delight.

"He was free! he was himself again, and what was the punishment to her?" She lay in a sort of extacy, fighting for him new battles and achieving more astounding conquests. Alas! the dreams of the young enthusiast were doomed to be quenched in the blood shed at Waterloo, when the gathering together of the nations, chained the imprisoned eagle to the lonely ocean rock.

Chapter VIII

Rachel had just entered her tenth year, but many changes had taken place in the fortunes of her family. Her father had given his name as security to a gentleman, nearly related to his wife, who betrayed his trust, and dragged his generous benefactor down in his own ruin.

Involved in difficulties, with a failing constitution and broken heart, Mr. Wilde still morally great, battled bravely with the waves of misfortune, which threatened to overwhelm him on all sides.

To reduce his comfortable establishment; dismiss the larger portion of his servants; and lay down pleasure horses, and equipages, was to him a command of duty to which he submitted without a sigh.

Released from the tyranny of a governess, Rachel continued her studies, together with Dorothea, and her two brothers, under the care of her elder sister.

In the distraction of their affairs, Miss Wilde, had so many more important things to attend to, that we cannot wonder that the children were left in a great measure to teach themselves. They were shut up for part of the day in the school-room, to do as they pleased, so that they were out of mischief: or they wandered over the estate, building huts in the plantations with boughs of trees, and thatching them with moss.

To pass away the weary hours, they all crowded together into one of these wigwams, and related stories and romances of their own invention, to amuse each other.

It would have formed a curious subject for a painter, — these girls and boys seated beneath their rude structure, o'er-canopied with forest trees, and eagerly relating the imaginary events in their histories as they flashed into their young minds — their eyes shining, their cheeks glowing, and their faces lighted up with the inspiration of the moment. If the interest of the tale flagged, or the reciter appeared at all at a loss for an adventure; one of the others took up the thread of the narrative as if perfectly acquainted with the plan of its originator, and continued the story. Some of these impromptu romances, were carried on for weeks and even months in this manner; and so eager were the children to develope all the mysteries of their plot, that the moment they had concluded their tasks, and the door closed upon Miss Wilde, and they were once more alone, the boys would cry out, "Come girls! — let us go on with the story!"

After having been so long successful narrators of fiction, although with no other audience than the two young brothers; Dorothea and Rachel, consulted together, as to the possibility of writing down one of their favorite tales. Poor children, they knew nothing about authors and authoresses, they had no ambition at that early period of their lives, of being known to the world. It was to them, merely a matter of diversion; a play which was to amuse themselves and their little brothers.

Dorothea thought that the scheme was practicable — that it would be a nice thing for them daily to write a portion of their history, and at night to read aloud what each had written.

"But," said she, "What shall we do for paper? — The pens and ink that we write our copies with will do, but we have no paper; and, you know, dear Rachel, that Lilla will never give us paper for such nonsense."

Rachel was now puzzled, she sat down and thought for a while. "Dorothea," she cried eagerly, rising and pushing her fingers through the dark masses of her chestnut hair; "Would blue paper do?"

Dorothea laughed heartily, "But wherefore blue?"

"Oh because we can get plenty of that, and Mamma and Lilla will never miss it; and would not care a fig for it if they did. You know the great Indian chest in Selina's room."

"Capital!" cried Dorothea now fully entering into the scheme.

"If we can read them ourselves, that is all we want," said Rachel. "We will call them the '*Blue Paper Manuscripts*' and we will keep the secret to ourselves."

To the great chest they went, hand in hand, to extract from its depths, materials for their first essay in authorship.

Alas! poor children, they little knew the troubles and trials that beset the dangerous path they were about to tread. The love and approbation of the few, and the envy and hatred of the many. To resign the joys of the present, and to live alone for the future. To be the scorn of vulgar and common minds; the dread of the weak and sensitive, to stand alone and without sympathy, misunderstood and maligned by most of their species.

This was the talisman they sought, the good they so recklessly coveted, in the blessed days of literary ignorance, and the blue paper manuscripts.

But of what, I hear my readers exclaim, were these manuscripts formed, and how came they blue?

In my hurry to get on with my tale, and my sage reflections on the same, I had forgotten to offer the necessary explanation.

This India chest, which was some seven feet long and three deep, was covered with *papier-maché* splendidly illustrated in black and gold, which at the present day, would have been prized by the collectors of Indian curiosities as a treasure; but which was suffered to hide its diminished head in a sleeping room; and to form a general repository for all the odd articles in the family. The wedding dresses, formed of rich brocaded silks, and interwoven with silver and gold, of several generations were there.

Beautiful specimens of fruits and flowers, embroidered on silk and satin, and fine linen, by fair hands now mouldering into dust, lay side by side, with long flapped waistcoats, fly caps, and muslin aprons, the latter curiously wrought in a thousand different stitches — and at the bottom of all this fading and useless finery, were several reams of blotting and blue paper, such as is used to line drawers and cover bandboxes. How the paper came there the girls never knew, or what business it had among the tarnished dresses of their ancestors; but to them it was a treasure far surpassing in value the bugled and spangled petticoats and gowns, in which they used to play at Queens, sailing about their bedrooms in the fine summer evenings, in the long trained dresses of a former age.

From the family chest, they abstracted a couple of quires of the blue paper which they privately conveyed to the school room, and hid behind an old fashioned cupboard which contained their school books.

That very afternoon they commenced their first written story. The scene of both was laid in Germany. Dorothea called her tale, "The Brothers," and Rachel sported the title of, "Harold of Hohenstien, or the spoilt child." Never was a story written in after years, so enthusiastically commenced, or so zealously continued. After her lessons were over, she flew to the task with the most intense delight, and often continued writing until the gray twilight obliterated from her sight, the characters that she still endeavored to trace upon the dusky looking paper.

With what pride she read over to the patient listening Dorothea, the wild outpourings of her untutored brain, and in her turn considered Dorothea's story divine. Harold was a soldier under Prince Eugene. Prince Eugene was one of Rachel's heroes, and her fancy, which at that period, was of a very warlike cast, luxuriated in drawing descriptions of battles and seiges, at all, and each of which, her spoilt child performed unheard of prodigies of valor, receiving and recovering from more desperate wounds, than would have killed a hundred champions like Goliah.

But nothing was impossible to Rachel in those days. She had faith in the wild and wonderful. Ghosts were her familiars, and with witches and fairies she was well acquainted. She had vague notions of the truth of the second sight, and was sorry that the gods of the old mythology were entirely banished from the world. It was at this period of her life, that she first read Milton's Paradise Lost, and was so deeply interested in his sublime delineation of Satan, that all her sympathies went with the fallen. She literally fell in love with the devil, and upon his being turned into a serpent, flung down the book and refused to read any farther, to the great amusement of Dorothea.

But to return to the blue paper manuscripts, they soon grew too cumbrous to be concealed behind the cupboard, and Rachel having let her sister Selina into the secret, who had just returned from the city of ——, where business detained her father the greater part of the year. Selina had removed the papers into the drawer of a sideboard in which she kept many articles that belonged to herself, and where she concluded the M.S., which she regarded as a wonderful performance from the pen of such a child, would be perfectly safe.

A few days after the removal of the M.S., Miss Wilde returned home, and expecting friends to dinner, she had been superintending the arrangements with the cook in the Kitchen. Wanting a piece of paper to cover a roasting pig, she went to look for some in Selina's drawer of litters. Rachel and Selina were at work by the fire, with their backs to the sideboard, and they had no idea of their sister's design until their attention was aroused by an exclamation of surprise from Miss Wilde.

Imagine the consternation of Rachel — for she was no favourite with Lilla, when she beheld her reading her sacred Manuscript, and evidently much amused at its contents.

"What are you about at my drawer Lilla?" said Selina.

"I want some waste paper, to cover the pig, to keep it from burning!"

"There is none there," said Selina pettishly, trembling for the fate of her poor protege's manuscript.

"Who in the world wrote this?" asked Lilla — "and on such paper. It really seems very interesting, was it Annie?"

Selina laughed and shook her head, "You must guess again — no it was Rachel." This was said with an air of triumph.

A frown gathered upon the brow of Lilla. — "That chit, ridiculous; indulge her in making such a fool of herself. I wish papa would put a stop to her nonsense, and if he does not I will. It will just do to cover the pig." She was about to rend the papers, but the kind Selina, starting from her seat, rescued the doomed manuscript from her hands.

And there sat the hapless author, the tears swelling up in her eyes, not that she had been found fault with for writing; she was too much the general scape-goat to wonder at that; but she felt keenly the injustice which had stamped the writing interesting, while supposed to have emanated from the pen of a more favored sister — and nonsense — only fit for the flames, or worse — to keep a vile pig from burning, as coming from her. And ah! how much of this spirit was put in force against her. The bitter sneer, the sarcastic critique, the scornful laugh, all that could wound the pride and repress the genius of the young candidate for fame, she had to bear in silence, and shroud in the depths of her own heart.

Time rolled on. The world, as umpire, decided the question of her capacity, and gave the meed of praise so long denied by those whom true wisdom and benevolence should have taught the policy of a more generous course.

Little recked Rachel for the change in her prospects. The desire to be loved by one noble heart was dearer to her than ambition, than the applause of the world; and she resigned the tempting wreath it offered her, to follow the adverse fortunes of the beloved — to toil in poverty and sorrow by his side — a stranger and an exile in a foreign land.

Victoria Magazine 1 (1848): 113–15, 126–28, 156–59, 183–87, 212–14, 234–37, 250–52.

The Quiet Horse; A Domestic Sketch

"A horse, a horse! My kingdom for a horse!"

Mrs. Harrowby had taken it into her head that she must pay a flying visit to her husband, who had been absent for some weeks from home, superintending the arrangement of a very complicated mercantile business, which had involved his brother-in-law in bankruptcy.

There was no immediate necessity for the premeditated visit of Mrs. Harrowby to the city of N——, but she suddenly formed the wish of going thither; and, like most of her sex when placed in similar circumstances, she determined to go.

The city of N—— was thirty miles off; and Mr. Harrowby, when at home, resided on a small estate in the county of S——, which he amused himself by cultivating. A most expensive recreation, by the by, to one unacquainted with the practical and useful science of agriculture, and who derived his information upon the subject entirely from books. The poor folks called him the gentleman farmer; the rich laughed at his speculative turn of mind, and prophesied his ruin. Well, he was absent and every thing at Harrowby was at a stand still. Mrs. H. was dull, for she had never before been separated from her husband. The boys were rude and troublesome, and the heavy rains had clouded the fair prospects of an abundant harvest; and without the master, all went wrong together.

"I wish your father were at home," said the anxious

wife, to her eldest daughter. "If nothing happens to prevent it, I must positively go and see him to-morrow."

"But, Mamma, what horse can you take? The gardener has ridden Billy to Ipswich, and will not be back before to-morrow night. The mare Phoebe is lame, and Wellington has been so recently broken in that it would be very dangerous for you to attempt to drive him."

"Well, I know all that, Eliza. I would not drive Wellington for a thousand pounds: but there are other horses in the stable besides that wild thing."

"You are not surely speculating upon the cart-horses? You had better hire a post-chaise from the village."

"Phoo, phoo! how your father would stare to see me drive up to his lodgings in a post-chaise. He would imagine that some one was dead; that some calamity had happened in his absence. Besides, think of the trouble of sending all the way to W—— for the chaise. The useless expense. No, no. I have a plan of my own worth two of that. Run, Harry, to the stable, and tell old Coulter that I want him."

Harry, a bright-eyed, fair-haired, imp of six years old, scampered off to do as he was bid, and quickly returned with the old man.

Coulter was the driver of the team of five Suffolk sorrels, only used for farm work. He had lived for seven years in a small cottage upon the estate, and regarded the three horses he had in charge with as much affection as his own children, bestowing more pains upon them, in currying, brushing and cleaning, than he had ever expended on his own person during a long and laborious life. Joe Coulter was a tall, lank-haired, athletic-looking man, on the wrong side of sixty, wrinkled and weather-beaten, but strong and active still. His face bore a striking resemblance to the physiognomy of his favorite animal, and had a simple honest expression.

Pulling the front lock of his rusty black hair, as a substitute for a bow, and scratching the back of his head with his left hand, the worthy peasant drew himself straight up at the back of Mrs. Harrowby's chair, and drawled out, in the true Suffolk whine, "Missus, here bees I. What are yer commands?"

"Joe, I want to go to N —— to-morrow, to see your master. What horse can I take for the journey?"

"None, as I knows of," returned the old man, shaking his head. "Work and pleasure require different servants. Measter's riding hoss is away. The mear is lame, and that ere Wellington is perfectly unmanageable. And now, though I'm sure ye'd like to see measter, I'm afeard that ye must bide at home."

"But I'll do no such thing. I have set my mind upon going to N —— , and I mean to go. What should prevent me from taking your fore-horse, Sharper. He is a beautiful animal."

The old man started a pace or two back, in utter amazement. "Take Shearper! The Lord save us. What put it into yer mind to take him? Why, Marm, he's as wild as the old un. I do think that the soul of a lord has some how got into that beast. Like all handsum folk, he's so proud and so tricky, and he do rear and plunge, and caper about like a mad thing. It is as much as I and my boy Jonathan can do to hold him in, when he have a mind to go his own way. He'd smash the chay all to shivers in a brace of shakes. Although," and the old man's eyes brightened "he's a bonny beast, and 'maist fit for a gentleman's carriage; he'd kill you and the young missuses in the twinkling of an eye."

"I certainly will dispense with his services," said Mrs. Harrowby. "But what of Boxer?"

"Why, Marm, he do well enough as middle hoss in the team. He's as dull as tother's spunky. Shearper starts him, and Captain drives him on. He's so fat and lazy-like, it would take you two days going to N —— ."

"And Captain?"

"Aye, he's the quieat beast. He's gentle as a lamb. A child might drive him. If you take any of my horses, it must e'en be the colt." For so Coulter designated a horse ten years old, who happened to be a colt when he came to the place; and the colt he still remained in the old man's estimation.

"The colt let it be; and mind me, Joe, let him be well fed and well cleaned, and in the chaise by six o'clock to-morrow morning. In the plated harness, he will look almost as well as Billy."

"Na, na," said the old man, "there is about as much difference between them as between you and the cook. Every hoss has his own place; and the colt is about as fit for the chay, as I be for the tea-parlor. If you take man or beast out of the situation God meant him for, you do him a bad sarvice." And with this eloquent harangue, old Joe Coulter retreated to the stable, to prepare his darling for the alarming prospect of the morrow.

Great were the preparations for the approaching journey. Mistress, and maids, and young ladies, were up by sunrise, making ready for the great event; gathering choice fruit, and collecting all sorts of dainties for the absent owner of the mansion. As to old Joe, he was stirring by daybreak, brightening the chaise harness, and braiding her long flowing mane of the unconscious victim of female caprice; and after all was done, and the old man declared that the colt looked a perfect beauty, that his skin shone like satin, and he'd not disgrace a carriage, he found more difficulty in preparing him for the journey than he had at first anticipated. The plated harness was far too small for the vast proportions of the ponderous beast, and had to be let out to the utmost extent into which a hole could be punched in the leather. The shafts of the slight and elegant vehicle were far too tight, and greatly curtailed his powers of locomotion. The poor animal looked sadly out of place, and cut but a sorry figure in his ill-fitting finery.

"I knew how he'd look in your trumpery," cried old Joe, shaking his head, "Just as Nan would look in Missuses best silk gownd. It don't fit him; and how can they 'spect for him to look himsel. And then as to going; them shafts be so tight, they hold him like a vice, he can't draw a breath in comfort. He'll puff and blow along the load, like them ugly black things at sea, that turn about like a cart-wheel, that the fishers call pomposses. Well Captain, boy, (patting him affectionately,) yer a gentleman now. How do ye like the gear?" The horse rubbed his white nose (for he had the misfortune to have a white face) affectionately against the caressing hand of the old man. "Aye, yer a sensible cratur, as wise as a human and as queeat as a child; but I do pities ye from my very soul. When these women folk do take a notion into their heads, they are the most unreasonable animals in the world."

His colloquy was here interrupted by the appearance of the mistress, with two of the young ladies and the maid servant, bearing a hamper full of good things from the farm.

The girls were in high spirits at the prospect of their ride, and they laughed and joked alternately with their mother and the maid, at the appearance of their equipage.

The great size of the horse elevated the forepart of the chaise to such a degree, that it seemed in the very act of falling backwards.

"Is it safe, Joe," asked Miss Sarah, pausing on the step and looking doubtingly at the old man.

"It can't go over while the hoss keeps his legs," said Coulter, sulkily; "an its no trifle that would capsize him."

"He looks just like an elephant in harness," cried little Anna, clapping her hands and bursting into a merry laugh, as she bounded into the chaise. "I am sure we need not fear his running away with us."

"He is very queeat, very queeat," muttered old Joe. "He'll go as he likes, in spite of ye, and no mistake."

Mrs. Harrowby now mounted, reins in hand; and though the horse presented the loftiest portion in the strange group, and their seat slanted inconveniently back, and had a very awkward appearance, she was not a nervous timid woman, and she apprehended no danger. Bidding Coulter let Captain's head go, she lightly touched him with the whip, and in a cheerful voice urged him forward. She might as well have tickled the hide of a rhinoceros with a feather, or spoken in Greek to a Cherokee Indian. The quiet horse neither felt her whip nor understood her language. He shook his mane, pricked up his ears, and whisked his long tail into the laps of the young ladies in the carriage. Anna, mischievous thing, was in convulsions of laughter; while Mrs. Harrowby, provoked by the obstinacy of her Bucephalus, applied the butt end of the whip to his fat, round back, and so far forgot her breeding as to exclaim, in no silver tone, "Get on, you stupid brute!"

The energy of her address set the great animal in motion; and in a pace between an amble and a high trot, he floundered round the carriage drive that led to the front of the house, and plunged into the road.

"Hold him up well, Marm!" was the last exhortation of old Joe, as his shaft-horse jolted off at a tremendous heavy gallop. "He's cruel hard in the mouth: and the Lord send ye a safe journey home."

"Amen," ejaculated Miss Sarah, who considered that the prayer of old Joe was not indispensable under existing circumstances. "Dear Mamma, do you not think that we had better return? It will be impossible to drive that horse thirty miles."

"I'll try my best," said Mrs. Harrowby. "I don't choose to be conquered by a brute." And on they went, at a pace so hard and rough that they were soon as much out of breath as the astonished horse, who, never accustomed to any vehicle but a heavy waggon or a dung cart, seemed to feel very much in the same predicament as a dog with a tin kettle tied to his tail. The shafts held him so closely, that his huge frame panted and swelled as if it would burst, at every step, the impediments that restrained him; and he often stopped, and shook both shafts and harness, with an angry impatience quite incompatible with his character of a quiet horse. Out of the heavy ruts he refused to go; his mouth was as hard as leather, so that to make him quarter the road, while passing other vehicles, was an operation attended with no small difficulty and danger; and then he hung his head so low, that he looked as if he were momentarily contemplating making a somerset, in order to free himself from his galling position. Fatigued with jerking the reins, and urging on the brute with voice and whip, poor Mrs. Harrowby's vexations did not end here. Every idle fellow that passed had some uncourteous remark to make upon the driver and her steed.

"Hard work, that?" cried one.

"Prime lady's horse," said another.

"Hollo, old lady!" vociferated a third. "What will you take for yer hoss? I want a racer to enter at Newmarket. Isn't he a spanker for the Derby?"

Tired, mortified, and thoroughly disgusted with the doings of the quiet horse, yet, like a true woman, determined not to give up, Mrs. Harrowby consoled herself and her girls with the idea, that they were not known in that part of the country and need not mind the provoking speeches of a set of vulgar fools. As to the girls, they were just young enough to laugh at their misadventure, and to regard it as an excellent frolic.

But to return to Captain. When he had succeeded in toiling up a hill, he took the liberty of stopping as long as he thought fit, in order to recover himself and take breath; and it required the united efforts of the whole party to urge him on; and when he did make a start, he went off at a ferocious pace, which threatened to jolt them to pieces. At every farm yard he stopped and neighed; and once, when it unfortunately happened that the gate that led from the road had been left open to admit a load of wheat, he rushed with headlong speed to the barn, and it required the farmer and his men to force him back into the road.

At mid-day, they had only accomplished fifteen miles of their journey; and after dining and resting, and feeding the unmanageable animal for two hours, at an inn by the road side, with heavy hearts they proceeded on their journey. Mrs. Harrowby's head ached, she was tired and out of spirits, the fair Sarah was busied with her own thoughts, and even the gay Anna had ceased to laugh at Captain and his absurdities.

The shades of night were darkening the beautiful landscape, which spreads far and wide round the ancient city, when the travellers caught a glimpse of their temporary home, and blessed their stars that they had been conducted thus far in safety: but their trials were not quite ended. The horse, who had been brought up in the country, and had never been in a large town in his life, was strongly agitated, and shewed unequivocal symptoms of alarm, when turned into the broad and lamp-lighted thoroughfare. He snorted, reared, and rushed from side to side, refusing to yield the least obedience to the feminine hand and voice that strove in vain to guide him and restrain the impetuosity of his movements; and would in all probability have been the death of his driver, had not the reins been grasped in a bolder hand, and the ladies rescued from their perilous situation, by a gentleman to whom they were known.

"My dearest Betsy," cried Mr. Harrowby, after the first affectionate salutations had passed between him and his wife and daughters, "what tempted you to risk your lives by driving over with that horse?"

"Ah, my dear John, I will allow that it was very foolish — but I did so long to see you; and I apprehended no danger, when Coulter assured me that Captain was such a quiet horse."

"And so he is, when confined to his proper place, in the farm yard; but there is always danger in taking either man or animal out of the sphere, where education and circumstances can alone render him useful, as you have proved, my dear old woman, by your late experience."

Three days passed happily away at N —— , and no one remembered Captain, but the servant who supplied his wants in the stable. The fourth morning was a glorious day for the harvest, and Mr. Harrowby reminded his wife that the service of Captain would be required at home.

Once more the mighty brute was forced between the narrow shafts; and Mrs. Harrowby, with less confidence in his gentle propensities, undertook the task of driving him home. The man servant led the horse beyond the bounds of the city, and saw him fairly started upon the turnpike road. But so impatient was the country-bred horse of the restraint and imprisonment of the close stable at the inn, that he needed neither whip nor voice to urge him to return to the beloved haunts of his youth, and the comrades who shared his daily labors. He literally set his face homeward, and his pace kept time with his wishes. He bounded forward at the top of his rough ungainly speed, making his anxiety to reach the anticipated goal known to the travellers by his loud and frequent neighing. The nearer he approached his native pastures, the more excentric did these manifestations become; and when at length within half a mile of his own stable, his shrill signals were answered by his comrades from the field, the poor brute jolted along with a velocity which shook the occupants of the chaise up and down, with that rolling motion of a ship struggling through a short heavy sea.

"Thank God! we are once more safe at home!" cried Mrs. Harrowby, to the gardener, who had ridden to meet them upon Billy: and the affectionate animals saluted each other with almost human sagacity. "I did not think that it was possible for a quiet horse to make so much noise."

"You forget, Mamma, that he belongs to the farm-yard," said Anna, laughing, "and the moral that Papa drew from our adventure. 'No one looks well or acts well out of his own sphere.'"

Victoria Magazine 1 (1848): 265–68.

Trifles from the Burthen of a Life

A Talk about Emigration

"Rachel, have you forgotten the talk we had about emigration, the morning before our marriage?" was a question rather suddenly put to his young wife, by Lieutenant M ——, as he paused in his rapid walk to and fro the room. The fact is, that the Lieutenant had been pondering over that conversation for the last hour. It had long been forgotten by his wife, who was seated upon the sofa with a young infant of three months old upon her lap, whose calm, sleeping face she was watching with inexpressible delight.

"Ah, we have been so happy ever since, that to tell you the truth, dear John, I have never given it a second thought; what put it into your head just now?"

"That child, and thinking how I could provide for her in any other way."

"Dear little pet. She cannot add much to our expenses;" And the mother stooped down and kissed her babe with a zest which mothers alone know.

"Not at present. But the little pet will in time grow into a tall girl; and other little pets may be treading upon her footsteps and they must all be clothed and fed, and educated."

Rachel in her overflowing happiness had dismissed all such cruel realities. "Emigration," she said, "is a terrible word. I wish that it could be expunged from the dictionary."

"I am afraid, my dear girl, that you are destined to learn the practical illustrations of its meaning. Nay, do not look so despondingly. If you intended to remain in England you should not have married a poor man."

"Don't say that, my beloved. That union made me rich in treasures which gold could not buy. But seriously, I do not see this urgent necessity for emigrating, we are not rich, but we have enough to be comfortable, and are surrounded with many blessings. Our dear little girl, whose presence seems to have conjured before you the gaunt image of poverty, has added greatly to our domestic happiness, — Yes, — little Miss Innocence, you are awake, are you — come crow to papa, and drive these ugly thoughts out of his head." The good father kissed fondly the smiling cherub seducingly held up to him, but he did not yield to the temptation, though Rachel kissed him with eyes brimful of tears.

"We are indeed happy, Rachel. But, will it last!"

"Why not!"

"Our income, love, is very, very small."

"It is enough for our present wants, and we have no debts."

"Thanks to your prudent management. Yes, we have no debts. But it has been a hard battle, only gained by great self denial and much pinching. We have kind friends, but I am too proud to be indebted to friends for the common necessaries of life. The narrow income which has barely supplied our wants, this year, without the encumbrance of a family, will not do so next. There remains no alternative but to emigrate."

Rachel felt that this was pressing her hard. "Let us drop this hateful subject," she said, "I cannot bear to think upon it."

"But we must force ourselves to think about it, — calmly and dispassionately. And having determined which is the path of duty we must follow it out without any reference to our own likes or dislikes. Our marriage would have been a most imprudent one, had it been contracted on any other terms, and we are both to blame that we have loitered away so many months of valuable time in indolent ease, when we should have been earning independence for ourselves and our family."

"You may be right, John. But it is not such an easy matter to leave your country and home, and the dear friends whose society renders life endurable, a certain good, for an uncertain better, to be sought for among untried difficulties. I would rather live in a cottage in England upon a crust of bread a day, than occupy a palace on the other side of the Atlantic."

"This sounds very prettily in poetry, Rachel. But, alas, for us, life is made up of stern realities, which press upon the mind and brain too forcibly to be neglected. I have thought long and painfully upon this subject, and I have come to the determination to emigrate this Spring."

"So soon!"

"The sooner the better. The longer we defer it, the more difficulties we shall have to encounter. The legacy left us by your Aunt will pay our expenses out and enable us to purchase a farm in Canada, a more propitious time could not be chosen, the only obstacle in the way is your reluctance to leave your friends. Am I less dear to you, Rachel, than friends and country?"

"Oh! no, no. You are more to me than all the world. I will try and reconcile myself to the change."

"Shall I go first, and leave you with your mother until I have arranged matters in Canada?"

"Such a separation would be worse than death. Yes, I will go, since it must be." Here followed a heavy sigh, the husband kissed the tears from her eyes, and whispered, that she was his dear good girl, and poor Rachel would have followed him to the deserts of Arabia.

Rachel remained for a long time in deep thought, after the door had closed upon her husband. She could now recal every word of that eventful conversation upon the subject of emigration which they had held together before their marriage, and, in the blessed prospect of becoming his wife, it had not then appeared to her so terrible. Faithfully had he reminded her of the evils she must encounter in uniting her destiny to a poor man; and he had pointed out emigration as the only remedy to counteract the imprudence of such a step, and Rachel, full of love and faith, was not hard to be persuaded. She considered, that to be his wife, endowed as he was by nature with so many moral and intellectual qualities, would make her the richest woman in the world. That there was in him a mine of mental wealth, which could never decrease, but which time and experience would augment, and come what might, she, in the end, was sure to be the gainer. For, she argued, did I marry a man, whom I could not love, merely for his wealth, and the position he held in society, misfortune might deprive me of these, and nothing but a disagreeable companion for life would remain. We think Rachel, after all, reasoned rightly, though the world would scarcely agree with us. But in matters of the heart, the world is seldom consulted.

After the marriage, our young friends retired to a pretty cottage upon the coast, and for upwards of a year they had been so happy, so much in love with each other and so contented with their humble lot, that all thoughts upon the dreaded subject of emigration had been banished.

Rachel knew her husband too well, to suspect him of changing his resolution. She felt that he was in the right, and painful as the struggle was, to part from all her dear friends, it was already made. Opening her writing desk, she took from its most sacred nook a copy of verses written by her husband a few days before their marriage, which but too faithfully coincided with his remarks that morning.

Oh can you leave your native land,
  An exile's bride to be?
Your mother's home and cheerful hearth,
  To tempt the main with me,
Across the wide and stormy sea,
  To trace our foaming track:
And know the wave that heaves us on,
  Will never bear us back.

And can you in Canadian woods
With me the harvest bind;
Nor feel one lingering fond regret
For all you leave behind?
Can those dear hands, unused to toil,
The woodman's wants supply;
Nor shrink beneath the chilly blast,
When wintry storms are nigh.

Amid the shade of forests dark,
Thy loved Isle will appear,
An Eden whose delicious bloom,
Will make the wild more drear;
And you in solitude may weep,
O'er scenes beloved in vain;
And pine away your soul to view, —
Once more your native plain.

Then pause, my girl — e're those dear lips
Your wanderer's fate decide;
My spirit spurns the selfish wish —
You must not be my bride! —
But oh, that smile — those tearful eyes,
My former purpose move;
Our hearts are one, and we will dare
All perils, thus to love! —

"Yes, I can and will dare them, dearest husband," said Rachel, carefully replacing the paper. "I am ready to follow wherever you lead, — England! my country! the worst trial will be to part from thee!"

The Old Captain

Rachel's reveries, were abruptly dispelled by a knock at the door, and her "come in;" was answered by a tall, portly, handsome, old lady, who sailed into the room, in all the conscious dignity of rich black silk, and stiff white lawn.

The handsome old lady, was Mrs. Kitson, the wife of the naval officer, whose ready furnished lodgings they had occupied for the last year. Rachel thrust aside her desk, and rose to meet her visitor. "Pray take the easy chair by the fire; Mrs. Kitson, I am happy to see you, I hope your cough is better?" "No chance of that," said the healthy old lady who had never known a fit of dangerous sickness in her life, "while I continue so weak, Hu, hu, hu, you see my dear, that it is as bad as ever." Rachel thought, that she never had seen an old lady, at her advanced stage of life, look so well. But every one has some pet weakness, and Mrs. Kitson's, was that of always fancying herself ever ill. Now Rachel had no very benignant feeling towards the old lady's long catalogue of imaginary ailments, so changed the subject by enquiring very affectionately after the health of the old Captain.

"Ah, my dear, he is just as well as ever. Nothing in the world ever ails him, and little he cares for the suffering of another. This is a great day with him. He is all bustle and fuss, just step to the window, and look at his doings. It is enough to drive one mad. Talk of women wearing the smalls, indeed. It is a libel on the sex! Captain Kitson, is not content with putting on my apron, but he appropriates my petticoats also. I cannot give an order to my maid, but he contradicts it, or buy a pound of tea, but he weighs it after the grocer; now my dear what would you do if the Lieutenant was like my husband?"

"Really I dont know," and Rachel laughed heartily; "It must be rather a trial of patience to a good housekeeper like you. But what is he about. He and old Kelly seem up to their eyes in business. What an assemblage of pots and kettles and household stuff there is upon the lawn. Are you going to have an auction?"

"You may well think so. But were that the case there might be some excuse for his folly. No. All this dirt and confusion, which once a week drives me out of the house, is what Kitson calls clearing up the ship, when he and his man Friday, (as he calls Kelly) turn every thing topsy turvy, and to make the muddle more complete they always choose my washing day for their frolic. Pantries and cellars are rummaged over, and every thing is dragged out of its place for the mere pleasure of making a litter and dragging it in again. The lawn covered with broken dishes, earless jugs, cracked plates and bottomless saucepans, to the great amusement of my neighbors, who enjoy a hearty laugh at my expense when they behold the poverty of the land. But what does Kitson care for my distress. In vain I hide up all the broken crocks in the darkest nooks of the cellar and pantry, nothing escapes his prying eyes. And then, he has such a memory that if he misses an old gallipot, he raises a storm loud enough to shake down the house.

"The last time he was in London, I collected a great quantity of useless trash and had it thrown into the pond in the garden. Well, when he cleared the decks next time, if he did not miss the old broken trumpery. All of which he said, he meant to mend with white lead on rainy days, while the broken bottles, forsooth, he had saved to put on the top of the brick wall, to hinder the little boys from climbing over to steal the apples. Oh, dear, dear, there was no end to his bawling and swearing and calling me hard names, while he had the impudence to tell Kelly, in my hearing, that I was the most extravagant woman in the world. Now, I, that have borne him seventeen children should know something about economy and good management, but he gives me no credit for that.

"He began scolding again to day, but my poor head could not stand it any longer, so I came over to spend a few minutes with you."

The handsome old lady paused to draw breath, and looked so much excited at this recapitulation of her domestic wrongs, that Rachel thought it not improbable that she had performed her part in the scolding.

As to Rachel, she was highly amused by the old Captain's vagaries, "By the by," she said, "Had he any luck in shooting this morning? He was out at sun-rise with his gun."

The old lady fell back in her chair and laughed immoderately.

"Shooting! Yes! yes, that was another frolic of his. But Kitson is an old fool and I have told him so a thousand times. So you saw him this morning with the gun?"

"Why I was afraid that he would shoot my husband, who was shaving at the window. The Captain pointed his gun sometimes at the window and sometimes at the eaves of the house, but as the gun always missed fire, I began to regain my courage and so did the sparrows, for they only chattered at him in defiance."

"As well they ought, for he had no powder in his gun. Now Mrs. M —— you will scarcely believe what I am going to tell you. But you know the man. When my poor Betsy died, she left all her little effects to her father, as she was not acquainted with any of her late husband's relations. In her dressing case, he found a box of charcoal for cleaning teeth, and in spite of all I could say or do, he would insist it was gunpowder.

"Gunpowder! says I, what should our Betsy do with gunpowder. It's charcoal, I tell you."

"Then he smelt it and smelt it; "'Tis gunpowder, dont you think I know the smell of gunpowder. I, that was with Nelson at Copenhagen and Trafalgar!'

"'Tis the snuff in your nose, makes every thing smell alike, says I, do you think Betsy would clean her beautiful white teeth with gunpowder.

"'Why not,' says he, 'there's charcoal in gunpowder, and now, madam if you contradict me again, I will shoot you with it, to prove the truth of what I say.'

"Well, I saw that there was no help for it, so I e'en let him have his own way, and he spent an hour last night in cleaning his old rusty gun, and rose this morning by day-break with the intention of murdering all the sparrows. No wonder that the sparrows laughed at him. I have done nothing but laugh ever since, so out of sheer revenge he proclaimed a cleaning day, and he and Kelly are now hard at it."

Rachel was delighted with this anecdote of their whimsical landlord, but before she could answer his indignant partner, the door was suddenly opened, and the sharp keen face of the little officer was thrust into the room.

"Mrs. M —— my dear, that nurse of yours is going to

hang out your clothes in front of the sea. Now it is hardly decent of her, to expose your garments to every boat that may be passing."

The Captain's delicacy threw Rachel almost into convulsions.

"Besides" he continued pettishly, "she knows no more how to handle a rope than a pig. If you will just tell her to wait a bit until I have overhauled my vessel, I will put up the ropes for you myself."

"And hang out the clothes for you, Mrs. M —— if you will only give him the treat. Besides he will not shock the sailors by hanging them near the sea," sneered the handsome old lady.

"I hate to see things done in a lubberly manner."

"Now pray oblige him, Mrs. M —— he is such an old woman I wonder he does not ask you to let him wash the clothes."

"Fresh water is not my element, Mrs. Kitson, I never suffer a woman to touch my ropes. Attend to your business, and leave me to mine, and put a stopper upon that clapper of yours, which goes at the rate of ten knots an hour, or look out for squalls."

In the hope of averting the storm which Rachel saw was gathering upon the old lady's brow, she assured the Captain that he might take the command of her nurse, ropes, clothes, and all.

"You are a sensible woman, my dear, which is more than I can say of some folks," glancing at his wife, "and I hope that you mean to submit patiently to the yoke of matrimony, and not pull one way, while your husband pulls another. To sail well together on the sea of life, you must hold fast to the right end of the rope and haul in the same direction." His hand was upon the back of the door, and the old lady had made herself sure of his exit, when he suddenly returned to the sofa, upon which Rachel was seated, and putting his mouth quite close to her ear, while his little inquisitive eyes sparkled with intense curiosity, said in a mysterious whisper: "How is this, my dear, I hear that you are going to leave us!"

Rachel started. Not a word had transpired of the conversation she had lately held with her husband. Did the old Captain possess the gift of second sight? "Captain Kitson!" she said in rather an excited tone, "who could have told you so?"

"Then it is true!" and the old fox nodded his head at the success of his stratagem; "Who told me — why I cannot exactly say who told me. But, you know where there are servants living in the house, and walls are thin — news travels fast."

"And when people have sharp ears, to listen to what is passing in their neighbors' houses," muttered the old lady in a provoking aside.

Rachel was amazed beyond measure at the impertinent curiosity of the old man. Her husband had only mentioned the subject to her, that morning; and she felt certain that their conversation must have been over-heard. Captain Kitson and his help-mate were notable gossips, and it was mortifying to know that their secret plans, in a few hours, would be made public. She replied coldly: "Captain Kitson you have been misinformed."

"Now my dear, that wont do. Leave an old sailor to find out a rat. I tell you, that it is the common report of the day. Besides, is not the *Leaftenant* gone this morning with that scapegrace Tom Wilson, to hear some lying land-shark preach about Canada."

"Lecture, Kitson," said the old lady, who was not a whit behind her spouse in wishing to extract the news, though she suffered him to be the active agent in the matter.

"Lecture or preach, it's all one. Only the parson takes a text out of the Bible to hold forth upon, and these pick-pockets say what they can out of their own heads. The object in both is to make money. I thought the Leaftenant was too sensible to be caught by chaff."

"My husband is of age to judge for himself," said Rachel coloring; "He does not need the advice of a third person."

"To be sure. To be sure," said the crafty old man without taking the least notice of her displeasure; "But what is Canada to you my dear. A fine settler's wife you will make, nervous, and delicate. Half the time confined to your bed with some complaint or another, and then, when you are well, the whole blessed day is wasted in reading and writing and coddling up the baby. I tell you that this sort of business will not do in a new country like Canada. I was there, often enough, during the American war, and I know that the country will neither suit you, nor you the country." Finding that Rachel returned no answer to this burst of eloquence, he continued in a coaxing tone; "Now just once in your life be guided by wiser and older heads than your own, and give up this foolish project altogether. Let well alone. You are happy and comfortable where you are. This is a nice house, quite big enough for your small family. Fine view of the sea from these windows, and all ready furnished to your hand. Nothing to find of your own but plate and linen. A pump, wood-house and coal-bin, all under one roof. An oven," —

"Stop," said the old lady; "You need say nothing about that, Kitson. The oven is good for nothing. It has no draft, and you cannot put a fire into it without filling the house with smoke."

"Pshaw!" muttered the old man; "A little contrivance would soon put that to rights."

"I tried my best," retorted the wife, "and I could never bake a loaf of bread fit to eat."

"We all know what bad bread you make, Mrs. Kitson," said the Captain; "But I know that it can be baked in it — so hold your tongue, madam, and don't contradict me again. At any rate there is not a smoky chimney in the house, which is complete from the cellar to the garret. And then the rent. Why what is it — a mere trifle — too cheap by one half. Only twenty five pounds per annum, what can you wish for more. And then, the privilege which you enjoy in my beautiful flower garden and lawn, there is not every lodging house which can offer such advantages, and all for the paltry sum of twenty five pounds a year."

"The cottage is pretty, and the rent moderate," said Rachel, "we have no fault to find, and you have not found us very difficult to please."

"Oh, I am quite contented with my tenants, I only want them to know when they are well off. Look twice, before you leap once, that's my manner; and give up this mad Canadian project, which I am certain will end in disappointment." And with this piece of disinterested advice, away toddled the gallant naval commander to finish the arrangement of his pots and kettles, and to superintend the hanging out of Rachel's clothes.

Do not imagine, gentle reader, that the picture is over charged. Captain Kitson, is no creature of romance; or was, we should rather say, for he has, long since, been gathered to his fathers; but a brave uneducated man, who during the war had risen from before the mast to the rank of Post Captain. He had fought at Copenhagen and Trafalgar, and distinguished himself in many a severe contest on the main, and bore the reputation of a dashing naval officer. At the advanced age of eighty, he retained all his original ignorance and vulgarity, and was never admitted into the society which his rank in the service entitled him to claim.

The restless activity which, in the vigor of manhood, had rendered him a useful and enterprising seaman, was now displayed in the most ridiculous interference in his own domestic affairs, and those of his neighbors. With a great deal of low cunning, he mingled the most insatiable curiosity, while his habits were so penurious, that he would stoop to any meanness to gain a trifling pecuniary advantage for his family.

He speculated largely in old ropes, condemned boats, and sea-tackles of all descriptions, while, as consul for the port, he had many opportunities of purchasing the wreck of the sea, and the damaged cargoes of foreign vessels at a cheap rate, and not a stone was left unturned by old Kitson, if, by the turning of it, a copper could be secured.

The meddling disposition of the Captain, rendered him the terror of all the fishermen on the coast, over whom he maintained a despotic sway, superintending and ordering their proceedings with an authority, as absolute as though he were still upon the deck of his own war ship. Not a boat could be put off, or a flag hoisted without he was consulted. Not a funeral could take place in the town without his calling upon the bereaved and offering his services upon the mournful occasion, securing to himself by this simple manoeuvre, an abundant supply of black silk cravats and kid gloves.

"Never lose any thing, my dear, for the want of asking," he would say; "A refusal breaks no bones and there is always a chance of getting what you ask for."

Acting upon this principle, he had begged favors of all the great men in power, and had solicited the interest of every influential person who had visited the town, during the bathing season, for the last twenty years. His favorite maxim, practically carried out in his instance, had been very successful, for by it, he had obtained commissions for all his sons, and had got all his grandsons comfortably placed in the Greenwich, or Christ Church Schools.

He had a garden too, which was at once his torment and his pride. During the Spring and Summer months, the beds were dug up and remodelled, three or four times during the season to suit the caprice of the owner, while the poor drooping flowers were ranged along the grass plot to wither in the sun during the process. This he called putting his borders into ship shape.

The flower beds that skirted the lawn, a pretty grass plot containing about an acre of ground, and surrounded by poplar trees, were regularly sown with a succession of annuals all for the time of one sort and color.

For several weeks, innumerable quantities of double crimson stocks flaunted before your eyes, so densely packed that scarcely a shade of green relieved the brilliant monotony. These were succeeded by larkspurs of all colors, and lastly by poppies which reared their tall gorgeous heads above the low white paling, and looked defiance on all beholders. Year after year presented the same spectacle, and pounds of stock, larkspur and poppy seed, were saved annually by the old man to renew the floral show. Tom Wilson, who was highly delighted by the Captain's oddities, had nick-named the Marine Cottage, *Larkspur Lodge*.

The Doctor's Wife

The news of the Lieutenant's projected emigration, soon spread through the village, and for several days formed the theme of conversation among friends and acquaintances. The timid blamed, the harsh criticized, and the wise applauded. The worldly sneered and made it a subject of ridicule, and prophesied his early repentance and quick return. John M —— listened to all their remarks, combatted vigorously their objections, and finally determined to abide by the conclusion that he had formed; — that he was in the right.

Rachel, who, like most women, was more guided by her feeling than her reason, was terribly annoyed by the impertinent interference of others, in what she peculiarly considered her own affairs; but day after day, she was tormented by visitors, who came to condole with her on the shocking prospect before her. Some of these were kind, well-meaning people, who really thought it a dreadful thing to be forced, at the caprice of a husband, to leave home and all its kindred joys. To these, Rachel listened with patience, for she believed that their fears were genuine, and their sympathy sincere.

There was only one person in the whole town, whose comments she dreaded, and whose pretended concern, she looked upon as a real bore. This person was Mrs. Saunders, the wife of the second best surgeon in the town.

The dreaded interview came at last. Mrs. Saunders had been absent in the country, the moment she heard the news, she rushed to the rescue of her friend. And here I must explain what sort of friendship it was, that existed between Henrietta Saunders and Rachel M —— , and why the latter had such a repugnance to the visit.

Mrs. Saunders was a woman of great pretensions, and had acquired a sort of influence in the society of which she formed a part, by assuming a superiority to which, in reality, she had not the slightest claim.

She considered herself a beauty, a wit, a person of great literary taste, and extraordinary genius. She talked of her person, her paintings, her music, her poetry, for by these names she designated a handsome, but masculine face and figure, a few wretched daubs, some miserable attempts at rhyme, and the performance of a few airs upon the piano. She claimed so much, and her temper was so fierce and vindictive, that her acquaintance, for friends she had none, in order to live in peace with her, yielded to her all, and many good credulous people, really believed that she was the talented person that she pretended to be.

A person of very moderate abilities can be spiteful, and Mrs. Saunders was so censorious, and said such bitter things, that her neighbors tolerated her impertinence, out of a weak fear, lest they should become the victims of her malicious tongue.

Though occupying the same house with her husband, whose third wife she was, they had long been separated, only meeting in public and at their joyless meals. Three children had been the fruits of this ill-starred union — two girls and one strange uncouth looking boy, who, really clever, was hated and ill-treated by his mother, for the great likeness which he bore to the despised and neglected father.

Rachel had no feeling in common with Mrs. Saunders, she neither courted her good opinion, nor wished for her society. To say that she hated her, would be too strong a term; but there had always existed a secret antipathy, a certain antagonism between them, unobserved by careless acquaintances, but well understood by the parties concerned.

Her loud, harsh voice, her ungentle, unfeminine manners, her assumption of learning and superiority without any real pretensions to either, was very offensive to a proud, sensitive mind, that could not brook the patronage of such a woman. Rachel had too much self respect, not to say vanity, to tolerate for a moment the insolence of a Mrs. Saunders. She treated her advances to friendship with a marked coldness, which, instead of repelling, only seemed to provoke a repetition of the vulgar, forcing familiarity from which she intuitively shrunk. The dislike was mutual — but Mrs. Saunders would not be affronted. Rachel belonged to an old and highly respectable family — Mrs. Saunders was a tin-smith's daughter, and she wished people to forget her acquaintance with pots and kettles, and she constantly boasted of her intimacy with her dear friend, Mrs. M —— .

"She is a young person of some literary note," she would say, "who deserves to be encouraged. Her verses are really, rather pretty, and with the advice and assistance of some friend, well versed in these matters, (herself, of course,) she may one day make a tolerable writer."

M —— was highly amused by the league offensive and defensive, which was carried on between his wife and Mrs. Saunders, who was the only real blue stocking in the place, and he was wont to call her, Rachel's *Mrs. Grundy*.

Mrs. Saunders was really glad that her dear friends, at the Marine Cottage, were going, but as she always spoke in direct opposition to her real sentiments, she feigned the most intense astonishment and grief.

"Mrs. M —— ," she exclaimed, the moment she sank into a chair, lifting up her hands and eyes: "Is it true? True that you are going to leave us? I cannot believe it! Tell me that I am misinformed! That it is one of old Kitson's idle gossip. For really I have not felt well since I heard it. What a blow to your mother? What a shock to the whole family? What a loss to society — to the world? What a dreadful sacrifice of yourself?"

Mrs. Saunders paused for breath, and applied a snowy cambric handkerchief to the glassy eyes, over whose hard surface no tears had stolen for years.

Rachel remained silent and embarrassed. She knew not what to say. She felt no confidence in Mrs. Saunders. She disbelieved her affectation of woe, until the weeping lady again gasped forth:

"Do not leave me in suspense, I beseech you. Tell me if you are really going to Canada?"

"Is that all, Mrs. Saunders? I could not imagine the cause of your distress."

"All! Is it not enough to agonize your friend? It is impossible that you can regard such a dreadful event with such stoical indifference! No, no, I see through it. It is only assumed to hide an aching heart. I pity you, my dear friend. I sympathize with you from my very heart. I know what your feelings are. I can realize it all."

"It is of no use lamenting over what is irremediable. Emigration is a matter of necessity, not choice. Did we consult our own feelings, Mrs. Saunders, we should certainly prefer staying at home."

"Your husband is mad, to draw you away from all your friends at a moment's warning. I would remonstrate. I would not go. I would exert a proper spirit, and make him abandon this idiotic scheme."

"Mrs. Saunders, you speak too warmly. Why should I endeavor to prevent an undertaking, which Mr. M —— considers, would greatly benefit his family?"

"Nonsense! I hate — I repudiate such passive obedience, as beneath the dignity of woman. I am none of your bread and butter wives, who consider it their duty to become the mere echo of their husbands. If I did not wish to go, no tyrannical lord of the creation, falsely so called, should compel me to act against my inclinations."

"No compulsion is necessary, when both parties are agreed."

"Oh, yes, I see how it is," with a contemptuous curl of the lip; "You are determined to bear Mr. M —— out, like a good dutiful wife, who aspires to become an example of enduring patience, to all the refractory conjugals in the place. Myself among the rest. I understand it all. How amiable some people can make themselves at the expense of others."

"Indeed Mrs. Saunders, I meant no reflections upon you. I never talk *at* any one."

"Certainly not. You are not aware I suppose," with a strong sneer, "that differences exist between Mr. Saunders and me, and will continue to exist, as long as mind claims a superiority over matter, that we are only husband and wife in name. But I forgive you."

"You have nothing to forgive," said Rachel, indignantly; "Nor do I ever trouble my head with what does not concern me."

"Oh, no! You are too selfishly engrossed with your own happiness, to have any sympathy for the sorrows of a friend. Ah! well, it is early days with you yet. Let a few short years of domestic care pass over your head; and all this honey will be changed to gall. Matrimony, is matrimony, husbands are husbands, and wives will strive to have their own way, and will fight to get it, too. You will *then* find, however, little of the sugar of love remains to sweeten your cup, and in the bitterness of your soul, you will think of me."

"This must be a false picture," said Rachel; "Or who would marry?"

"It is true in my case."

"But there are exceptions to all rules."

"Humph!" responded Mrs. Saunders: "This is another compliment at my expense."

"My dear Madam, I do not wish to quarrel with you; but you seem determined to take all my words amiss."

A long silence ensued. Mrs. Saunders smoothed down her ruffled plumes, and said in a pitying, patronizing tone:

"You will be disgusted with Canada. We shall see you back in twelve months."

"Not very likely. That is, if I know anything of John and myself."

"What will you do for society?"

Rachel thought that solitude would be a luxury, and Mrs. Saunders away.

"You may be twelve miles from the nearest habitation. No church — no schools — no markets — no medical attendant — think on that, Mrs. M —— . And worse, far worse, — no sympathizing friends to condole with you in distress and difficulty."

"These may be evils," said Rachel, losing all patience; "but we shall, at least, be spared the annoyance of disagreeable visitors."

"Oh, Rachel, how could you be so imprudent as to speak your thoughts aloud, and before such a woman as Mrs. Saunders." That lady took the hint and rose indignantly from her chair, and haughtily wishing

Mrs. M —— good morning, swept out of the room.

Rachel was astonished at her own want of caution, but she knew that it was useless to apologize, and she felt perfectly indifferent as to the result. Nor did she care if she never saw Mrs. Saunders again.

"Thank God she's gone!" involuntarily burst from her lips when she found herself once more alone.

It was impossible for Rachel to contemplate leaving England without great pain. The subject was so distressing to her feelings, that she endeavored to forget it as much as possible. When the great struggle came, she hoped to meet it with becoming fortitude, not only for her own, but for her husband's sake. The manner in which it had been forced upon her by Mrs. Saunders, was like probing a deep wound with a jagged instrument, and after that lady's departure, she covered her face with her hands, and wept long and bitterly.

The True Friend

Rachel was aroused from the passionate indulgence of grief by two arms passed softly round her neck and someone pulling back her head and gently kissing her brow, while a sweet, low woman's voice whispered in her ear — "Rachel, dear Rachel, I am come at last — What, no word of welcome — no kiss for Mary — In tears too. What is the matter? Are you ill? — Is the baby well? Do speak to me." This was said so rapidly, that Rachel was in the arms of her friend before she ceased speaking.

"A thousand welcomes, dear girl! You are the very person I wanted to see. The very sight of you is an antidote to grief. When did you come?"

"About an hour ago, by the mail."

"And your dear sister?"

"Is gone to a happier home," said Mary Grey, in a subdued voice and glancing at her black dress. "Ah, dear Rachel, I too have need of sympathy, I have suffered much since we parted. The dear creature died happy, so happy, and now, dear Rachel, she is happier still. But we will not speak of her just now, I cannot bear it. Time, which reconciles us to every change, will teach me resignation to the Divine will! But ah, it is a sore trial to part with the cherished friend and companion of our early years. Our hearts were always one — and now — " There was a pause, both friends wept. Mary first regained her composure.

"How is dear M —— . Has he finished his book? and where is my darling God-child?"

"Both are well. The book is finished and accepted by Bentley."

"Good, but I must scold the author for sending it away before Mary heard the conclusion. But here comes the delinquent to answer for himself."

"Our dear Mary returned?" cried the Lieutenant; "It seems an age since you left us."

"It has been a melancholy separation to me," said Mary; "But this parting I hope will be the last; my father has consented to come and live with my brother, and now that dear Charlotte is gone, I shall have no inducement to leave home. So you will have me all to yourselves, and we shall once more be happy together."

M —— looked at Rachel, but neither spoke. Mary saw in a moment that something was wrong; and she turned anxiously first to the one and then to the other.

"What mischief have you been plotting during my absence?" cried the affectionate girl, taking a hand of each; "Some mystery is here, I read it in your eyes, I come home forgetting my own heavy sorrows in the anticipation of our happy meeting, I find Rachel in tears, and you my dear friend grave and sad."

"Has not Rachel told you?"

"Told me what?"

"That we are about to start for Canada."

"Alas, no. This is sad news to me, worse than I expected."

"Our arrangements are already made."

"Worse and worse."

"Let us draw back," said Rachel, "The trial is too great."

"It is too late now," returned M —— . "All is for the best."

"If it is the work of Providence, far be it from me to persuade you to stay," said Mary: "Our destinies are in the hand of God, who does all things for our good. The present moment is the prophet of the future. It must decide your fate."

"I have not acted hastily in this matter," said M —— . "I have pondered over it long and anxiously and I feel that my decision is right. The grief that Rachel feels at parting with her friends is the greatest drawback. I have passed through the ordeal before, when I left Scotland for the Cape, and when we once lose sight of the English shores, I know my dear girl will submit cheerfully to the change."

"This then was the cause of Rachel's tears?"

"Not exactly," said Rachel laughing, "that odious Mrs. Saunders has been here torturing me with impertinent questions."

"You surely were not annoyed by that stupid woman," said M.

"Worse than that, John, I got into a passion and affronted her."

"And what did Mrs. Grundy say?"

"Ah, it's fine fun to you, but if you had been baited by her for a couple of hours as I was, you could not have stood it better than I did. Why she had the impudence to tell me to set your authority at defiance, if it were at variance with my wishes."

"A very serious offence, Rachel. Instigating my wife to an act of open rebellion. But I am sure you do not mean to profit by her example."

"She is the last person in the world I should wish to imitate; still I am sorry that I let my temper get the better of prudence."

"What a pity you did not fight it out," continued M —— laughing, "I will back you, Rachel, against Mrs. Grundy."

"She would scratch my eyes out, and then scribble a horrid sonnet to celebrate the catastrophe."

"Nobody would read it."

"But she would read it to every body. It is a good thing she went away as she did."

"Let her go, I am tired of Mrs. Grundy. Let us talk about your Canadian scheme," said Mary, "when do you go?"

"In three weeks," said M——.

"So soon. The time is too short to prepare one to part with friends so dear. If it were not for my poor old father, I would go with you."

"What a blessing it would be," said M.

"Oh, do go, dear Mary!" cried Rachel, flinging her arms about her friend. "It would make us so happy."

"It is impossible!" said the dear Mary with a sigh; "my heart goes with you, but duty keeps me here. My father's increasing age and infirmities demand my ceaseless care, and then I have the charge of my brother's orphan children. But I will not waste the time in useless regrets. I can work for you, and cheer you during the last days of your sojourn in your native land. Employment is the best remedy for aching hearts."

His plans once matured, Lieutenant M—— was not long in carrying them into execution. Leaving Rachel and her friend Mary Grey to prepare all the necessaries for their voyage; he hurried to London, to obtain permission from head quarters to settle in Canada as an unattached officer on half-pay, to arrange pecuniary matters and take leave of a few old and tried friends. During his absence Rachel was not idle. The mornings were devoted to making purchases, and the evenings in converting them into articles of domestic use. There were so many towels to hem, sheets to make, handkerchiefs and stockings to mark, that Rachel saw no end to her work, although assisted by kind sisters and the undefatigable Mary. Ignorant of the manners and customs of the colony to which she was about to emigrate, and of which she had formed the most erroneous and laughable notions, many of her purchases were not only useless but ridiculous. Things were overlooked which would have been of the greatest service, while others could have been procured in the colony for less than the expense of transportation.

Twenty years ago, the idea of anything decent being required in a barbarous desert, such as the woods of Canada, was repudiated as nonsense. Settlers were supposed to live twenty or thirty miles apart, in dense forests, and to subsist upon game and the wild fruits of the country. Common sense and reflection would have pointed this out as impossible. But common sense is very rare, and the majority of persons, seldom take the trouble to think. Rachel, who ought to have known better, believed these reports; and fancied that her lot would be cast in one of these remote settlements, where no sounds of human life were to meet her ears, and the ringing of her husband's axe would alone awake the echoes of the forest. She had yet to learn, that the proximity of fellow-laborers in the great work of clearing is indispensable, that man cannot work alone in the wilderness, where his best efforts require the aid of his fellow men.

The oft repeated assertion, that anything would do for Canada, was the cause of more blunders in her choice of an outfit, than the most exaggerated statements in its praise.

Of the fine towns and villages, and the well dressed population of the improved Districts in Upper Canada, she had not formed the slightest conception. To her it was a vast region of cheerless forests, inhabited by unreclaimed savages, and rude settlers doomed to perpetual toil. A climate of stern vicissitudes, alternating between intense heat and freezing cold, which presented at all seasons a gloomy picture. No land of Goshen, no paradise of fruits and flowers, rose in the distance to console her for the sacrifice she was about to make. The ideal was far worse than the reality.

Guided by these false impressions, she made choice of articles of dress too good for domestic occupations, and not fine enough for the rank to which she belonged. In this case extremes would have suited her better than a medium course.

Though fine clothes in the Backwoods are useless lumber; and warm merinos for winter, and washing calicoes for summer, are more to be prized than silks and satins, which a few days exposure to the rough flooring of a log cabin would effectually destroy; yet it is absolutely necessary to have both rich and handsome dresses, when visiting the large towns, where the wealthier classes not only dress well, but expensively.

In a country destitute of an hereditary aristocracy, the appearance which individuals make, and the style in which they live, determines their claims to superiority with the public. The aristocracy of England may be divided into three distinct classes, that of family, of wealth, and of talent. All powerful in their order. The one that ranks the last, however, should be the first, for it originally produced it; and the second, which is far inferior to the last, is likewise able to buy the first. The heads of old families are more tolerant to the great men of genius, than they are to the accumulators of wealth; and a wide distinction is made by them, between the purse-proud millionaire, and the poor man of genius, whose tastes and feelings are more in unison with their own.

In America, the man of money would have it all his own way. His dollars would be irresistible — and much the same might be said of Canada where the dress makes the man. Fine clothes are understood to express the wealth of the possessor; and a lady's gown determines her claims to the title. Theirs is the aristocracy of dress which after all, presents the lowest claims to gentility. A run-away thief may wear a fashionably cut coat, and a well paid domestic flaunt in silks and satins.

Rachel committed a great error in choosing neat but respectable clothing — the handsome, and the very ordinary, would have better answered her purpose. If necessity is the mother of invention, experience is the hand-maid of wisdom, and her garments fit well. Rachel was as yet a novice to the world and its ways; she had much to learn from a stern preceptress, in a cold calculating school.

To bid farewell to her mother and sisters, she regarded as her greatest trial. Mr. Wilde had long been dead, and her mother was in the vale of life. Rachel had fondly hoped to reside near her until the holy ties which united them should be dissolved by death.

Mrs. Wilde was greatly attached to her baby grandchild. The little Kate was the only grandchild she had ever seen, her eldest son who had a young family being separated from her by the Atlantic; and the heart of the old woman clung to her infant relative. To mention the approaching separation threw her into paroxysms of grief.

"Let the dear child stay with me," she said, covering its dimpled hands with kisses: "Let me not lose you both in one day."

"Dearest mother, how can I grant your request. How can I part with my child — my only one. Whatever our fortunes may be, she must share them with us. I could not bear up against the trials that await me, with a divided heart."

"But the advantage it would be to the child?"

"In the loss of both her parents?"

"In her exemption from hardships, and the education she would receive."

"I grant, dear mother, that she would be brought up with care, and would enjoy many advantages that we could not bestow; yet, nature points out that the interests of a child cannot be separated from those of its parents."

"You argue selfishly, Rachel, the child would be much better off with me."

"I speak from my heart, the heart of a mother which cannot, without it belongs to a monster, plead against its child. — I know how you love her, and that she would possess those comforts and luxuries which for her sake we are about to resign; but if we leave her behind, we part with her for ever. She is too young to remember us; and without knowing us, how could she love us?"

"She would be taught to love you."

"Her love would be of a very indefinite character. She would be told that she had a father and a mother in a distant land; and you would teach her to mention us daily in her prayers, but where would be the simple faith, the endearing confidence, the holy love, with which a child, brought up beneath the parental roof, regards the authors of its being. The love which falls like dew from heaven upon the weary heart, which forms a balm for every sorrow, a solace for every care. Without its refreshing influence, what would the wealth of the world be to us." Rachel's heart swelled and her eyes filled with tears; the eloquence of an angel at that moment, would have failed in persuading her to part with her child.

As each day brought nearer the hour of separation, the prospect became more intensely painful and fraught with melancholy anticipations, which haunted her even in sleep; she often awoke sick and faint at heart with the tears she had shed in a dream. Often she exclaimed with fervor: "Oh! that this dreadful parting was over." And never did these feelings press more heavily than when all was done in the way of preparation, when her trunks were all packed, her little bills in the town all paid, her faithful domestic discharged, and nothing remained of active employment to divert her mind from praying upon the sad prospect before her, and she only awaited the return of her husband to make those final adieus which in anticipation overwhelmed her with grief.

"Come and spend the last week with us, dear Rachel," said her sister Caroline, as she kissed her anxious brow. "You let this parting weigh too heavily upon your heart. We shall all meet again."

"I hope in heaven."

"Yes, and there too — but here on earth."

"Oh, no. It is useless to let hope deceive us. No, never again on earth."

"We shall see, Rachel, who is the true prophet, I always hope for the best, and find it true wisdom. But put on your bonnet and come with me to R —— . Mamma expects you to spend this last sad week with her. We will roam together once more through the gardens, the lanes, the meadows and the beautiful wood paths which made you a poet, and which you love so well."

"I cannot go. I shall never be able to turn myself away. The sight of these dear old haunts would only add a bitterness to grief."

"It will do you good to weep. These beautiful moonlight nights will refresh your wearied spirit after so many harrassing thoughts, and so much toil. Your favorite hawthorn tree is in blossom, and the nightingale sings every evening in the beautiful wood lane. In spite of yourself, Rachel you could not feel miserable among such sights and sounds, in the glorious month of May."

"It will make my heart ache half over the Atlantic."

"You deceive yourself. Your greatest happiness will be the recollection of such scenes in a savage land."

"Well, I will go to please you. But for myself — " the remainder of the sentence was lost in a sigh; and the sisters in silence took the oft trodden path that led them to the home of their infancy.

R —— Hall, was an old fashioned house, large, rambling, picturesque and cold. The rude stone figures which formed a kind of finish to the high pointed gable told it to have been built in the first year of the reign of the good queen Bess. The back part of the mansion appeared to have belonged to a period still more remote. The building was embosomed in fine old trees, and surrounded with lawn-like meadows adorned with groups of noble oak and beech. It was beneath the shadow of these trees, and reposing upon the velvet-like sward at their feet, that Rachel had first indulged in those delicious reveries, those lovely ideal visions of beauty and perfection, which cover with a tissue of morning beams all the rugged highways of life; and the soul, bowing down with intense adoration to the deified reality of the material world, pours forth its lofty aspirations on the altar of nature in a language unknown to common minds, and the voice which it utters is poetry.

For the first three and twenty years of her life, she had known no other home but this beloved spot. Every noble sentiment of her soul, every fault which threw its baneful shadow on the sunlight of her mind, had been fostered, or grown upon her in these pastoral solitudes. The trees around her, had witnessed a thousand bursts of passionate eloquence, a thousand gushes of bitter heart-humbling tears. Silent bosom friends were those dear old trees, to whom she had revealed all the joys and sorrows, the hopes and fears which she could not confide to the sneering and unsympathizing of her own species. The solemn druidical groves were not more holy to their imaginative and mysterious worshippers than were these old oaks to the weeping Rachel.

The summer wind as it swept their lofty branches seemed to utter a voice of thrilling lamentation, a sad, soul-touching farewell. "Home of my childhood must I visit you no more?" sobbed Rachel. "Are ye to become tomorrow, a vision of the past. When my heart has been bursting with the sorrows of the world, ye ever smiled upon me. Your loving arms were ever held out to welcome me, and I found a solace for all my cares upon your tranquil breast. Oh, that the glory of the spring was not upon the earth, that I had to leave you mid winter's chilling gloom, and not in this lovely blushing month of May.

"To hear the birds singing so sweetly, to see the young lambs frisking through the green meadows, and the fields and hedgerows bright with their first glad flush of blossoms, breaks my heart."

And the poor emigrant sank down upon the green grass, and burying her face among the fragrant daisies, imprinted a passionate kiss upon the sod that was never in time or eternity to form a resting place for her again.

But a beam is in the dark cloud, even for thee, poor Rachel, thou heart-sick lover of nature. Time will reconcile thee to a change which now appears so dreadful. The human flowers destined to spring around thy hut in the wilderness, will gladden thy bosom in the strange land to which thy course now tends, and the image of God in his glorious creation, will smile upon thee as graciously in the woods of Canada, as it now does in thy British Paradise. Yea, the hour shall come, when you shall say with fervor; "Thank God, I am the denizen of a free land. A land of beauty and progression. A land unpolluted by the groans of starving millions. A land that opens her fostering arms to receive and restore to his long lost birthright, the trampled and abused child of man. To bid him stand up a free inheritor of the soil, who so long labored for a scanty pittance of bread, as an ignorant and degraded slave."

When Rachel returned from an extended ramble through all her favorite haunts, she was agreeably surprised to find her husband conversing with her mother in the parlor.

The unexpected sight of the beloved who had returned to cheer her, some days sooner than the one he had named for his arrival, soon dried all regretful tears; and the sorrows of the future were forgotten in the present joy.

M —— had a thousand little incidents and anecdotes to relate of his journey, and his visit to the great metropolis; and Rachel was a delighted and interested listener. He had satisfactorily arranged all his pecuniary matters, and without sacrificing his half pay, was master of about three hundred and fifty pounds sterling, in ready money, which he thought, prudently managed, would enable them to make a tolerably comfortable settlement in Canada, as he would not have to purchase a farm, being entitled to four hundred acres of land.

All things looked well, and promised well and M —— who was naturally of a cheerful, hopeful disposition, was in high spirits. His reliance upon the protecting care of a merciful and superintending Providence was so firm, that he chid his desponding Rachel for her want of faith.

"I must confess that I found it rather a severe trial to part with my good Uncle," said M ——. "The dear old gentleman presented me with his favorite fowling piece, a splendid Manton, that cost him fifty guineas, and he has not forgotten you Rachel. Look at this elegant ruby pen. I was with him when he bought it. It cost him three sovereigns."

"Beautiful!" exclaimed Rachel examining the fine workmanship of the pretty toy, "I know I should love that kind Uncle of yours. But I question whether I shall have much occasion for his splendid gift. Besides, John, did you ever hear of an author whose works were worth reading, ever sporting such a luxury as a ruby pen?"

"My Uncle at least thought you deserved one. But to business, Madam Rachel. I have taken our passage to

Montreal in a fine vessel, that sails from Leith, the latter end of next week. I found that by going from Scotland we could be as well accommodated for half price, and it would give you the opportunity of seeing Edinburgh, and me, the melancholy satisfaction of taking a last look at the land of my birth.

"One of the London steamers will call for us on Thursday morning on her way to Scotland, and I must hire a boat to meet her in the roadstead and put us and our luggage on board. And now that all is settled, and the day named for our departure, promise me Rachel, to keep up your spirits and make yourself as comfortable as you can for my sake dear girl."

Rachel promised to do her best, but Rachel, as my readers must long ago have found out, was no heroine of romance, but a veritable human creature, subject to all the faults and weakness of her sex, and this announcement threw her into a fit of deep musing. Now that all things were prepared for their departure, she knew that the sooner they went the better, both for themselves and for the friends from whom they were forced to part. That delay was now as useless as it was dangerous and unwise; that a short notice to a sad, but inevitable necessity, was better than a long anticipation of grief. Now though all this struck her very forcibly, and ought to have produced a cheerful resignation to the Divine will, she felt both sad, and discontented, and drew her head from her husband's supporting arm and her chair from the family circle, in order to indulge her grief.

M —— roused her from this fit of melancholy, by enquiring, if she had found a woman to accompany her to Canada in the capacity of nurse, during his absence.

"Oh John, you cannot think what numbers applied. But I have not seen one whom I would like to take with me. If you and Mamma will agree to my plan, I would much rather be without."

"What, in your delicate health, and just recovered from a dangerous illness? The thing is impossible," said M —— rather impetuously.

"Oh not at all impossible."

"And who is to nurse the baby, and take care of you?"

"Myself will perform the first office, my dear husband the last."

"Nonsense Rachel!" said Mrs. Wilde. "You cannot do without a woman to attend upon you. M —— will never suffer you to go to sea without. You may be very ill, and unable to attend upon the child; or even to help yourself."

"There will be plenty of women in the steerage, who for a few dollars, would gladly give their assistance."

"You must not trust, Rachel, to such contingencies," said her husband. "Your mother is right, I must insist upon your taking a servant."

"But consider the expense?"

"I will pay that."

"I should like to have my own way in this matter," pouted Rachel, "for I feel that I am in the right."

"And those who love you are wrong, in wishing to spare you fatigue and pain. Is it not so Rachel?"

This silenced Rachel, yet, had her advice been acted upon, our emigrants would have been spared great trouble and inconvenience.

Perhaps of all follies, that of persons taking servants out with them to a colony, is the greatest; and is sure to end in loss and disappointment. If we consider the different position in which domestics are placed in the new and in the old world, we shall cease to wonder at this.

In Britain they are dependent upon the caprice of their employers for bread. They are brought up in the most servile dread and admiration of the higher classes; and feel most keenly their hopeless degradation. They know that if they lose their character for honesty or obedience, they must starve, or go to the work-house, a doom more dreaded by some than transportation or the gallows. To this cause we owe their fidelity and laborious services, more than to any moral perception of the fitness of submission in a situation which they are unable to better. The number of unemployed females in the lower classes at home, makes it more difficult for a girl to obtain a good place; and the very assurance that she will be well lodged and fed, and secure for herself a comfortable home in a respectable family as long as she performs her part well, forms a strong bond of union between her and her employer. For well she knows that if she loses her situation through her own misconduct, it is not an easy matter to get another.

But in Canada, the serving class is a small one. It admits of very little, if of any, competition, for the demand is larger than the means of supply, and the choice as to character and capability very limited indeed. Servants that understand the work of the country, are always hard to be procured, and can at all times command good wages. The dread of starving, or incarceration in the workhouse no longer frightens them into a servile submission. They will only obey your orders as far as they consider them reasonable. Ask a female domestic to blacken your shoes, or clean the knives, or bring in an armful of wood, or a pail of water; and she turns upon you like a lioness, and flatly tells you that she will do no such thing — that it is not woman's work — that you may do it yourself — and that you may get another as soon as you like, for she is sure of twenty good places to-morrow.

And she is right in her assertion. Her insolent rejection of your commands will not stand at all in her way in procuring another situation, and although blacking a lady's shoes is by no means such dirty work as cleaning the pots, or bringing in a pail of water so laborious as scrubbing the floor, she considers it a degradation, and she is now the inhabitant of a free country, and she will not submit to degradation.

When we look upon this as the reaction rising out of their former miserable and slavish state, we cannot so much blame them; but are obliged to own that it is the natural result of a sudden emancipation from their former bondage.

Upon the whole, though less agreeable to the prejudices of old country people, we much prefer the Canadian servants to the English; for if they prove respectful and obedient, it generally springs from a higher moral feeling; that of affection and gratitude.

Servants brought out to the colony in that capacity scarcely put their foot upon the American shore, than they become suddenly possessed by an ultra republican spirit. The chrysalis has burnt its dingy shell, they are no longer caterpillars, but gay butterflies, anxious to bask in the sun-blaze of popular rights. The master before whom they lately bowed in reverence, and whose slightest word was a law, now degenerates into the *man*; and their mistress, the *dear lady*, whom they strove by every attention to please, is the *woman* — while persons in their own rank are addressed as ma'am and sir. How particular they are in enforcing these assumed titles; how persevering in depriving their employers of their title. One would imagine that they not only considered themselves equal to their masters and mistresses, but that ignorance and vulgarity made them vastly their superiors.

It is highly amusing to watch from a distance, these self-made ladies and gentlemen, sporting their borrowed plumes.

True to their human nature, the picture may be humiliating, but it is a faithful representation of the vanity inherent in the heart of man.

It happened unfortunately for Rachel, that her mother had in her employment, a girl whose pretty feminine person and easy pliable manners had rendered her a great favorite in the family. Whenever Rachel visited R —— Hall, Hannah had taken charge of the baby, on whom she lavished the most endearing epithets and caresses. This girl had formed an imprudent intimacy with a young farmer in the neighborhood, and was in a situation which made their marriage a matter of necessity. The man, however, who in all probability knew more of the girl's worthlessness than her credulous employers, refused to make her his wife; and Hannah, in an agony of rage and grief, had confided her situation to her kind and benevolent mistress, imploring her not to turn her from her doors, or she would end her misery by self-destruction.

She had no home — no parents to receive or shelter her from the world, and she dared not return to the Aunt, who had previous to her going into service, offered her the shelter of her roof.

Shocked at the girl's melancholy situation, and anxious to save her from utter ruin, Mrs. Wilde proposed to Rachel, taking the forlorn creature with her to Canada. To this proposition the girl joyfully acceded; declaring, that if Mrs. M —— would take pity upon her, and remove her from the scene of her shame, she would ask no wages of her, but serve her and her child upon her knees. Though really sorry for a fellow creature in distress, Rachel for a long time resisted the earnest request of her mother and sisters. There was something about the girl that she did not like; and though much was said in praise of her gentle amiable temper, Rachel could not convince herself, that the being before her was worthy of the sympathy manifested in her behalf. She was reluctant to entail upon herself the trouble and responsibility which must arise from this woman's situation, and the scandal which it might involve. But all her arguments were borne down by her mother's earnest entreaties to save, if possible, a fellow creature from ruin.

The false notions formed by most persons at home, of Canada, made Mrs. Wilde reject as mere bug-bears all Rachel's fears. In a barbarous country so thinly peopled, that settlers seldom resided within a day's drive of each other, what was to be dreaded in the way of scandal. If the girl kept her own secret, who would take the trouble to find it out — children are a blessing in such a wilderness, and Hannah's child brought up in the family, would be no trouble or additional expense, but prove a grateful, attached servant, forming a lasting tie of union between the mother and her benefactors. The mother was an excellent worker, and, until this misfortune happened, a good faithful girl. She was *weak* to be sure, but then — (what a fatal mistake) — the more easily managed; they were certain that she would prove a treasure. And so Rachel was persuaded, and a bond was drawn up by the Lieutenant, that Hannah Turner was to serve his family for five years, at the rate of four dollars per month, after her arrival in Canada, and the expense of her outfit and passage across had been deducted from the period of her servitude.

The girl signed this document with tears of joy, and Rachel was provided with a servant.

Rachel remained with her mother until the day previous to their embarkation, when she bade a sorrowful farewell to home and all her friends — we will not dwell on such partings, they, as the poet has truly described them — "Wring the blood from out young hearts, making the snows of age descend upon the rose-crowned brow of youth."

Sorrowfully Rachel returned to her pretty little cottage, which now presented a scene of bustle and confusion that baffles description.

Every thing was out of place and turned up side down. Corded trunks and packages filled up the passages and doorways, and formed stumbling blocks for kind friends and curious neighbors, that crowded the house. Strange dogs forced their way in after their masters, and fought and yelped in undisturbed pugnacity. The baby cried, and no one was at leisure to pacify her, and a cheerless and uncomfortable spirit filled the once peaceful and happy home.

Old Kitson was in his glory, hurrying here and there, ordering, superintending, and assisting in the general confusion, without in the least degree helping on the work. He had taken upon himself the charge of hiring the boat, which was to convey the emigrants on board the steamer, and he stood chaffering for a couple of hours with the sailors to whom she belonged, to induce them to take a shilling less than the price proposed.

Tired with the altercation, and sorry for the honest tars, M —— took the master of the boat to one side, and told him to yield to the old Captain's terms, and he would make up the difference. The sailor answered with a knowing wink, and appeared reluctantly to consent to old Kitson's wishes.

"There, Mrs. M —— my dear! I told you that those fellows would come to my terms, rather than lose a customer," cried the old man, rubbing his hands together in an ecstasy of delight, "I am the man for making a bargain. The rogues cannot cheat me. The Lieutenant is too soft with those chaps. I'm an old stager, they can't come over me. I have made them take one pound for the use of their craft, instead of one and twenty shillings. Take care of the pence, and the pounds will take care of themselves, I found that out, long before poor Richard set it down in his log."

Then sideling close up to Rachel, and putting his long nose into her face, he whispered in her ear — "Now my dear gall, if there are any old coats or hats that Lieutenant M —— does not think worth picking up; I shall be very glad of them for my George. Mrs. K —— is an excellent hand at transmogrifying old things, and in a large family, such articles are always serviceable."

George was the Captain's youngest son, a poor idiot, who though upwards of thirty, had the appearance of an over-grown boy.

Rachel felt ashamed of the old man's meanness, but was glad of this opportunity of repaying his trifling services in his own way, and that suggested by himself.

The weather for the last three weeks had been unusually fine, but towards the evening of the 30th of May, large masses of clouds began to rise in the north east, and the sea changed its azure hue to a dull livid grey. Old Kitson shook his head prophetically.

"There is a change of weather at hand. You may look out for squalls before six o'clock to-morrow. The wind shifts every minute, and there is an ugly swell rolling in upon the shore."

"I hope it will be fine to-morrow," said Rachel, looking anxiously at the troubled sky. "It may pass off in a thunder shower."

The old man whistled, shut one eye, and looked at the sea with the eye of a connoisseur. "Women know about as much of the weather, as your nurse does of handling a rope. Whew! but there's a gale coming — I'll down to the beach and tell the lads to haul up the boats, and make all snug before it comes." And away toddled the old man, full of the importance of his mission.

An Open Boat at Sea

It was the last night at home. The last social meeting of kindred friends on this side the grave. Rachel tried to be cheerful, but the forced smile upon the tutored lips rendered doubly painful the tears kept back in the swollen eyes, the vain efforts of the sorrowful in heart, to be gay, or to look hopefully upon a parting, which forced open;

> Those flood gates of the soul that sever,
> In passions tide, to part for ever.

Alas! for the warm hearts, the generous friendships, the kindly greetings of dear old England, when would they be hers again. Mother — sisters — friends — all took leave and Rachel was left with her husband alone.

It was the dawn of day, when Rachel started from a broken sleep; aroused to consciousness, by the heavy roaring of the sea, as the huge billows burst with the noise of thunder upon the stony beach. To spring from her bed and draw back the curtain of the window that commanded a full view of the bay was but the work of a moment. Her worst fears were confirmed. Far as the eye could reach, the sea was covered with foam. Not a sail was visible, and a dark, leaden sky, was pouring down torrents of rain —

> High on the groaning shore,
> Upsprang the wreathed spray;
> Tremendous was the roar,
> Of the angry echoing bay —

"What a morning!" she muttered to herself, as she stole again to bed, "It will be impossible to put to sea today."

The sleep which had shunned her eyelids during the greater part of the night, gently stole over her, and wrapped her senses in forgetfulness. Old Kitson, two hours later, thrice threw a pebble against the window, before she again awoke.

"Leeftenant M ——! Leeftenant M ——!" shouted old Kitson in a voice like a speaking trumpet — "wind and tide wait for no man. Up, up, and be doing!"

"Aye! Aye!" responded M —— rubbing his eyes, and going to the window.

"See what a storm the night has been breeding for you;" continued old Kitson. "It blows great guns, and there's rain enough to float Noah's Ark. Waters is here, and wants to see you. He fears that his small craft won't live in a sea like this. So, I fear you must put off your voyage till the steamer takes her next trip."

"That is bad," said M —— hurrying on his clothes, and joining the old sailor on the lawn. "Is there any chance of this clearing up?"

"None. This is paying us off for three weeks fine weather, and may last for several days, at all events till night. The steamer will be rattling down upon us in an hour, with the wind and tide in her favor. Were you once on board, you might snap your fingers at this capful of wind."

"We must make up our minds to lose our places."

"You have taken your places there?"

"Yes, and made a deposit of half the passage money."

"Humph! Now, Leeftenant, that's a thing I never do. I always take my chance! I would rather lose my place in a boat, or a coach, than lose my money. But young fellows like you, never learn wisdom. Experience is all thrown away upon you. But as you can't remedy the evil, we had better step in and get a morsel of breakfast, this raw air makes one hungry. The wind may lull by that time." Shutting one eye he gazed intently at the sky with his other keen orb. "It rains too hard for it to blow long at this rate, and the season of the year is all in your favor. Go in, go in, and get something to eat; and we will settle over your wife's good coffee, what is best to be done." M —— thought with the Captain, that the storm would abate; and he returned to the anxious Rachel, to report the aspect of things without.

"It is a bad omen," said Rachel, as she poured out the coffee.

"The belief in omens has vanished from the earth, Rachel. It is an exploded superstition. Don't provoke me into impatience by talking in such a childish manner," said her husband.

"Women are so fond of prognosticating evil, that I believe they are disappointed if it does not happen as they say."

"Reason may find fault with us," said Rachel, "if she will. But we are all more or less influenced by these mysterious presentiments, and suffer, what to others appears a trifling circumstance, to give a coloring for good or evil to the passing hour."

Rachel's defence of her favorite theory was interrupted by the arrival of two friends, who had come from a distance through the storm to bid her good bye.

The elder, Mr. Hawke, an author of considerable celebrity in his native country, and a most kind, and excellent man, brought with him a young son, a fine lad of thirteen years of age, to place under the Lieutenant's charge.

James Hawke had taken a fancy to settle in Canada, and a friend of the family, who was settled in the Backwoods of that far region had written to his father, that he would take the lad, and teach him the mysteries of the axe, if he could find a person to bring him over. M —— had promised to do this, and the boy who had that day parted with his mother and little brothers and sisters, for the first time, in spite of the elastic spirits of youth, looked sad and dejected.

Allen Ritson, a young quaker gentleman, who had known Rachel for some years, and who felt for her the most sincere esteem, accompanied the Hawkes to see her off. "Friend Rachel," he said, taking her hand and shaking it affectionately, "This is a sad day for those who have known thee long and loved thee well; and a foul day for the commencement of thy long journey. Bad beginnings, they say, make bright endings, so there is hope for thee yet, in the dark cloud."

"Rachel, where are your bad omens now?" said M —— rather triumphantly.

"Either you, or friend Allen, must be wrong."

"Or the proverb I quoted, say rather," returned Allen, "Proverbs are but the wisdom and experience of past ages condensed. But the ancients might err as well as us poor moderns, some of their proverbs, even those of Solomon, involve strange contradictions."

"What a day," said the poet, turning from the window, while his eye fell sadly upon his son. "It is enough to chill the heart."

"When I was a boy at school," said Allen, "I used to think that God sent all the rain upon holidays, on purpose to disappoint us of our sport. I found that most things in life happened contrary to our wishes; and I used to pray devoutly, that all the Saturdays might prove wet days; firmly believing that it would be sure to turn out the reverse."

"According to your theory, Allen, Mrs. M —— must have prayed for a very fine day," said Hawke.

"Do you call this a holyday," returned the Quaker, slily. Poor Mr. Hawke suppressed a sigh, and his eyes again turned to his boy, then hurrying to the window, he mechanically drew his hand across his brow.

Here the old Captain again bustled in, full of importance, rubbing his hands and shaking his dripping fearnaught, with an air of great satisfaction.

"You will not be disappointed, my dear," he said, addressing Rachel; "The wind has fallen off a bit; and though the sea is too rough for the small craft, Palmer, the Captain of the pilot boat, has been with me; and for the consideration of two pounds, forty shillings (a large sum of money by the bye, I will try and beat him down to thirty) he says, that he will launch the great boat, and man her with twelve stout young fellows, and will take you, bag and baggage, safely on board the steamer, though the gale were blowing twice as stiff. You have no more to fear in that fine boat, than you have sitting at your ease in that arm-chair. So make up your mind my dear, for you have no time to lose."

Rachel looked anxiously at her husband and child, and then at the black pouring sky and the raging waters.

"There is no danger, Rachel," said the Lieutenant, "These fine boats can live in almost any sea. But, the rain will make it very uncomfortable for you and the child."

"Oh, I don't mind a little discomfort," said Rachel, "It

is better to bear a ducking than to lose our passage in the Chieftain. There cannot be much to apprehend from the violence of the storm, or twelve men would never risk their lives for the value of forty shillings. Our trunks are all in the boat house. Our servants are discharged, our friends have taken leave. We have no longer a home and I am impatient to commence our voyage."

"You are right Rachel, I will engage the boat immediately," and away bounded the Lieutenant to make the final arrangements, and see all the luggage safely stowed away in the boat.

Captain Kitson, seated himself at the table, and began discussing a beef steak with all the earnestness of a hungry man, from time to time, as his appetite began to slacken, addressing a word of comfort or encouragement to Mrs. M —— , who was wrapping up the baby for her perilous voyage.

"That's right, my dear, take care of the young un, 'tis the most troublesome piece of lumber you have with you. A child and a cat, are two things which never ought to come on board ship. But, take courage, my dear. Be like our brave Nelson, never look behind you after entering upon difficulties. It only makes bad worse and does no manner of good. You will encounter rougher gales than this before you have crossed the Atlantic."

"I hope we shall not have to wait long for the steamer," said Rachel. "I dread this drenching rain, for the dear child, far more than the stormy sea."

"Wait!" said the old man speaking with his mouth quite full. "The steamer will be rattling down in no time. But, Mrs. M —— my dear," hastily pushing from him his empty plate, "I have one word to say to you in private before you go." Rachel followed her leader into the kitchen, wondering what this private communication might be; when the old man shutting the door carefully behind him, said in his usual mysterious whisper: "The old clothes. Do you remember, what I said to you last night?"

Rachel colored, and looked down hesitatingly, as if fearful of wounding his feelings. Simple Rachel, she might have spared herself such apprehensions. The man was without delicacy, and had no feelings to wound.

"There is a bundle of things, Captain Kitson," as she at last faultered out, "in that press, for Mr. George. Coats, trowsers, and other things, I was ashamed to mention such trifles."

"Never mind, never mind, I am past blushing at my time of life; and really, (he always called it *reelly*,) I am much obliged to you, my dear." After a pause in which they both looked supremely foolish, the old man said: "There was a china cup, and two plates (pity to spoil the set,) that your careless maid broke the other day, in the wash-house, did Mrs. Kitson mention them to you, my dear?"

"Yes, Sir, and they are *paid* for," said Rachel, turning from the avaricious old man in deep disgust, "Have you any thing else to communicate?"

"All right," returned the Captain. "Here is your husband looking for you."

"Rachel, we only wait for you," said M——.

"I am ready," said Rachel, and placing the precious babe in her husband's arms, she descended to the beach.

Inspite of the inclemency of the weather, a crowd of old and young had assembled upon the beach, to witness their embarkation; and to bid them farewell.

The hearty "God bless you! — God grant you a prosperous voyage, and as good a home as the one you leave now, on the other side of the Atlantic," burst from the lips of many an honest tar, and brought the tears into Rachel's eyes, as the sailors crowded round the emigrants to shake hands with them before they stepped into the noble boat that lay rocking in the surf.

Rachel did not disdain the pressure of those hard, rough, weatherbeaten hands, that never could have come in contact with her own, under other circumstances — they expressed the warm sympathy felt by a true hearted set of poor men in her present situation, and she was grateful for the interest they took in her welfare.

"My good friends," she said; "I thank you sincerely for your good wishes. I have been brought up among you. I leave you all with regret, and I shall long remember with gratitude and pleasure your affectionate farewell."

"You are not going without one parting word with me!" cried Mary Grey, springing down the steep bank of stones against which thundered the tremendous surf; her hat thrown back upon her shoulders, and her bright auburn curls streaming in the wind.

The agitated, weeping girl, was alternately clasped in the arms of the Lieutenant and his wife.

"We bade you good bye last night, Mary. Why did you expose yourself to weather like this?"

"Don't talk of weather," sobbed Mary; "I only know that we must part. Do you begrudge me the last look. God bless you both!"

Before Rachel could speak another word, she was caught up in the arms of a stout seaman, who carried her through the surf, and safely deposited both the mother and her baby in the boat. M —— followed with Mr. Hawke, and Allen Ritson, who were determined to see them safe on board the steamer. Three cheers rose from the sailors on the beach; the gallant boat dashed through the surf, and was soon bounding over the giant billows.

Rachel resolutely turned her back to the shore.

"I will never," she said "take a last look of the dear home where I have been so happy."

The novelty of her situation soon roused her from the indulgence of useless grief. The parting, which, while far off, had weighed so heavily upon her heart was over. The certainty of her present situation rendered it not only tolerable, but invested it with strange interest. The magnificence of the stormy ocean. The consciousness that they were actually upon their way to a distant clime, and the necessity of exertion braced her mind, and stimulated her to bear with becoming fortitude this great epoch in her life.

The effects of the stormy weather, soon became very apparent among the passengers in the pilot boat. Sickness laid its leaden grasp upon all the fresh-water sailors. Even the Lieutenant, a hardy islander, and used to boats and boating all his life, was unable in this instance to contend with the unrelenting fiend — pale as a sheet, he sat with his head bowed forward upon his clasped hands, and Rachel often lifted the cape of the cloak which partially concealed his rigid features, to convince herself that he was still alive. The anxiety she felt in endeavoring to protect her infant from the pouring rain, perhaps acted as an antidote to this affecting malady; for Rachel, although a weakly creature, and just out of a sick bed, did not suffer from it.

Hannah, the maid, lay stretched at the bottom of the boat, her head supported by the ballast bags, in a state too miserable to describe; while James Hawke, the lad that was to accompany them on their long voyage, had sunk into a state of happy unconsciousness, after having vainly wished for the hundreth time, that he was safe on shore, scampering over the village green with his twelve brothers and sisters; and not tempting the angry main in an open boat, with the windows of heaven discharging waters enough upon his defenceless head to drown him; letting alone the big waves, which every moment burst into the boat, and gave him a salt bath upon a gigantic scale. After an hour's hard pulling, the King William, (for so their boat was called,) cast anchor in the roads, distant about eight miles from the town, and lay to, waiting for the coming up of the steamer.

Hours passed away — the day wore onward, but still the vessel they expected did not appear. The storm which had lulled at noon, toward evening increased to a gale, and signs of uneasiness began to be manifested by the crew of the pilot boat.

"Some accident must have happened to the steamer," remarked Palmer, the Captain of the King William, to Craigie, a fine, handsome young seaman, as he handed him the bucket to bail the water from the boat. "I don't like this. If the wind increases and remains in the present quarter, we may be thankful if we escape with our lives."

"Is there any danger?" demanded Rachel, eagerly, as she clasped her poor cold baby closer to her own wet bosom. The child had been crying piteously for the last hour.

"Yes, Madam," he returned, respectfully; "we have been in considerable danger all day. But do you see, if night comes on, and we do not fall in with the Soho, we shall have to haul up the anchor, and run before the gale; and with all our knowledge of the coast, we may be driven ashore, and the boat swamped in the surf."

Rachel sighed, and wished herself safe at home in her dear snug little parlor, the baby asleep in the cradle, and M—— reading aloud to her, or playing on his flute.

The rain again burst down in torrents; and the dull leaden sky looked as if it contained a second deluge. Rachel shivered with the cold, and bent over the now sleeping child to protect her as much as possible by the exposure of her own person to the drenching rain and spray.

"Ah! this is sad work for woman and children," said the honest tar, drawing a large tarpaulin over the mother and her infant, who, blinded and drenched by the pelting of the pitiless shower, crouched down in the bottom of the boat, in patient endurance of what might befal. The wind blew piercingly cold, and the spray of the huge billows enveloped the small craft in a feathery cloud, effectually concealing from her weary passengers, the black waste of raging waters that thundered around, above and beneath her. The baby again awoke, starving with hunger; and all its mother's efforts to keep it quiet proved unavailing. The gentlemen were as sick and helpless as the infant, and nothing could increase their wretchedness. They had been now ten hours at sea, and not expecting the least detention, or anticipating the non-arrival of the steamer, nothing in the way of provisions or drink had formed any part of their luggage. Those who had escaped the evils of sea-sickness, of which, Rachel was one, were dying with thirst, while the keen air had sharpened their appetites to a ravenous degree of hunger. Inspite of her forlorn situation, Rachel could not help being amused by the lively conversation of the crew, and the gay, careless manner in which they contended with these difficulties.

"Well, I'll be blow'd if I an't hungry!" cried Craigie as he stood up in the boat, with his arms folded, and his nor-wester pulled over his eyes, to ward off the down pouring of the rain. "Nothing would come amiss to me now, in the way of prog. I could digest a bit of the shark that swallowed Jonah, or pick a rib of the old prophet himself without making wry faces."

"I wonder which would prove the tougher morsel of the two?" said Mr. Hawke, raising his languid head from the bench before him, and whose love of fun overcame the deadly pangs of sea sickness.

"If the flesh of the prophet was as hard as his heart," said Craigie, "the fish would prove the tenderer bit of the two."

"A dish of good beef steaks from the Crown Inn, would be worth them both, friend," said Allen Ritson, who, getting the better of the sea-sickness, like Craigie, began to feel the pangs of hunger.

"Keep you the plate, Mister; but give me the grub."

"Ah! how bitter!" groaned James Hawke, raising himself up from the furled sail which had formed his bed, and yielding to the horrible nausea that oppressed him.

"Aye, Aye, my lad," said old Howe, an ancient mariner, on whose tanned face, time and exposure to sun and storm, had traced a thousand hierogliphics, "Nothing's sweet that's so contrary to nature. Among the bitter things of life, there's scarcely a worse than the one that now troubles you. Sick at sea — well on shore. So, there's comfort for you."

"Cold comfort," sighed the boy, as he again fell prostrate upon the wet sail. A huge billow broke over the side of the boat, and deluged him with brine, he did not heed it, having again relapsed into his former insensible state.

Night was fast closing over the storm tossed voyagers. The boat was half full of water which flowed over Rachel's lap as she sat, and she began to feel very apprehensive for the safety of her child. At this critical moment, a large retriever dog that belonged to Captain Palmer, crept into her lap, and she joyfully placed the poor wet baby upon his shaggy back, and the warmth of the animal seemed to revive the cold shivering babe.

Palmer now roused the Lieutenant from his stupor, and suggested the propriety of their return to S ——.

"You see, Sir," he said; "I am willing to wait the arrival of the 'Soho;' but something must have happened her, or she would have been down before this. Under existing circumstances I think it advisable to return."

"By all means," said M ——, and the next minute to the inexpressible joy of Rachel, the anchor was pulled up, and the gallant boat was once more careering over the mighty billows,

Those things of life, and light, and motion,
Spirits of the unfathomed ocean.

Yes, her head was once more turned towards that dear home to which she had bid adieu, in the morning, as she imagined for ever. "England! dear England!" she cried, stretching her arms towards the dusky shore. "The winds and waves forbid our leaving thee! Welcome! welcome once more!"

As they neared the beach, the stormy clouds parted in rifted masses; and the deep blue heavens studded here and there with a paly star, gleamed lovingly down upon them. The rain ceased its pitiless pelting, and the very elements seemed to smile upon their return.

The pilot boat had been reported lost, and the beach was crowded with anxious men and women, to hail its return. The wives and children of her crew pressed forward to greet them with joyful acclamations, and Rachel's depressed spirits rose with the excitement of the scene. "Hold fast the babby, Mrs. M ——, while the boat clears the surf," cried Palmer. "I warrant you, that you'll get a fresh ducking!"

As he spoke, the noble boat cut like an arrow through the line of formidable breakers that thundered on the beach; the foam flew in feathery volumes high above their heads, drenching them with a misty shower, the keel grated upon the shingles, and a strong arm lifted Rachel once more upon her native land. Benumbed and cramped with their long immersion in the salt water, her limbs had lost the power of motion, and Mr. Grey and Captain Kitson, carried her between them up the steps that led from the beach, to the top of the cliffs, and deposited her safely on the sofa in the little parlor of her deserted home. A cheerful fire was blazing in the grate, the fragrant tea was smoking upon the well covered table, and dear and familiar voices, rang in her ears, as sisters and friends, crowded about her to congratulate her upon her safe return and proffer their assistance.

And did not this repay the poor wanderers for all their past sufferings?

"The baby! where is the baby!" cried Rachel, after the first rapturous salutations were over.

The baby was laughing and crowing in the arms of her old nurse; looking as fresh and as rosy, as if nothing had happened to disturb her repose.

"Welcome once more to old England, dear Rachel," said Mary Grey, kissing the cold cheek of her friend. "I said, that we should meet again. I did not, however, think that it would be so soon. Thank God! you are all safe. For many hours it was reported at the look-out house, that the boat was swamped in the gale. You may imagine our distress, the anguish endured by your mother and sisters, and how we all rejoiced at the blessed news that the boat was returning, and that her crew was safe. But come up stairs my Rachel, and change these dripping clothes. There is a fire in your bed-room, and I have dry things all ready for you."

"Don't talk of changing her clothes, Miss Grey," said old Kitson, bursting in. "Undress and put her to bed immediately between hot blankets; and I will make her a good stiff glass of hot brandy and water, to drive the cold out of her; or she may fall into a sickness which no doctor could cure."

"The Captain is right," said M —— who just then entered, accompanied by a group of friends all anxious to congratulate Rachel on her safe return to S ——. "My dear girl go instantly to bed."

"It will be so dull," said Rachel, glancing round the happy group of friendly faces. "I should enjoy myself here so much. Now, John, do not poke me away to bed, and keep all the fun to yourself. The bright cheery fire, and all the good things."

The Lieutenant looked grave, and whispered something in her ear about the baby, and the madness of risking a bad cold, and his wishes were instantly obeyed.

"Ah Mary!" she said, as Miss Grey safely deposited her and the precious baby, between the hot blankets; "It was worth braving a thousand storms to receive such a welcome back. I never knew how much our dear kind friends loved us before."

Whilst sipping the potion prescribed by the old Captain, Nurse came running up stairs, to say that Captain Kitson thought that the Steamer was just rounding the point; and wanted to know, that if it really proved to be her, whether Mrs. M —— would get up and once more trust herself upon the waves to meet her?

"Not if a fortune depended upon it, Nurse. Tell the good Captain, that I had enough of the sea for one day, and mean to spend the night on shore."

But, Rachel, was not put to the trial. The Captain had mistaken the craft, and she was permitted to enjoy the warmth and comfort of a sound sleep, unbroken by the peals of laughter, that from time to time, ascended from the room beneath, where the gentlemen seemed determined to make the night recompense them for the dangers and privations of the day.

A Game at Hide and Seek

The morning brought its own train of troubles; and when do they ever come singly? Upon examination, the Lieutenant found that the salt water had penetrated into all their trunks and cases; and every thing had to be unpacked and hung out to dry. This was dull work, the disappointment and loss attending upon it, rendering it doubly irksome. M —— lost no time in writing to the Steamboat Company informing them of his disastrous attempt to meet the "Soho," and the loss he had incurred by missing the vessel. They stated in reply, that the boat had been wrecked at the mouth of the Thames in the gale, and another vessel would supply her place on the Sunday following. That she would pass the town at noon, and hoist a signal in time for them to get on board.

The intervening days passed heavily along. A restless fever of expectation preyed upon Rachel. She could settle to no regular occupation. She knew that they must go, and she longed to be off. The efforts made by her friends to amuse and divert her mind, only increased her melancholy. But time, however slowly it passes to the expectant, swiftly and surely ushers in the appointed day. The twenty-ninth of May dawned at last and proved one of the loveliest mornings of that delightful season. The lark carolled high in air, the swallows darted on light wings to and fro, and the sea vast and beautiful, gently heaved and undulated against the shore, with scarcely a ripple to break the long line of golden sun-beams, that danced and sparkled on its breast.

The church bells were chiming for morning prayer; and the cliffs were covered with happy groups in their holiday attire. Rachel, surrounded by her friends, strove to look cheerful. All eyes were turned towards the old ruined city of D. in which direction the steamer was first expected to appear. A small boat, which had been engaged to put their baggage on board, lay rocking on the surf, and all was ready for a start.

In the midst of an animated discussion upon their future prospects, the signal was given, that the Steamer was in sight, and had already rounded the point. How audibly to herself did Rachel's heart beat, as a small black speck upon the horizon, gradually increased to a dark cloud of trailing smoke, and not a doubt remained that this was the expected vessel.

Then came the blinding tears, the re-enactment of the last passionate adieu and they were once more afloat upon the water.

But the bitterness of parting was already past. The human heart can scarcely experience for the same event an equal intensity of grief. Repetition had softened the anguish of this second parting, and hope was calmly rising above the clouds of sorrow that had hung for the last weary days so loweringly above our poor emigrants. Mr. Hawke and James, alone accompanied them in their second expedition. Allen Ritson, had had enough of the sea, during their late adventure, and thought it most prudent to make his adieus upon the shore.

James Hawke was in high spirits, anticipating with boyish enthusiasm, the adventures which he thought would befall him, during a long voyage and his sojourn in that distant land, which was to prove to him a very land of Goshen. Thus many gay hopes smiled upon him, which like that bright day, were doomed to have a gloomy ending although at the beginning it promised so fair.

The owner of the boat, a morose old seaman, grumbled out his commands to the two sailors who rowed, in such a dogged sulky tone, that it attracted the attention of Mr. Hawke, and being naturally fond of fun, he endeavored to draw the old man out — but an abrupt monosyllable was all the reply he could obtain to his many questions.

The Lieutenant, who was highly amused by his surly humor, thought that he might prove more successful than his friend, by startling him into conversation.

"Friend," he cried, "I have forgotten your name?"

"Sam Rogers," — was the brief reply, uttered in a sort of short growl.

The ice once broken, Hawke chimed in. "Have you a wife?"

"She's in the church yard," with another growl.

"So much the better for Mrs. Rogers," whispered Hawke to Mrs. M——.

"You had better let the sea bear alone," returned Rachel in the same key. "The animal is sworn to silence."

In a few minutes, the little boat came along side the huge Leviathan of the deep; a rope was thrown from her deck, which having been secured, the following brief dialogue ensued:

"The City of Edinburgh for Edinburgh?"

"The Queen of Scotland for Aberdeen, Captain Fraser."

This announcement was followed by a look of blank astonishment and disappointment from the party in the boat. "Where is the City of Edinburgh?"

"We left her in the river. You had better take a passage to Aberdeen?" said Captain Fraser advancing to the side of the boat.

"Two hundred miles out of my way," said M ——, "fall off." The tow rope was cut loose, and the floating castle resumed her thundering course, leaving the party in the boat not a little disconcerted by the misadventure.

"The city of Edinburgh must soon be here," said M ——, addressing himself once more to the surly owner of the boat. That sociable individual continued smoking a short pipe, without deigning to notice the speaker. "Had we not better lay to and wait for her coming up."

"No, we should be run down by her. Do you see that," and he pointed with the short pipe to a grey cloud that was rolling over the surface of the sea towards them. "It is them sea rake; in three minutes, in less than three minutes, you will not be able to see three yards beyond the boat."

Even while the old man was speaking, the dense fog was rapidly spreading over the water, blotting the sun from the heavens, and enfolding every object in its chilly embrace. The shores faded from their view, the very waters upon which they floated were heard, but no longer seen. Rachel strove in vain to penetrate the thick, white curtain, which covered them like a shroud; her whole world was now confined to the little boat, and the figures it contained; the rest was a blank. The mist wetted like rain, and was more penetrating, and the constant efforts she made to see through it, made her eyes and head ache, and threw a damp upon her spirits, which almost amounted to despondency.

"What's to be done," asked M ——.

"Nothing that I know of," responded Sam Rogers, "but to return."

As he spoke, a dark shadow loomed through the mist which proved a small trading vessel, bound from London to Yarmouth. The sailors hailed her, and with some difficulty, ran the boat along side. "Have you passed the 'City of Edinburgh.'" "We spoke her in the river. She run foul of the Courier Steamer, and unshipped her rudder. She put back for repairs, and won't be down till tomorrow morning."

"Pleasant news for us," sighed Rachel. "This is worse than the storm, and it is so unexpected. I should be quite disheartened if I did not believe that Providence directed these untoward events."

"I am inclined to be of your opinion," said M ——, "in spite of my disbelief in signs and omens, to think that there is something beyond mere accident in this second disappointment."

The sailors, now turned the boat homewards, and took to their oars; the dead calm, precluding the use of the sail. The fog was so dense and bewildering, that they made little way, and the long day was spent in wandering to and fro, without being able to ascertain where they were.

"Hark!" cried one of the men laying his ear to the water. "I hear the flippers of the steamer."

"It is the roar of the accursed Barnet," cried the other; "I know its voice of old, having twice been wrecked upon the reef, we must change our course, we are on a wrong tack altogether."

It was near midnight before a breeze sprang up, and dispelled the ominous fog, the moon showed her wan face through the driving rack, the sail was at last hoisted, and cold, and hungry, and sick at heart, the wanderers once more returned to their old post.

This time, however, the beach was silent and deserted, and no friendly voice welcomed them back. Old Captain Kitson looked cross at being routed out of his bed at one o'clock in the morning, to admit them into their old house, and muttered as he did so, something about unlucky folks, and the deal of trouble they gave. That they had better give up going altogether, and hire their old lodgings again. That it was no joke, having his rest broken at his time of life. That he could not afford to keep open house at all hours for people who were no ways related to him. With such consoling expressions of sympathy in their forlorn condition, did the worldly, hard old man proceed to unlock the door of their former domicile; but food, lights and firing he would not produce until M —— had promised an exorbitant remuneration for the same.

Exhausted in mind and body, for she had not broken her fast since eight o'clock that morning, Rachel for a long time refused to partake of the warm cup of tea, her loving partner provided, while her tears continued to fall involuntary over the sleeping babe that lay upon her lap. Mr. Hawke, who saw that her nerves were quite unstrung with the fatigue and disappointment of the day, ran across the green, and roused up Rachel's nurse, who hurried to take charge of the babe, and assist her once dear mistress. Little Kate was soon well warmed and fed by the good old woman, and Rachel smiled through her tears when the husband made his appearance with a plate of ham which he had extorted from their stingy landlord.

"Come, Rachel," he cried, "you are ill for the want of food, I am going to make some sandwiches for you, and you must be a good girl and eat them, or I will never turn cook for you again."

The sandwiches proved excellent. Mr. Hawke exerted all his powers of drollery to enliven their miscellaneous meal. Rachel got over the hysterical affection, and retired to bed, fully determined to bear the crosses of life with more fortitude for the future.

The sun was not above the horizon when she was roused from a deep sleep, by the stentorian voice of old Kitson, who, anxious to get rid of his troublesome visitors, cried out with great glee: "Hollo! I say, here is the right steamer at last. Better late than never. The red flag is hoisted fore and aft, and she is standing in for the bay. Tell Mrs. M —— to dress as fast as she can. These big dons wait for no one. I have got all your trunks stowed away into the boat, and the lads are waiting. Quick! Quick, Lieutenant M —— or you'll be too late."

With all possible despatch, Rachel dressed herself, though baffled by anxiety from exerting unusual celerity, every button insinuating itself into a wrong hole; and every string tying into a knot. The business of the toilet was at last completed, and she hurried down to the beach. In a few minutes she was seated by her husband's side in the boat, uncheered by any parting blessing, but the cold farewell, and for ever, of old Captain Kitson, who could scarcely conceal the joy he felt at their departure.

The morning was wet and misty, and altogether comfortless, and Rachel was glad when the bustle of getting on board the steamer was over; and they were safe upon her deck.

The Steamer

A variety of groups occupied the deck of the steamer, and early as the hour was, all who were able to leave the close confinement of the cabins were enjoying the fresh air. Some walking to and fro, others leaning over the bulwarks, regarding the aspect of the country they were rapidly passing; or talking in small knots in a loud declamatory tone, intended more for the by-standers than to edify their own immediate listeners. Here, a pretty, insipid looking girl, sauntered the deck with a book in her hand, from which she never read, and another, more vivacious, but equally intent on attracting her share of admiration, raved to an elderly gentleman of the beauty and magnificence of the ocean. The young and good looking of either sex were flirting. The more wily and experienced, coquetting at a distance, while the ugly and the middle-aged were gossiping to some congenial spirit on the supposed merits or demerits of their neighbors. Not a few prostrate forms might be seen reclining upon cloaks and supported by pillows, whose languid, pale faces, and disarranged tresses, showed that the demon of the waters had remorselessly stricken them down.

Rachel's eye ranged from group to group of those strange faces, with a mechanical, uninterested gaze. Among several hundreds who sauntered the spacious deck of the City of Edinburgh, she did not recognize a single friendly face.

Standing near the seat she occupied, a lively fashionably dressed woman, apparently about five and twenty, was laughing and chatting in the most familiar manner with a tall, handsome man of forty, in a military surtout.

The person of the lady was agreeable, but her manners were so singular, that she attracted Rachel's attention.

When she first took her seat upon deck, Mrs. Dalton had left off her flirtations with Major F ——, and regarded the new arrival, with a long, cool, determined stare, then smiling meaningly to her companion, let slip with a slight elevation of the shoulders, the word "*nobody*!"

"He is a gentleman — a fine intelligent looking man," remarked her companion, in an aside, "and I like the appearance of his wife."

"My, dear sir, she has on a *stuff gown*! What lady would come on board these fine vessels, where they meet with so many fashionable people in a *stuff gown*?"

"A very suitable dress, I think, for a sea voyage," responded the Major.

"Pshaw!" muttered Mrs. Dalton, "I tell you, Major, that they are *nobody*!"

"You shall have it your own way. You know how easy it is for you to bring me to the same opinion."

This dialogue drew Rachel's attention to her dress, and she found that in her hurry she had put on a dark merino dress, which in the place of a silk one, had stamped her with the epithet of *nobody*.

Now, Rachel, it must be confessed, was rather annoyed at these remarks; and felt very much the reverse of benevolently, towards the person by whom they were made.

"Do you think that a pretty woman?" she said, directing her husband's eyes to the lady in question.

"Tolerable," said he coldly, "but very sophisticated," and Rachel responded like a true woman — "I am glad to hear you say so. Is that gentleman her husband?"

"No — do husbands and wives seek to attract each other's attention in public, as that man and woman are doing. I have no doubt, that they are strangers who never met before."

"Impossible!"

"Nothing more probable. — People who meet on short journeys, and voyages like this, often throw aside the restraints imposed by society; and act and talk in a manner, which would be severely censured in circles where they were known. Did you never hear persons relate their history in a stage coach?"

"Yes, often — and thought it very odd."

"It is a common occurrence, which I believe originates in vanity, and that love of display, that leads people at all hazards to make themselves the subject of conversation. Trusting to the ignorance of the parties they address, they communicate their most private affairs, without any regard to prudence or decorum. I have been greatly amused by some of these autobiographies."

"Ah, I remember getting into a sad scrape," said Rachel, "while travelling to London from R —— in a mail coach. One of those uncomfortable occurrences, which one hates to think of for the rest of a life. There were three gentlemen in the coach, two of them perfect strangers to me, the other a lawyer of some note, who had me under his charge during the journey; and was an old friend of the family. One of the strange gentlemen talked much upon literary matters; and from his conversation, led you to understand that he was well acquainted, and on intimate terms with all the celebrated authors of the day. After giving us a very frank critique upon the works of Scott and Byron whom he called, my friend, sir Walter; my companion, Lord Byron; — he suddenly turned to me and asked me, what I thought of the Rev. Mr. B ——'s poems.

"This reverend gentleman was a young man of considerable fortune, whose contributions to the county papers were never read but to be laughed at, and I answered very innocently: 'Oh, he is a stupid fellow. It is a pity that he has not some friend to tell him what a fool he makes of himself, whenever he appears in print.' Mr. C —— was stuffing his handkerchief into his mouth to avoid laughing out; while the poor man, for it was the author himself, drew back with an air of offended dignity, alternately red and pale, and regarded me as an ogre prepared to devour, at one mouthful, him and his literary fame. He spoke no more during his journey, and I sat upon thorns, until a handsome plain carriage met us upon the road and delivered us from his presence. This circumstance, made me feel so miserable, that I never ventured upon giving an opinion of the works of another, to a person unknown."

"He deserved what he got," said the Lieutenant. "For my part I do not pity him at all. It afforded you both a good lesson for the future."

At this moment, a young negro lad, fantastically dressed, and evidently very much in love with himself, strutted past. As he swaggered along, rolling his jet black eyes from side to side, and shewing his white teeth to the spectators, by humming some nigger ditty, an indolent looking young man, dressed in the extreme of the fashion, called lazily after him:

"Hollo, Blackey. What color's the Devil?"

"White," responded the imp of darkness, "and wears red whiskers like you."

Every one laughed. The dandy shrunk back confounded, while the negro snapped his fingers and crowed with delight.

"Ceasar! go down into the lady's cabin, and wait there until I call for you," said Mrs. Dalton in an angry voice. "I did not bring you here to insult gentlemen."

"De buckra! affront me first," returned the sable page, as he sullenly withdrew.

"That boy is very pert," continued his mistress, addressing Major F ——, "this is the effect of the stir made by the English people against slavery. The fellow knows that he is free the moment he touches the British shores — I hope that he will not leave me, for he saves me all the trouble of taking care of the children."

The Major laughed, while Rachel pitied the poor children, and wondered how any mother could confide them to the care of such a nurse.

The clouds that had been rising for some time gave very unequivocal notice of an approaching storm. The rain began to fall, and the decks were quickly cleared of their motley groups.

In the lady's cabin, all was helplessness and confusion. The larger portion of the berths were already occupied by invalids in every stage of sea-sickness. The floor and sofas were strewn with bonnets and shawls, and articles of dress were scattered about in all directions. Some of the ladies were stretched upon the carpet — others in a sitting posture were supporting their aching heads upon their knees, and appeared perfectly indifferent to all that was passing around them, and only alive to their own misery. Others there were, who beginning to recover from the effects of the prevailing malady, were employing their returning faculties in quizzing and making remarks half aloud on their prostrate companions particularly, if their dress and manners, were not exactly in accordance with their pre-conceived notions of gentility.

The centre of such a group, was a little, sharp faced, dark eyed, sallow, old maid of forty, whose skinny figure was arrayed in black silk, cut very low in the bust, and exposing a portion of her person, which in all ladies of her age, is better hid. She was travelling companion to a large showily dressed matron of fifty, who occupied the best sofa in the cabin, and who although evidently convalescent, commanded the principal attendance of the stewardess, while she graciously received the gratuitous services of all who were well enough to render her their homage. She was evidently the great lady of the cabin; and round her couch a knot of gossips had collected, when Rachel and her maid entered upon the scene.

The character of Mrs. Dalton formed the topic of conversation. The little old maid, was remorselessly tearing it to tatters. "No woman who valued her reputation," she said, "would flirt in the disgraceful manner, that Mrs. D. was doing."

"There is some excuse for her conduct," remarked an interesting looking woman, not herself in the early spring of youth. "Mrs. Dalton is a West Indian, and has not been brought up with our ideas of refinement and delicacy."

"I consider it none," exclaimed the other, vehemently glancing up as the door opened, at Rachel, to be sure that the object of her censure was absent. "Don't tell me, she knows very well, that she is doing wrong. My dear Mrs. F ——" turning to the great lady, "I wonder that you can bear so calmly her flirtations with the Major. If it was me, now, I should be ready to tear her eyes out. Do speak to Mrs. Dalton, and remonstrate with her, on her scandalous conduct."

"Ah, my dear! I am used to these things. No conduct of Major F's can give me the least uneasiness. Nor do I think, that Mrs. Dalton is aware that she is trying to seduce the affections of a married man."

"That she is, though!" exclaimed the old maid, "I took good care to interrupt one of their lively conversations, by telling Major F. that his wife was very ill. The creature colored and moved away, but the moment my back was turned, she recommenced her attack. If she were a widow, one might make some allowance for her. But a young married woman, with two small children. I have no doubt that she has left her husband for no good."

"I know Mrs. Dalton well," said a third lady. "She is not a native of the West Indies, as you supposed, Miss Leigh, she was born in Edinburgh, but married very young, to a man, nearly double her own age. A match made for her by her friends; especially by her grandmother, who is a person of considerable property. She was always a gay, flighty girl, and her lot I consider peculiarly hard, in being bound while quite a child, to a man she did not love."

"Her conduct is very creditable for a clergyman's wife," chimed in the old maid, "I wonder the rain don't bring her down into the cabin; but the society of ladies would prove very insipid to a person of her taste. I should like to know what brings her from Jamaica?"

"To place her two children with her grandmother, in order that they may receive a European education. She is a thoughtless being, but hardly deserves, Miss Man, your severe censure," said Miss Leigh.

The amiable manner, in which the last speaker tried

to defend the absent, without wholly excusing her levity, interested Rachel greatly in her favor; although Mrs. Dalton's conduct upon deck, had awakened in her own bosom, feelings of disgust and aversion.

"It is not in my power, to do justice to her vanity and frivolity," cried the indignant spinster. "No one ever before accused me of being censorious. But that woman is the vainest woman I ever saw. How she values herself upon her fine clothes. Did you notice Mrs. F. that she changed her dress four times yesterday and twice to day. She knelt a whole hour before the cheval glass arranging her hair; and trying on a variety of different head dresses, before she could fix upon one for the saloon. I should be ashamed to be the only lady among so many men — but she has a face of brass."

"She has, and so plain too" — murmured Mrs. Major F.

"Bless me!" cried the old maid; "if there is not her black imp sitting under the table. He will be sure to tell her all that we have said about her! What a nuisance he is!" she continued in a whisper. "I do not think that it is proper for him, a great boy of sixteen, to be admitted into the ladies' cabin."

"Pshaw! nobody cares for him — A black — "

"But, my dear Mrs. F ——, though he is black, the boy has eyes and ears, like the rest of his sex, and my sense of female propriety is shocked by his presence. But who are these people?" glancing at Rachel and her maid — "and why is that woman admitted into the ladies' cabin — servants have no business here."

"She is the nurse; that alters the case. The plea of being the children's attendant, brought master Ceasar, into the cabin," said Miss Leigh. "The boy is a black, and has on that score neither rank nor sex," continued the waspish Miss Man, contradicting the assertion, she had made only a few minutes before. "I will not submit to this insult, nor occupy the same apartment with a servant."

"My dear Madam, you strangely forget yourself," said the benevolent Miss Leigh. "This lady has a young infant, and cannot do without the aid of her nurse. A decent, tidy young woman, is not quite such a nuisance, as the noisy black boy that Mrs. Dalton has entailed upon us."

"But then — she is a woman of *fashion*," whispered Miss Man; "and we know nothing about these people — and if I were to judge by the young person's dress."

"A very poor criterion," said Miss Leigh; "I draw my inferences from a higher source." Rachel glanced once more at her dress, and a sarcastic smile passed over her face. It did not escape the observation of Miss Leigh, who in a friendly, kind manner enquired, "if she were going to Edinburgh — the age of the baby, and how she was affected by the sea?"

Before Rachel could well answer these questions, Miss Man addressed her, and said in a haughty, supercilious manner: "Perhaps, madam, you are not aware, that it is against the regulations of these vessels, to admit servants into the state cabins?"

"I am sorry, ladies, that the presence of mine, should incommode you," said Rachel; "but I have only just recovered from a dangerous illness and I am unable to attend upon the child myself. I have paid for my servant's attendance upon me here; and I am certain, that she will conduct herself with the greatest propriety."

"How unpleasant," grumbled forth the old maid; "but, what can we expect from underbred people."

"*In stuff gowns*," said Rachel, maliciously. Miss Leigh, smiled approvingly; and the little woman in black retreated behind the couch of the big lady.

"Send away your servant girl," said Miss Leigh, "and I will help you take care of the baby. If I may judge by her pale looks, she will be of little service to you; while her presence gives great offence to certain *little* people."

Rachel immediately complied, and Hannah was dismissed; in a short time, she became so ill, that she was unable to assist herself or attend to the child. Miss Leigh, like a good Samaritan, sat with her during the greater part of the night; but towards morning, Rachel grew so alarmingly worse that she earnestly requested that her husband might be allowed to speak with her.

Her petition was seconded by Miss Leigh.

A decided refusal on the part of the other ladies, was the result of poor Rachel's request.

Mrs. Dalton who had taken a very decided part in the matter, now sprang from her berth, and putting her back against the cabin door, declared that no man, save the surgeon, should gain, with her consent, an entrance there.

"Then pray, madam," said Miss Leigh, who was supporting Rachel in her arms, "adhere to your own regulations, and dismiss your black boy."

"I shall do no such thing. My objections are to men, not to boys. Ceasar, remain where you are."

"How consistent," sneered the old maid.

"The poor lady may die," said Miss Leigh; "how cruel it is of you, to deny her the consolation of speaking to her husband."

"Who is her husband?" said the old maid pettishly.

"A very handsome, gentlemanly man, I assure you," said Mrs. Dalton, "an officer in the army, with whom, I had a long chat upon deck, this evening."

"Very consoling to his sick wife," whispered Miss Man, to Mrs. Major F —— ; loud enough to be overheard by Mrs. Dalton, "it must have made the Major jealous."

"What a noise, that squalling child makes," cried a fat woman, popping her head out of an upper berth; "Can't it be removed. It hinders me from getting a wink of sleep."

"Children are a great nuisance," said the old maid, glancing at Mrs. Dalton, "and the older they are the worse they behave."

"Stewardess! where are you! Stewardess! send that noisy child to the nurse," again called the fat woman from her berth. "The nurse is as ill, as the mistress."

"Oh dear, oh dear, my poor head. Cannot you take charge of it, stewardess?"

"Oh, la, ladies, I've too much upon my hands already; what with Mrs. Dalton's children; and all this sickness."

"I will take care of the babe," said Miss Leigh.

"That will not stop its cries."

"I will do my best," said the benevolent lady, "we are

all strange to it, and it wants its mother."

"Oh, do not let them send away my baby!" cried Rachel recovering from the stupor into which she had fallen. "If it must be expelled, let us go together. If I could but get upon the deck to my husband, we should not meet with the treatment there, that we have received here."

"Don't fatigue yourself. They have no power to send either you or the dear little baby away," said Miss Leigh, "I will nurse you both. See, the pretty darling is already asleep."

She carried the infant to her own berth in an inner cabin, then undressed Rachel and put her to bed.

What a difference there is in women. Some, like ministering angels, strew flowers, and scatter blessings along the rugged paths of life; while others, by their malevolence and pride, increase its sorrows an hundred fold.

The next day continued stormy, and the violence of the gale and the unsteady motion of the vessel, did not tend to improve the health of the occupants of the ladies' cabin. Those who had been well the day before, were now as helpless and miserable as their companions. Miss Leigh alone seemed to retain her usual composure. Mrs. Dalton could scarcely be named in this catalogue, as she only slept and dressed in the cabin; the rest of her time was devoted to her friends upon the deck; and in spite of the boisterous wind and heavy sea, she was as gay and airy as ever.

Her children, the most noisy of their species, were confined to the cabin, where they amused themselves by running races round the table and shouting at the top of their shrill voices; greatly to the annoyance of the sick women. In all their pranks they were encouraged and abetted by Ceasar, who regardless of the entreaties of the invalids, did his best to increase the uproar. Ceasar cared for nobody but his mistress; and his mistress was in the saloon playing billiards with Major F——.

Little James Dalton, had discovered the baby, and Rachel was terrified whenever he approached her berth, which was on a level with the floor; as that young gentleman seemed bent upon mischief. Twice he had crept into her berth on hands and knees, and levelled a blow at the sleeping child, with the leg of a broken chair, which he had found beneath the sofa. The blows had been warded off by Rachel, but not before she had received a severe bruise on her arm. While the ladies slept, Ceasar stole from berth to berth, robbing them of all their stores of oranges and lemons, cayenne lozenges, sharing the spoils with the troublesome, spoilt monkeys left by their careful mamma in his keeping.

Towards evening, Rachel assisted by Miss Leigh, contrived to dress herself and go upon deck. The rain was still falling in large heavy drops; but the sun was struggling to take a farewell glance of the world before he sunk beneath the dense masses of black clouds piled in the west; and cast an uncertain gleam upon the wild scenery, over which Bamborough castle frowns in savage sublimity. That was the last look Rachel gave to the shores of dear old England. The angry storm vexed ocean, the lowering sky and falling rain, were they not emblems of her own sad destiny. Her head sunk upon her husband's shoulder; and as he silently clasped her to his breast, her tears fell fast, and she returned his affectionate greeting with heavy sobs. For his sake, for the sake of his child, whose little form was pressed convulsively to her throbbing heart — she had consented to leave those shores for ever — why did she repine — why did that last look of her native land fill her with such unutterable woe. Visions of the dim future floated before her, prophetic of all the trials and sorrows that awaited her on that unknown region to which they were journeying. She had obeyed the call of duty, but had not yet tasted the reward of well doing. All was still and dark in her bewildered mind.

The kind voice of the beloved, roused her from her gloomy foreboding; the night was raw and cold, the decks wet and slippery from the increasing rain; and with an affectionate pressure of the hand, that almost reconciled her to her lot; he whispered — "This is no place for you, Rachel, return to the Cabin."

With what reluctance Rachel re-entered that splendid apartment. Miss Leigh was the only person among the number by which it was occupied, who possessed a spirit at all in unison with her own. Short as her acquaintance with this lady had been, she regarded her with affection and esteem. It was not till after Miss Leigh had left the vessel, that Rachel discovered, that she was a connexion of her husband's, which would greatly have enhanced the pleasure of this accidental meeting. Had Miss Leigh, or Rachel, been in the habit of recounting their histories to strangers, they would not have met, and parted for ever as such.

The ladies early retired to their berths, and Rachel enjoyed, for several hours, a tranquil and refreshing sleep.

About midnight she awoke. A profound stillness reigned in the cabin; but seated on the ground in front of her berth, she discovered Mrs. Dalton wrapped in a loose dressing gown and engaged in reading a letter. She sighed deeply, as she folded and slipped it into her bosom; and, for some minutes, appeared in deep thought! All her accustomed gaiety had fled, and her face looked more interesting from the sad expression which had stolen over it. Her eye caught the earnest glance with which Rachel regarded her.

"I thought no one was awake but myself," she said, "I am a bad sleeper. If you are the same, get up, and let us have a little chat."

Surprised at this invitation from a woman towards whom she felt none of that mysterious attraction which marked her brief intercourse with Miss Leigh; she rather coldly replied, —

"I fear our conversation would not suit each other."

"That is as much as to say, that you don't like me, and that you conclude from that circumstance that I don't like you."

"You are right."

"Well, that is candid; when I first saw you, I thought you a very common looking person, and judged by your dress, that you held an inferior rank in society. I was wrong."

"I fancy that you overheard my observations to the Major."

"I did."

"Then I forgive you for disliking me. You think me a

vain, foolish woman."

Rachel nodded her head.

"Oh, you may speak out, I don't like you the worse for speaking the truth. But I am a strange creature, subject, at times, to the most dreadful depression of spirits, and it is only by excessive gaiety that I hinder myself from falling into a state of hopeless despondency."

"This state of mind is not natural. There must be some cause for these fits of depression."

"Yes, many, I am not quite the heartless coquette I seem. I was an only child and greatly indulged by both my parents. This circumstance made me irritable and volatile; I expected that every body would yield to me and let me have my own way as my parents had done; hence I was exposed to constant mortification and disappointment. I left school at sixteen, and was introduced to my husband, a worthy kind man, but old enough to be my father. I was easily persuaded to marry him, for it was a good match, and I, who had never been in love, thought it was such a fine thing to be married at sixteen. Our union has been one of esteem, and I have never swerved from the path of rectitude, but, oh Madam, I have been severely tried. My own sex speak slightingly of me; but I do not deserve their ill-natured censures. These women, I learn from Ceasar, have made a thousand malicious remarks about me, and you and Miss Leigh alone spared me."

"My conduct was perfectly negative. I said nothing either in praise or blame, I may have injured you by thinking hardly of you."

"I thank you for your forbearance in keeping your thoughts to yourself. The conversation that Ceasar repeated to me, greatly annoyed me. It has brought on one of my fits of gloom. If I did flirt with Major F ——, it was more to provoke that ill-natured old maid, and his proud, pompous wife, than from any wish to attract his attention."

"It is better," said Rachel, her heart softening towards her companion, "to avoid all appearance of evil; superficial observers only judge by what they see, and your conduct must have appeared strange to a jealous woman."

"She was jealous of me, then?" said the volatile woman, clapping her hands. "Oh, I am glad I annoyed her."

Rachel could hardly help laughing at the vivacity with which Mrs. Dalton spoke. She turned the conversation into a different channel; and they began to talk of the state of the slaves in the West Indies.

"Ah, I perceive that you know nothing about it," said Mrs. Dalton, "you are infected with the bigotry and prejudices of the anti-slavery advocates. Negroes are an inferior race, they were made to work for civilized men, in climates where labour would be death to those of a different nature and complexion."

"This is reducing the African to a mere beast of burden — a machine in the form of man. The just God never made a race of beings purposely to drag out a painful existence in perpetual slavery!"

"They are better off than your peasants at home — better fed, and taken care of. As to the idle tales they tell you about flogging, starving, and killing slaves, they are fearful exaggerations, not worthy of credit. Do you think a farmer would kill a horse that he knew was worth a hundred pounds? A planter would not disable a slave, if by so doing he injured himself. I have had many slaves, but I never ill-used one of them in my life."

"Ceasar is an example," said Rachel, "of over-indulgence. But, still, he is only a pet animal in your estimation. Do you believe that a negro has a soul?"

"I think it doubtful."

"And you the wife of a christian minister — " and Rachel drew back with a look of horror.

"If they had immortal souls and reasoning minds, we should not be permitted to hold them as slaves. Their degradation proves their inferiority."

"It only proves the brutalizing effect of your immoral system," said Rachel, waxing warm. "I taught a black man from the island of St. Vincent to read the Bible fluently in ten weeks; was that a proof of mental incapacity? I never met with an uneducated white man, who learned to read so rapidly, or pursued his studies with the ardour that this poor, despised, soulless negro did. His motive for this exertion was a noble one (and I believe that it cost him his life), the hope of carrying the glad tidings of salvation to his benighted and unfortunate countrymen, which he considered the best means of improving their condition, and rendering less burdensome their oppressive yoke."

"This is all very well in theory, but it will never do in practice. If the British Government, urged on by a set of fanatics, madly insist upon freeing the slaves, it will involve the West India Islands in ruin."

"May He hasten their emancipation in his own good time. It were better that the whole group of islands were sunk in the depths of the sea than continue to present to the world a system of injustice and cruelty, that is a disgrace to a christian community — a spectacle of infamy to the civilized world. Nor think that the wise and good men, who are engaged heart and hand in this holy cause, will cease their exertions until their great object is accomplished, and slavery is banished from the earth."

Mrs. Dalton stared at Rachel in amazement. She could not comprehend her enthusiasm — "Who cared for a slave?" "One would think," she said, "that you belonged to the Anti-Slavery Society. By the by, have you read a canting tract published by that *pious* fraternity called 'The History of Mary P ——.' It is set forth to be an authentic narrative, while I know it to be a tissue of falsehoods from beginning to end."

"Did you know Mary P ——?"

"Pshaw! — who does? It is an imaginary tale, got up for party purposes."

"But I do know Mary P ——, and I know that narrative to be strictly true, for I took it down myself from the woman's own lips."

"You?" — and Mrs. Dalton started from the ground, as though she had been bitten by a serpent.

"Yes, me."

"You belong to that odious society."

"I have many dear friends who are among its staunch supporters, whose motives are purely benevolent, who have nothing to gain by the freedom of the slave, beyond the restoration of a large portion of the human family to their rights as men."

"Mere cant — the vanity of making a noise in the world. One of the refined hypocricies of life. Good night, Mrs. M. — I don't want to know any more of the writer of Mary P ——."

Mrs. Dalton retired to the inner cabin; and Rachel retired to her berth, where she lay pondering over her conversation with Mrs. Dalton, until the morning broke, and the steamer cast anchor off Newhaven.

Edinburgh

The storm had passed away during the night; and at daybreak Rachel hurried upon deck to catch the first glance of

> "The glorious land of flood and fell,
> The noble north countrie, lassie."

The sun was still below the horizon, and a thick mist hung over the waters, and hid the city from her view.

Oh, for the rising of that white curtain! How Rachel tried to peer through its vapoury folds, to "Hail Old Scotia's darling seat," the abode of brave, intelligent, true-hearted men, and fair good women.

Beautiful Edinburgh! Who ever beheld thee for the first time with indifference, and felt not his eyes brighten, and his heart thrill with a proud ecstacy, the mingling of his spirit with a scene which, in romantic sublimity, has not its equal in the wide world.

"Who would not dare," exclaims the patriotic wizard of the north, "to fight for such a land!"

Aye, and die for it, if need be, as every true-hearted Scot would die rather than see one stain cast upon the national glory of his noble country.

It cannot be doubted that the character of a people is greatly influenced by the local features of the country to which it belongs. The inhabitants of mountainous districts have ever evaded, most effectually the encroachments of a foreign power, and the Scot may derive from his romantic land much of that poetic temperament and stern uncompromising love of independence, which has placed him in the first rank as a man.

The sun at length rose, the fog rolled its grey masses upwards, and the glorious castle emerged from the clouds, like some fabled palace of the Gods, its antique towers glittering like gold in the sun burst.

"Beautiful! most beautiful!" — and Rachel's cheek crimsoned with delight.

"The situation of Quebec is almost as fine," said the Captain, addressing her. "It will lose little by comparison."

"Indeed!" said Rachel eagerly. "You have been there?"

"Yes, many times; and always with increased pleasure. It combines every object that is requisite to make a magnificent scene — woods, mountains, rivers, cataracts, and all on the most stupendous scale. A lover of nature, like you, cannot fail to be delighted with the rock-defended fortress of British North America."

"You have made me quite happy," said Rachel. "I can never hate a country which abounds in natural beauty," — and she felt quite reconciled to Canada from this saying of the Captain's.

Boats were now constantly plying to and from the shore, conveying passengers and their luggage from the ship to the pier. The Captain, who had recognised a countryman in M ——, insisted on the voyagers taking breakfast with him, before they left the vessel. Rachel had suffered so much from sickness, that she had not tasted food since she came on board; early rising and the keen invigorating air had sharpened her appetite; and the refreshing smell of the rasher of ham and fried eggs made the offer too tempting to be refused. A small table was placed under an awning upon the deck, at which the honest Scotch tar presided; and never was a meal more heartily enjoyed. James Hawke, who had been confined, during the whole voyage, to his berth, now joined his friends, and ate of the savoury things before him with such downright goodwill, that the Captain declared that it was a pleasure to watch him handle his knife and fork.

"When a fellow has been starving for eight and forty hours, it is not a trifle that can satisfy his hunger," said Jim, making a vigorous onslaught into a leg of Scotch mutton. "Oh, but I never was so hungry in my life."

"Why, James, you make a worse sailor than I thought you would," said Rachel. "How shall we get you safe to Canada?"

"Never fear; I mean to leave all these qualms behind me, when once we lose sight of the British shores. I have been very ill, but 'tis all over now, and I feel as light as a feather."

On returning to the ladies' cabin to point out her luggage, Rachel found the stewardess walking about in high disdain. That important personage had bestowed very little attention upon Rachel, for which, in all probability, the merino gown had to answer. She had waited with most obsequious fawning politeness on Mrs. Major F. and Mrs. Dalton, because she fancied that they were rich people, who would amply reward her services; and they had given her all the trouble they possibly could. She had received few commands from Rachel, and those few she had neglected to perform. Still, as Rachel well knew that the salary of these people mainly depends upon the trifles bestowed upon them by the passengers, she slipped half a crown into her hand, and begged her to see that her trunks were carried upon deck.

The woman dropped a low curtsey. "Madam, you are one of the very few of our passengers, who has been kind enough to remember the stewardess. And all the trouble that that Mrs. Dalton gave, with her spoilt children, and her nasty black vagabond. I was out of my bed all last night with those noisy brats; and thinks I to myself, she cannot do less than give me a half sovereign for my services. But would you believe me, she went off without bestowing on me a single penny. And worse than that; I heard her tell the big, fat woman, that never rose up in her berth, but to drink brandy and water: 'That it was a bad fashion the Hinglish had of paying servants, and the sooner it was got rid of the better.'

"'I perfectly hagrees with you,' said the fat woman; and so she gave me nothing, not even thanks. Mrs. Major F. pretended not to see me, though I am sure I'm no midge; and I stood in the door-way on purpose to give her a hint; but the hideous, little old maid, told me to get out of the way, as she wanted to go upon deck. Oh the meanness of these would be fine ladies. But if ever they come in this boat again, won't I pay them hoff."

Now, it must be confessed, that Rachel rather enjoyed the discomfort of the disappointed stewardess; and she was forced to turn away her head for fear of betraying her inclination to laugh.

A fine boat landed the party of emigrants on the chain pier, at New Haven, from thence they proceeded to Leith in a hackney coach; as M —— wished to procure lodgings as near the place of embarcation as possible. Leaving Rachel and her maid at the inn, he set off with James Hawke in search of lodgings. In about an hour he returned, and conducted his wife to the house of a respectable woman, the widow of a surgeon, who resided near the bank, and only a few minutes walk from the wharf.

Great was the surprise of Rachel, when, instead of entering the house by a front door, they walked up an interminable flight of stone stairs; every landing comprising a distinct dwelling, with the names of the proprietors marked on the doors. At last they reached the flat that was occupied by good Mistress Waddell, who showed them into a comfortable sitting room, in which a bright fire was blazing, and welcomed her new lodgers with a torrent of kindly words, which were only half understood by the English portion of her audience.

A large, portly personage, was Mistress Waddell. Ugly, amiable, and by no means over particular in her dress. She was eloquent in the praise of her apartments; which she said, had been occupied by my Leddy Weymes, when his majesty, George the Fourth, God bless his sonsy face, landed at Leith, on his visit to Scotland. Her lodgings, it seems, had acquired quite an aristocratic character since the above named circumstance; and not a day passed but the good woman enumerated all the particulars of that visit. But her own autobiography was the stock theme with our good hostess. The most minute particulars of her private history, she daily divulged, to the unspeakable delight of the mischievous, laughter loving James; who, because he saw that it annoyed Rachel, was sure to lead slily to some circumstance that never failed to place the lady upon her high horse. And then she would talk — Ye gods! how she would talk and splutter away in her broad Scotch, until the wicked boy was in convulsions of laughter.

"Aye, Mister Jeames," she would say: "Ye will a' be m'akeng yer fun of a pure auld bodie, but 'tis na' cannie o' ye."

"Making fun of you, Mrs. Waddell," with a sly look at Rachel; "How can you take such a fancy into your head. It is so good of you to tell me all about your courtship; it's giving me a hint of how I am to go about it, when I am a man. I am sure you were a very pretty smart girl (with another sly look) in your young day?"

The old lady drew herself up and smiled approvingly at her black eyed tormenter: "Na' na', Mister Jeames, my gude man, who's dead and gane', said to me on the day that he made me his ain: Katie, ye are no bonnie, but ye a' gude, which is a hantle better."

"No doubt he was right, but, really, I think he was very ungallant, and did not do you half justice."

"Weel, weel," said the good dame, "every ain to his taste. He was not owr gifted that way himsel', but we are nane sensible of our ain defects."

The great attraction in the small windowless closet, in which James slept, was an enormous calabash, which her son, the idol of the poor woman's heart, had brought from the South Seas. Over this calabash, she daily rehearsed all the adventures which she had gathered from that individual, during his short visits home. But as she possessed a wonderfully retentive memory, she could have filled volumes with these maternal reminiscences. To which James listened with the most earnest attention; not on account of the adventures, for they were common place enough, but for the mere pleasure of hearing her talk Scotch, from which he seemed to derive the most ludicrous enjoyment.

Mrs. Waddell, had, in common with most of her sex, a great predilection for going to auctions; and scarcely a day passed without her making some wonderful bargains. For a mere trifle, she had bought a gude pot, only upon inspection, it turned out to be incurably leaky. A nice palliasse, which, on more intimate acquaintance, proved alive with gentry, with whom the most republican body could not endure to be on familiar terms. Jim was always joking the old lady upon her bargains, greatly to the edification of Betty Fraser, her black eyed prime minister in the culinary department.

"Weel, Mister Jeames, just ha' yer laugh out; but when ye get a glint o' the bonnie table, I bought this morning, for three-an-sixpence, ye'll no be making game o' me any mair. Betty, ye maun just step o'ur the curb stane to the broker's an bring the table hame."

Away sped the nimble-footed damsel, and we soon heard the clattering of the table, as the leaves flapped to and fro, as she lugged it up the public stairs.

"Now for the great bargain!" exclaimed the saucy lad, "I think, Mother Waddell, I'll buy it of you as my venture to Canada."

"Did ye ever," said the old lady, her eyes brightening, as Betty dragged in the last purchase, and placed it triumphantly before her mistress. Like the Marquis of Anglesea, it had been in the wars; and with a terrible clatter fell prostrate to the floor. Betty opened wide her great black eyes with a glance of blank astonishment; and raising her hands with a tragic air, that was perfectly irresistible, exclaimed:

"Marcy me! but it wants a fut!"

"A what!" screamed Jim, as he sank beside the fallen table in convulsions of laughter. "Do, for heaven's sake, tell me the English for a fut? Oh, dear, I shall die. Why do you make such funny purchases, Mrs. Waddell, you will be the death of me, and then, what will my mammie say?"

To add to this ridiculous scene, Mrs. Waddell's parrot, who was not the least important person in the establishment, fraternized with the prostrate lad, and echoed his laughter in the most outrageous manner.

"Whist Poll, hauld yer clatter, it's no laughing matter to lose three and sixpence in buying the like o' that." Mrs. Waddell did not attend another auction during the month that M. remained at her lodgings.

Unfortunately, on their arrival at Leith, they found that the Chieftain had sailed two days before, and Mrs. Waddell averred, that it was the last vessel that would leave that port for Canada.

This was bad news enough, but M., who never yielded to despondency, took it very philosophically, and lost no time in making enquiries among the ship-owners as to what vessels were still to sail; and, after several days of almost hopeless search, he was informed that the Rachel, Captain Irving, was to leave for Canada in a fortnight. The name seemed propitious; and that very afternoon they walked down to the wharf to inspect the vessel. She was a small brig, very old, very dirty, and with wretched accommodations. The Captain was a brutal looking person, blind of one eye, and very lame. Every third word he uttered was an oath; and, instead of answering their enquiries, he was engaged in a blasphemous dialogue with his two sons, who were his first and second mates; their whole conversation being interlarded with frightful imprecations on the limbs and souls of each other. They had a large number of steerage passengers, for the very small size of the vessel, and those of the lowest description.

"Don't go in this horrible vessel," whispered Rachel; "what a captain, what a crew; we shall be miserable, if we form any part of her live cargo."

"I fear, my dear girl, there is no alternative. We may, perhaps, hear of another before she sails. I won't engage places in her until the last moment."

The dread of going in the Rachel, took a prophetic hold of the mind of her namesake; and she begged Jim to be on the constant look out for another vessel.

During their stay at Leith, M —— was busily engaged in writing the concluding chapters of his book, and James and Rachel amused themselves by exploring the beauties of Edinburgh. The lad, who was very clever, possessed a wonderful faculty for remembering places, and before a week had passed away, he knew every street in Edinburgh and Leith, had twice or thrice climbed the heights of Arthur's Seat, and explored every nook of the old castle.

With James for a guide and Hannah following with the baby, one fine June afternoon, Rachel set forth to climb the mountain, the view of which, from her chamber window, she was never tired of contemplating. Her husband told her that she had better wait until he was able to accompany her, but, in spite of a perfect knowledge of the tale of the "dog Ball," Rachel, unable to control her impatience, gave him the slip, and set off on her mountain-climbing expedition.

Now be it known unto our readers, that Rachel was a native of a low pastoral country, very beautiful in running brooks, smooth meadows, and majestic parks, where the fat sleek cattle, so celebrated in the London markets, grazed knee deep in luxuriant grass, and the fallow deer browzed and gambolled through the long summer; but she had never seen a mountain before in her life, had never climbed a very high hill; and when she arrived at the foot of this grand upheaval of nature, she began to think the task more formidable than she had imagined at a distance, and made haste to dismiss Hannah and the baby while she commenced the ascent of the mountain, following the steps of her young conductor who, agile as a kid, bounded up the steep aclivity as if it were a bowling green.

"Not so fast, James, I cannot climb like you!"

But Jim was already beyond hearing, and was leaning over a projecting crag far over her head, laughing at the slow progress she made; meanwhile the narrow path that led round the mountain to the summit, became narrower and narrower, and the ascent more steep. Rachel had paused at the ruins of the chapel, to admire the magnificent prospect and to take breath, when a lovely boy of four years of age in a kilt and hose, his golden curls flying in the wind, ran at full speed up the steep side of the hill, a panting woman without bonnet or shawl, following hard upon his track shaking her fist at him and vociferating her commands (doubtless for him to retrace his steps) in gaelic. On fled the laughing child, the mother after him; but, as well might a giant pursue a fairy. Rachel followed the path they had taken, and was beginning to enjoy the keen bracing air of the hills, when she happened to cast her eyes below to the far off meadows beneath. Her head grew suddenly dizzy, and she could not divest herself of the idea that one false step would send her down to the plains below. Here was a most ridiculous and unromantic position; she neither dared to advance or retreat, and she stood grasping a ledge of the rocky wall in an agony of cowardice, irresolution, and despair. At this critical moment, the mother of the run-away child returned panting from a higher ledge of the hill, and, perceiving Rachel pale and trembling, very kindly speered what ailed her? Rachel could not refrain from laughing while she confessed her fear, lest she should fall from the narrow footpath on which she stood. The woman seemed highly amused at her distress, but her native kindliness of heart, which is the mother of genuine politeness, restrained the outburst of merriment that hovered about her lips.

"Ye are na' accustomed to the hills, if ye dread a hillock like this. Ye suld ha' been born where I was born to know a mountain fra' a mole-hill. There is my bairn, no, I canna keep him fra' the mountain. He will gang awa' to the tap, and only laughs at me when I speer him to come doon. But it is because he was sae weel gotten, an' all his forbears were reared amang the hills."

The good woman sat down upon a piece of loose rock and commenced a long history of herself, of her husband, and of the great clan of Macdonald, to which they belonged, that at last ended in the ignoble discovery that her aristocratic spouse was a common soldier in the highland regiment then stationed in Edinburgh; and that Flora, his wife, washed for the officers of the regiment; that the little Donald, with his wild goat propensities, was their only child, and so attached to the hills that she could not keep him confined to the meadows below, and the moment her eye was off him his great delight was to lead her a dance up the mountain, which as she, by her own account, never succeeded in catching him, was quite labour in vain. All this, and more, the good-natured woman communicated as she lead the fear-stricken Rachel down the narrow path to the meadow below; and her kindness did not end here, for she walked some way up the road to put her in the right track to regain her lodgings, for Rachel, trusting to the pilotage of Jim, was perfectly ignorant of the locality.

This highland Samaritan indignantly refused the piece of silver Rachel proffered in return for her services.

"Hout, leddy, keep the siller, I would not take ought fra' ye on the sabbath day for a trifling act o' courtesy. Na' na', I come of too guid bluid for that."

There was a noble simplicity about the honest-hearted woman that delighted Rachel. What a fine country, what a fine people! No smooth-tongued flatterers are these Scotch; with them an act of kindness is an act of duty, and they scorn payment for what they give gratuitously, without display and without ostentation. If I were not English, I should like to be a Scot. So thought Rachel, as she presented herself before her Scotch husband, who laughed heartily over her misadventure, and did not cease to teaze her about her expedition to the mountain, as long as they remained in Edinburgh.

This did not deter her from taking a long stroll on the sands the next afternoon with James, and delighted with collecting shells and specimens of sea-weed, they wandered on until Rachel remarked that her footprints were filled with water at each step, and the roaring of the sea gave notice of the return of the tide. What a race they had to gain the pier of Leith before they were overtaken by the waves, and how thankful they were that they were safe as the billows chased madly past, over the very ground which a few minutes before they had carelessly and fearlessly trod.

"This is rather worse than the mountain, and might have been more fatal to us both," whispered James, "I think Mr. M—— would scold this time if he knew of our danger."

"Thank God! the baby is safe at home," said Rachel, "I forgot all about the tide; what a mercy we were not both drowned."

"Yes, and no one would have known what had become of us."

"How miserable M —— would have been."

"And the poor baby — but what is this?" — "To sail on the 1st of July, for Quebec and Montreal, the fast sailing brig, the Ann, Captain Rogers; for particulars, inquire at the office of P. Glover, Bank Street, Leith. Hurra, a fig for Captain Irwine and the Rachel."

"Let us go James and look at the vessel. If it had not been for our fright on the sands we should not have seen this."

Before half an hour had elapsed, Rachel and her young friend had explored the Ann and held a long conversation with her Captain, who, though a rough sailor, seemed a hearty honest man. He had no cabin passengers, though a great many in the steerage, and he assured Rachel that she could have his state-cabin for herself and child, while her husband could occupy a berth with him in the cabin.

The state cabin was just big enough to hold the captain's chest of drawers, the top of which formed the berth which Rachel was to occupy. Small as the place was, it was neat and clean; and possessed to Rachel one great advantage, the charm of privacy, and she hastened home to report matters to her husband. But he had taken a fancy to go in the Rachel, because she was to sail a fortnight earlier, and it took a great deal of coaxing to induce him to change his determination, but he did change it, at the earnest solicitations of his wife, and took their passage in the Ann. For those who doubt the agency of an overruling providence in the ordinary affairs of life, these trifling reminiscences have been chiefly penned. From trifling circumstances the greatest events often spring. Musa, King of Grenada, owed his elevation to the throne to a delay of five minutes, when he requested the executioner whom his brother had sent to the prison to take his head, to wait for five minutes until he had checkmated the gaoler, with whom he was playing a game at chess. The grim official reluctantly consented.

Before the brief term expired, a tumult in the city dethroned his brother and placed Musa on the throne. How much he owed to one move at chess. Could that be accidental on which the fate of a nation, and the lives of thousands were staked?

So with our emigrants' disasterous trips to sea. The delay saved them from taking their passage in the "Chieftain." That ill fated ship lost all her crew and most of her numerous passengers with cholera, on the voyage out. The "Rachel" put to sea a fortnight before the "Ann;" she was wrecked upon the banks of Newfoundland, and was sixteen weeks at sea, her captain was made a prisoner in his cabin, by his own brutal sons; and most of her passengers died of small pox and the hardships they endured on the voyage. How kind was the providence that watched over our poor emigrants; although, like the rest of the world, they murmured at their provoking delay, and could not see the beam in the dark cloud, until the danger was over-past; and they had leisure to reflect on the great mercies they had received at the hands of the Almighty.

It was with deep regret, that Rachel bade farewell to the beautiful capital of Scotland. How happy would she have been, if her pilgrimage could have terminated in that land of poetry and romance, and she could have spent the residue of her days, among its truthful, highminded and hospitable people. But vain are regrets, the inexorable spirit of progress, points onward, and the beings she chooses to be the parents of a new people in a new land, must fulfil their august destiny.

On the 1st of July, they embarked on board the "Ann," and bade adieu to their country for ever, while the glory of summer was upon the earth, to seek a new home beyond the Atlantic, and friends in a land of strangers.

Literary Garland ns 9 (1851): 97–104, 170–77, 228–35, 258–62, 308–14. Expanded to become *Flora Lyndsay, or Passages in an Eventful Life* (London: Bentley, 1854).

My Cousin Tom. A Sketch from Life

My cousin was an artist. An odd man in the fullest acceptation of the word. He was odd in his appearance, in his manners, in his expressions, and ways of thinking. A perfect original, for I never met with any one like him, in my long journey through life.

He had served his apprenticeship with the great Bartolozzy, who was the first copper-plate engraver of his time.

He had so won the esteem of his celebrated master, that on the expiration of his apprenticeship, he returned to him the £400 premium he had received with him, together with a pair of handsome gold kneebuckles, which were indispensable articles in a gentleman's dress of the last century.

During his long residence with the Italians, he had imbibed a great dislike to every thing English. He wrote and spoke in the Italian language. I verily believe, that he thought in Italian; and being an exquisite musician, both on the viol to Gomba and the violin, never played any but Italian music. He was a Catholic too, although born of Protestant parents. Not that he had any particular preference for that religion, for I don't think that he troubled his mind at all about it; but it was, he said, "The religion of Kings and Emperors. The only one fit for a gentleman, and a man of taste."

He admired the grandeur of the ceremonial, which he considered highly picturesque; and the works of art that adorned the beautiful chapel in Spanish Place; and above all, the exquisite music and singing.

When staying with him and his niece, during the winter of 1826, he always insisted upon our going with him to this place of worship. It was there that my soul thrilled to the inspired notes of the divine Malabran, and many of the great musical celebrities of that day.

"You Protestants," he would say, "give your best music to the Devil; we Catholics to God."

He used to repeat an anecdote of a friend of his, a Mr. Nugent, who was also a Catholic, and a brother artist, with great glee. Some gentleman, who was sitting for his portrait, was laughing at him about his religion.

"You believe in Purgatory too?"

"Yes sir," replied Nugent, "and let me tell you, that you may go farther and fare worse!"

Cousin was considerably more than sixty when I first knew him. He was above the middle size, of a thin spare figure, and had the finest dark eyes I ever saw in a human head. His features were regular, and very handsome; but his face was sadly marred by the small-pox — a matter to him of deep and lasting regret.

"Beauty is God's greatest gift," he would say. "It is rank, wealth, power. What compensation can the world give to one who is cursed with hopeless ugliness?"

No one could look into his intelligent face, and think him ugly. But then, he dressed in such a queer fashion, and paid so little attention to his toilet, that days would pass without his combing his hair or washing his hands and face. The young artists, who loved him for his benevolence, and to whom he was a father in times of distress, had nicknamed him "Dirty Dick." He knew it, but did not reform his slovenly habits. "Pho! Pho! what does it matter. I am an old man. Who cares for old men? Let them call me what they like. I mean to do as I please."

Every thing was dirty about him. His studio was a dark den, in which every thing was covered with a deep layer of dust. The floor was strewed with dirty music and dirty old books, for he was an antiquarian, among his other accomplishments, and he sat at a dirty easel, in an old thread-bare black coat and pants, now brown with age. His fine iron-grey hair, curling round his lofty temples in tangled masses — his left hand serving for a palette, and covered with patches of color most laughable to behold.

I used to laugh at him and quiz him most outrageously. I was a great favorite with the old man, and he took it all in good part. His walking costume was still more ridiculous, and consisted of a blue dress coat and gilt buttons, buff leather breeches and Hessian military boots, a yellow Cassimere waistcoat, and a high, stiff black stock. I was really ashamed of being seen with him in the streets. Every one turned round and looked at us. He walked so rapidly, that as we went up Oxford street, every coachman threw open the door of his vehicle.

"A coach — want a coach, sir. Camberwell — Peckham, sir."

Cousin would laugh, put out his tongue — an ugly fashion he had — and reply: —

"Coach be —— I prefer the Apostles' horses!"

An Irishman answered him very pertly — "An' bedad they can travel purty fast!"

Cousin was a confirmed old bachelor, but he had once been in love. But I will tell the story as it was told to me.

"The rich banker, Mr. H ——, had an only daughter — a very beautiful girl. You know how Tom C —— admires beauty! He met the young lady at her father's table, and fell head over ears in love. He was a fine clever young fellow in those days. The old gentleman was greatly pleased with his wit and talent, and gave him a *carte blanche* to his house. Tom availed himself of the privilege, and went every day to look at Arabella H —— ; for naturally shy with women, he seldom plucked up courage enough to speak to her, still less to inform her of his passion. The young lady, I have every reason to know, loved him too; but as it is not customary for women to make the first advances, she patiently waited from day to day, expecting the young artist to declare himself. This state of things lasted for seven years. The young lady grew tired of her tardy wooer.

One day he went as usual, and missed his idol from her place at table. 'Where is Arabella — is she ill?' he enquired anxiously of her father.

"'Have you not heard the news, Tom? Arabella is married!'

"'Is she!' with a great oath. 'Then what business have I here!'

"He started up from the table, and ran through the streets like a madman, without his hat, and making the most vehement gesticulations, and never entered the house again. Poor Tom! It was a dreadful disappointment; he has never studied the graces, except in pictures, since. He, however, has not forgotten his first love: I can trace her likeness in every female head he paints."

He had a collection of very fine paintings from the old masters, which covered the walls of his dining-room; but they were so covered with the accumulated dust of years, that it hid the pictures more effectually than any veil. One day, when he was absent at a sale of books, I took upon myself to clean the neglected master-pieces. I wish I had let it alone; they were only fit for a bachelor artist's private studio. His old housekeeper, a character in her way, stood by, quietly watching the progress of the work.

"Now you see what you have done! My dear old mistress, master's mother, always kept them naked figures behind muslin curtains; but master is so absent-minded, he'll never notice them coming staring out upon us, in broad daylight."

Fortunately for me, her prediction was verified. He never noticed the brilliancy of the restored pictures. He had a habit of talking aloud to himself; but as it was always in a foreign language — for he was a great linguist — he had the talk all to himself. He was once coming down to ——, to spend the Christmas with us, and it so happened, that he was the only passenger in the mail. Finding the time hang heavily on his hands, he began repeating, in a loud sonorous voice, the first canto in the "Jerusalem Delivered" of Tasso. When the coach stopped to change horses, old Jey, the guard, and father of the present celebrated marine artist, put his head in at the window. "For God-sake, Mr. C ——, tell me to whom you are talking. I am sure there is no one but yourself in the coach."

"To the Devil!" was the curt reply.

"Indeed, sir — He does not often travel this road. — I hope you may find him a pleasant companion!"

Cousin laughed for a week over this adventure. When speaking of his younger days, it was always with deep regret that they had so soon vanished; and he generally ended such reminiscenses with blasphemously cursing his old age.

Another of his oddities consisted in his wishing to be the last man, that he might see the destruction of the earth. "What a grand spectacle," he would say. "It would be worth living for a thousand years to witness."

He was the first artist that used the pencil in water-color portraits. These he executed so well, that his studio never wanted a subject. Five and twenty guineas was his usual price for a likeness; which, as he worked very rapidly, was generally finished in two sittings. He was a master in his art. His pictures were very elegant; and he had a peculiar faculty of conveying to paper or canvass the exact expression of the sitter's face. He hated to paint an ugly person, and as a consequence, his likenesses were always flattering.

"You can never make a woman as good looking as she thinks herself. They like to be flattered. It is only improving the features a *little*, and giving a better complexion than nature gave. While you retain the expression in which the real identity lies, you must get a good likeness — a picture that will please every one."

"But, cousin, is that right?"

"Yes, it pleases them, and fills my pockets, and both parties are satisfied. I never painted but one person whose vanity it was impossible to gratify. He was the ugliest man in London, and had the worst countenance I ever saw. In fact, a perfect brute! Lord George Gordon, of Wilkes and Liberty notoriety. He sat to me fourteen times, for his portrait. I improved his coarse features as much as I could; but with all my skill, he made a vile picture. His face was covered with warts. I omitted them, and gave nature the lie, by giving him an expression which she had not given. He was still unsatisfied. I then drew him just as he was — warts and all. He was in a furious rage, and said 'I had painted him like the Devil!'

"'I do not think, my Lord, that the Devil would be flattered with the likeness. You are a —— ugly fellow. You may take the portraits or leave them; but you shall pay me for the time I have wasted on such a disagreeable subject.' He tore the pictures to pieces, and left me, foaming with passion. 'But I made him pay me,' he said, rubbing his hands with glee. 'Yes; I made him pay me!'"

He had a beautiful half-length portrait of Lady Hamilton. It was taken at the time she was struggling for bread, and sitting as a model to young artists. It was a charming face. I was never tired of looking at it.

"Ah, poor Emma!" he said, gloomily. "She was one of nature's master-pieces — a Queen of Beauty! Like Absalom, from the crown of her head to the sole of her foot, she was without spot or blemish. You will find the models of her foot and hand in that closet. The Venus *de Medici* could not show finer. And what was her fate?"

"She deserved it!" I said, coldly.

"Bah! that's the way women judge each other. They are merciless. She married for bread — to obtain a home — a kind, talented man, double her age. The result might have been anticipated. Clever, fascinating, beautiful — think of the temptations that surrounded her! the admiration she excited wherever she went! She made Nelson a hero! He dying, bequeathed her to his country; and that country left her to perish in poverty, heart-broken and alone. When I was last in France, I went to see her grave. No stone marks the spot; and the grave was so shallow, that by putting down my stick through the loose sand, I could touch the coffin. It makes me savage to think of it."

With all his eccentricities, cousin Tom had a large, generous heart. He heard that a young, promising artist, whom he had not seen for some time, was without employment, and starving in a garret. He sent him, anonymously, thirty pounds; and rubbing his hands, and laughing, said, as if to himself, "Poor Devil, he will get a good supper to-night, without feeling obliged to any one!"

In one of his rambles, he found two forlorn cats locked up in the area of an old stone house in Charlotte street. The creatures could neither get out of the area, nor back into the house. "They were perfect skeletons — mad with hunger," he said. "I had to buy them meat, or they would have devoured each other."

For more than a month he visited these cats every day, bearing on a skewer a supply of cat's meat. The animals knew his step, and used to greet him with a chorus of affectionate mews. One night we were just sitting down to tea, when he suddenly started up, with an oath. "I have forgotten to feed my prisoners!" and rushed out to supply their wants.

New tenants came to the house. The cats were released from durance vile; but he called upon the fresh occupants, and recommended his poor pensioners to their protection.

While I am upon the subject of cats, I will relate one of the drollest things that cousin did, while I was staying at his house. He had a large cat, whom he called "Black Tom." The creature was without a white hair — as black as night. It had a weird, ghost-like appearance, sitting, silently staring at you, with its large yellow eyes, in the dim twilight of a dingy London house. Cousin was very fond of his black namesake, and made him the sharer of both his bed and board. The attachment was mutual. Tom always followed close at his master's heels, or sat perched upon his knee, by the hour together.

It was droll to see cousin nursing his favourite. He had a habit of leaning back in his chair, with his hands clasped behind his head — his eyes closed, and himself in a half-dreamy state, — only that he kept up a perpetual tattooing with both his feet, which not only made him shake all over, but jarred the room and every thing in it. As the motion increased in violence, Tom actually danced up and down upon his master's knee, uttering now and then a plaintive remonstrance, in sundry low mews. It was impossible to witness this without laughing.

For three days Black Tom disappeared. At the end of the first, cousin began to grow fidgety; at the close of the second, he speculated sadly about his pet, and went out into the street calling "Tom! Tom!" in a melancholy voice, and enquiring of the wondering foot passengers, if they had "seen his black cat?"

The people, I have no doubt, thought him mad.

The next day his anxiety and grief grew desperate. He wrote a large placard, describing Tom's personal peculiarities, and offering the reward of a sovereign to any one who would restore him to his rightful owner. This he pasted, with his own hands, upon a large iron gate opposite, that closed a short cut from Newman street into Rathbone Place.

Before three hours had elapsed, the house was beseiged with boys, bringing (in hope of getting the reward) cats in baskets — cats in bags, or lugged by the neck and tail. Dire were the mewings, as each poor puss was held up for inspection; and loud the execrations of cousin, when a red or gray cat was offered to his notice, or a slim, lean cat of the genus feminine. At length a boy more fortunate than the rest, presented a black cat in a pillowcase, which cousin was determined must be Tom, because it was black; and he paid the joyful bearer the sovereign, without further parley. The animal was set loose in the hall; but instead of answering to the call of the delighted owner, it gave a loud squall, and rushed down into the kitchen, taking refuge in the copper-hole.

An hour after, I found cousin's housekeeper, Jane, upon her knees, peering under the copper, and talking thus: — "Is it Tom? No, it isn't. Well, I think it is; but he don't seem to me to behave like him. Tom! Tom!"

"Mew!" from the frightened puss. "Law! I don't think it can be he. That's not his way of mewing. It isn't Tom. I believe master has thrown that sovereign of his into the dirt. Do, Miss S ——, just look here, and tell me if that is our own Tom!"

I was soon down on my knees beside her, peeping at the rescued Tom, whose eyes glared at us, like two burning coals, from his dingy retreat.

"Had Tom a white patch on his breast, Jane?"

"No, no. He was as black as soot!"

I fell a laughing. "Mercy! what will cousin say to this beast with a white shirt-frill?"

"It isn't Tom, then? He shan't stay a moment here," cried Jane, starting up, and seizing the broom. "I knew it wasn't our own decent-behaved cat. Out, brute!" One touch of the broom, away rushed the surreptitious Tom. I opened the door, and he passed like a flash into the street.

"Law! how shall I tell master? He'll be so mad; and when he gets angry, he swears so. It is awful to hear him."

"I'll tell him."

To me young and full of mischief, it was a capital joke. I heard the floor shaking as I approached the parlour. Cousin was tattooing as usual, with both his feet, and talking to himself. I opened the door; was it ghost or demon! The real Simon Pure was dancing up and down on his master's knee!

"Where did you find Tom?"

"Oh, he came home of himself. I was sitting thinking of him, when he jumped up upon my knee, and began drumming with all his might."

"But it was not Tom for whom you gave the sovereign."

"I know it," said cousin, quietly. "It's all the same. I gave the sovereign to recover Tom, and he is here. I should have lost it anyhow; and that poor boy has got a famous price for the lean family cat. I'm contented; Tom's happy; and that young imp is rejoicing over his good fortune — perhaps buying bread for his starving mother."

Tom played his master a sad trick a few weeks after this, which in the first moments of exasperation, nearly cost puss his life.

Cousin had been four years painting a half-length picture in oils, of the Madonna. Many beautiful faces had looked out from that canvass, but none satisfied the artist.

Whenever the picture was nearly finished, he expunged it, and commenced a new one. His old friend, C. G ——, the Consul-General for Prussia, used to step in every day for a chat with him. "Ah! dere he is, at de everlastin' virgin," was the common salutation he gave the artist.

It was during my stay with him that the picture was finished to his entire satisfaction. It wanted but a few days for the opening of the Exhibition at Somerset House, and he was anxious to send something.

"Ah! she will do now!" he cried, after giving the last touches. "What do you think S ——," to me.

"She is divine! But how will you get the picture dry in time to send?"

"I will manage that." And he whistled, sung, rubbed his hands, and tattooed with his feet, more vigorously than ever.

I was going out to a party in the evening with my cousin Eliza, his niece. We had washed some lace edge to trim the front of our dresses. There was a paved court behind the house, into which the studio opened. Against the dingy brick wall, cousin had tried to cherish a few stunted rose trees. Upon the still leafless boughs of said trees, I had hung our small wash to dry. Opposite the dingy brick wall on the one side, was the steep side of the next house, with no window looking into our court, but a blank, which was meant to represent one. In this blank, brick recess, cousin had placed the Madonna to dry in the shade; and truly no sun ever peered into that narrow court, surrounded by lofty walls.

After we had dined, I went to fetch in the lace, and prepare for the evening.

"What are you laughing at, in that outrageous manner? Girl, you will kill yourself!" and cousin Tom emerged out of the studio. I was holding to the iron rails, on either side of the stone steps, that led down into the court.

The tears were running down my cheeks. I pointed up to the picture. "Did you ever see before a Madonna with a moustache?"

How he storm'd, and raged, and stamped — and how

I laughed! I knew it was cruel. I tried to stop it. I was sorry — really sorry — but if I had had to die for it, laugh I must. The Madonna had been placed head downwards in the blind window. Black Tom, who had followed his master into the court when he put up the picture, no sooner found the court clear than he jumped up to the stone ledge of the blank recess, and began walking to and fro in front of the painting, touching it every time he passed; and as the color was quite wet, he not only took that off, but left a patch of black hairs in its stead. One of the virgin's eyes had been wiped out with his tail; and he had bestowed upon the elegant chin, a regular beard. She looked everything but divine — the most ridiculous and disreputable caricature of beauty.

In the meanwhile, the author of the mischief, unconscious of the heretical sacrilege of which he had been guilty, jumped down from his lofty perch, and began rubbing himself against the poor artist's legs — bestowing upon the old shabby pants a layer of paint, mingled with black hairs. "Tom, you rascal! You have ruined me! I will kill you!"

He would have kept his word, had not Tom looked up in his face, and uttered one of his little affectionate greetings. This softened his master's ire.

"Take him out of my sight, S ——. You were worse than him, for laughing at the destruction of my best picture, for *you knew* how it would annoy me!"

"I plead guilty; but just look at it yourself. How could any one help it?"

He looked — fell a laughing; took down the unlucky picture, and flung it back into the studio, then turning to me, said, with his usual air of quiet drollery: "I forgive you, Gipsy! I wonder the transfiguration did not make the cat laugh!"

He came home one night very gloomy and sad, and began walking to and fro the long drawing-room, with rapid steps, and talking half-aloud to himself. "John Milton dead — dead in the workhouse — and I not know it! I his old friend and fellow-student. Dear me! it's too dreadful to be true! A man of his talent to be allowed to perish thus! It's a disgrace to the country. Yes! yes! such is the fate of genius."

This Milton was a landscape painter and engraver of some eminence. Cousin Tom brooded for months over his sad fate.

Dear old cousin, — some of the happiest months I ever spent in London were spent in that dirty house in Newman street. Though I laughed at your oddities, I loved you for your real worth. I was young then — full of hope, and ambitious of future fame. You encouraged all my scribbling propensities, and prophesied — . Ah, well! it never came to pass. Like you, I shall sink to an unknown and unhonored grave, and be forgotten in the land of my exile.

British American Magazine 1 (1863): 12–20.

Washing the Black-A-Moor White. A Page from Life

This useless unprofitable speculation has become proverbial. I wonder if any one had ever the folly to undertake it! It is one of those hard uncompromising facts that leaves no opening for pugnacious disputants to fight about. Even the celebrated individual, "that swore I was not I, and made a ghost of personal identity" would have to give it up. Still it strikes me, that the experiment must have been tried, or the satire contained in the old proverb would lose half its stinging pungency. I am more inclined to believe this, from a rude illustration of the subject, that gave its name to a portion of a street in the old city of Norwich, England, which was called *Labor in vain Hill*, and divided the Court House from the County Jail opposite.

Well I remember when a child, viewing this barbarous relic of a by-gone age, with the greatest admiration. I had never seen a darkie, and I took the picture for a likeness of his satanic majesty.

How it came there I do not know, or for what purpose it served as a sign, and I have often wondered if it is still hanging in the same place, and teaching the same trite truism to the passers by. I wonder if "Notes and Queries" ever took note of it, or the reverend antiquarian society let it depart in peace.

It was the portrait of a negro, certainly drawn from the dark side of nature, with no flattering pencil, sitting in a tub, making shocking big mouths and wry faces, while a sturdy John Bull, a genuine pup of the old bull dog breed, applied a scrubbing brush with vigorous energy to the bare shoulders of the dark-skinned African, grinning with supreme delight at the chained and helpless victim.

At the base of this odd picture, was appended in red letters, the moral of the benevolent intentions of the operators:

LABOR IN VAIN!

Whether the ancient fathers of the city intended this as a reflection upon the whole African race, or meant it to convey a gentle hint to the inmates of the jail, that the task of attempting to whiten characters blackened by years of crime was hopeless or to admonish the gentlemen of the long robe, who assembled in the Court House twice a year, to sit in judgment upon the rebellious weavers, — who were fond of kicking up a row and breaking the windows and heads of the lieges, — not to reverse the picture by turning white into black, we are not aware.

The nearest approach to solving this difficult problem was achieved by a negro lad of twelve years of age. The boy had been taken off the wreck of a slaver near the Guinea coast by a Captain Brown who commanded a merchant vessel, "the John Bull of Portsmouth." The young negro was the only living creature left in the doomed ship. The captain was a friend of Mr. C ——, of B ——, in the county of S ——, England, to whom he recommended the poor lad, who took him into his service, and he soon became an especial favorite with his master.

It was during the time when phrenology was making a great stir in the scientific world, and the writings of Gall and Spursheim had produced a perfect mania for the new science. Mr. C —— was an enthusiastic advocate of the new theory, and saw no sacrilege in Home disintering the body of his mother, in order to obtain a cast of her head. Mr. C —— had fitted up a large hall for casts and skulls, the latter ranged in ghastly rows, seemed to laugh at death and show their grinning teeth in defiance of decay. This horrid charnel house, which Mr. C —— appropriately termed his *scullery*, was the favorite resort of all the disciples of the marvellous new theory. And rotting bones and casts from living heads were daily consulted to attest its truth. John Bull — for the lad had been named after the vessel that had proved to him an ark of safety — Mr. C —— considered to have a very finely developed Negro cranium. He must take a cast of his head.

John Bull placed no impediments in the way, he was in ecstacies, and submitted to the unpleasant operation with the meekness of a black sheep.

When the bust was put together, Mr. C —— had it painted black, to make the likeness more apparent. John watched the proceedings with intense disgust, considering them a black injustice, and he expressed his dissent by sullen shakes of the head and low murmurs in his native tongue. John slept in the *scullery*, the keeping of it in order being entrusted to his care. The day after the cast had been placed on the shelf, Mr. C —— brought several gentlemen to look at it.

To his surprise and mortification, the black model was nowhere to be seen. Who had stole it? He rang the bell violently. John's woolly head instantly appeared.

"Vat massa ring for?"

"John, what's become of your head."

"La mass," grins the boy with a look of uncomparable simplicity. "Him war God Almighty put him, on John's neck."

"The cast I mean, the cast I took of you yesterday."

"Ough, dat black ugly nigger."

"The same. Where is it?"

"Duppies fly off wi dat head, him gone to de debil."

"Now John you must produce that head or I will have you whipped."

John saw a glare in massa's eye he didn't like, stepping up to the shelf which Mr. C —— had just reconnoitered, he quietly handed down the white cast of himself.

"How John. How is this. How came the black bust white?"

"Lors, massa fust make white boy, den turn 'em black. By am by de moon get up, John get up too, and scrape all de black off and turn de nigger white."

Mr. C —— turned laughingly to his companion. "I believe the boy has solved at last the difficult problem, not by applying the brush, but an oyster shell."

Canadian Literary Magazine 1 (1871): 163–65.

The Canadian Short Story Library, Series 2

The revitalized Canadian Short Story Library undertakes to publish fiction of importance to a fuller appreciation of Canadian literary history and the developing Canadian tradition. Work by major writers that has fallen into obscurity will be restored to canonical significance, and short stories by writers of lapsed renown will be gathered in collections or appropriate anthologies.

John Moss
General Editor

The Canadian Short Story Library

SERIES 1

Selected Stories of Duncan Campbell Scott
Edited by Glenn Clever

Selected Stories of Raymond Knister
Edited by Michael Gnarowski

Selected Stories of E.W. Thomson
Edited by Lorraine McMullen

Waken, Lords and Ladies Gay: Selected Stories of Desmond Pacey
Edited by Frank M. Tierney

Selected Stories of Isabella Valancy Crawford
Edited by Penny Petrone

Many Mansions: Selected Stories of Douglas O. Spettigue
Edited by Leo Simpson

The Lady and the Travelling Salesman: Stories by Leo Simpson
Edited by Henry Imbleau

Selected Stories of Robert Barr
Edited by John Parr

Selected Stories of Ernest Thompson Seton
Edited by Patricia Morley

Selected Stories of Mazo de la Roche
Edited by Douglas Daymond

Short Stories by Thomas Murtha
Edited by William Murtha

The Race and Other Stories by Sinclair Ross
Edited by Lorraine McMullen

Selected Stories of Norman Duncan
Edited by John Coldwell Adams

SERIES 2

New Women: Short Stories by Canadian Women, 1900–1920
Edited by Sandra Campbell and Lorraine McMullen

Voyages: Short Narratives of Susanna Moodie
Edited by John Thurston

Printed on paper
containing over 50%
recycled paper including
5% post-consumer fibre.